Fanny

A Mansfield Park Story

Amelia Marie Logan

With gratitude to:

Alida *for proofreading and providing very valuable feedback,*
Sofie *for brainstorming the idea for this story with me many years ago, and to all my friends and family who have supported me in this endeavor.*

Cover drawing by Hugh Thomson 1897.

Copyright 2021. All rights reserved.
ISBN: 978-1-7362080-1-4

ameliamarielogan.com

Preface

The following story is an alternative to the ending of Jane Austen's *Mansfield Park*, beginning immediately after Chapter 44 of the original novel and replacing Chapters 45 through 48. This story is a continuation of the novel which assumes the reader has read *Mansfield Park*, with all preceding events from Chapters 1 through 44, intact and referenced throughout.

In order to weave Austen's story into my own, I have used her original language heavily in the first chapter, changing what was necessary to take the story in a different direction. In addition, I have used many of Austen's sentences and turns of phrase from *Mansfield Park* as well as her other works throughout. And, imitation being "the sincerest form of flattery that mediocrity can pay to greatness,"[1] my own writing strives to emulate Austen's style to the extent of my ability.

When I first read the complete novels of Jane Austen, *Mansfield Park* was my least favorite; and I find that generally to be its rank among other Austen fans. In fact, more than one fellow Austen enthusiast has expressed surprise that I do not still rank *Mansfield Park* last among the completed novels. The truth is *Mansfield Park* is a masterful work; and though it stands in stark contrast to the "light and bright and sparkling"[2] *Pride and Prejudice*, it has its own laugh-out-loud moments in spite of the weight and depth of its tone. Whenever an Austen fan expresses distaste for *Mansfield Park*, I recommend reading it again.

The purpose of this work, therefore, is not to presume to improve on *Mansfield Park* – rather, it is only to answer the possibility offered by Austen herself at the end of her novel. In order to avoid spoilers, I have placed the excerpt from *Mansfield Park* that inspired this story at the end of it.

I have been working on this novel off and on for several years, and having completed it, I'm still not sure of my success in doing what Austen said could be done, though I wouldn't put it past her to have been toying with me all along.

~ The Author

---

1 Originally written by Charles Caleb Colton; expanded and made famous by Oscar Wilde.

2 Austen's own description of *Pride and Prejudice*.

Chapter 1

At about the week's end from his return to Mansfield, Tom's danger was such that the family had begun to fear the worst. Lady Bertram's next letter to Fanny was sent express to advise her of the news and acquaint her with the apprehensions which Sir Thomas and the physician had with respect to Tom's lungs. The letter also contained the news that arrangements had been made for Fanny's return to Mansfield. The situation was so grim and Lady Bertram so anxious, that she could no longer be done without. She was to be fetched home by Edmund as soon as may be. He would be in Portsmouth the very next morning. She wondered that the family was willing to do without him during such a crisis, and could not help but view it as a testament to her importance to their family circle that he should have been sent to fetch her. She was to leave Portsmouth tomorrow. She felt she was in some danger of feeling happy while so many were miserable. The evil which brought such good to her! To be going so soon, to be thought of and sent for as a comfort at such a desperate time, was a blessing to be felt even under the pain and distress which had occasioned the urgency to bring her home.

Fanny's only regret in departing Portsmouth, aside from the sorrowful tableau that awaited her at Mansfield, was that she was obliged to leave behind her sister, Susan. Yet, her observations gave her to believe that she had already been so much an influence in the past two months to have effected an improvement in Susan in that short time. The intimacy which had formed between the sisters was open and honest, but precariously new. If Susan could but maintain her end of a correspondence, Fanny had every reason to hope for a continuation of her improvement and of their mutual affection.

In the midst of preparing to be gone, Fanny chose to hope for her cousin Tom's recovery even though the news she had received had given her reason to fear that it was unlikely. And in such meditations, her mind could not help but wander back to Miss Crawford. That young lady had always given Fanny the idea of being the child of good luck, and to her selfishness and vanity it would be good luck to have Edmund the only son. Fanny stopped herself. Such meditations would not do. Tom had shown her kindness, in his way, and his death would be truly grievous. She knew that should such an unfortunately early demise befall him, those she held dearest would be inconsolable. Even Miss Crawford, she believed, must feel some despondence on such an occasion. And if she could not for her own sake – or for any feeling of friendship towards Tom – be sensible of his loss, then certainly for Edmund's sake, she must feel genuine sorrow. But Fanny could not long dwell on such melancholy expectations; and instead made a valiant effort to assure herself of his eventual recovery.

She was wild to be at home, to be of service to every creature in the house, to be of use to all, to save all of them some trouble of head or hand; and were it only in supporting the spirits of her aunt Bertram, keeping her from the evil of solitude, or the still greater evil of a restless, officious companion in her aunt Norris, who was too apt to be heightening danger in order to enhance her own importance, her being there would be a general good. She spent the evening fancying how she would read to her aunt, how she would talk to her, and how she would try at once to make her feel the hope of what might be and to prepare her mind for what was more likely to occur.

She was certain too that Tom's sisters must be then preparing for a similar journey. She could even suppose Miss Crawford to be soon contemplating her return to Mansfield as well. She had always said she planned on taking up her residence again at the Parsonage when the Grants should return from Bath. What Fanny imagined as the likely result of such an event could only give her pain. Yet she reflected that Miss Crawford's attachment to Edmund had been respectable, the most respectable part of her character; and her friendship for herself, had at least been blameless. But where was either sentiment now? It was so long since Fanny had had any letter from her that she had some reason to think lightly of the friendship which had been so dwelt on. It was weeks since she had heard anything of Miss Crawford or of her other connections in town, except through Mansfield, and she had begun to suppose that she might never know whether Mr. Crawford had gone into Norfolk again and might never hear from his sister any more this spring. But the relief she felt on behalf of herself and those at home to whom she could be of service outweighed all other feelings and she easily reconciled herself to the added delay of having any correspondence from that quarter forwarded to her from Portsmouth.

The affliction of the Bertrams was little felt in the Price family. Mrs. Price talked of her poor sister for a few minutes but her own domestic concerns soon prevailed. Rather than adding to her sympathy for her sister, having herself recovered from the death of a young child only hardened her against the prospect of such a loss. Fanny, who recalled with what little sensibility her aunts Bertram and Norris had borne the news of their sister's loss all those years ago, could overlook her mother's lack of any violent concern for the well-being of a nephew she had never known.

Instead, Fanny turned her attention to imparting as much advice to Susan as there was time for and preparation for her journey. And as nothing was really left for the decision of Mrs. Price, everything was rationally and duly accomplished, and Fanny was soon ready for the morrow. The advantage of much sleep to prepare her for the journey was impossible. The cousin who was suffering at Mansfield as well as the one who was travelling towards her could hardly have less than visited her agitated spirits, afflicted with all varying and indescribable perturbation. She was restless, her mind preoccupied with concern both for Tom's health and for the resultant suffering of all who loved him.

By eight in the morning, Edmund was in the house. Fanny heard his entrance from above and went down. The idea of immediately seeing him, with the knowledge of what he must be suffering, brought back all her own first feelings. He so near her, and in misery. She was ready to sink as she entered the parlour. He was alone and met her instantly; and she found herself pressed to his heart with only these words, just articulate, "My Fanny—my sister—my comfort." She could say nothing; nor for some minutes could he say more.

He turned away to recover himself, and when he spoke again, though his voice still faltered, his manner showed the wish of self-command. "Have you breakfasted? When shall you be ready?"—were questions following each other rapidly. His great object was to be off as soon as possible. When Mansfield was considered, time was precious; and the state of his own mind made him find relief only in motion. It was settled that he should order the carriage to the door in half an hour; Fanny answered for having breakfasted, and being quite ready in half an hour. He had already eaten, and declined any sustenance. He would walk round the ramparts, and return with the carriage. He was gone again, glad to get away even from Fanny.

He looked very ill; evidently suffering from grief and lack of sleep and, she had no doubt, varying painful emotions. The agitation of fear and suspense, together with weariness, were in his every feature; and some sense of consciousness of the benefit to himself that would result from the worst possible outcome, must be plaguing him as well. She knew it must be so, and it was terrible to her.

She was soon ready to go. The carriage came and he entered the house again at the same moment, just in time to spend a few minutes with the family, and be a witness—but that he saw nothing—of the tranquil manner in which the eldest daughter was parted with. Fanny's departure from her father's house was in character with her arrival, she was dismissed from it as hospitably as she had been welcomed.

How her heart swelled with relief and gratitude as she passed the barriers of Portsmouth, may be easily conceived. They shared little in the way of conversation during the journey. Edmund conveyed again all that he had witnessed of his brother's wretched condition, the physician's anxieties, and his own concerns for the well-being of his parents. She listened to him with never-failing solicitude and sometimes received in return an affectionate smile, which comforted her. And he expressed what a great comfort it was to him, to be with her again. It warmed her heart to know of what importance she was to him, even if he had used the word "sister." To her relief, he did not even mention Miss Crawford.

The first division of their journey occupied a long day and brought them, almost knocked up, to Oxford; but the second was over at a much earlier hour. They were in the environs of Mansfield long before the usual dinner-time on the second day; and as they approached the beloved place, the hearts of both sank a little. What news could there be? What had happened since Edmund's departure? As a distraction, Fanny had been everywhere awake to the difference of the country since February; but, when they entered the Park, her perceptions were of the keenest sort. It was more than two months since her quitting it; and the change was from winter to spring. Her eye fell everywhere on lawns and plantations of the freshest green; and the trees were in that delightful state, when farther beauty is known to be at hand, and when, while some is actually given to the sight, more yet remains for the imagination. She could observe, she could admire, but she could not enjoy the views. The grimness of Tom's situation seemed to imbue the entire park with a sadness that no amount of fresh greenery could conceal.

She looked at Edmund, he was leaning back, sunk in a deeper gloom than ever, and with eyes closed as if the view of cheerfulness oppressed him, and the lovely scenes of home must be shut out. It made her more melancholy; and the knowledge of what must be enduring there, invested even the house, modern, airy, and well situated as it was, with a melancholy aspect. By one of the suffering party within, they were expected with such impatience as she had never known before. Fanny had scarcely passed the solemn-looking servants, when Lady Bertram came from the drawing room to meet her; came with no indolent step; and falling on her neck, said, "Dear Fanny! My only comfort! What shall I do?"

Fanny did not readily know how to answer such a query, but there was no need as the more pressing business of exchanging salutations and the

4

latest news of the invalid was immediately engaged in. Edmund hurriedly retired to his brother's room without taking any refreshment after the journey. Fanny devoted herself to her aunt Bertram, returning to every former office with more than former zeal, and thinking she could never do enough for one who seemed so much to want her. She sat in her usual place next to her aunt to listen again to all the dreadful details of Tom's illness that had already been canvassed in her letters. The entire family was exhausted by the constant suspense that had hung over the house for the past week or so. And still, as Fanny soon learned, there was no material change in poor Tom's condition.

Over the next few days Fanny was continually expecting to receive her female cousins, but she heard nothing of their coming or of their having any intention of doing so. She could not readily comprehend their continued absence, imagining as she did that if the family had sent Edmund to fetch herself home they must likewise have written to Maria and Julia with the same urgent request. If *her* presence at home had been so necessary as to send Edmund away, surely theirs was of even greater importance. It astonished her that they had not returned to Mansfield, that they could be satisfied with remaining away from home at such a time, through an illness which had now, under different degrees of danger, lasted several weeks. *They* might return whenever they chose, travelling could be no difficulty to *them*. Yet, it seemed evident they would rather stay where they were.

The first fortnight after Fanny's return to Mansfield passed quietly with nothing occurring related to Tom's illness to give the family any definite idea of whether he would live or die. The physician came every day with fewer words and more shakes of the head than Sir Thomas liked. Fanny continued next to Lady Bertram earnestly attempting to forestall Mrs. Norris' prophecies of doom. The mood at Mansfield was sober and smiles were few. The dreadful suspense afflicted everyone, making each more agitated and less patient than usual. Fanny tried to lift spirits where she could without appearing indelicate or insensitive to Poor Tom – the appellation now commonly applied to him by well-meaning neighbours who called on Lady Bertram, hoping to be of comfort where none was possible.

In the third week since her return home, Fanny finally received a letter from Miss Crawford. It had been first directed to Portsmouth and forwarded to her at Mansfield. But after reading it Fanny would rather have never heard from Miss Crawford again. The letter was as follows:

Forgive me, my dear Fanny, as soon as you can, for my long silence, and behave as if you could forgive me directly. This is my modest request and expectation, for you are so good, that I depend upon being treated better than I deserve—and I write now to beg an immediate answer. I want to know the state of things at Mansfield Park, and you, no doubt, are perfectly able to give it. One should be a brute not to feel for the distress they are in—and from what I hear poor Mr. Bertram has a bad chance of ultimate recovery. I thought little of his illness at first. I looked upon him as the sort of person to be made a fuss with, and to make a fuss himself in any trifling disorder, and was chiefly concerned for those who had to nurse him; but now it is confidently asserted that he is really in a decline, that the symptoms are most alarming, and that the family are aware of it. If it be so, I am sure you must be familiar with all the particulars, and so I entreat you to let me know how far I have been rightly informed. I need not say how rejoiced I shall be to hear there has been any mistake, but the report is so prevalent, that I confess I cannot help trembling. To have such a fine young man cut off in the flower of his days, is most melancholy. Poor Sir Thomas will feel it dreadfully. I really am quite agitated on the subject. Fanny, Fanny, I see you smile, and look cunning, but upon my honour, I never bribed a physician in my life. Poor young man!—If he is to die, there will be *two* poor young men less in the world; and with a fearless face and bold voice would I say to any one, that wealth and consequence could fall into no hands more deserving of them. It was a foolish precipitation last Christmas, but the evil of a few days may be blotted out in part. Varnish and gilding hide many stains. It will be but the loss of the Esquire after his name. With real affection, Fanny, like mine, more might be overlooked. Write to me by return of post, judge of my anxiety, and do not trifle with it. Tell me the real truth, as you have it from the fountain head. And now, do not trouble yourself to be ashamed of either my feelings or your own. Believe me, they are not only natural, they are philanthropic and virtuous. I put it to your conscience, whether 'Sir Edmund' would not do more good with all the Bertram property, than any other possible

'Sir.' Had the Grants been at home, I would not have troubled you, but you are now the only one I can apply to for the truth, his sisters not being within my reach. Mrs. R. has been spending the Easter with the Aylmers at Twickenham (as to be sure you know), and is not yet returned; and Julia is with the cousins who live near Bedford Square; but I forget their name and street. Could I immediately apply to either, however, I should still prefer you, because it strikes me, that they have all along been so unwilling to have their own amusements cut up, as to shut their eyes to the truth. I suppose, Mrs. R.'s Easter holidays will not last much longer; no doubt they are thorough holidays to her. The Aylmers are pleasant people; and her husband away, she can have nothing but enjoyment. I give her credit for promoting his going dutifully down to Bath, to fetch his mother; but how will she and the dowager agree in one house? Henry is not at hand, he returned to Norfolk after the Frasers' party. He did not even wish to stay that long, but I begged him most fervently (and you know he can refuse me nothing). So to Everingham he has gone and there he stays. He would not even stir himself to go down to Richmond for Easter as he does every year, which was a great deprivation to me, as he certainly would have stopped in London on the way. My only solace, therefore, is in knowing how furious the admiral must have been in being so neglected. I would have had Henry remain in London, but he would go to Everingham to resolve some dispute there, though I suppose the business could have been deferred; at the very least it must be resolved by now, yet there he remains. And I begin to think his real reason for staying so long at Everingham must be to console himself by envisioning its future mistress walking its halls and pleasure gardens. Oh how he suffers on your account! He did wish for me to renew in my next letter and more eagerly, what he said at Portsmouth, about our conveying you home, and I join him in it with all my soul. Dear Fanny, write directly and tell us to come. It will do us all good. He and I can go to the Parsonage, you know, and be no trouble to our friends at Mansfield Park. It would really be gratifying to see them all again, and a little addition of society might be of infinite use to them; and, as to yourself, you must feel yourself to be so wanted there, that you cannot in conscience (conscientious as you are) keep away, when you have the means of returning. I have not time or patience to give you half the messages with which Henry charged me before he left; be satisfied, that the spirit of each and every one is unalterable affection. Do not you think Edmund would have been in town again long ago, but for this illness? – Yours ever, Mary.

Fanny's disgust at the greater part of this letter together with her extreme reluctance to bring the writer of it and her cousin Edmund together, would have made her (as she felt), incapable of any consideration of acceptance of the concluding offer had she not already been conveyed home. She saw so much to condemn in Miss Crawford's thinly veiled and cold-hearted ambition. As for what was related about the brother, Fanny felt Miss Crawford was indecorously liberal in conveying her thoughts and observations, but it was a source of information about which Fanny must admit some curiosity. She was disappointed to learn that he had not immediately gone to Norfolk after leaving her, but the rest of the account was admittedly to his credit; that Miss Crawford seemed to disapprove his conduct was little to hers. Fanny wondered, however, at his not going to Richmond as was his yearly habit; she could not help but suspect that his object had been to avoid a meeting with Mrs. Rushworth. And while this forbearance must do credit to his good judgement, it only confirmed the strength of that temptation, that continued interest, which must exist for such avoidance to be necessary. He must have reckoned his danger in going to be very great indeed, that he should be willing to offend his uncle to such a degree in order to avoid it. But the most alarming and disappointing news in the letter was what it related about Mrs. Rushworth and Miss Bertram. Neither of them, it appeared, had any intention of returning home on account of their brother's condition.

Fanny's reply to the letter was short. She thanked Miss Crawford, but assured her that she had already been conveyed home. As for her cousin's illness, she wrote that the situation was grave but that she and *all* the family continued in the expectation of a full recovery. This, she supposed would convey to the sanguine mind of her correspondent the hope of everything she was wishing for. Edmund would be forgiven for being a clergyman, it seemed, under certain conditions of wealth; and this, she suspected, was all the conquest of prejudice which he was so ready to

8

congratulate himself upon. She had only learnt to think nothing of consequence but money.

The letter in reply to Miss Crawford's was not long gone when Lady Bertram received word from the Grants of the date fixed for their return from Bath. Fanny hardly imagined that with the fulfilment of all her possible desires so palpably close, Miss Crawford would be able to stay away long after the return of her relations to Mansfield Parsonage. Little did Miss Crawford know, as she perused a letter from her sister communicating the same news, how very close at hand such desires were. For on the very same morning the Grants were expected back in the country, Edmund came down to breakfast from spending the night at his brother's bedside, his appearance haggard, and whispered something into his father's ear. The physician was sent for, but only to confirm what was already known. It was over. Tom Bertram was dead.

Chapter 2

The state in which the death of the heir placed the Bertram family can be well imagined. The spirits of everyone were sufficiently affected to make them all forget how little Tom had done in life to contribute to anyone's happiness and comfort save his own. He was now and forever to be known only as "Dear Tom" and "Poor Tom." There was no end to the suffering and agony to be endured. There was no end to the tears shed on his behalf by mother and aunt alike. Fanny, too, cried bitterly and perhaps more than her dearly departed cousin deserved. Her first opportunity of being alone in the East room was given to reliving the memories associated with each of the treasured gifts Tom had bestowed upon her over the years. Each box and trinket was touched and cradled and sobbed over in turn. Poor, dear Tom had always thought of her and she could not help but feel that she had never loved or cared for him enough.

His sisters, who had not troubled themselves to come home on account of his illness, were now summoned home on account of his death. Fanny almost dreaded their arrival – for she had not seen either since before the horrible business with Mr. Crawford – but assured herself that the present circumstance would put every other consideration out of their minds. As it was, they scarcely looked at her – Mrs. Rushworth, especially, seemed intent on not acknowledging her existence – and as this was so little an alteration from their former treatment of her, Fanny found it perfectly acceptable and was only relieved that none of the other family members seemed to notice.

Poor Tom was now the dearest brother in the world, and the kindest gentleman anyone could have known. Memories of childhood, long buried, now surfaced of his kind solicitude and gentle attentions, of a thousand acts of selflessness, of all the blessings and favours of every kind he had bestowed upon his dear family. Such recollections, though perhaps not wholly accurate, were dwelt on with all the fervour appropriate to the situation. His perfections were unceasingly repeated by everyone. At least in death, he became the man he should have been but never was while living. Both sisters lamented how greatly he would be missed by all the family. They would never recover from this loss and never cease to feel most acutely his absence from their lives. These declarations gave some credibility to Fanny's notions of what the sisters must be feeling on account of the loss of their brother. She perhaps attributed feelings to them more like what she might have felt for William than what could reasonably have been supposed drawing only from her knowledge of both the sisters and the departed brother. Julia's and Maria's effusions of fraternal sentiment soon gave way to wondering how they could possibly find tolerably suitable mourning clothes outside of London, how much adornment they might get away with in their dress, and how long they would be required to wear them. Thanks to the attentions of Mrs. Norris, which were no less economical than expedient, however, everyone very soon had appropriate clothing to be seen in by their neighbours and friends.

Sir Thomas attended to the arrangement of the house, the preparation of the body, and the funeral, which took place as quickly as was practicable. After he was washed, dressed and laid in a room downstairs, Lady Bertram would scarcely leave Tom's side until the funeral carriage came for him. Fanny watched the procession from an upstairs window, as she stood with Lady Bertram's head pressed to her shoulder. When the gentlemen returned, Lady Bertram wished to hear every detail of the service. Sir Thomas and Edmund sat with her and quietly answered her queries until she was satisfied, or at least exhausted by the emotional anguish of listening to their descriptions.

After the funeral, the visits began. Lady Bertram refused all callers for the first three days; then sent around her cards when she was ready to receive condolences. Well-meaning neighbours and friends called at Mansfield Park in respectable numbers, especially for a lady who had scarcely visited anyone in above ten years. It was a trying time for everyone, to be constantly visited by compassionate but uncomfortable friends, unsure whether the departed member of the family could be talked about, but unable to think of anything else that could fill the requisite quarter hour visit with conversation. The weather and the roads were often talked of, but inevitably the subject on everyone's mind was mentioned. Fanny stayed with her aunt through each of these visits, as she felt her very presence lifted Lady Bertram's spirits and gave her strength. Stories of Tom's youth were told and retold fondly, and Fanny observed that talking of him seemed to have a favourable effect on her aunt's feelings.

Sir Thomas now divided his time between sitting at his wife's side, meditating in his room, and staring at his elder son's portrait in the gallery. Edmund, who had the most capacity for feeling among his family, took the loss of his brother the hardest, and perhaps so much the harder from knowing what he must gain by it. What a burden to bear: to benefit so much from the loss of a loved one! Fanny knew how he must feel and chose not to attribute to him any thought of how the event would make possible his marriage to "the only woman in the world whom he could ever think of as his wife." The remembrance of everything Miss Crawford had written was an additional source of pain reserved only to Fanny. Her disgust and repulsion were so much greater now that the event had occurred than they had been even on her first reading the letter.

Thus, it was with extreme disappointment that she heard the news from Mrs. Grant that Miss Crawford would be returning thither and had sent her sincerest sympathies to the family until she was able to convey them personally. Fanny indulged herself in imagining Miss Crawford's smiles of delight as she wrote those lines. The very thought made her shudder, however, and she determined to think of it no more. Instead, she would devote herself to her aunt Bertram, her uncle, and Edmund; to supporting their spirits and being whatever comfort to them was within her power, as none of the other inhabitants of the house had any use for her. In contemplating Miss Crawford's arrival, Fanny could not help but consider it most likely that she would be conveyed to Mansfield by her brother and she hoped to avoid his company as much as possible.

It appeared that Mrs. Rushworth's mind was similarly bent as, upon hearing the news of Miss Crawford's return, she immediately quitted the room. Mr. Rushworth looked a little confused and uncertain as to what to do; but, after a moment of indecision, he followed her. Julia was bent quietly over her work, but shook her head, perhaps unconsciously, when her sister left the room, and sighed heavily when her brother-in-law followed. To Fanny's mind, no good could come from any of this. To have Mrs. Rushworth and Mr. Crawford meet and under such circumstances, was an evil to be avoided. Yet, with the Crawfords situated so near at the Parsonage, some intercourse must result. There was no reason to think either brother or sister would have the delicacy to leave the family to grieve in peace.

The Grants stayed only a half hour during the call which brought this news to the Bertram family. After they were gone, Edmund approached Fanny, "Come, you must have some fresh air, let us walk out." Fanny could not desire to leave her aunt Bertram's side, but as there had been little chance for her to speak privately with Edmund since Tom's death, and she could see that he wished to talk to her in confidence, she felt she should go. Edmund, seeing her hesitation, added, "You see my aunt Norris and Julia are here to attend Lady Bertram, she can spare you for a little while." Fanny glanced at her aunt Bertram, leaning back on the sofa, her eyes closed but damp, a handkerchief clutched in one hand, a look of sorrow overspreading her features. She ran upstairs to fetch her things, then taking Edmund's offered arm, walked out with him.

12

Once outdoors, they walked in silence for some minutes before Edmund began thus, "It must give you some pleasure at a time like this to know your friend will soon be nearby. I am sure her presence will give you solace and serve to support all of our spirits."

Fanny little expected such an introduction to their conversation, and preferring to change the subject, she replied, "*Your* spirits must be truly shaken by this unfortunate event. I can only imagine what you must be feeling. The loss of a brother …"

"The loss of a brother is a great sorrow to me, but it is of a piece with what we must all endure. Yet, …" he paused, "my own pain is doubled by the guilt of gaining an inheritance by it." And, proving he would not be deterred from speaking of Miss Crawford, he added, "And you alone know how much more I shall gain." He sighed. "What a relief it is to speak to you Fanny. You are the only one in whom I have confided my feelings and my intentions." Of course, he would persist in talking of *her*. Another sigh escaped him. "I cannot deny that her presence at such a time will be a comfort to me. I am sure she must know how I am suffering, and I cannot doubt she comprehends at least some share of my burden of guilt."

Such were the thoughts at present torturing Fanny's beloved Edmund. As for his last supposition, Fanny knew better than to believe Miss Crawford had any sensation of guilt about the prospect of living quite comfortably off of Poor Tom's inheritance. She was now at the point of wondering whether the contents of Miss Crawford's letter would have any effect on him. Would it open his eyes? Or would he continue to excuse her? Would it be right to show it to him? Were her motives in contemplating it selfish? He was expecting her to say something. "I know you must feel everything a brother ought to feel on account of Tom. You took such great care of him during his illness, staying by his bedside, reading to him, comforting him. You did more for him than anyone, but I know you could never have done less for a brother. And, at the end, he must have known he was loved."

"I take great comfort in supposing as much." He then added quietly, "But, was not it my duty as his brother to do everything I could for his comfort?"

"Duty yes, but fraternal love as well, must have been your motivation."

"Yes," he replied with a sigh, "but perhaps they are one and the same. The truth is, Tom and I have never been on intimate terms; we have such dissimilar dispositions and tastes, and interests. We spent so much of our time apart; and when together, we often disagreed. But, he was my brother, and as such was deserving of all that was in my power to give."

The conversation made Fanny uncomfortable. Intending to change the subject somewhat, she said, "I am concerned for my aunt Bertram. She has been so overpowered by her grief."

"You are her greatest comfort."

"It is my greatest comfort to hear you say so."

"Dearest Fanny, you are truly angelic."

Edmund's observation called to mind something Mr. Crawford had once said to her: "*You have some touches of the angel in you.*" She only expressed her wish to return to her aunt and could not regret that the conversation was over.

After dinner, that evening, when all the family were in the drawing room, Mr. Rushworth mentioned casually, "I believe it is time for us to return to Sotherton."

Fanny felt for him, a husband should not have to resort to such measures – to risk seeming insensitive to his wife's family in a difficult time – only to avoid her meeting with a former suitor.

Lady Bertram immediately protested and was supported by Mrs. Norris. Could not they stay but a fortnight longer? Dear Maria was so necessary to their comfort and to the serenity of the family circle during such a crisis. He attempted to explain the urgency of their going by relating that he had received a letter from his steward and had business to attend to that could not be delayed. However, the two ladies immediately suggested that he leave Mrs. Rushworth at Mansfield Park, if he could do without her, and return for her when his business was concluded. Perhaps in the course of inventing his excuses, Mr. Rushworth should have anticipated this suggestion. However, as it turned out, he in fact could not do without Mrs. Rushworth at all and leaving her behind was out of the question. Yet, he could no more refuse his acquiescence to so reasonable a solution than conjure a better excuse in the moment. And, in the end, the ladies' continued pleas together with Sir Thomas' look of disapprobation were too much for a man of Mr. Rushworth's stamp to withstand. He submitted with all the appropriate apologies and assurances that he felt their loss as keenly as any member of the family. He believed, after all, that the business at Sotherton could be handled by letter. Mrs. Rushworth was silent throughout the conversation.

Fanny, to whom the motivation behind Mr. Rushworth's eagerness to be gone was so clear, found it almost shocking that her other cousins did not seem to apprehend it. She had expected either or both of them to enter the conversation in support of Mr. Rushworth at every moment, but neither did; yet upon further reflection she could readily attribute their neglect to the burden of grief that afflicted everyone in the house.

The following morning brought another letter from Miss Crawford. Fanny was so little disposed to read anything it might contain that she could not but accept it with trepidation. She would almost have tossed it into the fire without so much as breaking the seal but for Edmund's eager expression as he sat across the breakfast table from her. He was waiting for her to open it. Hoping that if she did come across anything for which the writer ought to be ashamed her expression would not betray it, she unfolded the letter. It contained the following:

My dear Fanny, I cannot tell you how genuinely pleased I am to hear that you are safe at home, though you did deprive Henry and me the pleasure of taking you. We are both quite delighted to know you will be one of the party at Mansfield. How kind it was of your cousin to perform the office. Oh Fanny, you must know that I have heard the terrible news about poor Mr. Bertram. It is a sad business and my heart and soul are with my friends at Mansfield. Although I have sent my condolences with my sister, I implore you to convey them as well to Sir Thomas and Lady Bertram and all the family on my behalf. I hope to be with all of you very soon to condole with the family personally. We will again take our little walks together in the shrubbery outside the Parsonage. You cannot know how I miss the days of our intimacy. I have begged Henry to take me to Mansfield as soon as possible that we may both be with our friends at this distressing time. But what do you think? He says he will not do it! He is too busy at Everingham! Now do not be alarmed that his earnest desire to be near you has abated in any measure, for when I particularly asked him how he could neglect you at such a time he gave me every assurance of his constancy – but no further explanation of his refusal to be of service to me. He has become a Henry I scarcely know since the last time I saw him. I attribute it to his spending too much time in the country, for he has not yet returned from Norfolk. But I have written to tell him that I am resolved to go to Mansfield Parsonage even without his protection. I am sure I have quite shocked him and, as he will never abide his sister travelling post alone, I will prevail in the end.

Therefore, I expect him at every moment and hope to be with you all very soon. Until then, I am authorized to send you Henry's affectionate regard as well as my own. But before I close, I must ask: How does Mrs. Rushworth? I understand that she and her husband are at Mansfield Park. Do you suppose they will still be in residence when we arrive? Yours, etc., Mary.

There was no time for reflection on the contents of this letter, for when Fanny looked up from it she saw Edmund's eyes still fixed on her. "She sends her condolences to all the family," she replied to his unasked question, "and hopes to be among us soon."

He seemed satisfied and smiled.

Mr. Rushworth, with affected tranquillity, said, "Does she give a date for her arrival?"

"No," said Fanny, trying not to communicate in her features all the sympathy she felt for him. "She is still uncertain of when she will be able to travel; as she expects her brother to convey her, it is upon him that her date of travel depends." Then, in an effort to relieve his anxiety, she added, "He is still in Norfolk."

Now it was Mr. Rushworth who seemed satisfied, though Fanny could not entertain any hope of the delay being at least a fortnight in length. Her surmise was correct, Mr. Rushworth could only rejoice in the first week of his remaining time at Mansfield passing without the imposition of the Crawfords. The Mansfield family had the earliest intelligence of the appointed date for their arrival from Mrs. Grant and it was soon upon them.

The morning after their arrival, both Mr. and Miss Crawford paid their respects to the Bertram family. They were all collected in the drawing room, Edmund in the seat closest to the door, Mr. Rushworth immediately next to his wife, and Fanny in her usual place next to Lady Bertram. All three anxious about the impending visit, but for very different reasons. For her part, Fanny could have no wish to see either brother or sister. Miss Crawford had completely lost all of her regard and she did not feel equal to the effort of appearing friendly and polite to someone she could not respect. She likewise felt out of humour to withstand Mr. Crawford's indelicate attentions, especially under the present circumstances. Yet, her own disinclination for the visit could not prevent it and at last the callers arrived. Mr. and Miss Crawford were amongst them once again, for good or evil.

Chapter 3

Upon entering the drawing room, Miss Crawford's eyes flew directly to Edmund and her brother's to Fanny. He instantly withdrew them, however, and addressed himself to Lady Bertram and Sir Thomas with the utmost civility, and then to the others in turn. Fanny offered only a nod and a murmured "good morning" to both. When the company was invited to sit, Fanny steeled herself against an attack she felt was imminent. However, instead of sitting near her or seeking to engage her in conversation, Mr. Crawford sat between Lady Bertram and Mrs. Norris and spoke to them for the duration of the visit. Fanny scarcely lifted her eyes from her work. Miss Crawford had chosen a seat next to Edmund and they were engaged in quiet discourse for most of the visit, sometimes including the Rushworths and Julia in their conversation. It was now only a matter of getting through the next half hour.

As that time period drew to a close, Fanny began to feel the hope of getting through the visit without having to speak to either brother or sister – until Miss Crawford looked meaningfully at her and patted on the seat next to her. Fanny was obliged to move. "My dearest Fanny!" began Miss Crawford, turning away from the others. "How I have missed you!" Then lowering her voice to a whisper she added, "And – as you can imagine – I am not the only one." Here she glanced at her brother. "You must stop torturing him! I am sure he means to have everything settled with you on this visit."

"There is nothing to settle, Miss Crawford. And this is hardly the time."

"Oh yes, I know. The sad business of poor Mr. Bertram," she said with a smile. "How shall his family get on without him? But he was scarcely ever at home in any case. Even still, Lady Bertram appears positively inconsolable."

"I believe her spirits will improve with time."

"And what of the present Mr. Bertram? Ah, how well the appellation suits him. I was just telling him as much."

Ignoring the end of her speech, Fanny chose to respond only to her first inquiry. "His spirits have been tolerably good. I believe he tries to remain as cheerful as possible to make everyone else more comfortable."

"Yes, he seems to be in remarkably good cheer. It must be a blessing to all the rest of the family to have him so."

"Indeed." Fanny had no wish to talk more of Edmund so she asked the only thing she could think of, "How was your journey?"

"The roads were passable and the weather was indifferent, but Henry was intolerably solemn." Then she added more quietly, "And I believe it must all be on account of you!"

"Of me?" asked Fanny, unable to imagine that her previous admonitions had had any influence on the gentleman.

"Such modesty! You must know that all these months of unrequited love have taken their toll on him. And I should never say that he did not deserve it. I am certain that when he is secured of your affection and your hand he will become cheerful again and return to his former self."

"I am sure you must be mistaken. If he is not himself, it can have nothing to do with me."

Miss Crawford smiled, "Oh Fanny, how can you speak so? You cannot pretend to be so modest with me. I know you can be in no doubt of his regard."

"Indeed, I assure you, I do not pretend modesty. I simply can have no reason to presume having any influence over Mr. Crawford's moods." Although they were speaking in almost a whisper, she was uncomfortable discussing such a topic in front of so many others, but when she looked around the room everyone seemed to be talking amongst themselves and, thankfully, it appeared that no one was attending to their conversation. Mr. Crawford, she felt assured, was too far away to hear them, and Edmund seemed wholly engaged by Mr. Rushworth and Dr. Grant.

Again Miss Crawford smiled, and looked as if she might laugh at Fanny. "No influence? But my dear Fanny you must know you are the only influence on his moods now. He can do nothing without considering your judgement or your approbation. Truly, I have never seen him so affected by anyone. And, for all your protestations to the contrary, I know you cannot be insensible of it."

Fanny knew Miss Crawford tended to exaggeration and therefore took nothing she said seriously. After all that Fanny had read to Miss Crawford's discredit from her own pen, it was easy to dismiss such fanciful descriptions that were so contrary to Fanny's understanding of the gentleman in question and so distasteful to her delicate sense of propriety. Desperately wishing to change the subject, Fanny asked Miss Crawford how she had enjoyed London. "Oh now you wish to know all about how Henry behaved when away from you. Do not look so surprised that I perceive your purpose. But let me assure you, he did nothing to dishonour his affection for you. He could think and speak of nothing but Fanny!"

Fanny wondered how Miss Crawford could be insensible of the sincere distress she felt in her continuing such a subject. She longed to find something to speak of that could not be brought back to the topic her companion seemed determined to pursue. She could think of nothing, however, and was relieved beyond measure when Mr. Crawford, in the next moment, stood to take his leave. His sister followed suit, quietly whispering to Fanny, as she rose from her seat, her disapprobation of Fanny's failure to pay any attention to Mr. Crawford during the entire visit. And, before she quitted the house, Miss Crawford engaged Fanny to join her at the Parsonage in the morning for a walk, saying, "My dear Fanny you must come to the Parsonage and walk out with me tomorrow." Then in an undervoice, she added, "I cannot talk to you properly in this sombre drawing room."

Fanny said quietly, "I am sure Lady Bertram cannot spare me. I should be here, with her."

"What? With both Mrs. Rushworth and Miss Bertram at home? I am sure she can spare you for an hour very well. Only think of me, dearest Fanny, Henry is to go out in the morning and I shall be quite desolate. You will not wish me to be alone and friendless at the Parsonage." More quietly she added, "I know you will not let his absence stop you from coming."

"Indeed not," said Fanny quietly, "but shall not you have Mrs. Grant's company?"

"Oh no, she will be making calls in the village with Dr. Grant."

"Do not you wish to go with her?"

"I am afraid I would be but a poor companion. I cannot abide … well, I am of little use, you know, in attending the poor and sick. I am afraid *I* was not formed for the work of a parson's wife." This was said with the hint of a smile as if to emphasize that such a prospect was no longer a consideration. "No, I am better off at home, though I will be all alone unless you rescue me from my solitude."

Fanny perceived that, though his eyes were directed elsewhere, Mr. Crawford was now attending to their conversation, and she was a little surprised that he did not intervene to press her. Edmund, however, hearing only the last part of Miss Crawford's speech, approached the two young ladies to learn more and upon hearing the invitation and Fanny's excuses, he interposed his opinion that Lady Bertram could certainly spare Fanny for an hour in the morning and advised that it would do her good to take some exercise out of doors. There was nothing Fanny could say to oppose the scheme, and she assured Miss Crawford that she would call at the Parsonage during the course of the morning.

Miss Crawford was perfectly satisfied and then, smiling, said, "But here is Henry! You have hardly spoken two words to him today and now there is nothing left to be said."

Upon hearing the words, Mr. Crawford stepped towards them and made his bow. "Good morning, Miss Price. I hope you are well."

"I am very well, thank you. I hope your journey hither was not unpleasant."

"Not in the least. We had fine weather and made very good time."

"I trust your business in Norfolk was resolved to your satisfaction."

"The matter of the mill was resolved entirely as it should have been, and so much the better for my having been there personally."

"Then you must be pleased you went."

"Yes, I am."

She wanted to ask how long he planned to stay in the neighbourhood, but dared not, lest he should misinterpret her interest as he had been wont to do in the past. As it was, she could think of nothing more to say, and he saved her the trouble by taking his sister's arm and quitting the house. At last they were gone. Fanny had not dared to venture a look at Mrs. Rushworth during the course of the meeting, but glancing at her now she had all the appearance of having behaved herself as she ought.

The rest of the day until dinner was spent in the drawing room in quiet employment or hushed conversation. Fanny was at leisure now to contemplate the morning's visit. Miss Crawford, it was clear, was unaltered. She thought only of herself and had been more lively, in Fanny's opinion, than the situation should have allowed. Mr. Crawford she could not understand so readily, for his manners were so altered she knew not what to make of him. She was relieved and pleased that he had not paid any particular attention to either Maria or Julia. And as for his having been equally inattentive to herself, she was just as relieved and just as pleased. It gave her hope that he had at last given up his suit – notwithstanding all his sister's assurances to the contrary. Fanny was more inclined to rely on her own perceptions of the gentleman than anything Miss Crawford had to say; after all, they had not been together for the past several weeks.

After dinner there was a brief alteration to the solemnity of the drawing room. When the ladies were free, for a time, from the company of the gentlemen, Maria and Julia sat together as far away from the others as they could contrive and appeared engaged in a quiet, though spirited conversation. Every now and then Fanny could even hear laughter coming from their corner of the room and each time, she raised her head in surprise, hoping that such behaviour would not disturb Lady Bertram's serenity. About the third time of this happening, Mrs. Norris commented, to no one in particular, how pleasant it was to hear laughter again in the house and what a comfort it was to have her two lively nieces with them at such a time. "It is necessary to be sombre at such times as these, to be sure; but the occasional laughter of young people only serves to lift one's spirits. It does my heart good to hear it." Fanny said nothing. She was glad when the gentlemen returned, causing the other two young ladies to behave with more decorum.

The next morning, Fanny was alone in the East room before breakfast. Since Tom's death, Lady Bertram had been in the habit of staying in her room until breakfast so Fanny was at leisure to spend this time in solitude and quiet reflection, attending to her own correspondence or reading quietly. It was here that she was found by Julia.

"My dear Fanny," she began, rushing into the room unceremoniously, "I must speak to you. Here let us sit down." They did so and Julia immediately asked, "Is it true that you are really not at all in love with Mr. Crawford?"

Fanny was struck as much by the novelty of having been sought out by Julia in such a way as by the question she now posed. She did not think Julia had ever been in the East room since the dismissal of Miss Lee and never in their lives had Julia spoken with her in privacy or sought her confidence. She wondered how her cousin could now impose upon her to discuss such a topic. Although Fanny knew that everyone seemed to believe she loved, or at least *should* love, the gentleman in spite of her unequivocal denial, she had hoped her cousins were well-bred enough not to mention the matter. It seemed Fanny's most intimate friends and relations thought themselves more knowledgeable of her own feelings than even she could be. "It is true," said Fanny, without hesitation. "I do not love him."

"Then why does everyone suppose that you do?"

Fanny shrugged. "I have asked myself the same question. The only answer I can think of is that it is generally believed to be impossible for a woman not to return a man's affections, or even his professed affections."

"You speak as if you do not think he really loves you. I have not heard him say it myself, but it is well known that he has spoken openly of it."

"I cannot presume to know what his feelings might or might not be. I only mean to say that it appears from what I have seen of the world, which I confess is not much, that if a man claims to be in love then so must be the woman who is his object. It seems a woman is expected to need no other inducement to falling in love than to be told she is loved." Now remembering the sisters' private conversation the evening before, Fanny could not help but wonder if Maria had sent her sister to discover Fanny's feelings.

Julia replied, "Oh no. That cannot be right. For, while I was in town I was aware of many young ladies being in love with men who had not declared themselves!"

"I know nothing of how things are in town."

Here Julia paused in quiet contemplation, then began anew with, "What did you think of the Crawfords yesterday?"

"I thought Miss Crawford looked well and was much the same as I remembered her. Mr. Crawford's manners, however, were very different."

"Yes!" agreed Julia. "He was so quiet and serious, so unlike himself."

"Perhaps he felt it appropriate under the circumstances." Julia gave her a questioning look. "After the family's loss," prompted Fanny.

"Oh yes, perhaps," said Julia pensively. She then stood and walked about the room in an agitated manner as if struggling internally with some question. At length, seeming to have resolved the matter, she sat down again. After some further hesitation, she declared, "Maria is not happy."

"I am sorry to hear it."

"She is displeased with his treatment of her. She was cold to him in London when we saw him at Mrs. Fraser's party. She meant to punish him. She expected him to be affronted, to attempt to win back her favour. Instead, his behaviour towards her, and indeed towards both of us, was marked only by the appearance of indifference and forced civility. And *that*, she cannot abide. She would … she would have him smile at her as he used to do. She would have him jealous of her marriage. It is the only way she can be satisfied … after he disappointed her last year." Here she paused, but Fanny said nothing. "She sought another opportunity to try her powers on him by going to Richmond at Easter, knowing he would be there – that he was in the habit of going every year; but he never appeared. Yet, she has not given up." She stopped again, then after a long pause, she added, "She means to make him regret her."

"Julia," Fanny began quietly, but it was hardly within her power to reprimand a cousin whom she had been brought up to think of as her superior. And that cousin, though unlikely to be deterred by any such admonition, was not attending in any case.

Julia stood again and, walking to and fro, continued, "But she made her choice. She chose marriage without love solely for the independence it has afforded her and the means to exercise it. And it has been a fair trade for her I think. She is at liberty to do just as she pleases. Yet she is not content. Her satisfaction is not complete without the triumph of Mr.

Crawford's jealousy. She can think only of herself, of her own disappointed hopes. But what about me? *She* was already engaged when they met. She knew he was designed for me and I would have got him if she had not interfered. But, she could not be satisfied with one conquest. I wonder how she would feel if I were to win him after all!"

What could Fanny possibly say in response to such a speech? "I must go. I believe it must be time for breakfast," was all she could contrive, and she fled the room. Julia, having unburdened herself of feelings she had not been able to share with her usual confidante, was left to wonder whether perhaps she had said too much.

As for Fanny, how could she recover from such a conversation in time to meet the others in the breakfast room with tolerable composure? That the two girls could be thinking of such things so soon after the death of their brother was inconceivable. That they could still be rivals for Henry Crawford was such a source of disgust that it entirely took away her appetite. Edmund, noticing that she did not eat, wondered if she were unwell and expressed hope that she would not be prevented from calling on her friend in the course of the morning. Fanny assured him she was quite well and would make the promised call.

Edmund and Mr. Rushworth announced their intention of going to Northampton, where Edmund had an errand from his father, who was disinclined to go anywhere himself, and had asked his brother-in-law to accompany him. Once the gentlemen had settled on their plan, Maria declared that she and Julia would go for a ride in the Park.

"But your horse is at Sotherton," said Mr. Rushworth.

"True, but Edmund's mare will do for one of us, and as Julia will want to ride her own horse, I suppose it will have to be me."

Edmund looked at Fanny with concern, "I trust you were not planning to ride today as you will be calling at the Parsonage."

Fanny wondered to herself how long he expected her to stay at the Parsonage if he did not think she would have time to do both, but replied that she had no intention of riding during the course of the day.

The idea of going for a ride had been secretly contrived by the two sisters during their private conference the evening before, after gaining the intelligence that Mr. Crawford was to be out, as a scheme of encountering him alone. To the others, they simply expressed that they had been indoors too much lately and would benefit from the air and exercise. All remained oblivious to their true purpose and there could be no objection from anyone. For, while Maria had confided her resentments in Julia, she had long since forgotten that Mr. Crawford had once slighted Julia in favour of herself and could little imagine that her sister had resentments of her own that were not equally disclosed.

After breakfast Fanny was content to retire to the drawing room with only her two aunts for company. It was a time of peaceful reflection without any interruptions or unwanted confidences from anyone. She did not look forward to her engagement with Miss Crawford and based upon some of the lady's previous actions and declarations, she half expected to be ambushed by Mr. Crawford at the Parsonage, in spite of all the assurances given by his sister that he was to be out of the house. Yet, she was so disinclined to spend any time alone with Miss Crawford, she scarcely knew whether his presence would be a greater or lesser evil than enduring a private meeting with his sister, as that lady's two favourite topics of conversation – Edmund's attentions to Miss Crawford and Mr. Crawford's professed feelings for herself – could only bring pain to Fanny.

She had begun, after yesterday's meeting to indulge the belief that Mr. Crawford had given her up. Indeed, when he left her in Portsmouth she had hoped the gentle solicitude he had then shown for her health and comfort would lead him to abandon his suit on account of the distress it caused her. Equally likely to her mind was the possibility that he had simply grown tired of his pursuit, which had always been inevitable. His behaviour on their first meeting since her return from Portsmouth supported either supposition and she cared not which was his motivation, so long as he no longer importuned her with his addresses. Thus, she could only hope that if she did meet him again, his behaviour would continue to support her conviction that he had abandoned his suit; for, she was certain, that once the brother no longer found her an object of interest, the sister's friendly overtures towards her would cease. Fanny, however, could scarcely entertain the hope that an end to their intimacy might be possible, given her knowledge of Edmund's intentions and the opportunity recently bestowed that would make their accomplishment easy. That Edmund would marry Miss Crawford, she could not admit a doubt. That she would have to make herself stop loving him, was equally clear. He would never feel anything for her but what a brother feels for a sister; and Fanny's natural modesty and learned humility had always made it impossible for her to aspire to anything more than spending her life sitting at the side of Lady Bertram, being of use to her.

At last, when Fanny could put off the errand which gave her so much distress no longer, she excused herself from her two aunts, and with no more than a, "Take care not to overstay your welcome," from Mrs. Norris, she was off. It was with great trepidation that she then walked towards

Mansfield Parsonage, unsure of what she would find there but with every expectation of its being unpleasant.

Chapter 4

Fanny was at least relieved of one source of uneasiness in finding Miss Crawford alone at the Parsonage. She was greeted with the same friendly enthusiasm as the day before. "At last we can speak openly," said Miss Crawford, "come let us walk in the shrubbery as we used to do."

As they walked, Miss Crawford began thus, "I trust you left the family well this morning?"

"Yes, they were all quite well, thank you."

"All assembled in the drawing room as they were yesterday?"

"No, Mr. Bertram and Mr. Rushworth have gone to Northampton together and Mrs. Rushworth and Miss Bertram had gone riding before I came out. Only Lady Bertram and Mrs. Norris remained in the drawing room."

"And what of Sir Thomas? Did not he go out with the other gentlemen?"

"He was disinclined for it. He has taken to meditating in his room a great deal of late."

"I think it would be much better for him to go out, to be engaged in some active employment. The period of grief, I think passes more quickly when the mind is occupied by present activity, it saves one from thinking too much of the past."

"It is still so soon after the unhappy event, to expect either Sir Thomas or Lady Bertram to be able to fix their minds on anything else."

"But do you think they will be in such very deep mourning for long? I mean one must always follow the dictates of society in these things, one must dress according to the established custom and abstain from mixing too much in society for the necessary period of time, but how long do you suppose they will continue in this solemn state?"

"I do not believe it is possible to ever recover from the loss of a child," replied Fanny, forgetting the easy manner in which her sister Mary's death had been talked of in Portsmouth.

"No indeed, I believe it must be impossible. I do not think they shall ever fully recover, but certainly one would expect them to be restored to tolerably good cheer before long. I speak only in view of their well-being; such depressed spirits as I witnessed yesterday cannot be healthy for either of them."

"Each must grieve in his own time. I cannot presume to suppose how long it takes a parent to be reconciled to the death of a son."

"I hope your uncle has not been terribly inconvenienced by all those tedious matters of business that must accompany such an event."

"I have no knowledge of his business dealings."

"No of course you would not, but you must know if his attorney has been to call."

"Mr. Robinson and his wife did call to express their condolences."

"They are attentive and dutiful neighbours, I am sure."

"They have always been attentive. And though making a call of condolence upon a grieving neighbour may be a form of duty, I believe it was a duty carried out with genuine kindness and sympathy."

"I suppose then it was only a social call."

Fanny was a little confused but acknowledged it to be so.

Miss Crawford looked at Fanny and sighed, then said, "Well I do not envy you the duty of dressing in mourning clothes, but I must say you look as lovely in black as you do in every other colour I have seen you dressed in. But you must feel the good luck of being able to discard them sooner than Mrs. Rushworth or Miss Bertram. I know they cannot like having to wear them."

"I will observe the same mourning period as the rest of the family."

"Then you will mourn him as a sister! Dearest Fanny, I should have known you could do no less! You who have been a sister and confidante to the present Mr. Bertram; indeed, I believe he looks upon you as even more of a sister than those of his blood." This observation was too distressing to Fanny to permit her to make any reply. Miss Crawford, however, was not at a loss for words, "But what a shame for you to miss out on all the felicities of mixing in society, now that you are out."

"I assure you I will not regret missing any social intercourse."

"No, my dearest Fanny, I am not surprised to hear it, for you are too shy and modest. And what use are balls and parties but for finding a husband?" With a meaningful look, Miss Crawford added, "Happily, you have no need to look for one! But I imagine, nonetheless, that Lady Bertram, or at the very least, Sir Thomas would give enough thought to your happiness to go into half-mourning before long, on your account alone, if for no other reason."

Fanny was mortified by the suggestion. "I would never expect or desire such a thing, particularly on my account. I can only suppose that Sir Thomas and Lady Bertram will act in accordance with all the proper observances on the occasion. That they feel the loss inwardly every bit as much as their behaviour and manner of dress demonstrate it outwardly, I am certain. My own conduct will be ruled by their example."

Miss Crawford smiled. "You are too good, dearest Fanny. Too good for them, and even too good for Henry, I think. But I cannot imagine Mrs. Rushworth shares in your fastidious views. And, once she removes to Sotherton, free of any parental influence, I do not scruple to say with certainty equal to your own that *she* will not wear mourning clothes or stay out of society for very long."

"I can only hope that she will do what she judges to be right."

"Ah, because we are all the best guide of our own conduct! Henry told me you said as much." Fanny was surprised by this. She had hardly thought Mr. Crawford had heard her admonition in Portsmouth. "Do not be so surprised my dear friend, you are well aware that he hangs on your every word. If only those words had been true. Dear innocent Fanny, it is so like you to think well of everyone – though I believe you give dear Mrs. Rushworth too much credit. I cannot help but believe her an insufficient judge to be a guide to herself, even if she would attend her own judgement."

Fanny was taken aback by such easy criticism especially considering how well it applied to the speaker herself. "She certainly ought to have the ability to judge properly. There has been no deficiency in her education nor in the example provided by her parents. I hope that your conjecture is false, but if you can be supposed to be correct, then she must be guided by the judgement of her husband."

"Even if *he* possessed the ability to judge properly (a point upon which there must be considerable doubt), *she* has not enough respect for him to act according to his judgement. No, she would be governed by her own ill-judgement before his."

"Let us hope, then, that they will both be governed by the example of the rest of the family."

"I am perfectly willing to acquiesce, though I feel we will be hoping in excess of the abilities and inclinations of either." Then being ready to change the subject to one more pleasant to herself, Miss Crawford said, "Now tell me, my dearest friend, how has Mr. Bertram been since yesterday? Has he said anything to you about our visit?"

"He has not said anything to me about it."

"Not even so much as a 'Miss Crawford looked well did not she?' I should be extremely vexed with him for such an omission, but I will endeavour to forgive him ere I see him again." Fanny said nothing, so she continued. "But Fanny, your response to my inquiry is most unfair. You must be able to give me some encouraging news. I know he confides in you."

"I would never think of breaching his confidence."

"No, nor could I in good conscience ask it of you, but my dear Fanny, it must be within your power to give me a hint of his intentions. I had thought he was on the point of making a decision when we were in London and I expected that he would soon return before Tom's illness took precedence. And now … now that matters are resolved in such a way … now that there can be no obstacle to his finally coming to the point, it seems he is to be put off by the business of grieving. And I must endure this wretched suspense in the meanwhile. Thankfully, I have you, my dearest Fanny to commiserate with me."

Fanny had no intention of doing any such thing. That Miss Crawford could now complain of the delay in the achievement of her hopes occasioned by mourning the heir whose death made those very hopes possible was such an extreme of selfishness that Fanny could scarcely believe even in such a woman. "I beg you will excuse me from the office, Miss Crawford, I fear I would be ill-qualified to be of service to you."

"You have enough of commiseration at home, I imagine. I suppose then Mrs. Grant will have to do." Then, returning to her previous subject, she asked, "And what of the ladies of the house? What had Mrs. Rushworth and Miss Bertram to say of Henry and me? I can well imagine they view us as no less than interlopers!"

Fanny could hardly think of a better word to describe the Crawfords. In reply she simply said, "Mrs. Rushworth did not speak to me about it and Miss Bertram only asked me what I thought of the visit."

"And dare I ask what your reply was? I know it could not have been anything to our discredit."

"I told her only that you looked well and appeared as lively as ever, but that Mr. Crawford's manner seemed somewhat altered."

"What is this? It is you, my dear Fanny, who have caused the alteration, and cannot now be heard to complain of it! You know it is within your power alone to return his spirits to what they were."

"My observation was by no means a complaint."

"Henry will be happy to hear it," replied her companion with quickness.

Once again, Fanny's meaning had been wilfully mistaken. "Miss Crawford, I beg you would not repeat to him the substance of our conversation."

"Perhaps if you would talk to him more, I would not have to sustain him with second-hand repetitions of your every expression!"

"I do not imagine that he and I can have much of anything to say to one another."

"I am sure if you gave him the chance, you would find a thousand things to talk about."

"It does not signify in any case, as he seemed just as disinclined to talk to me." The moment it was spoken, Fanny regretted it. She knew the words would be misconstrued, particularly by one so desirous of interpreting them in a way they were never intended.

"Ah, dearest Fanny, I knew how it would be. I warned him yesterday that his conduct would cause you to doubt his constancy. But I can give you every assurance of his continued affection. I beg you would not take his neglect of you yesterday to heart."

"Indeed, you misunderstand me. I am not distressed by his disinclination to converse with me."

"That was exactly Henry's fear, that you would rather rejoice in his lack of attentions. But I gave him every reassurance to the contrary. Indeed, I told him you could not be so unfeeling, nor so undiscerning as to fail to appreciate his goodness and amiability and all the qualities for which he is universally adored."

Fanny was mortified by Miss Crawford's presumption. She had never said anything that could be construed as a basis for such representations; but her protestations to them were of no avail. She kept to herself her reflection that if Mr. Crawford commanded the adoration of so many, he could certainly have no use for her. That he should not be satisfied with such a superfluity of admirers was to his own discredit and misfortune.

The return of Mrs. Grant to the Parsonage provided Fanny with the opportunity to observe the lateness of the hour and declare that she must walk home. As she prepared to quit the Parsonage, Miss Crawford urged her to return on the morrow, and at first she could not be prevailed upon to leave her aunt's side again so soon; but Miss Crawford began to hint that she might pay a visit upon her to save her the uneasiness of giving her aunt any distress. This, Fanny considered an even greater evil, and she agreed to come again the next morning, provided that her uncle had no objection and her aunt could spare her. With that she left them and hurried home. After walking some distance, she looked back towards the Parsonage and perceived a gentleman on horseback who could only be Mr. Crawford, approaching it. She felt all the luck of having missed seeing him but dreaded the possibility that he might be there when she called tomorrow. She could not help wondering whether he had seen her walking back, and she imagined it must have been impossible not to. Yet, he had not taken the opportunity of finding her alone to impose himself on her. This boded well for her hopes that he had given her up.

When Fanny entered the drawing room she saw that Mrs. Rushworth and Miss Bertram had returned from their ride and were in high spirits, though affecting a sombre composure owing to their father being in the room. Fanny resumed her usual seat next to Lady Bertram where she remained until dinner. Edmund was home in time for dinner and within five minutes of entering the drawing room after its conclusion he sat close to Fanny and calmly asked about her visit with every appearance of disinterestedness. Fanny spoke enough to satisfy him, but felt she could repeat but little of her conversation with Miss Crawford. Some of that lady's expressions brought colour to Fanny's cheeks just in their remembrance – to speak them aloud was unthinkable. She did, upon being pressed, mention the invitation for the following morning and communicated her hesitation to leave her aunt again, but Edmund felt strongly that she should go, that it would do her good, and show her to be a grateful friend. Surely, she could not wish to disappoint Miss Crawford!

Before the gentlemen had entered the room, there had been more conspiratorial chatter between the sisters and the next morning they again announced their intent of going out riding. Again, there could be no objection. Mr. Rushworth, at first, suggested that he might accompany them. And at this juncture, Fanny noticed a look of alarm pass between the sisters. But Edmund announced that he had some business at Thornton Lacey and recalled that Mr. Rushworth had previously expressed a desire to see the place. Mr. Rushworth wondered if the ladies would take their ride to Thornton Lacey, to accompany him and Edmund, but both protested that it was too far, that they would be fatigued, and as Edmund did not know how long his business might take, the ladies felt their presence would be an inconvenience. Mr. Rushworth at last assented.

Chapter 5

Fanny set off for the Parsonage the following morning even more apprehensive than the day before and uncertain of what she was to find. Upon arriving she was greeted by Mrs. Grant with great affability and directed to walk outdoors and join her friends. Fanny almost cringed upon discerning the last letter of the word, knowing it meant she must encounter both brother and sister. They were not readily within view when Fanny walked out of the house, but upon hearing their voices she knew in which direction to walk. As Fanny approached, she was able to make out what they were saying before they came into view and she soon felt that she was intruding on a very private discussion.

"You know that I must go, Mary. It is the only thing to be done."

Fanny breathed a great sigh of relief as she heard Mr. Crawford's voice. One of her sources of distress would soon be gone.

"You are making too much of this, Henry, it is not cause to leave me here alone … and to leave Fanny. Only think of Fanny."

"You shall not be alone, and *she* will be happy to see me go, I assure you."

"It was nothing more than a little flirtation. It is not as though Mr. Rushworth would call you out."

At this Fanny stopped walking, overcome with surprise. She knew she should not listen to what was obviously a private conversation and had no desire to do so, but the shock of what she heard prevented her from being able to either advance forward or retreat.

"If he did, it would be no more than I deserve."

Fanny wondered what Mr. Crawford could have done to induce the possibility of such an extreme response in Mr. Rushworth.

"And if you make her a widow in a duel over her honour you might well be expected to marry her – and you do not deserve *that*!"

"Do not make light of this."

"Do not let *her* folly drive you away. It was she who purposefully set out to meet you yesterday. That alone might have gone undiscovered, but it was not enough for the foolish girl. And now *I* am made to suffer for it."

Fanny could listen no longer. The shocking discovery that Mrs. Rushworth had set out by design to meet Mr. Crawford the day before was enough to rouse her to her senses. She had no wish to hear what evil misdeeds that meeting had led to which now required Mr. Crawford to flee from a jealous husband. She quickly turned to walk back towards the house. But, before Mr. Crawford could make any reply to his sister, she perceived Fanny and called out to her. Fanny turned again, walked towards where the two stood and uttered an almost silent, "Good morning." They were both looking at her; each uncertain, perhaps, of how much she had heard. Miss Crawford asked, "My dearest Fanny, how long have you been hiding in the hedgerows?"

"I was not hiding," replied Fanny, in a voice barely above a whisper. She felt flushed.

Mr. Crawford said, "Mary, do not tease her."

Miss Crawford looked to her brother with a smile, looked back at Fanny, then suddenly felt that Mrs. Grant must have a great need for her at that particular moment and rushed inside, only pausing to hurriedly beg Fanny to convince her brother to stay.

Fanny must have looked as distressed as she felt, for Mr. Crawford immediately offered her his arm and led her to a seat saying, "Are you unwell?"

"I am quite well, thank you."

"Perhaps you heard too much of our conversation." She said nothing. "I had hoped that by being out here we would have had less chance of being overheard, and that Mrs. Grant would have given us notice of your arrival."

"It was my own fault for not making my presence known," she replied.

"No, I am sure you are not at fault," he replied. After a brief hesitation, but before she could make any response he added, "As you may have heard, I must leave the country."

"Yes. I confess I overheard as much."

"I … Miss Price, I would wish you to know …" he seemed to be searching for words, but he stopped himself. Instead, he stood and offered her his hand, saying, "Come, let us return inside." Whatever he had intended to say was abandoned and Fanny could not regret it. She had no desire to know anything more of the reason for his precipitous departure from the neighbourhood. She knew too much already. She took his hand very unwillingly and relinquished it immediately upon rising from the bench; then they walked silently back into the house. Once inside, he looked at her momentarily, then only said, "I will leave you to your visit," and turned away. He quit the room and a moment later Fanny heard his footfall on the stair.

There was scarcely any time for reflection following this exchange before Fanny was required to face Miss Crawford, who was sitting languidly with Mrs. Grant in the drawing room. When Fanny approached the pair, Miss Crawford leaned forward seeming to expect some disclosure from Fanny of her recent conversation. Receiving none, however, she had no choice but to inquire as to Fanny's success in changing Mr. Crawford's mind. Fanny only replied that he had mentioned to her his intent to leave the country. After a moment's pause, Miss Crawford – who seemed to have half expected that the brief conversation had settled everything between her brother and her friend – hoped to urge Fanny's confidence by entreating her to commiserate with her in her brother's going away. "My dear Fanny," said she with real despondence, "we must console one another as best we can." When thinking of consolation, Fanny's mind could only turn to those at home who were more deserving of it and for a cause more worthy. "What shall we do without our Henry?"

"I believe we shall do as we have done heretofore," was all Fanny said in reply, ignoring Miss Crawford's use of the word "our." She knew that any acknowledgement of a community of melancholy feeling regarding Mr. Crawford's departure, even a denial as to her share in it, would invite a conversation of greater length than the subject warranted.

Here Miss Crawford smiled and glancing at her sister, said, "Come now Fanny, you are with intimate friends. There can be no secrets between us. Especially concerning Henry."

Fanny was taken aback by such an invitation. "Indeed, Miss Crawford, I have no such secrets."

"Oh Fanny, I beg you to relieve my suffering by telling me you have finally relieved Henry's."

Fanny was visibly confused. "I have not the pleasure of understanding you," she said.

"I am sure you do but as you refuse to talk to me, I will desist. I will get it out of Henry before he leaves in any case." She then returned to the other subject of interest to her, "But it is so unfair that he should be going away." Then looking at Fanny she added, "I am sure you heard all about the unhappy business that has driven him from us; not that I agree to its being a reason for him to quit the country."

Fanny found the topic too distasteful to be able to form any response and only hoped she could soon turn the conversation to other matters. However, it was taken up by Mrs. Grant. "It is rather shocking," she agreed, "that Mrs. Rushworth should show such poor judgement but I think Henry need not leave us on account of it, as she will be going away herself in a few days."

Miss Crawford sighed. "I do not think it much signifies whether Henry leaves the country or not. Either way, I will be much surprised if the news does not spread about the neighbourhood before her escape. Everyone loves a scandalous rumour, after all."

"With both of the involved parties gone, there can be no reason for any rumours – if they do arise – to persist long enough to do any lasting damage."

Fanny felt she had endured quite enough for one morning but thought an immediate departure would result in so short a visit as to give offence. She listened to the sisters for a few minutes more and availed herself of every opportunity that opened to her to change the conversation. After a quarter hour of going on in this manner, she announced her intent to depart. This was met with protestations as to the shortness of her visit, but she was determined. At last her friends yielded and she left the Parsonage with all the contentment of returning to a home full of grievous despair.

She had much to contemplate on her walk back. That Henry Crawford's behaviour, to her mind, supported her supposition that he had given her up was the least of it. She could not deny that she had begun after his visit to Portsmouth to think he really loved her, and to fancy his affection for her something more than common – even to allow that the more recent withdrawal of his attentions may have been due to his solicitude for her own comfort – and his sister still said that he cared for nobody else; but his recent behaviour proved otherwise. So much for the proofs of constancy he had promised. She hoped, at least, that this event might give him knowledge of his own disposition, convince him that he was not capable of being steadily attached to any one woman in the world, and shame him from persisting any longer in addressing herself. And, although she could only rejoice in the withdrawal of his attentions, she could not help feeling some satisfaction in having been right about him. She was glad to be rid of him.

In considering all she had learned, she could not doubt that something reprehensible had occurred between him and her cousin; there must have been some marked display of attentions. For the other two ladies to have spoken of the event in such a way there must have been some strong indiscretion, since Miss Crawford was not of a sort to regard a slight one. Indeed, the conversation between brother and sister left little doubt as to the seriousness of the offence. Yet, Miss Crawford's chief concern in the matter had been in losing her brother's company. To Fanny's mind, his going away was the only circumstance mitigating against the evil of the affair.

That Maria and Julia had actually gone riding with the design of finding him and engaging him in a continued flirtation was horrid enough, but she knew there was more to it. What that encounter had led to, Fanny neither knew nor wished to know; but that it was enough to necessitate Mr. Crawford's leaving the country was sufficient to establish both his and Maria's guilt firmly in Fanny's mind.

Clearly there had been some meeting between the two after the first encounter. And it appeared that through some neglect on Maria's part, they had been discovered by someone. For there to be a danger of Mr. Rushworth challenging Mr. Crawford, the two must have been caught in some act of dishonour. Nothing less serious would justify the expectation of so extreme a measure or necessitate Mr. Crawford's departure. That Miss Crawford placed all the blame on Mrs. Rushworth, Fanny attributed to the bias of a sister, for the gentleman had said himself that he deserved to be called out. Fanny shook her head to herself as she reflected that Mr. Crawford and Mrs. Rushworth had not been in the same country for three days before being discovered in a compromising situation!

Poor Mr. Rushworth! How could Maria be so foolishly selfish? And now it had fallen to Fanny's lot to learn that some great indiscretion had been committed. What should she do? What could she do? To approach Sir Thomas on such a subject was unimaginable. She could speak to Edmund about it. But what could be done? She herself was thankfully unacquainted with any of the particulars and knew not of how much Mr. Rushworth might be aware. Adding to the suspicion Fanny knew he already felt might only make matters worse. Besides, the danger would be gone with Mr. Crawford out of the country.

At least he had acted rightly there, though it could not atone for whatever misdeed had precipitated his flight. And in trying to reconcile why he should decide to leave the country after such an indiscretion now when he had flagrantly remained last autumn to carry on a flirtation with both sisters, she could only attribute it to Sir Thomas being at home, and she was very glad of it.

And though Mr. Crawford was right to leave, whatever his motives, Fanny could not think so well of his sister's view of the matter. To have encouraged him to remain in the country and continue a flirtation – and anything else – with a married woman who was determined to make him regret her was simply another example of the extreme poor judgement Miss Crawford always exhibited. Indeed, if there was a woman in existence who could treat as a trifle an indiscretion of such magnitude, she could believe Miss Crawford to be that woman.

She thought of Edmund, and how he was so deceived by her; how ill-suited they were to one another. She thought of his strong principles and of her indifference to decorum and righteousness. If Fanny could but know for sure that showing Edmund her letter regarding Tom's prospects would undeceive him, she might consider it. Yet, she knew that it would be a violation of honour to show him the letter, that no one ought to be judged or known by such testimonies, that no private correspondence should bear the eye of others. And there was no reason to believe, even if she could bring herself to show it to him, that Edmund would not excuse Miss Crawford as he had done on so many other occasions when her indelicate views had been immediately before him. Fanny could not call her own motives in contemplating the disclosure selfish as it was quite out of her power to rate herself worthy of being within Edmund's sphere of choice. Yet, she could not trust herself to judge her own motives objectively. To breach the dictates of propriety and the confidence of the writer – even such a writer – was more than Fanny was equal to. How could a young woman in her position presume to appear to judge such a woman as Miss Crawford? – a woman who was her superior by every standard. She would be deemed officious, self-righteous, ungrateful, and perhaps even spiteful – should her own feelings ever come to light.

Oh that she had some guidance! Usually Edmund was her guide in matters of delicacy and uncertainty, but she could not turn to him now. Was there anyone with whom she was on so intimate a footing yet sufficiently detached from the Mansfield family and upon whose judgement and discretion she could trust? William. She would write to William. *He* could have no interest in any of the business to bias him and no particular like or dislike for anyone involved. She would write to William and rely on his counsel as to what, if anything, she should do.

She was now eager to get home and before joining her aunt in the drawing room she went to the East room for the privacy required to compose such a letter. She could not, of course, tell William everything. Her own feelings for Edmund she could not disclose, even to William; and she felt that such knowledge might bias him after all in favour of her happiness; that he might aspire to more on her behalf than she could ever hope for herself. She did tell him of the indelicacy of Miss Crawford's letter, of Edmund's blindness to her faults, of Maria's foolish ill-conduct, and of Miss Crawford's response to it. She wrote all and then urged him fervently to burn the letter once he'd written back. She felt better after this task was completed. She felt as if a great burden had been lifted from her. And she went down to her aunt with the lightest spirits she could be capable of under the circumstances.

At dinner, Sir Thomas announced that he had received a note from Mr. Crawford expressing that he had to leave the country on urgent business, that he would already have departed by the time they received his note, and that he regretted that it had not been within his power to make a farewell call before doing so. He hoped the family was well and again expressed his deepest condolences for their loss.

Fanny was a bit surprised by the expedience with which Mr. Crawford had carried out his resolution of quitting the neighbourhood, but could not be displeased by it. Maria and Julia attempted to appear unaffected by the news but shared a meaningful look. Edmund could only express concern for the sister Mr. Crawford was leaving behind and urge his cousin to be even more attentive to her to prevent loneliness, as he was certain no one could lift Miss Crawford's spirits as she could.

However, in the relative privacy of a quiet corner in the drawing room after dinner, he had more to say.

"My dear Fanny. I know how Mr. Crawford's departure must affect you."

Fanny could not help but be disappointed by his choice of subject. "Please Edmund," was all she could say.

"You do not wish to speak of it because it pains you."

Oh why would Edmund not believe that she was not in love with Mr. Crawford? How could he fail to perceive her discomfort whenever the matter was spoken of? "No, you are mistaken. I am not pained in the least by his going away. I think it is for the best."

"Your modesty and delicacy are exemplary, but you can be open with me." She protested again but to no avail. "I must confess, I was pleased by his having visited you in Portsmouth. For him to have gone out of his way to see you, says a great deal of the depth of his feelings and must have softened your feelings towards him; and now he has gone away again, just when you have resumed your acquaintance."

"Truly, you must believe me, nothing of any consequence happened at Portsmouth to change my feelings towards him. I have never been attached to him. We are not suited to one another."

"And who, I wonder, would you consider suitable if you cannot accept the man who has done so much for your dearest brother?"

"I trust you will not think me ungrateful," she said with real concern.

"I know your gratitude must give way to more precious feelings in the face of his constancy and devotion. You are too generous not to return his love."

Fanny could not receive this observation as the compliment it was clearly intended to be. "I cannot think well of him," she said firmly.

Edmund lowered his voice even more, though no one could have discerned a word of their conversation heretofore. "Do not place too much emphasis on his behaviour last autumn. It was wrong, but it was only a harmless flirtation which has come to nothing."

If Edmund could only know how mistaken he was! If he only knew the degree of danger that had arisen from the "harmless flirtation" to which he alluded. Fanny could say nothing to correct his supposition and instead gave him to understand her own opinion as to the change of Mr. Crawford's feelings and intentions towards herself.

Edmund would not agree with her. Fanny sighed, but as she was eager to change the subject she did not contradict him. Instead, she observed, "Your sisters seem to be more sedate this evening than the last two."

"Yes, and I cannot regret it. Their liveliness at a time like this seemed a bit indecorous to me. I am glad they have seen it as well and improved their conduct."

"I hope they had a pleasant ride today."

"I believe it must have been a strenuous one for, Lady Bertram tells me, they were tired out much more quickly than yesterday and returned home sooner."

"I wonder if they will go out again tomorrow."

"Do you intend to ride tomorrow? I know it has been some time since you have done so. Or, do you intend to call again at the Parsonage?"

"I am not engaged to call at the Parsonage tomorrow. But nor will I go riding. I have left my aunt two days in a row now; I am resolved to stay with her tomorrow. She did not send you to fetch me home in her time of need to have me everywhere but at her side."

Edmund could not help but smile his approval of her devotion to her aunt, though he had hoped to accompany her on one of her visits to the Parsonage and the following morning he happened to be unengaged. He sighed, knowing there would be other opportunities.

Chapter 6

Just such an opportunity came sooner than Fanny could have anticipated; for, the next morning before breakfast, Julia again sought her out in the East room for private conversation. "Fanny," she said, "I believe I shall walk with you to the Parsonage this morning."

"But I am not engaged to go to the Parsonage today."

"What? Not go? But you are such good friends with Miss Crawford, I cannot very well go without you."

"You have been on an intimate enough footing with her in the past. I am sure there can be no reason for you not to call on her alone."

"But that was so very long ago, and she was never my particular friend as she has been yours. I would feel awkward to go alone, uninvited. Yet, how else am I to become better acquainted with Mrs. Grant and Miss Crawford as you have done?" She paused, and on receiving no response, continued. "I dare say Mr. Crawford will invite his sisters to Everingham this summer. Do not you think Miss Crawford would wish to have an intimate friend with her on such a visit? And if Mrs. Grant goes with her, why should she not invite me as well?"

Fanny was surprised and disappointed by the extent of her cousin's scheming, but simply replied, "I fear I cannot leave my aunt's side for a third day. And to lose your company as well as mine, I think would be too much for her."

"Come now, Maria is still here. She is in low spirits and expects to sit in the drawing room with my mother all day. And I dare say my aunt Norris will be about as well. We shall only be gone an hour."

"I feel that I should be with Lady Bertram today, perhaps another day soon we can make the call."

"But once Maria has gone away you will not wish for both of us to leave my mother. If we are to call at the Parsonage together we should do so before Maria leaves Mansfield." Seeing she hadn't convinced Fanny she added, "Let us not decide hastily; we have not yet seen my mother today. I dare say if we find her in tolerably good spirits at breakfast you will be satisfied."

Fanny knew it was within Julia's power to elicit an acknowledgement from her mother that she could do without both of them for an hour during the course of the morning. Yet how could she refuse so reasonable a compromise? "Very well," she replied.

It happened, however, that the compromise was for naught, as Lady Bertram did not come down to breakfast at all. An upper maid had informed Edmund, in response to his inquiry, that Lady Bertram had the headache, was not in spirits to join the family at breakfast, and had declared her intent of staying in her rooms all day with only the inestimable Chapman to attend her.

While Mrs. Norris' extremity of concern for her sister prevented her from staying away from Lady Bertram's apartment the entire day, she did not hesitate to excuse the young ladies from making any appearance there. In fact, she was sure she could find errands enough to keep Fanny busy during the entirety of the morning and was making lists in her head of what use she could make of her even as she came back down the stairs from her first ascent to Lady Bertram's chamber. She had soon begun communicating her needs to Fanny with detailed instructions on the best way to carry out each task, but Julia was determined that Fanny should have little opportunity to test how well she could adhere to such minute instructions and was quick to tell Mrs. Norris of their intended visit to the Parsonage. It was then that Fanny discovered that Edmund was to accompany them as well. Mrs. Norris felt there was no need for Fanny to go with Julia and Edmund but they insisted on having her company. When pressed to join them by Edmund, Maria declined, making it clear that she had a great many things to do at home. Mr. Rushworth chose to remain with his wife. Very soon, the three were on their way to the Parsonage, much to Fanny's dismay. As they walked the short distance, Fanny reflected to herself that this would be her third visit to the Parsonage in as many days; it was not the habit she had wished to establish on her renewed acquaintance with Miss Crawford.

Not long after their arrival and once the necessary pleasantries had been exchanged, Edmund requested music of Miss Crawford, eagerly assuring her that he could think of no greater pleasure than listening to her play the harp. Julia and Fanny also expressed their delight at the suggestion, though with less enthusiasm. She played a few songs and Fanny enjoyed the music in spite of herself. What she could not bear was witnessing Edmund staring at Miss Crawford the way he did while she played. It was quite evident that he was enthralled. Even though she had long known of his feelings, it was still difficult for her to comprehend that he did not see Miss Crawford for what she truly was; that with his superior understanding and adherence to principle, he could love such a woman – a woman who flaunted her selfishness, her vanity and her abhorrence for the very principles he lived by and valued so greatly, the principles that he had always taught to Fanny. That the only person who had been able to perceive Fanny's suffering in her youth and show her any compassion, the only person who had exerted himself for her comfort, now showed so little perception when it came to this woman – a woman who never demonstrated the attributes Fanny admired in Edmund, who rarely showed compassion or selfless exertion on behalf of another, a woman who had openly criticized his values and his choices – was distressing to the extreme. Edmund had changed and Fanny began to feel he was lost to her – as a cousin, as a friend, even as a brother – forever.

Following the performance, and after the requisite amount of praise was bestowed on the performer – and then some by Edmund – Julia managed to turn the conversation to Mr. Crawford. She asked Miss Crawford several questions regarding the reason for his sudden removal, where he was going, and when he might return to the neighbourhood. Miss Crawford could scarcely contain her melancholy in replying to these inquiries, though she addressed herself to Fanny as if she had been the one inquiring, perhaps imagining that Fanny had asked Julia to make the inquiries on her behalf.

Such visits occurred more often than Fanny liked in the ensuing weeks, which must be attributed to the desire by both Miss and Mr. Bertram to improve their acquaintance with Miss Crawford; and within a fortnight the two women were calling each other by their Christian names. However, the blossoming friendship was suddenly cut short by an event which gave way to a more promising opportunity for Miss Bertram.

Mr. and Mrs. Rushworth had removed to Sotherton on the appointed date, and Fanny wondered that Julia had not contrived to go with them; she hoped she could attribute it to her cousin's desire to be with her family during their time of grief. But a different reason became apparent soon after the Rushworths' removal, when Fanny learned that Julia had requested Sir Thomas' permission to go back to those cousins with whom she had been staying in London. It was further revealed that the cousins had taken a country house for the summer – in Norfolk. This raised some alarm for Fanny but she could not suppose the location of the house to be due to anything but coincidence. Norfolk was a large county and the likelihood of their being in close enough proximity to Everingham for any kind of social intercourse must be very small. Yet, Fanny could not forget Julia's apparent determination to exact revenge upon her sister by catching Mr. Crawford, nor her scheme of securing an invitation to Everingham through friendship with its master's sisters, and could not help but wonder whether this move to Norfolk had been brought about, at least in part, by Julia's own design. Fanny had no knowledge of how far Julia's influence might hold sway with this particular family of cousins, but she knew that

Julia had been in constant communication with them since her departure from their home in London. Although Fanny could certainly not approve Julia's scheme to catch Mr. Crawford, and thought any permanent connection between the families highly undesirable – though hardly avoidable given Edmund's feelings – she knew it was not so great an evil as a clandestine connection between Mrs. Rushworth and Mr. Crawford would have been. She began to think an attachment between Julia and Mr. Crawford might not be a very bad thing so far as it would put an end to whatever ambitions Maria might still have towards Mr. Crawford and any feelings Mr. Crawford might still have for herself. But Fanny knew what kind of man Mr. Crawford was and she doubted that marriage to Julia could be his object; she only hoped her cousin would not allow herself to be ill-used by him.

Permission was readily given to Julia by Sir Thomas, whose first object now was the pleasure of his remaining children, and Lady Bertram could have no objection; thus, Edmund dutifully conveyed his sister to London whence she would travel with her cousins to Norfolk for the summer. And so it was that Fanny was soon receiving regular though unsolicited news from two sources regarding Mr. Crawford. For, as it turned out, the house rented by the family of cousins with whom Julia had gone to stay was in the very neighbourhood of Everingham, and Julia and Mr. Crawford were now constantly in company together. Julia could not be called a diligent correspondent, but even so, her letters were more frequent than Fanny could wish; from the first, they justified her fears:

My Dear Fanny, I hope this letter finds you and my parents well. I am quite well-settled here in Norfolk and within two miles of Everingham. Mr. Dixon's arrangements have answered my every hope. I have seen him already. He called on Mr. Dixon only two days after our arrival and we dined together in company yesterday where he met me with all the warmth of intimate friendship. We had a little ball after dinner and we danced together and remembered fondly our drive to Sotherton last year. I am so very glad I brought all my dresses with me. I shall be able to wear them after all. I see no reason to wear mourning clothes in a country where no one even knew Poor Tom, and Maria has given them up entirely, she told me in her last letter that she wears only black ribbons now. I have not yet been to Everingham as there is no lady in the house, but I am sure

Miss Dixon and I will contrive some way of seeing the place. As for the rest of the neighbourhood, everyone is quite intrigued by my prior connection with Mr. Crawford. All of the girls hereabouts are wild for him, but he looks at none of them. And Miss Webb – his neighbour and now my intimate friend – is certain he has never singled out anyone as he does me. I will write more of my progress as I am sure you will rejoice in my success – I will be ever so happy to relieve you of the speculation arising from his prior declarations to you. Give my love to all, and tell my mother I shall write to her very soon. Yours etc., Julia Bertram

There was nothing Fanny could approve in Julia's correspondence, or indeed in her scheme of going to Norfolk altogether. Fanny had no reason to doubt that Mr. Crawford was paying attentions to Julia, given her own prior observations of his behaviour; what she did doubt was that it would end as Julia hoped.

In spite of Julia's hints to the contrary, Miss Crawford continued to reassure Fanny of her brother's constancy and continued to impart to Fanny the minutiae of every letter she received from him. These assurances, however, Fanny attributed wholly to Miss Crawford's own desires and imagination, for Julia's letters told another story. Fanny was pleased with the news from Julia, insofar as it supported her supposition that Mr. Crawford no longer thought of herself. She might have been happy for Julia as well had she not been aware of her cousin's private motivation of securing Mr. Crawford to spite her sister. Miss Crawford's impression was clearly very different but Fanny simply supposed that Mr. Crawford did not share everything about his flirtation with Julia in his letters to his sister and therefore she was free to believe what she wished. Indeed, she remembered Miss Crawford once saying that her brother wrote short letters with little detail; these could hardly contain a full account of his social dealings, and Julia's letters withheld nothing.

The first such conversation between Fanny and Miss Crawford occurred one day, not long after Fanny had received Julia's first letter from Norfolk, when they were walking alone in the shrubbery at the Parsonage, Miss Crawford said, "So what do you think of Julia's going to Norfolk?"

"I do not think anything of it."

"Have you had a letter from her?"

"Yes, she wrote that she is having a pleasant time with her cousins and has enjoyed making new acquaintances in the neighbourhood."

"And meeting with old acquaintances as well, I am sure."

"She mentioned that she had seen Mr. Crawford, but you must have received news of their meeting from him."

"He said little about it, except that she behaves very differently when not in Mrs. Rushworth's company." Fanny made no reply. "He says she is less reserved, more open." She leaned forward as if imparting a great secret. "He wrote that her cousin Mr. Dixon told him that when he first considered taking a place in the country, it was Julia who suggested Norfolk to Miss Dixon by letter." Fanny was not surprised, but said nothing. "Henry also mentioned that a young gentleman in the neighbourhood – the second or third son of one of the families thereabouts – has been very particular in his inquiries about her." She paused, but on receiving no response, continued, "But I think she has other designs." Miss Crawford still could not provoke her friend's curiosity. "Do not you wish to know of my suspicions?"

"I would not wish to conjecture as to Miss Bertram's designs."

"But it is *my* conjecture, so you can have no objection to it," replied Miss Crawford teasingly. "At first I could not make Julia out at all. She seemed so intent on forwarding a friendship with me during her last few weeks at Mansfield, visiting with you at the Parsonage at every opportunity – which I confess, I found tiresome for it deprived me of any chance of ever speaking to you in confidence. And then she left so suddenly and so eagerly upon receiving the invitation from her cousins; I knew it had to be more than coincidence that took her so near to Everingham, but I did not fully apprehend her design until I received Henry's letter." She paused, then stated with great effect, "I think she still hopes to secure my brother." Miss Crawford waited for a response from her companion, but on receiving none, added, "This is, after all, Julia's first time being in company with him without Mrs. Rushworth around as a distraction. It was very clever of her to contrive to throw herself in his way without any of us in reach." Fanny still said nothing. "I know you would never think ill of your own cousin, but I can only view it as an affront to you. She knows as well as anyone that Henry is in love with you."

"I do not think he is," said Fanny earnestly, "and even if he was at one time, I have assured Julia – just as I have assured everyone else – that my feelings towards Mr. Crawford are and always have been nothing more than what is due to him as an acquaintance of the family. Even if your conjecture as to her motives is true, I am not affronted. On the contrary, I would welcome the match."

Miss Crawford looked gravely at Fanny and said, "We have been friends a long time, and I still hope for the day when you will confide your true feelings in me, my dear Fanny. Have not I been a good friend? Have not I confided all my secrets in you? You need not hide your feelings from me. As for your not loving Henry, I will never believe it, no matter how earnestly you try to convince me. It is impossible for any woman not to love him."

Fanny could protest no more. "I will not try to convince you. I speak only the truth. If you do not believe me then so it must be. In any case, I have reason to believe that any feelings he may have had for me have long since diminished. And it is for the best."

"You may claim to know your own feelings better than I do, but I know Henry better than anyone and his feelings for you are unabated, as I have assured you many times."

"Even so, I do not suppose that there are many men who could overlook the attentions of a pretty, good-natured girl who is frequently before him in favour of the memory of one who has refused him and whom he never sees. I beg of you to speak no more to me of Mr. Crawford's constancy."

Fanny of course wished only to put an end to a topic of conversation that always distressed her. Miss Crawford however, as was her wont, took this speech rather as a confirmation of her belief that Fanny loved Mr. Crawford than as a denial of it. In her view, Fanny's delicate heart was threatened by Julia's scheme.

"Then I will not tell you that he asked after you in his letter. Instead I will tell you what he said about Julia. He danced with her one evening after dinner at the home of one of his neighbours, which I am sure she told you. But he wrote of it with indifference, while she undoubtedly wrote of it with great enthusiasm." She waited for confirmation but Fanny only acknowledged that Julia had mentioned the dance. "He wrote that he had not been inclined for dancing at all, but had done so out of duty and politeness."

Fanny knew Mr. Crawford to only do what gave him pleasure and that his conduct was generally guided by neither duty nor politeness. If he had danced with Julia, it had been because he wanted to. If he had neglected to write to his sister of his own smiles during the dance then Miss Crawford could not make an accurate judgement of his inclinations.

Chapter 7

The days and weeks now passed in relative tranquillity. Sir Thomas and Lady Bertram were slowly becoming more animated as their prior dispositions gradually returned. Fanny spent most of her days indoors with Lady Bertram. Her frequent walks to the Parsonage left her little time for any other exercise; which was just as well, since Miss Crawford had again taken up riding and often urged Fanny to join her, observing that the availability of Julia's horse made it possible for them to ride together. This, Fanny acquiesced to as infrequently as she could contrive, particularly as Edmund often joined them when they rode out together; and on those occasions, neither seemed to notice Fanny at all. Nevertheless, Miss Crawford's zeal to go out riding together overthrew any possibility of Fanny ever being able to ride without her company. The family heard little from Julia, aside from her infrequent letters to Fanny, and less from Maria.

Edmund continued to go to Thornton Lacey on Sundays, as he had been doing since his ordination and even through his brother's illness and death, but he remained a resident of Mansfield from Monday through Saturday. It seemed natural, after the family's loss that he should remain with them, but Fanny knew he had another motive for staying. Indeed, the family's intercourse with the Parsonage at this time was as frequent as ever and Fanny could only anticipate with restless agitation the inevitable conclusion of the growing intimacy between Edmund and Miss Crawford. He took care not to make any indelicate display of his intent, given the family's circumstances, for even in the height of his passion he could not suppose it possible to become engaged within six months after his brother's death; but despite these efforts, their mutual attraction was obvious and before summer's end, it was openly accepted in the neighbourhood that they were engaged. It was commonly assumed that they had an understanding between themselves and had not made it public yet due only to the family's circumstances.

Fanny's indecision regarding whether to disclose the contents of Miss Crawford's letter to Edmund was put an end to by William's letter in response to hers, in which he wrote that their cousin Edmund must be left to manage his own affairs and advised Fanny not to interfere. She thus considered the matter settled.

Unfortunately, Miss Crawford did not show the same forbearance and spoke often to Fanny of Mr. Crawford on those occasions when Edmund was not present for their meetings – which were as infrequent as Fanny could contrive – imparting, unsolicited, all the information contained in his letters. Fanny happily found that she was scarcely mentioned in those letters; and in support of her conviction that he had given her up, Mr. Crawford no longer sent her messages through his sister. Yet she allowed herself to be so much interested in his doings as to feel somewhat pleased to hear he intended to remain in Norfolk through the summer. It seemed now that any meeting between him and Mrs. Rushworth was impossible, at least for the time being, and that was a relief. She wondered if the growing intimacy described in Julia's letters had anything to do with his decision to remain at Everingham. Although Julia could easily return to Mansfield should he visit the Parsonage, Fanny imagined both would prefer to carry out their courtship away from the eyes of either her family or his. Yet, Fanny could not believe that Mr. Crawford intended anything serious by his attentions to Julia, and could not forget her concerns for Julia's reputation. The longer Julia stayed within his influence, the more Fanny feared some evil would befall her. This fear grew with each letter from Julia, who wrote with ever increasing fervour of her conviction that Mr. Crawford would soon make her an offer. Fanny could not imagine that Julia would write with such certainty if she had not been receiving definite signs of encouragement from Mr. Crawford. She doubted neither that Mr. Crawford was giving Julia reason to hope nor that he had little intention of justifying her hopes. She wondered how, knowing of her sister's disappointment the previous year, Julia could have fallen into the same trap of expecting an offer that would not come.

Yet, as usual, Miss Crawford, who received her information from another source, viewed the matter in a very different light. As they were walking one day, Miss Crawford said suddenly, "I believe Henry is at his wit's end when it comes to your cousin Julia."

"Why do you say so? What can be the matter?"

"He writes that the neighbourhood is beginning to talk of a match between them, though he has never done anything to promote the idea."

"If his neighbours have formed an expectation of a match, then his behaviour must have given rise to it, at least in part."

"Or, she is trying to trap him. It is easy enough for a young lady to plant the seeds of expectation, especially in matters such as this. Did not I tell you how it would be? But he will not be so easily ensnared. He will not do it. Of that, I am certain."

Fanny could not disagree. She had long known Mr. Crawford was not of a disposition to marry, notwithstanding his proposals to herself. Julia would be disappointed and all Fanny could hope for was that her cousin would survive with her reputation intact. Fanny sought only to put an end to the conversation, as she always did.

It seemed she was surrounded by one source of pain after another – her grieving aunt and uncle reduced to shadows of the people they once were, another aunt constantly criticizing and making everyone more miserable, her deluded cousin blinded by love for a worthless woman, letters from another cousin filled with hopes that would inevitably be disappointed but whose motivations made compassion nearly impossible, and a friend and constant companion who gave her no pleasure and always imposed upon her with distasteful and uncomfortable conversation. Even her letters from Susan were filled with news of all the trials and tribulations of the Price household – and they were so few and far between, Fanny began to despair that her influence there was slipping away. Her one solace, her one source of unalloyed joy, and of escape from the sorrows that surrounded her, was her correspondence with William. Aside from her one request for his advice, his letters spoke only of his adventures, of his career, of the advancements he had made, the places he had seen, and the people he had encountered. They allowed Fanny to escape, to know there was a world outside of Mansfield where happiness and joy existed. William's letters, though not as frequent as she would have liked, always made her smile.

And so it was with great joy that she received a letter from him, the contents of which surprised her exceedingly. He wrote in his usual way of his doings, covering the front and almost the back of the paper. Then, at the end, he wrote the following:

My dear Fanny, I am pleased I had not yet closed my letter as I have just received news that I hope will please you as much as it has pleased me. Mr. Crawford has written to invite me to a shooting party. I mentioned in my last letter to him that my ship would put into port at Yarmouth and I would have a seven days' leave of absence. I had just reconciled myself to the impossibility of travelling into Northamptonshire during that time when I received his letter of invitation. He is attending a shooting party at the home of a friend who lives about twenty miles from Everingham at Hollingsworth. This friend has some connections in the navy and upon Mr. Crawford having mentioned me to him in a letter, insisted that he extend me an invitation to join them. I hope to have the good luck to be in port in time. I will write to you next from there. Yours, etc., W. Price

Fanny received the news with as much astonishment as pleasure. She had not even known that William and Mr. Crawford corresponded. Whatever Mr. Crawford's faults, it appeared he had a genuine attachment to William and desired to maintain a friendship with him. Given Mr. Crawford's connections in the navy, such a friendship could be invaluable to her brother.

William wrote from Hollingsworth as he promised. He spoke of Mr. Crawford and of his host, Mr. Blake, as well as the other gentlemen present, in the fondest of terms. Indeed, he was enjoying both the company and the sport a great deal. He made no reference to what had passed between Fanny and Mr. Crawford the previous winter, and for that Fanny was grateful, but he did mention that he and Mr. Crawford had spoken of her briefly.

In her reply letter, Fanny could not help but be conscious of who might be in the room when William read it. She had little news of Mansfield to send other than assuring him of the continued improvement in the spirits of their aunt and uncle. She encouraged him to enjoy his stay at Hollingsworth and wished him luck with his shooting. Then, after a great deal of indecision, she bade William to give her regards to Mr. Crawford. She felt it her duty to acknowledge their acquaintance for no other reason than his kindness to William. She had a reply from him written from Yarmouth before he sailed and she knew it would be some time before she heard from him again. This letter was of a piece with his last, informing her of how he had enjoyed both the sport and the company at Hollingsworth, and how grateful he had been for the opportunity to join the party. He mentioned that Mr. Crawford thanked her for remembering him and returned her salutation. Fanny breathed a sigh of relief. The exchange had been marked by no more than common civility. The whole unhappy matter of Mr. Crawford's suit now seemed behind her. She felt secure of never being importuned by his advances again and had only to wait for his sister to realize the truth and cease talking about it.

Chapter 8

The news that Julia would be returning to Mansfield came soon after Miss Crawford received word from Mr. Crawford that he would be leaving Everingham for an unspecified amount of time to attend a shooting party at a friend's estate. Miss Crawford spoke of the shooting party only as a means for her brother to escape Julia and the expectations of the neighbourhood. To Fanny, it was all too familiar. He had sported with Julia and run away just as he had done with Maria. But she was happy for her brother's sake. Miss Crawford however, professed her profound disappointment that her own brother had gone to stay at Hollingsworth but had made no plans to spend any part of the summer at Mansfield and now that the hunting season had begun, there was no hope of his coming this summer.

Julia, upon returning to Mansfield, resumed her overtures of friendship towards Miss Crawford and replaced Fanny as a riding companion. She joined in Miss Crawford's disappointment that Mr. Crawford would not be at Mansfield at all for the summer, and reflected fondly on her time in Norfolk where she had seen him regularly. She spoke of nothing but the pleasant times and delightful friends she had enjoyed there. She confided to Fanny that she felt she had made great progress in her plan of winning Mr. Crawford. Yet, though Julia attempted only to show cheerfulness, Fanny could sense that for all the encouragement she boasted of having received, she was disappointed. She had expected to come home an engaged woman.

The intimacy between Miss Crawford and Edmund continued to grow. It was evident that Miss Crawford intended to go from Mansfield Parsonage to Thornton Lacey. In early November her long wait was rewarded. Edmund, it seemed, now felt that he had honoured his brother's memory long enough by formally requesting the hand of the woman who had rejoiced in that brother's impending death. Though Sir Thomas was a little surprised by the news – or at least that the engagement had been announced scarcely more than half a year since Poor Tom's untimely death – a death that had made the union possible, or at least easy – he took it well and gave his blessing.

For Fanny it was a difficult blow. She now discovered the difference between the expectation of an unpleasant event, however certain the mind may be told to consider it, and certainty itself. She had known the marriage was inevitable in the privacy of her own thoughts, but to have the engagement accomplished and openly acknowledged by everyone made it real and imminent. There was no turning back now. It was done. Fanny had lost any chance of influencing Edmund's choice by exposing Miss Crawford – even though she had decided against doing so, the possibility had always been there. But now, there was nothing to be done. Edmund would be married, and to such a woman. Her friendship with him would never be the same. And, as if the one man she could love being lost to her forever was not enough, Fanny's distress was compounded by Miss Crawford's request soon after the engagement was formed to serve as her bridesmaid. "I have no unmarried sisters who can stand up with me, Fanny," she pleaded, "and I feel you are my sister already." Fanny could not decline the request. Instead, she accepted the office with remarkable grace and deferred her tears for the privacy of her own chamber.

The prospect of a wedding now gave the Mansfield family something with which to occupy themselves and served as somewhat of a diversion from the business of grieving. Miss Crawford and the Grants were now constantly at the Park. Edmund and Mary took long walks out alone together and Fanny's friendship now seemed less indispensable to either. In Miss Crawford's case, Fanny could only rejoice; in Edmund's case, it was a source of extreme pain. But she felt it was for the best as it would teach her to forget those feelings which she knew must now be forgotten.

Everyone seemed busier, more animated. There was the date to decide upon and the banns to be published; the marriage articles to be drawn up and the announcement for the papers to be written; there was a carriage to order, and Miss Crawford, of course, must go to London to buy wedding clothes. She first thought of writing to her brother to request that he escort her there, but a change of circumstances at Mansfield brought to mind a different idea entirely.

Julia received an invitation to Sotherton for a visit of indefinite length and anticipating more diversion there than she found at home, immediately accepted. Fanny reflected upon the event with disapprobation. After Mrs. Rushworth's indiscretion in the spring, Fanny could not help but feel that she was no person to have the charge of a younger sister, particularly one with a head full of schemes; she doubted that any part of Miss Bertram's conscience that could yet be guided by goodness or morality was likely to govern her behaviour while she was with the Rushworths. Yet, Sir Thomas saw no evil in the invitation and Fanny must be satisfied with his judgement. Nor could Fanny lament that Julia took her horse to Sotherton, as it prevented her having to ride together with Miss Crawford; and although sharing Edmund's mare between them lessened the frequency of Fanny's rides, it was far more preferable than riding with Miss Crawford.

Julia's departure from Mansfield, however, allowed Miss Crawford to settle upon a scheme for going to London which to her mind was most satisfactory, but might otherwise have given offence to Julia – Edmund could take both her and Fanny to London for a few days if Mrs. Fraser would be willing to receive the young ladies. Fanny, she thought, must want a new dress for the wedding. The suggestion was made shortly after the resolution was formed, during a morning call by the ladies of the Parsonage to those at the Park, but before Fanny could communicate her own disinclination for it Mrs. Norris quickly protested, stating that the dress Sir Thomas had so generously given Fanny for Maria's wedding would be suitable for her to wear to Edmund's wedding as well. Fanny enthusiastically agreed, adding that she could not think of leaving her Aunt Bertram. But Edmund and Miss Crawford were both against her and had soon won both Sir Thomas and Lady Bertram over to their view by observing that Fanny had had so little opportunity for amusement and had never been to London.

Mrs. Fraser was immediately applied to and within a few days Miss Crawford received her enthusiastic assent. Thus it was settled that Fanny would go to London for her own good, in spite of her sincere wishes and protestations to the contrary and much to the vexation of Mrs. Norris, who intimated more than once that Fanny had only been invited because Julia was away and had Julia been at home it would have been very acceptable, very proper for *her* to make such a visit with Miss Crawford and Edmund. The only pleasant association Fanny had when thinking of London was the knowledge that her brother John was there. But she did not know how or where to find him and felt all the misfortune of being in the same town yet unable to meet him.

Miss Crawford took the first opportunity for privacy with Fanny to explain that Mrs. Fraser had quite got over Mr. Crawford's neglect of her daughter-in-law – as the latter had very lately married a young man of title with a fortune almost equal to Henry's – and could thus receive Fanny cordially; and in consequence of the former Miss Fraser's recent marriage, Mrs. Fraser was quite in want of company at this particular time. Fanny was mortified by the suggestion that Mrs. Fraser would have any ill-feelings towards her as a result of Mr. Crawford's reputed attachment to herself and neglect of the former Miss Fraser and felt even more than ever that her presence would be an imposition. But when she voiced these concerns Miss Crawford laughed them off, assuring her that Mrs. Fraser was delighted with the idea of their coming for she had a great curiosity to see her. This assurance was of little comfort to Fanny.

Fanny had expected Edmund to object to the scheme on account of the strong disapprobation of Mrs. Fraser he had described in a previous letter to her. However, it seemed his engagement to Miss Crawford had completely done away with any scruple as to not only her lodging at the Frasers', but Fanny as well. Fanny was again expected only to show gratitude. She was to be grateful for the opportunity to go to London, because she had never been and therefore must want to go. She tried to be grateful, for she knew Edmund and Sir Thomas at least genuinely felt it would benefit her to go. In the end, everything was settled and arranged by Edmund and Miss Crawford to go to town for the first week in December.

In the midst of the activity and planning related to the wedding and the visit to London, Fanny was given further opportunity to think and reflect on what Edmund's marriage meant for her own future while sitting in the drawing room one morning with Mrs. Norris and Lady Bertram by the observation of the latter that all her children were leaving her. With Tom gone and both her daughters out of the house and now with Edmund engaged and soon to be married, she began to feel very lonely. She could scarcely bear the loss of Poor Tom and she missed her daughters exceedingly. The house now seemed so empty. Mrs. Norris agreed, the loss of Poor Tom was a terrible tragedy and Mansfield was not the same without her beloved Maria and her beloved Julia. "We will have to get used to the loneliness, I am afraid, Sister, now that Maria is married, and surely Julia will soon become engaged. I have no doubt she will meet a very eligible young man very soon and will be settled as happily as her sister is."

"And Edmund will be going to Thornton Lacey to live after he is married. But I still have Fanny."

"Yes, though it cannot compare to the company of your own dear children, at least you will always have Fanny."

Fanny reflected, perhaps for the first time in earnest, that her life at Mansfield was not just a life for the present, it was her future as well. She would always be here, always giving comfort to Lady Bertram. She did not know what would happen once Edmund inherited the house but she imagined Miss Crawford, for all her sisterly affection, would not wish Fanny to continue in residence; and nor could Fanny desire such an arrangement. But where would she go? It seemed natural that she would follow Lady Bertram, but she had never thought of her own future beyond that. Would she end up in the house presently occupied by Mrs. Norris? Fanny could easily foresee just such a future for herself. It was all predetermined for her. Though she had always known how it would be, the realization now was startling. She would always be with Lady Bertram and after that, she would finish her days a spinster, alone in a small house near Mansfield. Always closely connected to the man she loved and his wife, constantly witnessing their life together, and assisting perhaps with their children.

All of a sudden it was all so forcefully clear. There were no choices within her power, even for her own future. The only other option was marriage and the only man she would ever consider marrying was out of her reach forever. She smiled in spite of these grim meditations as she remembered fondly William's description of how they would live out their days together in a small cottage. Fanny was wise enough to know such a plan was unlikely to ever reach fruition. William would marry and even if it should be within his power to extend some kindness or assistance to his family there were so many other brothers and sisters in greater need than herself. She was the only one who had the patronage of Mansfield. But of one thing she was certain, whether at Mansfield Park or an idyllic cottage with William, she would always be dependent.

She could not help reflecting that she had once been offered a chance to avoid the fate that she now envisioned for herself, and she had rejected it. She thought of Julia's description of Maria's marriage as a sacrifice of being bound to a man she did not love in exchange for independence and freedom of choice. The chilling prospect that now lay before Fanny as she contemplated her future life made such an exchange seem almost bearable. Yet, to have her own home to manage and command of her own time and money, while appealing in some respects seemed just as daunting to her in others. Such lofty goals were unimaginable to her, having never had the charge of anything or anyone, her own self included. And she remembered again who had made the offer. She had long ago settled it within herself that she would much rather live amongst those dearest to her, being of use to them, and spend her last years alone than to abandon her friends and spend her life bound to a man she could neither love nor respect. She was better off where she was and could not help feeling a little guilty for meditations that could be construed as ingratitude.

After all, she was so little in the habit of making decisions or giving direction, she was sure she would not know where to begin in the task of managing a household. The manner of her upbringing had left her with the firm impression that she should never be mistress of anything. She was scarcely the mistress of her own time or her own whereabouts. She could not aspire to anything more than to repay the kindness of her aunt and uncle with her companionship. It was her place to accept the gifts that had been bestowed upon her with gratitude, unworthy as she was to have received even so much; there could be no expectation of anything more. In any case, she had rejected the offer with no regrets and it was very unlikely another offer would ever be made to her. She was resigned to her fate – no, not just resigned, she was grateful for the good will and generosity that had brought her to Mansfield Park and allowed her to partake of its blessings.

Fanny was resigned to her fate at Mansfield, but insomuch as that fate comprehended an intimacy with the future Mr. and Mrs. Bertram, it was difficult to imagine at present how she would ever manage it with any feeling approaching equanimity. She trusted she would become accustomed to it in time, but for now, the impending trip to London as their travelling companion was a daunting prospect. And, to make matters worse, just before departing for London, Fanny received the following letter from Julia:

My dearest cousin, You cannot know what merriment there is here at Sotherton – what a joy it is to escape the wretched solemnity of Mansfield! I had quite forgotten how cold and melancholy that house has become. The independence from Mansfield made possible by Maria's marriage is well worth every sacrifice she has endured! She told me herself, it was a small price to pay to be at liberty to do just as we please. For, you know, she has learnt to have her way in everything with Mr. R. And, you will never guess what surprise awaited me when I arrived here. Maria has convinced her husband to convert that old family chapel into a theatre. A real theatre, right here in the house! It is the perfect room, as it is fitted already with a balcony and doors on either side. And we are determined to perform *Lovers' Vows* properly this time – and with no intrusions. His mother was unhappy at first about the chapel, but she had to concede that it was never used. The Rushworths plan to invite a great many friends to Sotherton to be in the play, including Mr. Yates! Oh how I wish you and Miss Crawford could see the play when we finally perform it, but I know there is little chance of either of you being able to come here. Though I do not see why Mr. C should not be invited; he is such a great actor after all, and his involvement in our Mansfield theatre makes it natural that he should be included in our renewal of the scheme. Indeed, there can be nothing to prevent him. Perhaps I shall suggest it to Maria. She pretends she has got over him, but when Mr. R was not around she asked me a thousand questions about my visit to Norfolk, all the while attempting to appear disinterested. But I must go. Please give my love to all the family. Yours, etc., Julia Bertram

Fanny hardly knew what to make of such a letter. She could approve of none of its contents. To think that the Rushworths had decided to convert the lovely family chapel that had existed for so many generations into a theatre, to actually build a stage in it so that they could indulge in conduct that, at the very least, could easily lead to impropriety; and to fix on so lively a scheme, a scheme of such merriment, and involving so many, scarcely half a year after their brother's death! To undertake the performance of the very same play which that brother had been on the verge of performing with them only a year before! She would never have imagined it possible.

It seemed to Fanny that she was every day and from every quarter receiving news that gave her distress; and she wondered not for the first time why all her relations burdened her with the knowledge of these matters. She had struggled so many times with the question of whether to mention something that had been disclosed to her to Sir Thomas or to Edmund and had always decided against it. What could she do? If she told Sir Thomas of the goings on at Sotherton, it would only enrage and disappoint him. He would, perhaps, go there and fetch Julia home but he would see with displeasure the lifestyle of his other daughter and know that he was powerless to effect any change there. Marriage had given her the freedom she had wanted to do as she pleased regardless of the approbation of her parents; and her choice of husband had given her the means to do just about anything, no matter how frivolous, expensive, or ill-advised – the fact that she despised the man notwithstanding. Fanny could see no good in disturbing her uncle's mind and heart with the information contained in Julia's letter. And even aside from all this, she felt it was quite beyond her power to be so presumptuous as to bring such a matter to Sir Thomas' attention. She might have gone to Edmund but her confidence in his powers of judgement had begun to erode last year and was now completely lost. There was nothing she could do. She remembered William's advice regarding whether to disclose the contents of Miss Crawford's letter to Edmund and could see no reason that it should not hold true in this instance as well. The fact that someone had chosen to confide in her did not endow her with the power to presume to correct that person's conduct. Julia must be left to the management of her father, whose judgement in such matters must be superior to Fanny's.

Thus, she left Mansfield for London with a mind consumed by these meditations as her two companions conversed of the pleasures they expected over the course of the next several days. For her part, Fanny had no expectation of pleasure as everything she had heard of London made her believe she would not like being there. But she had to admit some curiosity to see it.

Chapter 9

The post carriage delivered the ladies to the Frasers' door, where Edmund stayed only a moment and agreed to return the following day for dinner. He then went to his hotel leaving Fanny to the companionship of Miss Crawford and Mrs. Fraser. The three sat in the drawing room and Mrs. Fraser quickly dispensed with the requisite questions about their journey and began the conversation in earnest by observing, "So this is the famous Miss Price."

"Yes," replied Miss Crawford, "is not she everything Henry described?"

"She is exactly as I imagined she would be!" Then addressing Fanny she said, "There are several ladies hereabouts who would very much like to know your secret."

"I do not understand what you mean," said Fanny, a little embarrassed.

"The secret of how to attach Henry Crawford."

"I did nothing, I assure you," said Fanny quietly but quickly.

"Ah," said Mrs. Fraser, "perhaps *that* is the secret."

"I think it may well be," laughed Miss Crawford, "but Fanny does not like to talk about poor, dear Henry. He is quite wretched on her account and she has no sympathy whatsoever."

Fanny was about to protest but found it unnecessary as Mrs. Fraser seemed perfectly willing to give up the subject, saying, "Very well, then tell me, how does Mrs. Rushworth get on?"

"I scarcely know. She and her husband ran away to Sotherton shortly after Poor Tom was buried and they have not been back since. Now Julia has gone to Sotherton as well to partake of their happiness."

"I can well imagine Miss Bertram brings as much cheer to her sister as Mrs. Rushworth finds at home."

"Indeed," smiled Miss Crawford, "And, pray how does Lady Hamilton?"

"She is quite satisfied with married life so far, and I have every hope that once the novelty of independence has worn away she will yet have no cause to repine. And as they are settled here in London we have had little opportunity to miss her at all. She and Sir James will be joining us for dinner tomorrow."

Mrs. Fraser and Miss Crawford began discussing news of their common acquaintance in London, while Fanny was content to sit quietly unnoticed. Mr. Fraser, having returned home shortly before dinner time, was the only addition to their small party. Fanny found him to be a man of few words who seemed little interested in the goings on of London society which so fascinated his wife. After dinner Fanny was especially pleased to hear a duet played by Miss Crawford and Mrs. Fraser and on the whole, except for some of the mortifyingly unkind things said between her two companions about their friends and acquaintances, she had no cause to complain pertaining to her first evening in London.

The following morning was Mrs. Fraser's morning in and they would all remain at home to receive callers. Fanny understood also that there would be a large party for dinner. The shopping would commence the day after. Fanny had little desire for the activity, but could not avoid making one purchase at least, as her uncle had given her some money for the purpose of buying a dress to wear to Edmund's wedding. She was pleased to retire early and looked forward to a morning of social calls during which she could sit quietly and unobtrusively by while the other two ladies conversed with their acquaintance. Since she did not expect to know anyone, she felt secure of not having to utter anything beyond how pleased she was to meet each caller.

Before breakfast Fanny was able to write to Lady Bertram, William, and Susan. The visits began after breakfast, and it all went forward as Fanny had expected. She had a chance to observe how morning visits were conducted in London, and it seemed to be done much more by rule than in the country, though she had little to compare it to as Lady Bertram visited no one. She was content not to be a participant, but was surprised to find that nearly everyone to whom she was introduced seemed to know who she was. Her name was familiar to almost all, and there was more than one, "So this is Miss Price," or "Ah, Miss Price," uttered during the course of the morning. Apparently, she had obtained some notoriety by having at one time been the reputed object of Mr. Crawford's affection. But luckily for her it was too delicate a subject for anyone to enter into openly on so short an acquaintance with her and she was spared any conversation regarding the unhappy events of the previous winter. But this wasn't the only source of mortification to Fanny, for after each lady left the house Miss Crawford and Mrs. Fraser would discuss her at length, and often not in the kindest of terms, until the arrival of the next caller. Fanny was sometimes applied to for her own impressions during these conversations and consistently replied that each lady she met seemed amiable and good-natured.

At one point in the course of the morning, while a Mrs. Baxter and her daughters were asking after Miss Crawford's brother, the butler entered and offered a card to Mrs. Fraser. She smiled upon reading the name and said, "Show him in." The butler nodded and left the room. Upon the entrance of the servant, Mrs. Baxter had seemed prepared to begin taking leave but when she heard the word "him," she apparently felt authorized to remain. Within a moment Mr. Crawford entered the room. Fanny was surprised, and certainly unprepared for his appearance; and she may have been inclined to suspect a conspiracy between brother and sister had she not observed that Miss Crawford was even more surprised to see him than herself. As he made his greetings to everyone, Mrs. Baxter looked from Mr. Crawford to Fanny as if she expected a scene of great interest to unfold at any moment. Miss Crawford meanwhile, scolded her brother for not having written of his intent to meet her in London. When they were all seated again, they talked pleasantly until Mrs. Baxter and her daughters were obliged to depart.

As soon as they were gone Miss Crawford observed, "Oh did you see how Miss Baxter looked when you walked in Henry?" He confessed that he had not. "I dare say she is still not recovered from when you broke her heart two years ago!" He ventured a fleeting glance at Fanny before protesting that he had done any such thing. "Very well, I will not argue with you," she replied with affected gallantry, "It must be as you say. We will not speak of it. But tell me, what has brought you into town?"

"I am here on a particular errand, if Miss Price would be so kind as to spare a moment of her time."

Fanny scarcely knew what to say, but she had no need to make a response, for Mrs. Fraser suddenly remembered that she had wished to show Miss Crawford a fine muslin she had purchased a few days before. They left the room before Fanny knew what was happening, perhaps on the assumption that Mr. Crawford intended to renew his addresses on the spot. The frightening possibility also occurred to Fanny who felt unequal to any such confrontation.

Seeing her distress, he immediately informed her of the purpose of his call. "I wish only to speak to you in regards to your brother," he began, moving to a seat next to her. "They need not have left the room, but I am pleased you will have the chance to receive his gift in privacy."

"Gift?" was the only response she could manage, though she was visibly relieved.

He now handed her a parcel he had brought in with him, saying, "He was with me, as you know, in August, and knowing of my connections at Mansfield, felt it was more likely I would have an opportunity of seeing you sooner than he would. Nor could he trust this to the post; instead, he asked me to make sure you received it whenever it should be within my power to put it into your hands."

She regarded him with some suspicion, remembering how he had tricked her into accepting a gift from him on a previous occasion. "There is a note from him there as well, I believe," he added, as if reading her mind. "I would have brought it to Mansfield sooner, but by the time I could be spared from Everingham, I had notice from my sister of your coming to London."

"I thank you for bringing it to me, but surely you had other business in town. You could not have come all this way only to deliver this."

"I only regret I could not give it to you sooner."

She opened the parcel and there was indeed a note within from William explaining as follows:

> My Dear Fanny, Enclosed you will find a gift I reserved for you upon our capture of an enemy merchant ship. When I found this among the items seized, when I saw the nature of the decoration, I knew it must be for you. I requested that I be allowed to keep it as a portion of my share of the prize. You will not be distressed on account of its previous owner as I can assure you he and his crew are quite well and have been sent home. So you can use it without guilt, and in the satisfaction of knowing that it would never be sold to profit a Frenchman or fund any battle against England. I trust your next letter to me will be written with this pen. I will not send this by post but will entrust it to Mr. Crawford to give you when he is next at Mansfield, as he is likely to be there sooner than I can be. Affectionately yours, William Price.

She opened the small box to find a silver writing set with ornate chasing in the design of angels. As she looked upon it, tears sprang unbidden to her eyes. She had never been given so fine a gift.

"William should not have given me such a gift."

"He hoped you would be pleased by it."

"I am. It is beautiful. It is just too much."

"I am sure it is not too much. But it is very lovely. I remember when he showed it to me agreeing with him how well, how particularly well," he said these words as he ran his fingers along the wings of an angel engraved on the handle of the letter opener, "it should suit you."

"Thank you again, sir," she said hoping she was not blushing and that he would soon be gone. Then she felt she was being unkind in wishing him to leave so quickly after the service he had performed for William.

"It has been my pleasure to be of service, I assure you," he replied. As she made no further comment, at length he said, "I hope you have been well since I last saw you."

"Yes, I thank you. I have been very well."

"And the family at Mansfield? Sir Thomas and Lady Bertram? Have they shown any improvement these past months?"

"I believe they are both returning to their former selves, gradually. But I fear they will never really recover from the loss of Poor Mr. Bertram."

"It is a sad business," he said with a sigh. "They did not deserve it."

As she said nothing, they sat in silence for a few moments until he asked, "This is your first visit to London?"

"Yes."

"And how do you like it?"

"So far it has not been unpleasant, but I have not yet been out of the house. Mrs. Fraser has been receiving callers this morning."

"I can imagine it must be somewhat tedious meeting so many ladies with whom you are not acquainted."

"I do not mind it; but, though all of the visitors were unknown to me, many of them were familiar with my name."

Had Fanny believed the gentleman capable of blushing she might have imagined she observed his colour heighten. "My sister has spoken of you amongst her acquaintance in town. She has a very high regard for your friendship. I assure you she could not have said anything to discredit you."

"It does not signify," she replied. "I will be home in a few days and I dare say will never see any of them again."

He smiled softly. "I was surprised when Mary told me you would be coming to London. I would not have thought you would wish for it."

"Miss Crawford desired me to come with her, and Edmund felt it would be good for me."

"And your wishes, I suppose, were not consulted." Fanny did not know what to say. He looked at her in silence for a long moment before speaking again, "I fear London will no more agree with your constitution than did Portsmouth."

"I thank you for your kind concern, sir. I confess I was not then in the best of health, but I have been better since returning home, and I shall be here less than a week."

"I suppose a week can do you no harm. But do not let Mary exhaust you running into all the shops and warehouses in town. You must tell her when you are weary and ready to come home, for she may not see it."

"I believe I shall be safe from becoming overtired."

He regarded her again in silence as if unsure what to say next, and she took the opportunity to thank him for his kindness to William in securing him the invitation to the shooting party. Mr. Crawford assured her it had been his pleasure and that Mr. Price's company had been a great improvement to the party.

Another pause ensued and in an effort to break the silence, she thought to ask him about his journey. He answered her with the expected report of the weather and the roads. "It is some time since I have been to town," he added. "I have been at Everingham since March, except for the short time I spent at Mansfield and the shooting party in August. The business with the mill I mentioned to you in Portsmouth was remedied soon after my return, and I have not yet had occasion to repent my decision."

"I am very glad to hear it, and that the delay occasioned by your staying in town for some little time before returning to Everingham did not result in any adverse consequences."

He smiled at this reminder. "My sister did persuade me to stay in town last March to attend an evening party." He paused contemplatively for a moment and his smile disappeared, then he said, "It did not turn out as I had hoped."

Fanny did not dare to ask what he had hoped for in that evening or how his hopes had been disappointed. After another brief silence she observed, "I understand you passed a pleasant summer." She could think of nothing else to say.

He sighed and looked at her earnestly. It was a look she had not seen before. But he was saved the trouble of making any response beyond a murmured, "Indeed," by the return of the other two ladies into the room who, of course, fully expected to find a newly engaged couple, overflowing with felicity. But it was not to be. Fanny immediately explained Mr. Crawford's errand and showed the writing set to her friends, who were quick to admire it. The notion of inviting Mr. Crawford to join the party for dinner soon occurred to Mrs. Fraser. The invitation having been made, he hesitated to accept it; and upon perceiving his hesitation, his sister said, "Surely you have not made another engagement for dinner!"

"No," he replied. "I am not engaged."

"Then it is settled, you shall dine with us," said Mrs. Fraser with satisfaction. She had a great curiosity to observe how Mr. Crawford behaved in company with the woman who by securing his affection and the offer of his hand had done what no other woman had succeeded in doing.

With the dinner arrangements settled, Miss Crawford again reprimanded her brother for the manner of his sudden appearance in Mrs. Fraser's house and asked about his journey and how he had left things at Everingham. When he had done answering these questions, she asked him, "And how are your little trees?"

"They are doing quite well. They have all grown better than expected since the planting."

"What is this?" asked Mrs. Fraser, "Have you been improving Everingham?"

"A little," he replied. "I have planted an avenue of trees on the south side of the house, beginning at the edge of the pleasure gardens and extending to a small pond beyond. I saw something similar when I was at Sotherton Court last year and it occurred to me that an avenue of trees would be quite suitable for that side of the house. It is much in the same style, except I planted evergreen trees. I thought perhaps they would add a little more life to the landscape."

"Henry was quite wild about the idea when he left me in March and has scarcely talked of anything else in his letters except how his little trees are getting on. The avenue at Sotherton was very lovely, was not it, Fanny?"

"I do not know," she replied, "I did not happen to see it when we were there."

"Oh, it is a shame you missed it, for I believe it is gone now. But Henry's I think will be better, for his trees will be alive year round. Of course, it will be some years before they are grown enough to add any real beauty or character to Everingham. The ones we saw at Sotherton had been there for ages. Nevertheless, you must come to see them with Edmund and me next summer."

To make such a visit was the last thing Fanny could desire, so she made no reply. The choice of evergreen trees for the avenue of Everingham was wholeheartedly approved by Mrs. Fraser and she confessed a great desire to see it as well. The conversation was interrupted at this point by another caller, and Mr. Crawford at last took leave of them. With the other two ladies engrossed in conversation, Fanny was at liberty to reflect on all that had passed.

The talk of the avenue at Everingham was a source of amusement as she recalled Mr. Crawford explicitly saying that his estate required no further improvement. Apparently, his visit to Sotherton had given him different ideas. She was not displeased with the conversation that had passed between herself and Mr. Crawford when they had been alone. He had come to her as the friend of her brother, had not taken advantage of suddenly finding himself alone with her, had made no attempt to renew his declarations, and had not so much as alluded to his prior attachment. Indeed, she could not have formed any expectation of his doing otherwise had she known he was to call given how much time had passed since his former declarations; it seemed impossible that a love, even one as strong as he had professed, could survive rejection, resolute discouragement, and an absence of so many months, especially to the mind of a girl as modest as Fanny and in a man so impulsive and unsteady as she knew Mr. Crawford to be. But given his sister's constant assurances on the subject, Fanny was relieved to have her views confirmed by his own behaviour. She finally felt that she could abandon any remaining doubt as to her conviction that he had given up his suit forever; and having satisfied herself on that point, her gratitude for his kindness to William even went so far as to support her acceptance of having to endure his company at dinner. She felt she could be in the same room with him without the anxiety the constant expectation of his unwanted addresses had formerly created. She could not forget his behaviour the previous autumn, nor his indiscretion with Mrs. Rushworth that had driven him away from Mansfield in the spring, nor his treatment of Julia over the summer; but she could be comfortable, or at least a little less ill at ease, after this conversation.

When the ladies retired to dress for dinner, Fanny took a few minutes to start a new letter to William using the writing set he had given her, in which she could only begin to attempt to express her feelings of gratitude.

Chapter 10

As the dinner hour approached Fanny dressed with some trepidation. She was unaccustomed to dining in company, and especially with those with whom she was not acquainted. She was not sure how many would be in the party but there would inevitably be some whom she did not know. In her determination to be punctual, she was in the drawing room before even Mr. or Mrs. Fraser. They soon came down, however, as did Miss Crawford. The first guest to arrive was Edmund, and Fanny was exceedingly happy to see him. Other guests arrived soon after and when they were all present a party of twelve was assembled. In addition to these five and Mr. Crawford, there was also Sir James and Lady Hamilton, Miss Hamilton, a sister of Sir James who had come to stay with them since their marriage, Mr. Fraser's brother, Colonel Fraser, whose wife was indisposed due to her seventh confinement, and Lord and Lady Stornaway.

Fanny was quite distressed to find herself sitting next to Mr. Crawford at dinner and only hoped he did not expect her to talk to him very much. When they were seated he asked whether she had had an opportunity to make use of the writing set William had given her. She acknowledged that she had just sent a letter to him that morning before Mr. Crawford's arrival, but had already used the new writing instruments to start her next one.

"Then he will have to settle for my letter giving him the earliest intelligence of it," he replied, "for I wrote to him as soon as I arrived at my uncle's house after leaving you this morning to inform him that my errand was finally discharged and that his sister was quite pleased with her gift."

"I am glad you were able to do so," she replied. She said nothing further, and hoped he would find someone else to talk to during the meal.

Thankfully, most of the other dinner guests had not seen Mr. Crawford since March when he had last been in London and had many things to say to him. Fanny was able to eat peacefully for the most part and was much relieved when Mrs. Fraser finally withdrew from the dining room. In the drawing room, Fanny took a seat as far away from the other ladies as civility would allow and only hoped she would not have to participate too much in the conversation.

Lady Hamilton, being lately married herself, again congratulated Miss Crawford on her engagement and after some further discussion of the delights of being engaged, asked, "But where will you live?"

"Mr. Bertram has a house at Thornton Lacey, about eight miles from Mansfield."

"Then you will divide your time between London and the country?"

"Yes, we shall, I believe, spend half the year in town." Fanny raised her head in surprise, but said nothing.

"I am quite envious. I shall speak to Sir James about finding a cottage in the country. I could never give up London entirely, but it is intolerable in the heat of summer."

The other ladies soon asked Lady Hamilton about her domestic concerns and she was very happy to give them all a very thorough account of her situation, her home, and her husband. After answering their questions, she added, "I am now qualified to speak on the marriage state and I assure you, I find it very agreeable. It is more delightful even than being engaged; and I could never have asked for a better husband than my own dear, Sir James. I now recommend marriage to everyone."

"I can attest to it," said Miss Hamilton. "She speaks of nothing but getting me married, and I begin to think she wants me out of the way."

"That is nonsense," replied Lady Hamilton, "as you know very well. I only wish to see you, and indeed all my friends, as happily settled as I am."

"But we cannot all marry to advantage equal to your own, or Miss Crawford's, for that matter," said Miss Hamilton.

"I dare say you shall be able to make a very advantageous match," said Mrs. Fraser, "you have charms enough."

"Yes, not the least of which being her fortune of fifteen thousand pounds," said Lady Hamilton.

"That is more than either Mrs. Fraser or I had," added Lady Stornaway, "and we have not done too badly, I think."

"Well Miss Price," said Miss Hamilton suddenly rising and moving to a seat next to Fanny, "as the only two single women in the room we must support one another. These ladies are all too well satisfied with their own situations to think rationally of the slightest reluctance by anyone else to enter into the marriage state."

Fanny was a little startled to be addressed in such a way and did not know what to say in response. But Lady Hamilton saved her the trouble by laughing again and saying, "The only reason for any reluctance, my dear Cassandra, would be in accepting an offer that is unwelcome; but that can be avoided easily enough. You need only choose the gentleman you want to marry and make yourself agreeable to him."

"You seem to forget, my dear sister, that women do not have the advantage of choice, only the power of refusal."

"Women have power enough," said Lady Stornaway, "they have but to use it."

"Allowing the possibility that it is as easy as you represent, I have not seen a man I *would* choose for myself even if I could."

"That is only because you have been too long in the country," said Mrs. Fraser. "Eligible gentlemen abound in London. They are to be found everywhere; one has only to look."

As soon as she spoke, the door to the drawing room opened and the gentlemen joined them, followed by general laughter among the ladies. Sir James wondered what all the merriment was about and his wife replied, "We were just talking about eligible men and in you all walked, with the most precise timing."

"But we, none of us, are eligible," laughed Sir James in reply, "save Mr. Crawford here; you may dispose of him as you please."

Miss Crawford laughed, "Oh no, he will have none of that, Sir James, I assure you."

"Oh? Have his views on matrimony changed again? I know he was against it at one time, but I was given to believe that he had begun to view it more favourably."

Fanny now turned scarlet, and could do nothing but look at her hands in her lap, hoping no one would notice.

"My views on the subject are entirely inconsequential," said Mr. Crawford. He then changed the conversation by making a general request for music.

Lady Hamilton replied saying, "Miss Hamilton shall play for you, Mr. Crawford, I am sure. She was at the pianoforte all morning practising something new; but you must turn the pages for her."

As she rose to move to the instrument, Miss Hamilton whispered to Fanny with a glance at Mr. Crawford, "And there is the embodiment of my sister's ambition for me!"

Fanny made no reply. The lady took her seat at the instrument and the gentleman seated himself next to her. Fanny did not look at either of them, but she was very happy to listen to the performance.

After two songs, Miss Hamilton returned to her seat next to Fanny and said quietly, "I hope that will satisfy Lady Hamilton on the point of Mr. Crawford. I must allow him to be an excellent page turner; in the strictest execution of the office, he has my hearty commendation; though I do not believe I have ever seen anyone turn pages with so little gallantry."

"Is that your objection to him?" asked Fanny, almost as surprised to hear herself talk as to hear Mr. Crawford described in such a way.

"My objection is only to Lady Hamilton's interference in my affairs," then lowering her voice further, "but what everyone here wants to know, not least the gentlemen we have been speaking of, I imagine, is what *your* objection to him was." Fanny only blushed again. "But you clearly have no wish to speak of it."

"No indeed. I was not sure whether you knew."

"My dear Miss Price, everyone knows, and I confess that circumstance alone makes me cautious; but let us speak of it no more."

"Thank you," whispered Fanny.

After musical performances by some of the other ladies, the card tables were placed and Fanny was pressed into playing. She played very ill and could be tranquil only when the evening at last came to an end and she could escape to the solitude of her bed chamber.

The next two days were spent wholly in shopping and Fanny was quite fatigued at the end of them. In spite of her previous assurances to Mr. Crawford, she found herself unequal to spending so many hours walking into and out of various shops and warehouses. Yet, she did not heed his advice as she also found herself unwilling to make any complaint to her friends who seemed genuinely to enjoy the exercise. She had ordered a new gown for the wedding early on the first day in one of the first shops they entered. Miss Crawford, however, declared that she liked nothing in any of the shops they visited, but never left one of them without making a purchase. Fanny felt certain after each stop that Miss Crawford would feel she had purchased enough, but even as they gave direction for delivery of all their packages, her two companions complained that they had not found what they were looking for. Fanny did not understand it at all.

The evenings were given to a review and examination of the purchases made during the day. Edmund joined them for tea during the evening on both days, but on the second day Fanny was too exhausted to stay up much past dinner and went to bed before tea was served. The next morning she awoke later than her usual time to find that the other ladies had gone out without her. Miss Crawford had left her a note urging her to spend the day resting at home. She could not help supposing such kindness had been suggested to Miss Crawford by Edmund the evening before. And, as Mr. Fraser was never at home by day, Fanny was perfectly content to have the house to herself and was at leisure to finish her letter to William which was very long but nevertheless very insufficient to contain her effusions of gratitude for his gift.

Having written her letter, she had been settled on one of the sofas with a book for some time, when a caller was shown into the drawing room. It was Mr. Crawford, who quickly explained that he had just stopped in for a moment to give Mrs. Fraser an answer to her invitation to tea. "I had expected to find you all in the house at this hour. I had not thought even Mary could do nothing but visit shops for three full days together! But I am glad to find you sitting here comfortably, rather than being dragged about London in search of finery, and looking well. I understand you were fatigued yesterday and retired before tea time."

As he spoke of his surprise at finding her alone, Fanny could not help but wonder if Miss Crawford had contrived for just such a meeting. His demeanour was marked by a cheerfulness not unlike what she had seen in him formerly.

"Yes, but as you can see I am well. And, I confess, I was happy to stay behind today. But I do hope Miss Crawford and Mrs. Fraser are enjoying themselves."

"I dare say they are," he replied. "And what about you, have you enjoyed your time in London?"

"It has not been unpleasant, but I prefer the country."

"I am not surprised, but what have you done in town to give you a favourable impression? You have had one dinner party with more strangers than friends, and two days of nothing but shopping. You have not been to any concerts or lectures or plays."

"I should have liked to see a play," said Fanny, before she realized what she was saying. When she did, she averted her eyes from him, a little embarrassed.

He could not repress a slight smile, but did not make further mention of plays. "London has much to offer that you might enjoy. It is a shame you did not have an opportunity to see more of it. Perhaps on your next visit."

She looked at him in surprise. "I doubt I will ever return."

"No?" he asked. "I believe you will very likely receive an invitation from Mr. and Mrs. Bertram after their marriage. I know how much my sister enjoys being in town, and I am sure they will spend some time here every year. Mary loves you as a sister and it is quite obvious Bertram cares for you as a brother. I imagine they will invite you to join them whenever they visit."

Fanny was as much unsettled by Mr. Crawford's description of Edmund's fraternal affection for her as by the picture he painted of Edmund's marriage to Miss Crawford. She knew she must become accustomed to the idea of their marriage; nevertheless, the thought of travelling anywhere with them after the event held no attraction for Fanny. "I have no such expectation," she replied quietly, hoping Mr. Crawford had not noticed her discomfort.

But he was regarding her carefully, as if trying to discern exactly what the source of her discomfort could be. Perhaps considering that it might be his own presence, he rose to take his leave. "Would you be so kind as to communicate my acceptance of Mrs. Fraser's invitation to tea again this evening?" He smiled broadly as he mentioned it as if with great anticipation of delight in what the evening might bring.

"Certainly."

"Thank you, Miss Price." He hesitated a moment then added, "And I am pleased to see you have had a restful day and will therefore have no need to retire early as you did last evening."

This gave her a little start, it was almost like a renewal of his former attentions. His words and his smile, his tone altogether in saying it, seemed to hint that he looked forward to her particular company in the evening. He made his bow, bade her good day, and quit the room, but left her feeling a little uneasy.

When the other ladies returned, Fanny dutifully communicated his acceptance of the invitation. When asked about how she enjoyed her day, she responded with grateful assurance that a quiet day of solitude had been exactly what she needed. Miss Crawford then observed, "That is just what Henry said last evening when he gave me a hint that you would be too exhausted for a third day of shopping." Fanny was surprised and a little disappointed that it had been Mr. Crawford rather than Edmund who had given Miss Crawford the hint. She had not even known that he had called the previous evening. Then she regretted that an act of kindness could make her feel uncomfortable.

Fanny, Miss Crawford, and Edmund were to leave London the following morning. Their last evening in town was spent quietly, making final preparations for their journey and sitting down to a family dinner with Edmund as the only guest until tea time when they expected Mr. Crawford. Fanny could not shake the uneasiness that had settled upon her after his visit earlier in the day; and by the time the ladies left the dining room after dinner she had worked herself into a state of dread, having allowed his parting statement to shatter the peace of mind she had so recently been congratulating herself on finally acquiring.

The gentleman arrived punctually, but was not alone. When the butler showed him into the drawing room, Fanny looked up and while his companion was familiar, she did not immediately recognize him; but when he was announced as Mr. John Price, she sprung forward to embrace him fondly. She could not help but express her extreme surprise at seeing him there. He told her he had been working in London for two years now.

"Yes," she replied, "I learned as much when I was in Portsmouth last winter." He was quickly introduced to the others and everyone was seated again before she was quite over her surprise.

Her first question to her brother was, "But, how is it possible that you came to call on me here?"

"Mr. Crawford appeared at my office today, introduced himself as a friend of William's and told me you were in town. He asked me to accompany him to see you this afternoon but I was not then at liberty. He proposed calling after dinner instead, which, as you see, I was perfectly able to do. Though as I am told it is your last day in London I am sure nothing would have stopped me."

Fanny was absolutely astonished. She looked at Mr. Crawford to find he was watching her with an expression of delight. Then she turned back to John, "But how did he know where to find you?"

"He and William were together in August. William told him of my position." Then, turning to Mr. Crawford, he added, "Though I understand he had a hard time of it."

Mr. Crawford laughed lightly. "Indeed! I began my search on Wednesday and did not locate him until this morning. He was not where his brother said he would be but we must excuse Mr. Price as he then had no knowledge of his brother's recent promotion."

"A promotion?" said Fanny, turning to her brother.

"A small promotion, which involved a change of location," he replied.

These questions and answers were exchanged in rapid succession, after which Fanny allowed Edmund and the others to talk to her brother. She was pleased to find him quite respectable looking, well-mannered, and well-spoken. His establishment in London seemed to have improved his situation. He expressed his regret that he had not been at home when she had been in Portsmouth and had not been able to meet her then. She was a little surprised to find him so well informed of her situation and learned that William had been giving John news of her. He had, by that means, learned of her visit to Portsmouth and heard much in her favour. He stayed with them the entirety of the evening and Fanny could hardly get enough of talking to him and listening to him. Edmund showed a great interest in getting to know John and the others made a polite effort to converse with him. Mr. Crawford however, said very little. If Fanny had been less enthralled with a brother she had not seen in above nine years she might have noticed his eyes fixed on her.

John left them only when the other two gentlemen also took their leave but not before promising to write to Fanny. The ladies retired almost immediately. Fanny was left with a very good impression of this brother, and had still not got over her shock at his appearance and the manner in which he had found her. It was such an amazing, unexpected turn of events. She felt gratitude towards Mr. Crawford and noted to herself that he had not mentioned a word of it to her when he had seen her that afternoon. It seemed incredible that he would undertake to find her brother and arrange a meeting with him while she was in town. She was, in fact, so astonished, so caught up in the surprise of the gesture and the joy of meeting her brother that, notwithstanding her earlier anxieties – which were now wholly forgotten – she was not at leisure to allow this most recent example of his kindness to disturb the sanguinity of her conviction that Mr. Crawford had given her up.

Fanny was almost as eager to leave London as she had been to quit Portsmouth. As she travelled, she reflected with wonder and satisfaction on having had the opportunity to meet her brother, John. She was reminded constantly by her companions of Mr. Crawford's very great kindness in finding Mr. John Price and bringing him to meet her. Fanny expressed her gratitude towards him for the gesture, but nevertheless could not be induced to converse further on the subject of Mr. Crawford. The journey was otherwise uneventful and the familiar sights that began to appear on either side of the carriage were most welcome, as were the happy greetings she received from her aunt and uncle Bertram.

A few days after their return home, Edmund sought Fanny out in the East room to speak with her privately. "My dear Fanny," he began solemnly, "I confess to being a little distressed at present. Miss Crawford and I … we have not exactly quarrelled, but there is such a disagreement between us. I am at a loss as to what can be done." Fanny appeared puzzled. "Ever since we returned from London she has been talking of going there for a few weeks in the spring."

"Does this surprise you? You have long known of her fondness for London life."

"I think she is just as happy in the country as she has ever been in town. It is only because she was so recently there that her feelings of attachment to the place have been given more consequence at present. But I am convinced it is only temporary, and that once we are settled at Thornton Lacey she will be exceedingly happy with her situation and give up the scheme."

"Then why should you be distressed?"

"Our discussion of that subject has led to one of more substance. In support of her argument, she observed that the income provided by her fortune would make it possible to go to London. And while I conceded the point, I reminded her of my own duties at Thornton Lacey. This is what has distressed me the most: she seems to expect me to give up the church altogether. In short, she has been expecting me to leave a curate to carry out the duties of the parish while we live entirely in retirement – dividing our time, I suppose, between Thornton Lacey and London."

Fanny, of course, had prior knowledge of this expectation, and was more surprised that the question should only be coming up between them now than by any other part of his disclosure. "But had not you discussed this with her previously?"

"No," cried he with feeling. "There was certainly no doubt as to our living at Thornton Lacey; but beyond that it has been all confusion on both sides! I believed that she understood my intention to continue my duties until … until I should inherit Mansfield; and she had convinced herself that I would relinquish the duties of the parish entirely to a curate whilst living in retirement off of the income of Thornton Lacey, her fortune, and a provision from my father. She went so far in her presumption as to believe that Sir Thomas would make over something to us on our marriage. She has great plans for improving Thornton Lacey, to implement some ideas of her brother's. She seems to expect that we shall live now as if I were already master of Mansfield Park!"

The only part of what Edmund related that surprised Fanny was *his* surprise by anything Miss Crawford had said. "Surely you can make her understand how unreasonable she is in such an expectation."

Edmund sighed heavily. "I have tried," he exclaimed with feeling, "do not you think I have tried?" Fanny was a little startled by his manner of expression. He took her hand. "Forgive me, dearest Fanny. I should not have burdened you with my troubles."

Fanny withdrew her hand and turning slightly away from him said softly, "But I am afraid there is nothing I can do." She paused, suddenly fearing he might ask her to speak to Miss Crawford on his behalf.

"It is enough to know that you understand why I am so distressed; that you believe I have the right of it."

"My view on the subject is of little consequence."

"It is of great worth to me to know that you comprehend my view of the matter. It gives me hope that I shall yet be able to convince another. She must be made to see how important, how necessary it is for me to fulfil my duties. Things will change for us in future; but until then, she must accept the situation in which we find ourselves. I do believe that she will come around and, in time, agree with me."

After this conversation, he sought out Miss Crawford, indulging in the vain hope of finding her as reasonable and agreeable as Fanny.

Chapter 11

The first week of the new year brought the wedding and with it yet another source of pain for Fanny. She learned that very morning of Edmund's plan to take his quiet mare to Thornton Lacey so that Mary might ride her. He rationalized it to himself by noting how little Fanny had been using the horse since Poor Tom's death. And he said it would be only for a short time and then he would return the horse to Mansfield for Fanny's use. Thus, he was confident the two ladies could continue to share the horse as they had been doing. Fanny could only hope that the arrangement would be as successful as Edmund envisioned. She watched sadly from the drawing room window as one of the grooms led the horse out of the stable and tied it to Edmund's new carriage which was to convey the happy couple to Thornton Lacey after the wedding. But, she reflected, this was how it should be. The horse was Edmund's; of course his wife should have it.

Fanny, having already spent a great number of tears in anticipation of the event, managed to arrive at the church with admirable equanimity. She stood in her place striving to think of anything but what was going forward, and scarcely hearing any of the service as it was read by Dr. Grant. The newly married Bertrams left for Thornton Lacey from the church door, and it was done. Sir Thomas, Lady Bertram, and Mrs. Norris returned home in the carriage where the Grants were to meet them to toast Mr. and Mrs. Bertram; but Fanny, in need of solitude and fresh air, assured them she would follow on foot.

She went into the churchyard while the remaining friends and neighbours who had attended the ceremony disbanded. She walked among the headstones noting those that were familiar to her – her uncle Norris, and of course, Poor Tom. She was lost in her own reverie, and after some time, she ventured quietly back into the now empty church. She sat in the first pew and the remembrance of all that had just happened there came flooding back – for as little as she had tried to attend to the ceremony, the image of her dear Edmund binding himself to Miss Crawford forever had not escaped her notice. It was hers to recall and relive at any future moment in which she might be in want of misery.

Now that she was alone, in this sacred place where Edmund's union to another had so recently occurred, her sorrow was at liberty to spill forth. She had suppressed it valiantly during the ceremony but now there was no need. The tears could be restrained no longer. She wept not for what might have been – for she had never truly thought it possible that Edmund might marry her – but for what she had lost, her beloved and dearest friend and confidant. She wept also for Edmund, for a great pain arose in her heart from the conviction that he had chosen ill, that his wife was wholly unworthy of him, wholly unsuited to him, and would bring him little happiness in life. Indeed, she felt he could only be miserable with such a woman.

By now, Fanny was leaning against the back of the pew, her face against the side panel on one end. She started when she heard footsteps behind her at the entrance to the church, and thinking it must be the caretaker, she looked up making a vain effort to compose herself and hoping to be able to acquit herself creditably. By then, the intruder was almost at her side and was just uttering the words, "Miss Price."

It was Mr. Crawford. He had come to Mansfield the day before for the wedding but she had scarcely taken notice of him until this moment. She said nothing, and merely covered her face again.

"Good God," he said, "what is the matter?" In a moment he was seated next to her. "You are unwell. Is there anything I can offer for your present relief? Please, you must allow me to escort you home."

This suggestion finally stirred her to speak. "No," she replied. "I am well."

"You are not well. Cannot you tell me what is distressing you? Tell me how I can be of service."

She was silenced by a sudden burst of more tears. He offered her his handkerchief, which she accepted only after hesitating, and afterwards he simply stared at her in wretched suspense, not knowing how else to assist.

When she was again able to speak she said, "Please, leave me be."

"I cannot. Of course, I have no wish to distress you further, but I cannot simply leave you alone in this state. Please, I beg you, allow me to be of service."

"I thank you, but truly, there is nothing you can do," she said firmly, trying to compose herself.

He continued looking at her, he looked around the church, at the altar, and back to her contemplatively, as if searching for an explanation. He thought of what had been going forward in that room only a few moments ago. At last he realized the truth and whispered at the same moment that it occurred to him, more to himself than to her, "You were in love with him." She did not confirm his suspicion, but nor did she deny it. She simply looked away, burying her face in his handkerchief, and again broke into sobs. "I am sorry, I should not have said that. I beg you would forgive me." As she made no reply, he was silent for a long moment, contemplating this new piece to the puzzle that was Fanny. This one realization made everything suddenly so clear to him. So many past conversations and interactions came back to him in a rush of comprehension under so simple yet so elucidating an epiphany. At length, with an expression of sincere compassion he said, "I am sorry, so sorry to see you suffer in this way."

"I have no right to suffer," she muttered, not really knowing what she was saying.

"You have every right," he replied quietly. "Yet, I wish you would not. I think you have had enough suffering."

"I have been very fortunate," she said, dabbing at her eyes and trying to compose herself, "and have received more blessings than were my due."

"So you have always been taught."

"Oh, what can you know about it?" she asked in frustration, still wishing he would leave her.

"Perhaps very little, but I do know something of what you are enduring at present." Here she finally raised her head but said nothing, though her look expressed doubt. He whispered, "Do not think I have never shed a tear from a broken heart." She again looked at him skeptically "Real tears," he said, pointing to his eyes.

She shook her head. "You are teasing me."

"I am not. I would not."

She looked at him, then looked down at his handkerchief in her hand. "I never believed that you really suffered."

"You never believed my feelings to be sincere."

"I had seen too much to think they could be."

"I behaved badly, very badly, especially during the time of the play." She was surprised by his acknowledgement "Little did I realize then," he continued, "how far reaching the consequences could be of what I looked upon at the time as nothing more than a diversion. I acted very foolishly."

She shook her head again. "A diversion indeed!" she replied, almost becoming angry, and at the risk of nearly forgetting her present distress. "A diversion to sport with the feelings of two women? The consequences of your foolishness have been far-reaching and felt by many."

"You are right, of course. I never meant to … It was never my intent to cause injury."

"You had to know the pain that would result from such behaviour. You could not have been so unaware."

"I should have known, perhaps, had I thought of it. But, I confess, I did not." He sighed. "To own the truth, I knew from almost the moment I arrived at Mansfield that I was intended for the present Miss Bertram. I had no desire to be married off by my sisters but they would hear nothing of my protestations and were quite determined that I should marry her. I was equally aware that Mrs. Rushworth was already engaged and I felt much safer bestowing my attentions there."

"But why bestow your attentions on either of them?" asked Fanny indignantly.

He could not help but smile. "Ah, because I did not then recognize the infinite superiority of the third young lady at Mansfield." Fanny blushed and turned away, shaking her head slightly. "You have perfectly identified my second greatest fault in the whole business, as I have just named my first. If I had shown indifference to both of them, I might be a happier man today." She made no reply. Thus, he continued with a sigh, "But as my sister once said, I had to have an object. And with Mrs. Rushworth engaged, I could never have imagined that I might encourage any real expectations there; I looked upon it as a way of avoiding any appearance of particularity towards her sister. To own the truth, when I perceived that she cared nothing for the man to whom she had pledged herself it was easier to justify myself. Had I seen any evidence of affection between them, I would not have tested their attachment."

"That does not excuse your behaviour!"

"No. It does not. My behaviour to both of them was wrong. Do not doubt that I know that much, Miss Price. I have learnt my lesson from it. I have suffered the very painful consequences of my own misconduct." He paused, and catching her eye, he added softly, "Your rejection was my penance."

They were both silent for a long moment. Then at length, she said in a whisper, "I never wished to punish you," still dabbing at her eyes with his handkerchief.

"No, I am sure you did not," he replied. Then, after a silence of a few moments he spoke again in a low voice. "I remember with what arrogance I told you that I deserved you. That I could win you by mere perseverance and not by my own merit. But you showed me how insufficient were all my pretensions to please a woman worthy of being pleased." She would not look at him, but she made no effort to stop him. "My object was only to persuade you to agree – the means of persuasion were wholly inconsequential and I would use everything and everyone at my disposal, regardless of your wishes or comfort; and I justified it all by supposing that if I could only convince you to agree to the engagement, I knew I could make you happy, that you would learn to rejoice in your acceptance." He paused. She was silent but not unaffected by his disclosure. Leaning forward a little, he continued in almost a whisper, "I would wish you to know now that it was never my intent to cause you pain. I did not see your pain. I saw only what I wished to see. Not merely for my own sake, but for yours as well. I wished to take you away from a situation of dependence which I judged to be oppressive to you, to liberate you, to give you a home, independence, and command of your own life. And in doing so much good – at least in my estimation – for a heart so deserving, I felt I would have earned the reward of your love."

Fanny was astonished by what she now heard, not only by his words but by the quiet sincerity with which he spoke, which was so different from the tone of his former declarations. Fresh tears threatened to spill forth; but these tears were not for Edmund. They sprang from a different emotion – from gratitude perhaps, for Mr. Crawford's having wanted to do so much for her, for his having given so much thought to her situation, to have had an active desire to improve it for her own sake. His intentions, as he represented them now, showed generosity – as misguided as his judgement had been.

"I had no idea you ever felt so much," she whispered.

"You may have seen me insincere, I have no doubt you have; but every word I have ever spoken to you of my own feelings has been truth." She looked at him skeptically but made no reply. "Though my design on you did not begin under such feelings. I confess that last winter, when I returned to Mansfield after Mrs. Rushworth and Miss Bertram had left it, I set out to engage your heart – with no serious intentions. It was all for my own amusement."

He had expected her to be affronted, but she only said simply, "That is exactly what I thought."

"But by the time you thought any such thing my feelings were quite real. I set out to trifle with your heart, but engaged my own instead. You were too good, too genuinely good to fall for the tricks that had succeeded with others. And it was my own heart, which I had till then thought untouchable, that was awakened."

"I never wished to cause you any pain," she said again softly.

"You have never been the cause of a moment's pain to anyone, I am sure, especially myself." He added, almost in a whisper, "All of my pain has been of my own doing." She did not know what to say in response. The last thing she had ever expected from such a man was any acknowledgement of wrongdoing. Having received no response he added only, "I hope I have not said too much."

"No," she replied. "I am not sorry to have a clearer view of past events.

And, I confess it is not so difficult to talk about it now … now that it is all over with and in the past."

He looked at her searchingly for a moment, then smiled softly. "You are determined to have me inconstant."

"No," she said, a little flustered. "But surely after all that has happened … after all these months …" She turned away from him. "Your behaviour towards me has been so different."

"Is it a wonder that I should behave differently towards you after having my eyes opened to your feelings regarding my former attentions? No. I suppose there is nothing you would imagine me incapable of." Her silence confirmed his supposition. "I see now that I made you uncomfortable not only by my addresses, but by making my hopes generally known to those around us. I thought only of my own wishes when involving your family and did not think of the consequences to you that would be occasioned by their disapprobation of your refusal. You were too strong to be swayed by the persuasion of even those closest to you; and I was too weak to forego the opportunity to use their influence to my advantage."

Fanny shuddered as she recalled her uncle's harsh words to her after her refusal of Mr. Crawford's proposal. He observed her response and said quietly, "They were unkind to you." She made no reply. "I am sorry." He leaned forward and seemed almost to reach for her hand. "You cannot know how it pains me to think I have caused you to suffer. You have endured the censure of those you love and respect the most for holding to the very principles they taught you and for having formed an opinion of me that was more just than anyone else's." He said it quietly but with feeling. Fanny could say nothing in response, whether from her astonishment that such a declaration could be made by such a man or simply the heightened emotion of the moment, she could not determine. She finally felt some vindication after all the disappointment she had caused her family, even if the acknowledgement that she had been justified came only from Mr. Crawford. "And you never told them your reasons," he continued. "Your uncle is still too civil towards me to know the truth. You did not tell him because it would also implicate your cousins. You would not spare yourself from unjust censure at their expense, even after all you have endured at their hands. They did not deserve so much kindness from you."

Fanny made no reply, but reflected at length upon his words. After a long silence, she felt out of danger of any further tears escaping her and believed she was quite ready to show her face amongst her family. "It is growing late," she said at last, "my aunt may be wondering where I am."

"Come," he said, rising and offering her his hand, "I will walk you home."

"Thank you," she replied, accepting his arm.

They walked back in silence.

Chapter 12

Fanny could not sleep the night of Edmund's wedding to Mary Crawford. Her mind was plagued by turbulent emotions – vacillating between pity for Edmund in being taken in, wonder at how he could have been so blind, genuine sorrow for the unhappiness that she was certain he would suffer, and sincere hope that they would both learn to be happy together. She was utterly wretched. After tossing and turning and trying to fix her mind on anything but Edmund, she crept into the East room to sit in front of the cooling embers that remained in the fireplace.

As a rational matter, she knew Edmund was married. She had witnessed the ceremony. Yet, her heart and even her head could not yet fully grasp that it had happened. That it was done. Edmund was unalterably and irrevocably lost to her forever. It was a painful acknowledgement. Her heart felt empty, hollow, and the tears would not stop. But the worst pain was the sense of helplessness that enveloped her. Everything that had happened leading up to this moment, the greatest moment of sorrow in her life, had occurred around her without any participation by her. No act or choice on her part had or could have had any influence on her present unhappy state. Loving Edmund had been as natural as breathing. And everything else had just happened. Her disappointment had resulted entirely from choices made by others. Then she caught herself and wondered if she was being selfish. How could she feel melancholy when Edmund was happy? She remembered his smiles, his happy glow, his special look just for her immediately after the ceremony, as if intending to share a confidence, to acknowledge that she especially must know how happy he was. Was it selfish of her to be unhappy on his behalf? To feel saddened by the prospect that a lifetime of discontent would be the reward for his love and faith in a woman who deserved neither? Her heart could have rejoiced for Edmund if she could have believed he had married a woman who would make him happy.

She tried to believe they would learn to be happy together. Perhaps Miss Crawford … Fanny shook her head at the thought … Mrs. Bertram, perhaps Mrs. Bertram would change. Perhaps she would learn better principles from Edmund as Fanny herself had done. Perhaps Edmund would not have to fully compromise all his principles to maintain peace at home. But the circumstances seemed against such hope. Tom's death had made it possible for them to marry with compromise from neither. The impediment of fortune done away with, they had not troubled themselves to consider how to reconcile the differences in their own characters which had made such an impediment material. That much was evident by their quarrel after returning from London.

Such thoughts continued to agitate her mind until sunlight began to filter into the room from the windows and a servant entered to light the fire. Fanny was exhausted, not so much from lack of sleep as from the emotional strain of the continuous turbulent thoughts which had occupied her all night. After dressing, she tried to divert her mind by reading. But no sooner did she begin a favourite passage than she remembered Edmund's recommendation of it, his opinions and impressions. She closed the book and put it down, arising to pace the room in frustration. But everything her eyes fixed on recalled a memory of Edmund.

Finally, she was able to join the family at breakfast, but there was no relief to be found there. All anyone could talk about were the events of the day before, how lovely the bride had appeared, how happy the groom had looked, and the general regret that dear Mrs. Rushworth and Miss Bertram had been prevented from coming to Mansfield for the occasion, as they had guests staying at Sotherton Court. This led to lamentations of the distance between Mansfield Park and Thornton Lacey and how much the family would miss seeing both Edmund and Mary every day; but Sir Thomas soon put an end to such unhappy observations by announcing that he expected them for dinner a week hence.

Fanny was not looking forward to the dinner, but she knew she must become accustomed to being in company with Edmund and his wife. She taught herself to think of it as an opportunity to complete the change of feelings that she had forced upon herself since their engagement. She had been sitting with her aunts since breakfast feeling restless as she considered this, and thus she went outdoors alone to walk in the shrubbery. Wanting to prolong her solitude, she sat down on a sunny bench still thinking of Edmund and his new wife. The same thoughts and feelings that had plagued her all night and all morning still consumed her mind and heart. And it was in this state that Mr. Crawford found her.

She was so lost in her agonizing reverie that she did not hear his approach and only became aware of him by the sudden loss of the sun's warmth caused by his shadow as he stepped in front of her. She looked up at him. "Good morning, Miss Price," he said. "Lady Bertram said I might find you out here. I wanted to make sure you were well … after yesterday."

She realized now that she had not thought of him at all since he had left her in the drawing room the previous day after the wedding. "Good morning, sir. As you can see, I am quite well."

"You look as if you have not slept," he said, sitting down beside her.

She would not admit that she had been awake all night so she simply did not reply. He quickly added, "I confess, I was not able to sleep last night either." She said nothing. "I could not stop thinking about our conversation yesterday."

Now she raised her eyes to him; she looked at him penetratingly, realizing that he was referring to his discovery of her feelings for Edmund. Her secret. For the first time since the day before she thought to be alarmed by his knowledge. Her eyes widened. Mr. Crawford had never shown any discretion. How in the world could she trust him with her most private, most intimate, most sacred secret? She felt a sudden dread come upon her and a knot grew in the pit of her stomach; her heart began to race with panic. From what she could discern of their relationship, he and his sister had no secrets between them. They shared everything. What if he should tell her? Fanny could hardly doubt the inevitability of such a disclosure. "Mr. Crawford ..." she began urgently. But he silenced her.

"Miss Price," he said quickly, "please be assured that I would never breathe a word of my suspicions to anyone."

He spoke with quiet sincerity, but she looked at him in disbelief, then turned away from him, doubtful of his ability to keep such a promise. She did not like the feeling that her heart's secret was at the mercy of his whim and she had no reason to rely on his words. But what choice did she have now? She had seen him insincere too many times to feel secure that he would keep his word. But perhaps it did not signify now if Edmund or anyone else should learn of her feelings, now that he was married to another. At length, she said quietly, "I fear sir, that I cannot trust your promise, but it seems I have little choice now."

"I am sorry that my supposition continues to distress you but you must remember that you have not confirmed it. I have no verification of its truth."

She turned back and looked at him again. She considered his changed manner and all the things he had said to her yesterday – which she had not taken any time to reflect on until now – his expressions of understanding of what he had done wrong, and of his regret. Perhaps he had changed, perhaps it was possible he could be trusted. No, she knew him too well. She shook her head and looked down at her hands in her lap.

Mr. Crawford watched the varying expressions cross her features. "What is it?" he asked. "That is not the first time you shake your head at me. Will you tell me why?"

She looked at him again. "I was just wondering if it is possible that you can really have changed so much as you seem to have done."

"I do not think I have changed so very much, but if you perceive a change in me, I hope it is a change for the better."

After a moment she said, "I have never known you to be so serious and contemplative as you were yesterday and as you continue to appear at present."

"It was serious contemplation that I formerly lacked." After a pause, he continued, "Despite what you may think of me, it has never been in my nature to deliberately cause injury. Rather, my defect was never to think of it. I did not reflect on how my actions affected others; or, to the extent I did think of it, I deceived myself into believing any pain occasioned by my actions to be trifling."

Fanny was astonished. To hear Henry Crawford speak in such a way – both yesterday and today – seemed so foreign to her, so different from what she knew of his character. And yet, his demeanour was of a piece with his behaviour in Portsmouth. She did not know what to make of him. "And what, I wonder, can have prompted this sudden surge of contemplation?"

"Do you wonder?" he asked with a half-smile. She made no reply, but withdrew her eyes from his. "I would very much like to give you a full history of it someday. But now is not the time. It is too cold for you to be out here much longer and I would address something else with you before I urge you to return indoors. I spoke to your uncle before I came in search of you." For a brief moment Fanny could not help but fear that Mr. Crawford had determined to renew his suit and had once again enlisted Sir Thomas' assistance. Then she remembered his expressions of regret the day before for having done so in the past. Surely, he could not still entertain any hopes of her. "He asked me to join the family for dinner next week. The Grants will be here, as well as Mr. and Mrs. Bertram." He paused a moment then added, "I did not give him a definite answer. I have no desire to give you discomfort and if my presence will cause you any, I will not come to dinner. Only say the word now, and I will make my excuses to Sir Thomas."

He said it quietly and as a matter of simple fact. Fanny thought it extraordinary that he should put such a question to her, that he should defer anything to her decision. The prospect of spending the evening with Mr. and Mrs. Bertram did make her apprehensive and Mr. Crawford's presence was not likely to make her more comfortable, especially given his knowledge of her heart. But Fanny could never put herself forward to such a degree. "If my uncle saw fit to invite you," she said, "I would not presume to differ with him."

He hesitated a moment before replying, "Very well then, I shall accept the invitation. Now, you really should not sit out here any longer. Shall we return to the drawing room?"

"Yes," she said, rising from the bench.

The following morning, before she ventured downstairs, Fanny was surprised when a servant brought word that Sir Thomas wished to see her in his room before breakfast. As she walked to meet him, she wondered what could be the reason for his summons. She remembered Mr. Crawford having mentioned a conversation with him and wondered if it were possible that he had said something that may have hinted at her true feelings for Edmund. She dreaded the possibility that her uncle had found out her secret. Then she wondered if perhaps Mr. Crawford had again asked Sir Thomas to intercede with her on his behalf after all. There was no telling what it could be, but her curiosity was soon satisfied after entering his room.

Once she was seated Sir Thomas regarded her for a long moment in silence, then began by saying, "I saw Mr. Crawford yesterday; he wished to speak to me on a particular matter. He, in fact, confessed to me that you had very valid reasons for rejecting his suit last year." Fanny could not suppress an expression of surprise, but said nothing. "He openly admits that his own behaviour justifiably led to your poor opinion of him and ultimately to your refusal. He even went so far as to suggest that he is now convinced he was unworthy of your hand. He, regrettably, would not give me particulars as to the nature of his objectionable conduct and urged me not to demand them of you either. I do not know what could have caused him to make such a confession to me now, after so many months, but it appears that I may have been too harsh in my censure of you last year. Instead of giving you credit for having good reasons to refuse Mr. Crawford and learning for myself what they were, I saw only that you were rejecting an advantageous match and I became angry." Tears were now flowing down Fanny's cheeks. "What I do not comprehend is why you would not explain your reasons for refusing him to me more fully at the time."

"I could not," was all she said, lowering her eyes.

"I will not deny that I wish you felt that you could confide in me," he replied, "but I will not press you. You are a good girl, Fanny," he said, "and I should be truly sorry if I caused you any undue pain."

"I know, Uncle," she cried, springing to her feet. "Please do not think of it any more."

"Come," he said waving her towards him as he arose as well. She walked to him obediently. "You are a good girl," he repeated, kissing her forehead.

"Thank you," she replied with renewed tears.

"You may go. I will see you at breakfast."

"Yes sir," she said, then hastily left the room.

Fanny felt more relieved after this conversation than she would have expected to feel had she known what he wished to discuss with her. How Mr. Crawford had managed to impart enough information to her uncle to effect such a conversation without revealing too much about the unhappy conduct of his daughters during the preceding year while convincing him not to press her for more details, and still retaining his friendship was a mystery to Fanny. But she was amazed not only that he had managed to do it, but that he had undertaken it. Moreover, she reflected that Mr. Crawford would only have made such a confession if he never intended to seek her uncle's consent to marry her again. This was a welcome realization. She was glad that she had not asked him to decline the invitation to dinner.

Chapter 13

The anticipated dinner with the newly married couple was soon upon Fanny. She had scarcely been able to think of anything but Edmund's marriage since it had occurred. Now, she dreaded seeing the one person who had been her dearest friend and closest confidant. Her anxiety was heightened by her apprehension that Mr. Crawford might somehow reveal her secret. That some other person, any other person, had knowledge of her true feelings was distressing enough; but that a man she felt to be dishonest and unprincipled and whose first loyalty must be to the last creature whom Fanny could wish the intelligence to reach, should be possessed of such knowledge was altogether terrifying. Fanny had never wished more fervently for Mr. Crawford to leave Mansfield. She had not thought to wonder why he was still in the neighbourhood or why, now that his sister had married, he had not spoken of leaving it.

The Grants and Mr. Crawford arrived before the Bertrams, and happily for Fanny she was very little noticed by anyone and was left to the leisure of agonizing anticipation as she awaited the arrival of her beloved Edmund and his new wife. At last they entered the room – the very picture of conjugal felicity. They were overflowing with joy and animation, smiling at everyone and exchanging meaningful looks with one another that showed how much they were in each other's confidence. Mrs. Bertram grasped Fanny's hands, calling her "my dearest Fanny," and telling her again and again how very happy she was. And with a meaningful look to her brother, she expressed to Fanny how much she looked forward to seeing her just as happy some day soon. There was little time for anything else before dinner and Fanny could not regret that she had not had a chance to talk to Edmund after their initial exchange of greetings.

She was dismayed, however, a moment later when Edmund sat next to her at the dinner table. "My dear Fanny," he began, as soon as they were seated, "I am so pleased to be seated next to you, as I am sure you are as eager to hear the extent of my joy as I am to tell you of it!" And thus, Fanny was forced to endure throughout the dinner Edmund's expressions of delight with the marriage state in general and with his own enchanting wife in particular. In describing their life of a full week together at Thornton Lacey he painted a picture of such exquisite contentment as he was sure no other two people had ever known or could ever know. And his bride, she was perfection itself. She had already shown such aptitude for her housekeeping duties and had so many ideas for improving their little household as delighted him immeasurably. Edmund's effusions continued from the soup through the dessert. Never in her life had Fanny been more relieved to see Lady Bertram stand to withdraw from the dining room.

In the drawing room, Fanny was able to sit quietly and listen to the others, but the topic of conversation did not change. The ladies alternated between asking about Mrs. Bertram's new situation in excruciating detail and giving her bits and pieces of indispensable advice that were sure to save her a substantial amount of expense or trouble at unspecified future times. Although the conversation in the drawing room was infinitely preferable to what she had endured at dinner, Fanny was beginning to suffer from the headache. She was just considering seriously the propriety of excusing herself and going to bed when the gentlemen joined them.

Fanny had never felt more alone. There was no one who could give her any comfort; no one who could shield her from the sources of pain and distress. That had always been Edmund's office, but those days were long gone. She must now rely on herself. She must be strong. And her strength was put to an early test as Mrs. Bertram soon moved to Fanny's side and began speaking to her quietly. Fanny felt as if she was reliving her dinner conversation but with another partner. The many joys and felicities of marriage to her own dear Edmund were dwelt on with such warmth and animation by Mrs. Bertram as made Fanny almost feel faint; and she could not help but conclude that with all this joy and felicity, the lovers' quarrel must have been wholly resolved, yet she could not conceive any resolution that would so completely satisfy both parties.

Not long after his sister appeared at Fanny's side, Mr. Crawford walked over to them, sat down next to Mrs. Bertram and engaged her attention almost entirely. Fanny leaned back and breathed a sigh of relief. She soon noticed with gratitude that Mr. Crawford was directing the conversation towards any subject other than Mrs. Bertram's connubial happiness.

The conversation between brother and sister soon revealed to Fanny that Mrs. Bertram fully intended to go to London in the spring. Her way of talking indicated that she considered it as quite a settled thing, and she was asking her brother's opinion as to what lodgings they should secure. Fanny looked at Edmund, but he was engaged in conversation with Dr. Grant and had apparently not heard his wife. She wondered that he had agreed to go to London after confiding in Fanny that he would not. So this was the end to the quarrel: Edmund had given in. It did not portend well for his ability to check his wife's unreasonable expectations in future. She was disappointed in Edmund, but then told herself she had no right to be, it was not her concern.

Music was soon requested of the ladies. There was no harp at Mansfield, but Mrs. Grant played the pianoforte well enough to accompany her sister's singing. As everyone settled in to listen in silence, Fanny was finally able to relax. If she did not look at Edmund as he gazed adoringly at his wife, she could even enjoy the music. In trying to avoid looking at Edmund, Fanny could not fix her eyes anywhere else. She looked at the others in the room and they were all watching the performers. The only exception was Mr. Crawford; when she glanced in his direction, she noticed that he was watching her intently.

She remembered what he had said to her in the church, that he understood her suffering. But this was something he could not understand. He may have understood unrequited love, but he had not suffered the irrevocable loss of the one he loved to another. Then she shook her head, remembering her conviction that he had given her up; surely, he no longer loved her. After hearing his expressions of remorse for his prior conduct she could attribute his recent kind gestures towards her as merely an attempt to redress his past wrongs. She saw that he noticed her shaking her head and she looked away, sighing to herself. She longed for an escape, and again thought of going to bed on account of the headache.

After two songs the ladies moved away from the instrument and the conversation of Thornton Lacey and its happy occupants was resumed. Fanny had never considered the Parsonage house so busy a place as it seemed at present. She began to wonder whether it was possible to exhaust all details of their living arrangements that were open for discussion. From the placement of the furniture to the size of the poultry to the shelves in the closet, nothing was overlooked in the conversation. Mrs. Grant was observing for at least the tenth time how very pleased she was to have Mary so near and so well settled and so very happy, then added with a sigh, "If only I could dispose of Henry so well. If only I could see him as happily settled." And then glancing ever so briefly at Fanny as if to emphasize her doubt of any hope there, she turned to Lady Bertram and asked how soon Miss Bertram would be returning home to Mansfield.

Since her own return from London, Fanny had received a letter from Julia to inform her that the stage had been completed, that they had obtained some very serviceable curtains for it, and that nearly all of the actors had gathered to begin rehearsals. Julia was undoubtedly too engaged with all the felicities of a large party of young people and a play to prepare for to think of writing much, and Fanny could not regret it. She chose not to think of the happenings at Sotherton, but was never completely successful. Even the brief intelligence communicated in the one short note was more news than Fanny wished for and it had been difficult for her to respond to Lady Bertram's inquiries regarding Julia's letters without disclosing the improprieties of conduct being engaged in at Sotherton. Finally, she had not been able to help mentioning to her aunts, with as little detail as possible, that a play was contemplated. Mrs. Norris expressed her delight that the girls were able to undertake such a pleasant diversion and wished she could travel to Sotherton to see the performance herself. Fanny could not share in this sentiment.

Lady Bertram replied to Mrs. Grant's inquiry by saying that Julia had no present plans of returning home, and that she was quite happy where she was, in the company of other young people and engaging in pursuits appropriate to her age and situation. Then, to Fanny's dismay, they began to speak of the possibility of their all travelling to Sotherton for the day very soon. This, thought Fanny, was an evil to be avoided. Seeing the style in which his daughters were choosing to live at Sotherton, she felt, could only bring disappointment to her uncle. Fanny had no wish to go, but if Lady Bertram went, as was now under discussion and very likely if Sir Thomas were to go, she knew she would have no choice.

The others were in favour of the idea. Both Mr. and Mrs. Bertram longed to walk again in the wilderness and exchanged a meaningful look of remembrance of the last time they were there together. Lady Bertram and Mrs. Norris both missed Maria and Julia enough to acquiesce to the scheme, the latter immediately and the former after some consideration of whether seeing her children would make venturing so far from home during the winter worthwhile, and some persuasion from her husband and sister. The only one who opposed the idea was Mr. Crawford who, when applied to by his sisters, acknowledged that he had seen all of Sotherton he had cared to see on his first visit; nor did he have the slightest curiosity to see any of the improvements that had since been made to it. Even Mrs. Bertram could not shake his resolute determination against going to Sotherton, but nor could he dissuade the others from going; and Fanny was left to hope this would be one of those schemes that was talked about but never undertaken.

Soon the card tables were placed and Dr. Grant sat down with Sir Thomas, Lady Bertram and Mrs. Norris. Mrs. Grant, Mr. Bertram and Mrs. Bertram had just determined to sit down together as well when Edmund, seeing Mr. Crawford with a newspaper, entreated Fanny to join them. She had no desire to play but being as she was accustomed to doing as she was bidden, she was rising to go to their table when Mr. Crawford laid down his newspaper and intervened. "Please Miss Price, if you do not mind, I would ask you to give me the chance to redeem myself." She looked at him curiously. He smiled. "I played very ill the last time I had a game with Bertram and must have my revenge, if you will indulge me."

"Of course," she said, returning to her seat very relieved. Something in his smile told her that he had done it to spare her from having to sit and play at cards with Edmund and Mary. She knew she would have to grow accustomed to spending evenings with them in such a way, but she felt it was too soon and she was grateful for his intervention. She picked up a book and read contentedly until the tea things were brought in, when Lady Bertram was perfectly satisfied with allowing her to make the tea.

At last the evening ended and Fanny was able to retire to her room, but she found that she could not relieve her headache, and her mind was still plagued with the same restless thoughts and agitations that had occupied her for the past week. After a few minutes of tossing and turning in bed she returned to the East room and set about pacing to and fro in front of the fire. After a while she sat down at her writing table and stared at the beautiful silver writing things that William had given her. Then, looking past them, her eyes rested on a small box at the back of the table. The box had been a gift from Poor Tom and it contained her most cherished treasure. She opened it, and inside was a scrap of paper: the unfinished note Edmund had written her when he had been meaning to leave the chain he bought her for William's cross in her room before she had interrupted him. She took out the paper and unfolded it, reading the familiar words, "My very dear Fanny, you must do me the favour to accept …" One hand moved to her throat and touched the chain and cross she now wore at all times – a token unifying the two men most dear to her. She felt a single tear spill forth down one cheek. She wiped it away and still holding the paper, she arose and walked to the fireplace. She stared a moment into the now dwindling flames and steeling herself with a deep, fortifying breath, she cast the paper into the fire.

Chapter 14

The distraction of the wedding over, Mansfield seemed to return to the quietude that had characterized it since Tom's death. The family saw nothing of the Parsonage inhabitants for some days and the cold weather prevented any exercise out of doors. After breakfast one morning, when the weather had begun to grow a little warmer, Fanny was sitting in the drawing room with her two aunts, when Mrs. Norris remembered that she had forgotten to bring a balm she had acquired which she was certain would do away entirely with the dark circles that had appeared under Lady Bertram's eyes since Poor Tom's death. Mrs. Norris authoritatively decided that her sister could not possibly go another day without the balm and that Fanny would just have to fetch it from her house. Fanny, who felt she had sat still for too long, not having had the opportunity to ride or take a long walk for several days and perhaps having spent too many hours with the same companions, welcomed the exercise.

Lady Bertram objected on account of the weather observing, "I am sure Sir Thomas said it looked like it would rain today. He was certain of it."

"But it is not raining now," replied her sister. "There are some clouds, but very few; I have never seen it rain in these parts with so few clouds. To be sure, no one has a better notion than me of what impending rain looks like at Mansfield. Imagine how much more often I am out of doors than yourself, walking the short distance to my own humble home and back sometimes two or three times a day. No one can say better than I can whether there is enough time. I dare say it might rain later. I have no doubt that Sir Thomas' prediction will hold true. But now there can be no danger. Certainly, if she hurries there is ample time to walk only to my house and back."

Lady Bertram, being satisfied in the assurance that Sir Thomas would be proven right at some point, could not say that Fanny did not have time to make the walk. And, it did seem a very short walk. It never seemed to take Mrs. Norris very long at all to go to her home and return again. "If you think it is best," was all she had to say in reply.

When Fanny stepped outside, she noticed that the sky was overcast and the wind blew strongly against her pelisse. Nevertheless, she trudged forward, confident that she would be back home before the rain. But she was to have no such luck. The clouds burst open just as she approached the walk to her aunt's house and she ran the rest of the way in.

By the time she found what she had come for, the rain was falling too hard outdoors for her to begin the walk home even with the umbrella. She lit a candle and sat down to occupy herself with Mrs. Norris' work basket. She had been sitting for a few minutes when the door was suddenly opened and Mr. Crawford was shown in. He was soaking wet. "Miss Price!" he said, "I am glad to have found you."

"Mr. Crawford," she said in surprise.

"I arrived at your uncle's house just as the storm broke and your aunts told me you had gone out," he explained. "I am relieved to see that you made it here in time."

"You are wet. Please sit down. I will get you something to dry off with."

Looking around the room, after Fanny left it, he saw a candle and her work lying next to where she had been sitting and noticed the cold fireplace. When she returned to the room with a towel in her hand and the housemaid trotting behind her, he looked at her pointedly and said, "You have been sitting here without a fire?"

"I was not very wet," she replied, handing him the towel. "But you will need one," she added, gesturing towards the maid who was already starting a fire. "You look as if you walked here without so much as an umbrella."

He thanked her for the towel, and then sitting down near the fireplace to dry off, he added, "Neither my umbrella nor my hat nor my great coat were of any use against this storm. The wind is far too violent to be reckoned with." He smiled at her, "I am afraid you will have to put up with my company until it passes."

Fanny only smiled back at him and resumed her work as the storm raged on outdoors. He watched her for a moment, then, once the maid had left them and closed the door behind her, he ventured to ask, "What possessed you to go out in such weather?"

"It was not raining when I left the house."

"But you must have seen that it would."

"And did not you venture out in the same weather?"

"I left the Parsonage early this morning on business I had in the village, but there was little sign of rain then; indeed, the weather looked so favourable that I went for a ride in the Park afterwards. I decided to stop in to visit you and your aunts before returning to the Parsonage and was shown into the house just as the storm broke. When I learned that you had gone out not long before, I truly wondered whether you had been able to make it here and whether you might have met with some trouble or inconvenience. Sir Thomas, having walked into the drawing room with me, heard of your errand at the same time, and was quite worried about you and not at all pleased that you had been sent out. When I suggested that perhaps I ought to go in search of you, he readily assented and Lady Bertram seemed eager for me to do so as well."

Fanny was a bit embarrassed to have been the cause of so much fuss, but only replied, "As you can see I am well."

"Yes. And I intend to see you home after the storm."

"That is not necessary," she said, attending diligently to her work.

"Determined as I am to never again act against your express wishes, I do hope you will allow me the honour of seeing you safely back to your aunt."

She was tempted to test the first part of his speech, but his offer was made with such kindness, she thought better of it and acquiesced.

"I do not know what Mrs. Norris can have been thinking, to send you out in such threatening weather." he said.

"She thought I would have sufficient time before the rain. Besides, I was quite happy for the exercise. I had not had a walk in several days."

"You have not had your usual exercise from riding either."

"No," she replied, "I have not been riding since —" she hesitated, not wanting to cast Edmund in an unfavourable light, "— since before the wedding." Then she added quickly, "But the weather has not been suitable for riding in any case."

"I did notice that Bertram took his mare to Thornton Lacey."

"Which is as it should be."

"That you would resort to walk out in a storm for exercise is not as it should be; and the exercise would not be beneficial if you were caught in the rain and took ill as a result."

"I thank you for your concern, but as you can see no harm has come to me. You do not seem concerned that you might take ill and you are wet through."

"My constitution is not so delicate as yours."

"Mine is not so delicate as you might think."

"You have strength of character, Miss Price, but I fear it is not matched by strength of constitution. I, on the other hand, have always had the latter," he hesitated, then added, "though perhaps I am still working on the former."

They were both quiet for several minutes following this observation, Fanny working and Mr. Crawford watching her. Suddenly, she stopped and looked at him. Then, resuming her work, she said, "I trust you enjoyed your card games the other evening."

He smiled. "I did. And I hope you enjoyed your book."

"It is one I have read before. I confess I was not inclined for cards."

"That is precisely why I offered to play."

"I am grateful."

"I was happy to do it. I enjoyed the game. But more importantly, I wanted to spare you from a pursuit you were not inclined for." He paused then added earnestly but quietly, "I would have spared you from the entire evening if it had been within my power."

She shook her head but did not say anything.

He leaned forward. "Are you displeased?"

"No," she replied without looking up, "I ... no."

He leaned back again and after another long moment, changed the subject. "I was surprised to hear of the scheme of going to Sotherton."

"Why should you be? Is not it natural that Sir Thomas would wish to call on his daughters?"

"Yes, of course, but I fear he may be disappointed by what he finds there."

She looked up at him a little surprised, wondering how much he knew.

"I have had a letter from Mr. Yates," he said. "He wrote to tell me that I must come to Sotherton to perform in their little theatre! He says it does not signify that I have received no invitation from his hosts. It will disappoint you to learn, if you have not already heard it from another source, that they have converted the family chapel into a theatre."

"I had already heard it from Miss Bertram."

"It is a shame."

"Do you really think so?" she asked doubtfully.

"I do think so."

"I am told the chapel at Sotherton was never used and everyone seems to be quite pleased with the change."

"Indeed, Mr. Yates described the theatre in great detail. And he wrote in very familiar terms of Miss Bertram. If things continue on the course his letter seemed to suggest, I think your uncle may be very disappointed."

Fanny was a little affronted by the easy way in which he could speak of Julia's prospects after disappointing her the previous summer. It seemed to her an impertinence, though in accord with what she knew of his character; but she could not disagree. "I do not think he was very fond of Mr. Yates."

"Poor Sir Thomas will have lost two daughters to two very unworthy gentlemen." It was, perhaps, not the kindest of things to say, but Fanny could not deny the truth of Mr. Crawford's observation; and, she thought to herself that Sir Thomas had lost his son to an unworthy wife as well, but said nothing. "But his niece will not be lost. She will not settle for an unworthy husband."

Fanny's colour heightened. "I doubt I will ever marry," she replied, her eyes fixed on her work. He made no reply. Feeling a little embarrassed, she sought to change the subject. "I wonder that Mr. Yates took it upon himself to invite you to Sotherton."

"It was rather unbecoming of him to be so presumptuous, though he cannot know how little I would be welcomed there; or perhaps he should know but was not observant enough in former times to comprehend it. But I would not go under any circumstance. I was surprised *you* did not wish to go, especially as you missed seeing some of the grounds during your last visit."

"I have no wish to go. I did not see everything I had hoped to see, but I saw enough."

"I cannot think of that day without regret. I know you were made uncomfortable by more than one circumstance. I was insensible of it until many months later when I reflected on it with a more open mind."

"It is in the past and of no consequence."

"It is of consequence," he protested. "I wish …" here he paused, then seeming to change direction he said, "I would have taken you to see the avenue."

She looked up at him sharply, but quickly returned her eyes to her work. "It was no great deprivation, Mr. Crawford, I was quite fatigued and … there will be other opportunities, there are other avenues."

She had said it only to show that it was no great loss and with no thought of his improvements at Everingham; but his thoughts were there immediately. "So there are," he replied.

She looked at him and remembered the conversation from London. "I did not mean …"

"I know you did not mean Everingham," he replied. "I know you well enough to be certain you would never make such a hint."

"I trust all is going well with your planting."

"Yes. I have had word from my steward that everything is proceeding as it should."

"It must be difficult to manage your affairs while away," she observed, not really knowing what to say.

He sighed. "Yes, I will have to return," he said. Then he added quietly, "Though I have no wish to quit Mansfield."

"I imagine you would not wish to leave your sisters."

Mr. Crawford did not immediately respond. After a moment of silent contemplation, he stood from his chair, walked over to the window and looked out at the storm. Fanny had resumed her work and was engaged in her own reverie by the time he spoke again. "I do not know what to say," he said quietly, turning to face her. "There is much I want to tell you, but it is exactly what you do not want to hear. And I certainly have no desire to cause you any further distress."

She glanced at him briefly but returned to her work saying quietly, "I thank you for that, sir." He took this as a confirmation of what he suspected: that she did not wish to hear what he had to say. He turned back to the window and watched the storm in silence. It was a long time before either of them spoke again.

Fanny broke the silence by suddenly raising her head and saying, "I have not yet thanked you for bringing my brother John to call on me in London. I feel ashamed for not having mentioned it sooner; indeed, I should have thanked you long ago. It was such an unexpected act of kindness."

He had turned to face her again upon hearing her speak. "It was my pleasure and you have no reason to feel ashamed. He seemed a very pleasant young man, and appears to be distinguishing himself in his position."

"I was quite surprised to see him. It was so very kind of you."

"As I said, I was happy to do it."

She was silent for a moment, then said, "I am grateful for the kindness, though I cannot imagine why you would put yourself to so much trouble."

"It was no trouble," he said simply.

"You were three days finding him!"

He laughed lightly, "I did not spend the whole of those three days finding him; but truly, having discharged my purpose in coming to town early in the week, I was quite at leisure to track him through all the public offices in London. And it was well worthwhile to witness your expression of delight as you met with him." Here she blushed. "I confess, it was more pleasing even than when I gave you the news of Mr. Price's promotion."

Her expression grew dark. "Please do not speak of that day."

"I speak only of the pleasant part of the day." He paused for a moment, then continued, "I would have to be permitted a broader scope of remembrance to give you my reason for having greater pleasure in the more recent of the two events; but as it has been forbidden, and as you show no sign of curiosity I will make no further mention of it."

His reference to what he had done for William only heightened her confusion resulting from the kindnesses he had lately shown her: bringing her brother's gift to her, bringing another brother to call on her, speaking to her uncle, even playing at cards with the Bertrams. What was his motivation if marriage was no longer his object? Was it perhaps to make some kind of amends? Or was he yet sporting with her? She shook her head in confusion.

He sat down across from her. "Will you tell me what you are thinking?" he asked.

She looked hesitant to speak, unsure, perhaps, of whether she should continue the openness that had marked their past few conversations. She reflected to herself, that he had already guessed at her deepest, most private secret. There could be no reason for reserve now. "I do not understand the motivation for your sudden kindness towards me."

He regarded her silently for a moment before replying, "Is my being kind to you such a novelty?"

She thought for a moment, then said, "No. You had shown me kindness before, but somehow, lately, you are different." She paused again. She had spoken to him before of his change of behaviour towards her – the withdrawal of his unwelcome and indelicate attentions. She looked back at him as the realization struck her. "Now, it is all kindness, only kindness." She blushed as she said it, then looked down to her work.

He smiled. "As it should be. You have indeed fixed precisely on the very reason I alluded to a moment ago. My joy in seeing you with Mr. John Price, was unalloyed by any other motive than to see you happy. The business with Mr. Price, I was happy to do for his own sake, but it was part of a larger scheme to …"

"I know," she said quietly.

"It is this circumstance that makes all the difference."

To her mind, he wished her to comprehend that his recent kindnesses were not part of a "larger scheme," as he had put it – and since the scheme he alluded to was his offer of marriage to her, it was clear that he had no intention of renewing those proposals. This confirmation of her conviction as to that point put her somewhat at ease.

She could not acknowledge this to him, but continued the conversation saying, "Bringing one brother's gift to me and bringing the other to visit me or playing at cards are all acts of kindness which might only involve sacrifices of your own time and convenience. But speaking to my uncle the way you did could not have been easy."

"Does not the difficulty of an act of kindness add to its value?" he asked with a smile. She said nothing. Then assuming a more serious tone, he added, "I spoke to Sir Thomas simply to right a past wrong and I spoke only the truth; though I know it does not and cannot make up for causing you to be unjustly censured by him."

His response did not diminish Fanny's confusion. His recent acts of kindness together with the confessions he had made to her since Edmund's wedding so wholly contradicted everything she knew of his character as to leave her quite perplexed. Yet, he seemed sincere, indeed she had never seen or heard him speak as he had been doing in their last few conversations. But what could be his purpose? He had all but admitted a moment ago that he had no intention of renewing his proposals to her. Was it possible that he was yet sporting with her, that his recent kind gestures and expressions were calculated to mislead her? Was he merely trying a different stratagem, one more finely tailored to her character and preferences? She shook her head again. "I do not know," she said as much to herself as to him. "I cannot make out your motives."

He stood and walked back to the window briskly, then turned to face her again. "Are you trying to press me into making a confession you have no desire to hear, Miss Price? I will say it most readily, most happily, if you wish."

She dropped her eyes back to her work and made no reply, but the colour rose in her cheeks.

He spoke again, more quietly and with less quickness, "I am well aware of your feelings. You have nothing to fear from me."

She said nothing and would not look up; he turned back to the window. After several more minutes of watching the storm in silence, he walked across the room to a bookshelf. He browsed the few books in Mrs. Norris' collection, then asked Fanny. "Shall I read to you?"

She raised her head abruptly, as if surprised to hear him speak after so long a silence. "If you like," she said.

"There are not many choices. Fordyce, Shakespeare, ..."

"You choose."

"Shakespeare," he said, picking up one of the books.

He sat back down in his chair and began paging through the volume; when he began reading, she was a little startled by his choice.

Let me not to the marriage of true minds
Admit impediments. Love is not love
Which alters when it alteration finds,
Or bends with the remover to remove:
O no! it is an ever-fixed mark
That looks on tempests and is never shaken;

It is the star to every wandering bark,
Whose worth's unknown, although his height be taken.
Love's not Time's fool, though rosy lips and cheeks
Within his bending sickle's compass come:
Love alters not with his brief hours and weeks,
But bears it out even to the edge of doom.
If this be error and upon me proved,
I never writ, nor no man ever loved.

Fanny could not help but blush. She dared not raise her eyes to him. There was no mistaking the meaning behind his choice. The poem was about constancy, and too pointed a reference to be considered a coincidence. He had selected it because of its meaning, yet he read it without a hint of consciousness. Did he, could he really understand it? She continued working as he read other sonnets out of the collection and she smiled in spite of herself at the irony of Mrs. Norris having a book of sonnets on her sparse bookshelf. She recollected Tom having brought it to her as a present after Mr. Norris' death and having joked to his sisters that it might be of use to her in finding a new husband. Fanny shook her head at the thought, but Mr. Crawford had not seemed to notice her distraction, as his eyes were fixed on the page. He read well, as he always did, and with feeling, but his tone was not so impassioned as to cause her any further embarrassment and she soon became so engaged in listening to him that her hands stopped moving without her realizing it, and she leaned forward a little. There was no denying his abilities. Then suddenly, he snapped the book closed. She looked at him in surprise and he nodded towards the window. "The storm has stopped. I will walk you home."

"Thank you," she said, rising. She put away the work basket, extinguished the candle, and ordered the fire to be put out as well, then remembered to get the balm she had come for.

When they arrived home, Lady Bertram was very relieved to see them. "Oh my dear Fanny," she cried. "Mr. Crawford, thank heaven you found her!"

"Thankfully, she had made it to Mrs. Norris' home before the storm," he said.

After Sir Thomas also expressed his relief in her safe return, Fanny handed the balm to Mrs. Norris, who observed, "The two of you were alone together at my house all this time?"

"Neither of us could leave on account of the storm," said Fanny.

Mrs. Norris looked suspiciously at Mr. Crawford, but Lady Bertram said to Fanny, "I am so pleased you did not have to wait out the storm alone." Then turning to Mr. Crawford she added, "I hope you did not get too wet."

"No," he said. "I was a little wet but I was able to dry off in front of the fire."

"You had a fire lit?" asked Mrs. Norris of Fanny.

Fanny appeared alarmed.

"You would not expect Miss Price to sit without a fire on a day like this," said Mr. Crawford with his customary cheerfulness. Mrs. Norris said nothing. "I believe she made quite a bit of progress with your work basket," he added.

"Well, I should hope so. I would not expect her to sit idly."

Mr. Crawford had nothing further to say to her. He declined Lady Bertram's invitation to sit, observing that he had better get back to the Parsonage.

Chapter 15

About a week later, Edmund came to Mansfield on some business with his father and took the opportunity for another private interview with Fanny. She was glad to see him. Mansfield had not been the same since he had moved away and she had missed his presence. Thus, after his meeting with Sir Thomas, while Mrs. Bertram was visiting at the Parsonage, she was gratified by his request to walk out with him. She prepared herself for either another appeal to go to Sotherton or more exclamations on his conjugal felicity. For a moment, she dared to hope that he might give her news of returning his mare to Mansfield Park so she could resume riding. Instead, Edmund spoke again of the disagreement between himself and Mrs. Bertram.

"I do not know what to do, Fanny. She is absolutely determined to go to London. She does not listen when I tell her the very sound reasons against it. She has written to make inquiries as to lodgings!"

"Perhaps you must be more firm," ventured Fanny quietly.

"I have been thinking that it might be best to go. This is the first year of our marriage. She will have a whole year afterwards to become accustomed to life in the country. She has not yet had a chance to do so."

"Do you believe if you agree to go this year, she will understand why you cannot go next year?"

"I believe she will not wish to go next year. Besides, she knows how I feel about it. She will understand what it means for me to agree to go now. And if I compromise on this point, perhaps it will be easier for her to accept that I must continue performing the duties of the parish once we return."

Fanny knew that any argument would be pointless. She was disappointed to see him give in against his better judgement, but then she checked herself. What did she know about the compromises that must be made in marriage?

"We would like for you to come with us," he said, to Fanny's surprise.

"No," she replied hastily but emphatically. "I cannot possibly go. I thank you for your kind invitation, but I would rather remain at home."

"If that is your wish, I will not press you. But I hope you will consider changing your mind. I know Mary truly desires for you to go and I cannot promise she will not try to convince you."

Mrs. Bertram did indeed press her, but Fanny stood firmly on her refusal. She had no wish to go back to town and even less desire to be there with Mary and Edmund – to be under the same roof with them. She did not wish them unhappy, but nor did she have any desire to be a constant witness to their felicity or a confidante to either of them when they disagreed.

Fanny was content to spend her days with Lady Bertram and had no wish to travel with the Bertrams to London or anywhere else. Nor could she regret that Thornton Lacey was too far off for daily intercourse. There was now less intimacy even with Mansfield Parsonage. Mr. Crawford remained there but Fanny saw comparatively little of him. When she did see him, he continued to exercise those improved manners she had seen in him since Tom's death. He was friendly and warm towards her, always solicitous of her comfort, but never showed any sign of particularity in front of the others, which was a great relief to Fanny. She was also relieved that, for the time being at least, the scheme of going to Sotherton had been abandoned. The weather had been too unpleasant for too many days in succession for anyone to think of making such a journey.

Fanny soon received tidings of the proceedings at Sotherton in the form of another letter from Julia. She hoped it contained news that the play had been abandoned and that they had all come to their senses, but even as the thought crossed her mind she knew such hopes were in vain. Instead, the letter read as follows:

Dear Fanny, We have had the best time these past few weeks. The new theatre is fitted up perfectly and everything was carried out as smoothly as can be imagined for our three performances of *Lovers' Vows*. All the neighbours came to watch us and everyone praised our little production. I do believe my Amelia was superior to any other I have seen, even if I do say it myself. But, I confess our Frederick was not so lively and we only had Mr. R's steward to play the butler, but now our company has grown! There has been such fun here, some of Mr. R's friends have wanted desperately to be a part of it, and Mr. Yates even invited his friend Sir Henry to join us here at Sotherton. You may remember Mr. Y talking of him – he was to play Anhalt at Ecclesford. Mr. Y had to have someone of the Ecclesford party see him in all his glory of performing the Baron! And now Sir Henry is determined to act in our theatre! He and Mr. Y and Mr. R are reading through the volume of Shakespeare to see what can be agreed upon. There was talk of *The Taming of the Shrew* but the gentlemen have doubts as to whether our small company is equal to it. I told them I would do it only if I am cast as Bianca and Mr. Y immediately announced his intent of playing Lucentio. He has been flirting with me since he has been here, you know. But I am starting to think Sir H a better conquest. He is not as handsome as Mr. Y, but he is richer. And I believe Sir H is ready to be conquered. He scolded Mr. Y about being so hasty in claiming Lucentio for himself. The only trouble is Maria says she has no wish to play Katherine. I believe she fears she will have to put up with her husband playing her husband! How intolerable that would be! I think she envies me. She has tried flirting with Sir H, but he does not even look at her. Tell me, how is everyone at Mansfield? I know that Mr. C returned to the Parsonage for the wedding. Mr. Y writes to him and tells me everything. Maria and I would have come but we could not leave Sotherton full of guests and there were so many friends here. I am sure Edmund did not mind our not being there. It was only a wedding after all. But you must tell everyone of the delightful times we are having here at Sotherton. And when you see Mrs. Bertram I am sure she will wish to hear all about how well I acquitted myself as Amelia. And I believe she will be diverted to hear of the competition among the gentleman of the company to play Lucentio in our next production. And to think they were such great friends when they came here! Her brother, I suppose, is often at Thornton Lacey. Perhaps I will write to her myself, and it would be so much the better if a certain gentleman were to be in the same room as she reads my letter. He might learn to regret passing up the opportunity he had in Norfolk. But, I must be off now, I cannot be late for breakfast or the others will arrange everything to suit themselves without a care for my wishes. Yours etc., J. Bertram

Once again, Fanny did not know what to make of such a letter. It was all nonsense, nothing but ill-judged nonsense. How could two women raised at Mansfield Park by Sir Thomas Bertram comport themselves in such a manner? It was incomprehensible! What could she do? She knew Julia would never heed any reproach from her own pen and there was no one else to turn to, no one to talk to. Edmund could not be counted on. The all too familiar feeling of helplessness was again upon her.

The days following the arrival of this letter brought an improvement in the weather and another meeting between the Mansfield and Thornton Lacey families. With all the interested parties together again and the promise of warmer weather approaching, the subject of going to Sotherton was renewed with even greater enthusiasm. Fanny could tell by his way of talking that Sir Thomas really meant to go this time. She dreaded the result of such a scheme – the perturbation of his peace of mind that was sure to follow his discovery of the Sotherton Theatrics. As the others worked out the details of the intended visit after dinner, Mr. Crawford approached Fanny and asked if he might sit next to her.

"As you wish," she replied quietly.

"There is no stopping Sir Thomas from making this visit, I suppose?"

"It is only natural that he would wish to go."

"Indeed. Yet I fear that only disappointment will come of it. Is he truly in the dark as to the whole theatrical business?"

"I cannot be certain. I was obliged to tell my aunts a small part of what had been described in one of Julia's letters, but Sir Thomas has never betrayed any knowledge of it. I dare to hope there will be some enjoyment in the visit. Surely my uncle will write of his intentions. If they expect him, perhaps they can make such preparations as would prevent any unpleasantness."

"Let us hope so."

"But I am surprised your sisters have not prevailed upon you to join the party."

"Are you?" he said, looking a little wounded. "I had thought I had managed to effect some small improvement in your opinion of me."

Fanny was relieved from having to respond by the general announcement which followed, with great delight, inviting them all to Thornton Lacey for dinner a week hence. Fanny did not receive the invitation with pleasure. She had avoided calling at Thornton Lacey since the wedding, which was made easy by Lady Bertram's not having stirred herself to wait upon her daughter-in-law in all the glory of her new establishment. But it could be avoided no longer. Fanny had always known it would be inevitable that she should have to go to Edmund's marital home. Mr. Crawford alone could guess at her distress. The invitation was duly accepted by Lady Bertram who required only a little persuasion on the part of her husband, son, and sister to acquiesce to the scheme. To Thornton Lacey they were all to go.

Fanny entered the house shared by Edmund and his new wife with some trepidation. The Mansfield party were met by their hostess with great dignity and, having arrived only a moment after the Grants and Mr. Crawford, they all immediately began a tour of the house. As Mrs. Bertram led them from one room to the next, Edmund continually pointed out each improvement his wife had made to the place with unconcealed pride. Fanny could not help but feel the house would have answered her every wish. She thought it was well situated, and to her it appeared comfortable and snug. The mistress' sitting room, she found especially pleasing. It was on a corner of the house and therefore had windows on two sides which provided a great deal of sunlight for most of the day, and looked out onto a well-appointed rose garden. Indeed, she could find nothing to disapprove.

Fanny was not surprised when Mr. Crawford sat down next to her at dinner. In truth, it relieved her. He had proven to be an ally in distracting her from Edmund and Mary's marital bliss. During and after dinner, there was so much talk of the Bertrams' domestic concerns that Fanny was reminded of the conversations she had endured when the newly married couple had first dined at Mansfield Park. And still, more than a month later, nothing seemed to be talked of more than their contentment and felicity. Fanny sincerely wished for their happiness but only desired that she should not have to bear witness to it quite so often. Yet, thankfully, the pain of seeing Edmund married to another had dulled since those first days following the wedding.

These thoughts occupied her mind as Mrs. Bertram played the harp after dinner. She glanced at Edmund as he watched his wife's performance with undisguised adoration. Did she still love him? She hardly knew. He certainly was not the same man she had loved for so many years. There had been a change in him, but she was aware that there had also been a change in her feelings. She was not sure whether she could credit the change to her efforts at driving away feelings which had been made inappropriate by his marriage, or whether the changes in him had made him less attractive to her. She had loved and admired him for so many years, it was difficult to admit any other feelings. Yet there were times when all she felt for him was pity, and since his marriage – since before his engagement even – there had been times when she felt she did not know him at all.

During the course of the evening, the company finalized the arrangements for going to Sotherton, a day being settled on in late February before the Bertrams and the Rushworths were to depart for London. While the others were thus engaged, Mr. Crawford and Fanny, as the only two not directly interested in the planning of the excursion, were left to each other's company. Slowly and gradually he drew her into a conversation. They talked of books at first, but he soon discerned that Edmund's name was mentioned often when she spoke of books. However, when she revealed that she had introduced some of her favourite books to her sister, Susan, he was able to direct the conversation away from unhappy reminders of Edmund. Fanny became more animated as, in response to his questions, she talked of her satisfaction with Susan's progress, as evidenced by her letters. She talked with an affection and cheerfulness he had only seen in her before when her brother William had been at Mansfield Park. It had been some time since Fanny had really enjoyed a conversation, and though she would scarcely admit it to herself, she enjoyed this one.

Chapter 16

The following morning, Sir Thomas wrote to Mr. Rushworth to notify him of their intent to visit Sotherton Court and appointing a date in late February. As far as he was concerned, it was a settled matter. He very soon received a response to his letter from Mrs. Rushworth advising that the chosen date would not be convenient at all and urging him to put off the visit until after their return from London. Her Ladyship would be much more comfortable travelling in late spring or early summer and Sotherton Court would appear to much greater advantage; moreover, the party would not be confined to the house and she was certain her mother would like to see the gardens. On the same day, Fanny received a letter from Julia, stating as follows:

> My Dearest Cousin, Maria has just this moment told me that Sir Thomas is contemplating a visit to Sotherton Court on the very day we intend to give our performance of *The Taming of the Shrew*! You must stop him from coming. He will ruin everything. We have invited everyone. The stage is set up perfectly. We are having such beautiful painted scenes made of Padua. And I shall be wearing the most exquisite gowns. It shall be an injustice beyond anything if my father is to appear here. Maria has written to him, but I know he has a mind of his own. You must prevent him from coming. I know you will find a way. We are counting on you. Yours etc., J. Bertram

Fanny was seriously considering never opening another letter again. She glanced over at Lady Bertram who was leaning her head against the back of the sofa with her eyes closed. Fanny stood, walked over to the fireplace and was tempted to extend her hand over the flames and drop the letter in. She stood thus for a moment contemplating whether to burn the letter when she heard a man's voice say, "I hope it is not bad news."

She turned to face her uncle. "No," she said quickly, placing the letter into her pocket.

"Is that Julia's letter?" he asked.

"Yes," she replied quietly.

"Does it say anything of our proposed visit? Maria has written to ask that we postpone the scheme on account of the date being inconvenient."

"I believe Julia is in agreement with her sister."

He sighed. "Then I suppose it is best to wait until after their return from London." For the first time in her life Fanny could perceive a sense of uncertainty and even helplessness in her uncle's countenance. He squeezed her shoulder affectionately, then walked over to sit with Lady Bertram.

Fanny heard nothing more about the matter and had considered it settled that there would be no visit to Sotherton, at least for the time being. But a few days after this exchange the subject was taken up again by Mrs. Grant, who had been to Thornton Lacey with her brother and settled all the details with Mr. and Mrs. Bertram; they were quite determined to go in spite of Maria's request. Edmund had written to his brother-in-law explaining that they wished to go to Sotherton before going to London, as they may not have a chance to do so during the summer due to the extended visit to Everingham they intended to make at that time; the Grants, likewise, contemplated a return to Bath in the spring and might not have a fairer opportunity. Thus, he felt they must take their chance for a visit sooner rather than later and proposed to go to Sotherton only a few days after the original date, which was still about a week before the Rushworths were to go to London. Mr. Rushworth wrote back with his acquiescence, since they were determined to come and the play would be over by then. Mrs. Norris, upon hearing that the scheme was revived, eagerly asked Mrs. Grant about the arrangements, saying how much she would wish to visit dear Maria and dear Julia. She was sure Mr. Rushworth's mother would be happy to see her again as well. It had been so long since she had seen any of them and it would be nothing to bring her along if they were going anyway.

Mrs. Grant replied, "It would be our great pleasure to accommodate you, if it can be contrived. As Henry refuses to join us and Dr. Grant remains at home, the three of us shall go in Edmund's carriage, but the carriage will only hold four and we must have a seat for Miss Price."

Mrs. Norris was quite vexed with this response, but before she could say anything, Fanny spoke. "Oh no," she cried, "I do not intend to go to Sotherton. I must remain at home with Lady Bertram. I am quite content to do so, I assure you."

"My goodness," said Mrs. Grant, a little surprised by the strength of Fanny's assertion, "you sound just like Henry. He has absolutely refused to go with us and could not be persuaded otherwise. But surely, Miss Price, you must come along. I am quite certain your aunt can spare you as Sir Thomas will be staying at home."

"Fanny would be better off at home," said Mrs. Norris. "And, I cannot speak for your brother, but I certainly agree he should be one of the party. I believe he enjoyed his last visit there. And I am quite sure he must be eager to meet with Mrs. Rushworth and Miss Bertram again." Then she remembered to add, "Of course he could easily go on horseback."

"I do not know what to make of it," replied Mrs. Grant, "but Mary and I will convince him in the end, I am sure. But nor do I wish to give up hope of changing Miss Price's mind."

"Fanny has already been to Sotherton once and should be satisfied with her good fortune."

But Mrs. Grant would not desist until Fanny hinted that as Sir Thomas had decided not to go, she felt it would be a defiance for her to go against his will. Mrs. Grant was at last resigned. Fanny's refusal forced her to offer the seat to Mrs. Norris.

Fanny could only rejoice in the manner in which things were settled. An attempt was made to persuade Sir Thomas to go, but luckily for Fanny, he could not be prevailed upon; not out of pride that the date he chose had been rejected, but out of a genuine feeling that his daughters preferred them all to wait. No alternative date had been offered to him and he had been particularly asked to wait until after their return from London. He felt the visit contemplated by the Bertrams and the Grants might be an imposition to which Mr. Rushworth had only acquiesced out of politeness, for he knew his son-in-law had little fortitude in such matters. Thus he would wait, and Fanny was saved from having to join the party.

The date appointed for this visit fell on a Friday; thus, the Bertrams were to drive to Mansfield on Thursday and spend the night at the Parsonage so that they could set off for Sotherton early the following morning with Mrs. Grant and Mrs. Norris. The Grants and Mr. Crawford came to the Park for tea on Wednesday evening. Mrs. Grant again lamented that neither Fanny nor Mr. Crawford would join the party to Sotherton. She could comprehend Fanny's reason for not going, but was at a loss as to why her brother was so adamantly against it. Both were steadfast in their refusal. However, Mr. Crawford gained her full attention when he announced with apparent delight that he could not possibly go to Sotherton as he must depart for Northampton very early the next morning and would not be back at Mansfield in time to join them.

"Northampton? But why? What business takes you there?"

"I can say nothing of my business at present," he said with a smile. "You will find out everything upon my return."

"But what can be the reason for all this secrecy?"

"I am not sure how it will all turn out. I would rather wait until I have carried my purpose before I make it known."

"But whatever your business may be, surely it can be concluded in one day."

"I do not know how long it will take, but I will be gone more than one day." He smiled again. "It is a delicate matter, requiring patience."

"Is it this business that has had you in such high spirits all day?"

"It has to do with that mysterious letter he received this morning, I'd wager," Dr. Grant called from the card table.

Mr. Crawford only smiled more, confirming his brother-in-law's conjecture. And the more his sister asked about his business the more he seemed to enjoy not sharing it with her. At last she gave up the inquiry and being left unsatisfied, she lamented the absence of her sister, whose assistance, she felt would have resulted more favourably. She was soon drawn into the conversation at the card table and pulled up a chair to observe the game.

Mr. Crawford moved closer to Fanny. He still appeared to be overflowing with good cheer. "I hope they shall have good weather for the journey," he said to her.

"I believe they will. I could perceive nothing in the air today that would portend bad weather but who knows what tomorrow and the day after may bring."

"Let us hope for a fair day for travelling both tomorrow and Friday – and perhaps for riding. But I suppose it is of no consequence on that point. You will stay with Lady Bertram all day as Mrs. Norris is going to Sotherton."

"Yes, even if I could ride, I would not leave my aunt alone in order to do so."

"But spring is nigh and there will be other fine days. I trust you will soon have ample opportunity for your regular exercise."

Fanny swelled with emotion. She had been forgotten by Edmund. Would he think to return the horse for her use as he had promised? She dared to hope he might do so before departing for London. Did Mr. Crawford intend to give him a hint? She would not have him do so for anything. "I hope you may be right."

He leaned towards her and spoke quietly, "If I may prevail upon your good will to give my view on the subject unsolicited – I think it is an abominable deprivation and most unfair to you."

"Please, I beg you would not say anything of the matter."

"Rest assured, I would not – but only because I know you do not wish it."

114

Fanny, desiring to change the subject, observed, "You seem to be in very good spirits today."

He smiled. "I am happy in anticipation of my errand tomorrow."

"I hope it will turn out well."

"Thank you, Miss Price. I believe it shall."

The following morning, while Fanny happened to be alone in the drawing room, she received a strange note from Maria by express which appeared to have been written hastily, and stated as follows:

> Fanny, You must tell me if Mr. C is still at Mansfield. There is no one else I can ask. Send word immediately by return express. I must know. It is urgent. M. R.

Fanny did not know what to make of such a note, but she could perceive no evil in satisfying Mrs. Rushworth on the question and so she wrote by return express:

> Mr. Crawford was here with the Grants last evening and spoke of his plans to travel to Northampton for an unspecified amount of time. He was to leave this morning. I have no reason to believe he has not done so. F. P.

The delivery of a letter by express was sufficiently rare at Mansfield to raise the curiosity of the household, and Fanny expected to be asked about it by someone throughout the day. But no inquiry came from either the family or the servants, much to her relief. Fanny, nevertheless, continued to be puzzled by the strange note from Maria. What could it signify? Why would she so urgently want to know Mr. Crawford's whereabouts? In the haste of the moment while the express rider waited for a reply she had seen no evil in responding; and she could still see no reason why she should have acted differently, but she felt strongly that nothing good could have led Maria to make the inquiry.

The Mansfield family dined at the Parsonage that evening along with the Bertrams and Mrs. Norris. During the course of the evening, Fanny perceived that Sir Thomas was dissatisfied by their choice to go to Sotherton even after he had decided against it. Fanny reflected that at least the intended performance would already be concluded; but who knew what manner of assemblage would be encountered at Sotherton? Julia's letters seemed to indicate that quite a large party had gathered there and Fanny hoped they would have dispersed by the time the travellers should arrive.

In the drawing room after dinner, Edmund and Mary did everything they could to persuade Fanny to go – they were sure they could find a way to accommodate her in the carriage. She adamantly declined but they continued to press her until Sir Thomas was obliged to intervene and put an end to their entreaties. In those moments, she had almost missed Mr. Crawford.

Mrs. Norris was to join them at the Parsonage for an early breakfast so they could all set forth together afterwards. Fanny reflected with gratitude that she had been able to escape the visit and retired that evening hopeful that it would have no ill consequences.

Chapter 17

The next day, just after the luncheon tray had been brought in, as Fanny sat working quietly in the drawing room with Lady Bertram, her reverie was interrupted by the sudden entrance of Mrs. Bertram and Mrs. Grant. Their manner was agitated and their expressions revealed severe distress. "What is the matter?" she asked, "Why have you come back so soon?"

Mrs. Grant glanced at the door, and once the servant had left the room and closed it, said, "Miss Bertram is gone. She has left Sotherton."

"Edmund has gone to tell Sir Thomas this moment," added Mrs. Bertram. "Mrs. Norris remains at Sotherton."

"Gone?" asked Lady Bertram with alarm.

"She has gone away. No one knows where, or with whom," said Mrs. Bertram.

"She left alone?" asked Fanny.

"She left a note for her sister that disclosed very little," replied Mrs. Grant. "She said she had run away with her one true love or some such thing."

"But it seems," added Mrs. Bertram, "both Sir Henry and Mr. Yates left Sotherton at the same time. Sir Henry's departure had been expected, but the Rushworths had no notice of Mr. Yates having any intent of going away. There is no telling which one of them Julia ran off with or what his intentions are."

"They must have left very early this morning," observed Lady Bertram, trembling.

The sisters glanced at one another before Mrs. Bertram said, "The Rushworths discovered that all three had gone when none of them appeared at breakfast *yesterday* morning."

"Since yesterday?" gasped Fanny. "How is it possible that we did not receive word sooner?"

"From what we could gather," said Mrs. Bertram, "Mrs. Rushworth convinced Mr. Rushworth that *he* should find Miss Bertram and return her to Sotherton without alarming the family. Mrs. Rushworth confessed that she had hoped to have her sister back at Sotherton before our arrival today and, failing that, she hoped to engage Edmund's assistance in the search. Edmund, instead, insisted on coming back at once to consult with Sir Thomas."

By now, Lady Bertram was extremely distraught. Fanny sat at her side and comforted her as best she could. Suddenly, she remembered Maria's short note to her the day before, urgently inquiring as to whether Mr. Crawford had left the country. Now Fanny understood. Julia's note had said she had eloped with the man she loved and Maria had feared it was Mr. Crawford. Maria, who upon discovering that her sister was missing had not bothered to send word to her father of Julia's disappearance, had sent such a note to Fanny! It was beyond anything. And now Fanny wondered at the coincidence of Mr. Crawford having gone to Northampton the previous morning. Was it possible that he had eloped with Julia? It had been said the previous evening that he had left the Parsonage at dawn that morning. Certainly, he would have had enough time to get to Sotherton and carry Julia away before she was missed. They may have planned the elopement for the same day Sir Henry was to leave in order to provide the cover of confusion; and he had been in communication with Mr. Yates, so he must have known of Sir Henry's plans. Indeed, Dr. Grant had mentioned a letter that had seemed to prompt his decision to go to Northampton.

Mrs. Bertram and Mrs. Grant had seated themselves on the other side of Lady Bertram and between the two of them and Fanny they had calmed her down somewhat. When she felt Lady Bertram could withstand her leaving the room, Fanny excused herself and ran to find the note from Maria. It occurred to her that Julia's letters from Norfolk and Sotherton might also shed light on the situation and she collected those as well. When she had them all in hand, she breathed deeply, convinced she was doing the right thing, and then walked determinedly to her uncle's room. Gathering up her courage, she knocked on the door. "Come in," came the stern voice of Sir Thomas from the other side.

When Fanny entered the room, she saw her uncle standing in the middle of it, as if he'd been pacing, and Edmund standing opposite him. Neither of them sitting, neither of them comfortable. She extended her hand holding the letters to her uncle with tears in her eyes. "I am sorry I did not show these to you sooner," she said softly "I believe they contain intelligence that may be of use." He took them from her. "I might have prevented ..."

"No," he said, stopping her. "This is not your fault. Now, go." She turned and fled the room as quickly as she could. She returned to the drawing room and resumed her seat next to Lady Bertram, still trembling from the encounter with Sir Thomas. About an hour later, the gentlemen entered the drawing room.

"I must go," said Sir Thomas to his wife. "I do not know if I will be home tonight or how soon I might return, but if I do not return tonight I will write." He looked to Mrs. Bertram. "Edmund will come with me." Both ladies acquiesced and the two men quit the room and soon thereafter, the house.

The ladies were left to speculate as to all the unknown facts pertaining to Julia's situation. Fanny dared not share her suspicions, but she was beginning to feel quite certain that Mr. Crawford must be to blame. How could there be any other explanation? She reminded herself that two other gentlemen had left Sotherton at the same time as Julia. Everyone else seemed to assume she had run off with one or the other of them. Mr. Crawford had hinted at an attachment between Julia and Mr. Yates and Julia herself had acknowledged flirting with both gentlemen. She might have run off with Mr. Yates and the timing with Sir Henry's departure could have been pure coincidence. Or she might have been planning to run off with Sir Henry and Mr. Yates, upon learning she was going with his rival, might have decided to be off as well.

In truth, there was a multitude of possibilities. But Maria's note together with Mr. Crawford's own admission of his communication with Mr. Yates made one possibility far more likely than any other. She wondered whether Mr. Crawford had tried to purposely mislead her when he suggested an attachment between Julia and Mr. Yates? It seemed like something he might do, if only for his own amusement. She remembered how Edmund and Mary had communicated with each other through letters to her and how Mr. Crawford had sent messages to herself through his sister; and Julia's most recent letter had revealed that Mr. Yates was communicating the substance of his letters from Mr. Crawford to her. Thus, she could not consider it an extraordinary conjecture to suppose the correspondence with Mr. Yates was used by design as a means of communication between Julia and Mr. Crawford. She could even conceive that Mr. Crawford and Julia had written directly. Certainly, there was no one at Sotherton who would have prevented it; in fact, a correspondence of that kind seemed a likely explanation for Maria's suspicion.

She thought of the evening before last, when Mr. Crawford had been bursting with anticipation for his errand the following day. His exuberance must have been the result of his impending elopement. And to make such an exhibition of it before them all was so much like him! His behaviour altogether was so telling of the event. He had spoken to her with such an air of concern for her lack of exercise, yet all the while scheming to ruin Julia's reputation and throw the entire Mansfield family, already afflicted, into a state of suspense and anguish. This was the Henry Crawford she knew and despised. So much for his professed changes – no, he had even told her himself he had not really changed. He had been sporting with her again after all.

There were too many unanswered questions and far too many coincidences for her to admit a doubt that Mr. Crawford was involved. And what was worse, she could not allow the possibility that he would marry Miss Bertram. The other ladies seemed confident that Julia would return a married woman. But Fanny knew it was not possible. Julia would be ruined. She reproached herself in the severest terms. That she had actually been tempted to believe Mr. Crawford and had even begun to view him more favourably was a source of disgust of herself and her judgement. How could she have been so foolish to think a man such as he could change, that he *had* changed? She was truly mortified for herself and for Julia.

Mrs. Grant and Mrs. Bertram remained for the better part of the day, then departed before dinner to dine at the Parsonage with Dr. Grant. Lady Bertram retired to her rooms after they left and ordered her dinner to be brought to her there, surrendering herself to the care of Mrs. Chapman. Fanny sat in the East room, utterly alone and helpless. She declined any food. She could not eat, she could not sleep, and she could not settle herself to any occupation. Instead, she paced the room restlessly. Her thoughts plagued her. She had known of Julia's designs on Mr. Crawford. And she had known of Mr. Crawford's nature, of his indiscretion last year with Maria, and who knew what had happened between him and Julia during the summer. Yet she had let him begin to sway her with his false sincerity and kind words. They all meant nothing. He remained every bit as contemptible as she had ever thought him to be. And she could not forgive herself for having remained silent.

Chapter 18

Sir Thomas did not return that evening. He sent word the following day from Sotherton of his safe arrival and his uncertainty as to when he would return home. His letter contained no further information. Mrs. Grant and Mrs. Bertram called on the ladies at the Park and, having received better intelligence, were able to shed more light on the matter. Edmund had written that his father had gone first to Sotherton to speak to Mr. and Mrs. Rushworth directly and interview any of the household who might have heard or seen anything; while he had gone to Northampton, as the fugitives would have to pass through it in order to reach Scotland. His search was made the more difficult, by not knowing which gentleman had accompanied Julia. At this Fanny wondered how there could be any doubt if they had read the letters she had given them, and knowing Mr. Crawford had gone to Northampton the very day of Julia's disappearance. She considered that Edmund certainly would not wish to accuse his wife's brother without absolute proof; yet, there was no mention of his having met with Mr. Crawford at Northampton. It seemed impossible to Fanny that Edmund would not immediately seek out his brother-in-law if they were in the same town, especially under such pressing circumstances.

And so the ladies waited. For three days they sat together talking, trying to pass the time, trying to comfort Lady Bertram, and separated only at dinner time. The only change in circumstances to occur in this interim was the arrival of Mrs. Norris from Sotherton.

The four ladies had been seated in the drawing room and, upon hearing a bustle in the hall, had at first wondered whether it might be Julia returned home. The mystery was soon solved however, when Mrs. Norris entered the room, having just arrived from Sotherton Court. Within the first five minutes of her being in the drawing room, she had explained all the circumstances of her return and every detail of the arrangement of her own journey – of the alacrity with which Mr. Rushworth had anticipated her desire to be at home and offered her the use of his own carriage and horses; and of the expedience with which everything was performed to convey her to Mansfield comfortably and speedily. She scrupled not to admit that she had been of great use to the Rushworths while she had been staying at Sotherton and Mr. Rushworth had spoken warmly of his regret in seeing her go away while attending her himself to the carriage. She had, of course, only to inform the driver of one modification in the plan by directing him to Mansfield Park first instead of her own house as she could by no means be anywhere but at her sister's side during such a trying time.

All of the various gifts and acquisitions she had obtained during her stay at Sotherton, were being delivered to her house by its coachman even as she spoke. Julia's horse also had been returned to Mansfield with her on Sir Thomas' order, as he had made it clear he had no expectation of Julia returning to Sotherton Court upon being recovered.

This news gave Fanny a little start. Was this what Mr. Crawford had been alluding to when he hinted that Fanny would soon have an opportunity to ride? Could he have known that Julia's horse would be returned home and Julia would not be there to ride it herself? But how could he be thinking such a thing at such a moment? It seemed very odd indeed that he could have anticipated such a turn of events when planning the elopement; yet, it seemed even more unlikely to be mere coincidence. Every revelation pertaining to the unhappy situation unfolding before her produced sensations of greater anxiety and disgust.

There was little else to talk about at such a time other than Julia's situation, and Mrs. Norris was soon informed of what little news there was to impart. She was then at liberty to again talk of all that had been happening at Sotherton Court while she was there; to speak with great approbation of all that the Rushworths had undertaken to recover poor Julia, and to defend their concern for Julia's reputation in preventing the news from spreading beyond the household. She had seen Sir Thomas only briefly and could certainly understand his anger at not being instantly informed of Julia's elopement, but she had not scrupled to remind him that it had been a decision made under great distress and with the view only of protecting Julia and the reputation of the family; but she could give them no news of where he had gone upon leaving Sotherton.

The addition of Mrs. Norris to the party of ladies did not diminish the attentions from the Parsonage. On the fourth day of this state of suspense, Mrs. Grant and Mrs. Bertram agreed that both Lady Bertram and Fanny appeared tired and worn and Fanny, they were sure, had grown thinner. Thus, after seeing that Dr. Grant was amply supplied with his favourite dishes and a backgammon opponent from amongst his acquaintance in Mansfield Village, they determined to stay for dinner and spent both the day and evening at the Park. After a quiet, solemn dinner in which the Parsonage ladies urged their friends to take sustenance, they returned to the drawing room to resume their vigil. Where silence had prevailed before, with Mrs. Grant and Mrs. Bertram trying quietly to distract Lady Bertram and lift her spirits, there was no shortage of conversation now. As they sat in the drawing room after dinner, Mrs. Norris was again telling the other ladies of her certainty that Julia would return a married woman; that while she had gone about the business in an ill-judged way, there could not be a doubt as to her being married upon returning home. Any young man must feel the good fortune of allying himself with the Bertram family and as to beauty and good-nature, there could be no young lady more eligible. She had no doubt as to the matter and considered it quite a settled thing that Julia would return home very soon and quite married.

Mrs. Norris had scarcely concluded these prognostications when they began to hear voices and movement outside the room. They were all instantly on their feet and in the next moment Julia was before them.

Lady Bertram embraced her daughter with a sigh of joyous relief. "Oh my dear Julia, you are home!" she cried.

Julia appeared downcast and her face showed that she had been crying. The other ladies instantly began asking questions of her companion and it was only then that Fanny noticed it was Mr. Crawford who had walked into the room behind her.

"She is well," he replied to their inquiries. "That is all I will say. I believe she may need to refresh herself after her journey."

Lady Bertram rang for Chapman herself, who was to minister to Julia's immediate needs and then return her to the drawing room. In the meantime, Mr. Crawford assured Lady Bertram that, if he could avail himself of Sir Thomas' study, he would write to both him and Edmund directly with the news. He then advised his sisters in response to their multitude of questions that he would give the particulars to Sir Thomas and that if they wanted to know anything further, they were to direct their inquiries to *Miss Bertram*. His use of the appellation was the first indication that they were not married. Fanny wondered how he could show his face, how he could speak so matter-of-factly to all of them of informing Sir Thomas without so much as a blush or any hint of shame. Only Henry Crawford could have the audacity to bring the young lady home himself, unmarried, after having eloped with her. Yet, perhaps it was a sign that he did intend to marry her. He was, after all, writing to her father.

When Julia returned to them, her looks were improved but her spirits were not. Mr. Crawford had gone out of the room to write his letters. Lady Bertram was too emotional to speak much and while Mrs. Norris was effusive in her concern, she would demand no information from her niece. Fanny sat in silence. Thus, it was up to the two sisters to get the whole story out of Julia.

"What happened to you, my dear sister?" asked Mrs. Bertram.

Julia looked at both of them and at first did not answer. She looked at her mother and for a moment seemed a little ashamed. She looked at Fanny briefly and her expression changed. She turned back to Mrs. Bertram who had renewed her inquiry and said, "He promised we would be married."

"Who?"

"Henry!" she cried, then buried her face in her hands and began sobbing.

Fanny could scarcely bear it. She had known something like this would happen. Julia would be ruined. Surely, she had not behaved as she should, but *he* must bear the blame. Yet the consequences would be so much worse for her. This was the wretched ending of all his careless, selfish games, her foolishness, and the excessive vanity of both. Fanny could not be surprised. She congratulated herself on having never trusted in his apparent reformation. It had all been meaningless, nothing but meaningless nonsense to ingratiate himself with her once again. This was all the reformation he had undertaken: transferring his nefarious attentions from one sister to the other.

She could listen no more, and excusing herself from the others, though they scarcely noticed her exit at such a moment, she ran into the rose garden for the relief of quiet and solitude. Yet, she wondered how this could have happened. Clearly, Julia and Mr. Crawford must have been carrying on some kind of clandestine correspondence. They must have run off together, and in the end, he had changed his mind or they had quarrelled; Fanny could not imagine he had ever actually intended to marry her. And, by bringing her home still unmarried, he made it perfectly clear that he did not mean to marry her. Yet, why bring her home at all? She could only suppose it was owing to his sister's connection to the family; and now he was deigning to write to Sir Thomas and Edmund! Could there be hope yet? She could not imagine any. It was all misery! Tom was dead, Maria in a loveless marriage and carrying on a lifestyle of indulgence, Edmund married to an unworthy, selfish woman, and now Julia was ruined and shamed. It seemed far more than her poor uncle and aunt should have to bear.

She did not know how long she had been sitting alone when Mr. Crawford himself walked towards her. She could scarcely perceive him in the moonlight, but when she did she stood and immediately moved away from him.

"Miss Price," he said.

"Do not speak to me," she cried, trembling, and ran into the house and into the sanctuary of the East room. She needed to be alone, she did not feel equal to witnessing any more misery. She felt a little guilty leaving her aunt, but Julia was home now, and Mrs. Norris was there, and the other ladies would stay until supper.

After the Parsonage party departed, Fanny finally returned to the drawing room. Neither of her aunts made any further inquiry of Julia; but seizing upon a moment while Lady Bertram was wholly engaged by her sister, Julia asked Fanny, "Why did you run off before? Do not you wish to know all about my adventure?"

"No," said Fanny, "I do not wish to know."

"He has quite broken my heart," said Julia with great feeling. Then she added with a tone of satisfaction, "but when my father comes home he will make him marry me."

Fanny could not believe that Mr. Crawford would be prevailed upon to do the right thing and she fully expected he would be long gone by the time of Sir Thomas' return.

Chapter 19

Sir Thomas and Edmund arrived home the next day. Edmund arrived first, and after paying his respects to his mother and checking on his sister, who had not come down from her room all day, went to the Parsonage. Sir Thomas came home while Edmund was at the Parsonage. He looked more severe than Fanny had ever seen him and his homecoming was a solemn, quiet affair. He immediately summoned Julia to his study, where they were locked up together for a long time. Her expression, when she emerged, was agitated and discontented; her face was stained with tears and her eyes were red and swollen. She sat heavily on the sofa next to her mother with a petulant expression and said not a word. Sir Thomas returned to the drawing room shortly after and explained to Lady Bertram that he would walk over to the Parsonage to, "hear what Mr. Crawford has to say." Fanny reflected that this, of course, must be done; and as expediently as possible. She fervently hoped that the interview would settle everything. But she doubted whether Mr. Crawford could be prevailed upon. Her uncle was an imposing figure, but could he convince a young man who was accustomed to doing as he pleased, to do what he ought instead? Fanny had little hope of his success. She doubted even that Sir Thomas would find Mr. Crawford at the Parsonage at all.

After some time, Sir Thomas returned with Edmund and expressed his intent of leaving for London in the morning. He gave strict instructions to Lady Bertram and Mrs. Norris that Julia was not to leave the house for any purpose, under any circumstances. His daughter began to protest but he instantly silenced her. "She is not to set foot outside of this house until I return. She is not to send or receive any correspondence."

Julia was agitated but dared not protest further. Sir Thomas spent the rest of the day in his study making preparations for his journey. Edmund and Mary returned home to Thornton Lacey the same day. After sending them off, Mrs. Grant again came to sit with the ladies at the Park. She could not stay long because Dr. Grant was quite alone and now that Julia was home safe she felt she ought to return to her own domestic concerns. The observation by Mrs. Grant that her husband was home alone confirmed what Fanny had suspected and explained Sir Thomas' planned trip to London: Mr. Crawford had not been at the Parsonage when Sir Thomas had sought him out. He had fled.

The following days comprised another period of suspense, though more tolerable, now that Julia was at home. The matter was little spoken of among the ladies of the house. Lady Bertram was happy to have Julia home and was not inclined to trouble herself with details she was sure her husband would take care of; Mrs. Norris would say nothing against Julia and therefore avoided the subject entirely; Mrs. Grant, who continued to call every day, would have entered into the subject had the others raised it, but her good manners and sense of delicacy prevented her from bringing it up; and Julia scarcely left her room. Thus, Fanny was saved from hearing anything more on the subject until Edmund rode to Mansfield a few days after Sir Thomas' departure to check on his mother and sister. He came alone, and upon arriving he found his sister unhappy but otherwise behaving with all the appearance of obedience and submission. After visiting with the ladies in the drawing room, he asked Fanny to walk with him to call at the Parsonage. Fanny soon discovered his purpose was to engage again in private discourse with her.

"Forgive me for demanding your attention in this way, my dear Fanny," began he when they were alone, "but you are the only person to whom I feel I can speak. Perhaps I am making too much of it; yet, I cannot help but feel very dissatisfied with the way in which Mary views this whole situation of Julia's."

Fanny was not surprised that Mrs. Bertram would perhaps take a different view from the perspective of a sister of one of the parties involved in the event than Edmund would have as a brother of the other party involved.

He then went on to communicate the substance of their conversation in more detail. Mary had introduced the subject the morning after their return to Thornton Lacey in a manner which he owned had shocked him a little. "'What a terrible time you must have had these past few days,' said she, 'but it is all done now. And what can be said of Julia's folly?'

"But I know she had been distressed by my being away for so long," continued Edmund, "and being in suspense with the family for so many days together. I am sure she must understand the severity of the indiscretion."

"Then what is it that troubles you so?" asked Fanny a little confused.

"I was dismayed by Mary's apparent view that news of the indiscretion reaching the public would be a greater evil than the elopement itself. She went so far as to say she did not blame Maria for keeping quiet about it, observing that her object had been to protect the family from publicity. 'Consider,' said she, 'that Maria must have felt Sir Thomas' inquiring after Julia in all parts of the country and perhaps so far as London would certainly have brought attention to the event.' She even hinted that I may have done better to assist in the search for Julia while maintaining the secrecy that Maria had at first employed. While avoiding a public scandal is important, I was a bit troubled that it appears to be Mary's chief concern in the whole business. It pained me to hear her refer to the event itself as mere folly and the resulting rumours as the real evil. But given her upbringing and the examples of her youth, her view on the matter is perhaps not surprising. I know she has good principles, Fanny, I only hope I can give her more guidance in following them than she has had. Her heart is too good, too pure not to feel all that she ought in reference to such a moral transgression, if not for such influences as she has been subject to."

Fanny could not help but believe it might be too late for Mrs. Bertram to receive a second education in morality. Yet, it was just like Edmund to undertake such a duty. She thought it strange that Edmund should dwell so much on his wife's response to Julia's offence while he did not even mention his own sister's want of principle in committing the offence to begin with. For all Fanny had been able to observe, Julia did not seem at all repentant and appeared to regret only that she was back home. She could not help but ask his opinion of Julia's feelings with regard to the situation in which she found herself, and whether he believed she had learned anything from it.

"Julia was very wrong," replied he, "but the whole ordeal has been hard on her. I have hope that it will be favourably resolved and that when the urgency has passed and she has more leisure to reflect on her actions, she will comprehend the full weight of her transgression. Yet, I cannot help but feel somewhat to blame for the incident myself."

"You?" gasped Fanny in surprise. "But surely you knew nothing of the matter."

"No, of course I had no idea of her plan to elope from Sotherton, but I had formerly received information about her which troubled me exceedingly and yet, I did not act on it. When we were in London I called on my cousins near Bedford Square and Mr. Dixon told me that it was Julia who had first suggested the part of the country in which he resided last summer. He only meant to spend the summer in the country and it did not matter much to him where, so when Miss Dixon told her father that Julia had a friend near Everingham he saw no harm in wanting to bring her close enough to call on her *friend*. It turns out the friend was Mr. Crawford. It seemed to have been her design all along to be near enough to him to create an expectation of a match. Mary later told me that she had suspected it at the time, but said nothing to me until after I mentioned to her my conversation with Mr. Dixon in December. So, you may see why I share some of the guilt: I knew since then the machinations and the scheming Julia had been capable of, yet I did nothing. To own the truth, with her at Sotherton and Crawford at Everingham and then here at Mansfield, I thought there could be no danger! I had no idea what had been going on there, what Maria was allowing. And when I saw your letters from her, they confirmed far worse than I had dared to fear."

"I should have given her letters to my uncle sooner."

"No, do not blame yourself, Fanny. You have done nothing wrong. You alone have been right all along; and I am very sorry I doubted your judgement when I supposed there could be no lasting effects from the folly of which we all – all but you – partook during the time of the play, for I do believe that is when all the mischief began. Indeed, we have all of us, except for you, been accessories to the present evil; I shall never cease to regret the dangerous intimacy of our unjustifiable theatre."

Fanny could not disagree, and found the subject too distasteful to pursue further. She was glad when the conversation ended upon their arrival at the Parsonage. On the walk home, after their visit, Edmund thankfully spoke of other things, primarily his plans for going to London the following week, but he made no mention of returning his mare to Mansfield.

A succession of tolerably fine days followed, which made Fanny think of how long it had been since she had ridden. It was more than two months since Edmund's marriage and she had been without a horse since then. She knew she had no claim to Edmund's mare, and would never dream of mentioning even a hint of her deprivation to him; but still, she suffered to think that he had forgotten her.

A few days after his conversation with Fanny, Edmund called at Mansfield again, this time with his wife. They arrived on horseback to make a farewell call the day before they were to depart for London. As soon as they entered the drawing room, Mrs. Bertram spoke enthusiastically of the favourable weather for riding on horseback. Julia quickly offered herself as a riding companion, but when Lady Bertram reminded her of her father's rule she protested, "But my father could not have intended even to prevent me from riding about the grounds with my own brother and sister! Surely, madam, there can be no objection."

Mrs. Norris looked as if she would take up Julia's cause but Edmund quickly intervened. "I am sorry Julia, my father was quite specific in saying you are not to leave the house. Do not press Lady Bertram to overrule him!"

Julia was silenced and left the room. Mrs. Bertram then urged Fanny to ride out with them. But Fanny would not use Julia's horse when she could not. To take advantage of Julia's deprivation, no matter how well deserved, was beyond Fanny's ability. Moreover, the idea having been foretold to her in such a way by Mr. Crawford the day before the unhappy business had unfolded gave her such disgust as to prevent her acquiescence. She wished only to stay with her aunt.

As Fanny would not be persuaded to ride, Mrs. Bertram, with a meaningful look at Edmund, urged her to at least walk out to the stables with her. Fanny complied and was happy to see Edmund's mare when they arrived at the stall. Mrs. Bertram was all smiles as she watched Fanny patting the horse. "It was always our intent to bring her to you when we set off for London," she said to Fanny. "But now, you are to consider her yours henceforth."

Fanny was confused. "But did not you ride her here? How will you get home?"

"Come," said her companion, walking down to another stall. Then, unable to contain her delight, she suddenly cried, "Oh my dear Fanny can you imagine my great surprise this morning when this beautiful mare was delivered to me at Thornton Lacey as a wedding present."

"Oh, Edmund has bought you a horse!"

"No, not Edmund! Henry. My own dear brother Henry. He never spoke a word of it, and then this morning this delightful creature arrived at Thornton Lacey, with a note from Henry offering it as a belated wedding present. Can you believe it? Now we shall be able to ride together on any fine day! Is not he the most thoughtful, most generous brother? And do not think me insensible of his wanting to please more than myself with such a gift." She said the last with a meaningful look that Fanny had not seen since they had been in London.

Fanny was mortified. She knew not what to say. She was stunned by the easy and effusive manner with which Mrs. Bertram now spoke of Mr. Crawford. He was her brother and he had given her a fine gift, but he had ruined Julia and run from the responsibility; and now to be hinting that he might still be attached to herself seemed beyond even Mrs. Bertram's liberal sense of propriety. Fanny could see that her companion was waiting for a response. "I hope you will enjoy your new horse exceedingly."

"And you will enjoy yours. You must forgive Edmund and me at once for keeping her for so long. But now, oh what lovely long rides we shall have together when I return from London. And it will just be the time of year for fine weather."

"I thank you for your kindness. I will, of course, make use of the horse as long as she is here, but I could never consider her as mine. She will always be Edmund's horse."

"But *we* will consider her your horse which, I suppose, will have to be good enough."

With that they returned indoors. As they walked into the drawing room Mrs. Norris was just exclaiming, "Give the horse to Fanny? What can you be thinking Edmund? This gift from Mr. Crawford is a very kind gesture to be sure, but there must be some other use for your mare."

"The horse was purchased for Fanny to ride. That is its best use. We should not have kept it this long."

He looked to the ladies who had just entered and Fanny thanked him warmly. She sat with them a while, but her thoughts were so wildly turbulent, that she could fix on nothing. She could scarcely follow the conversation. She needed to be alone to reflect on these events, to make sense of it all.

Mr. and Mrs. Bertram were with them most of the day but returned to Thornton Lacey to dine. Once they were gone, Fanny at last had leisure for contemplation. She had, of course, at first been delighted to learn of the mare's return. Her joy in that moment had been only a little alloyed by the realization immediately following, that Mrs. Bertram had not returned the mare until after acquiring a new horse of her own; yet Fanny had supposed she must have been at least somewhat in Edmund's thoughts when he had bought the new horse for his wife – for the brief moment of her believing that he had been the one who made the purchase.

Fanny had barely been able to contain her shock and dismay upon learning the truth. Edmund had not thought of her at all. It was all Mr. Crawford's doing! It was his gift of a horse, *his* thoughtfulness that had brought the return of the mare to Mansfield. Then to be struck immediately after by Mrs. Bertram's mortifying suggestion that he had done it for her, had been even more distressing. Yet, Mr. Crawford's sister had already been in possession of a horse to ride; what reason would he have for buying her another one except as a way of inducing Edmund to return his mare to Fanny's use? She began to feel faint as she considered the probable truth. She thought of the way he had managed to give her a necklace. It had been entirely his doing; he had used his sister to give her the gift to ensure that she would accept it. But this was different, there was no subterfuge now – and he had not actually given her a gift. She was reminded of her own solution to the dispute in Portsmouth between her sisters, Susan and Betsy, over Mary's knife. She had bought Betsy her own knife so that Susan might have the one Mary had given her. Mr. Crawford had done the same thing but on a larger scale.

That Mr. Crawford had been the only one to remember that Fanny had been without a horse for more than two months and to take action to rectify that situation was a source of pain, but the knowledge that he had done so while carrying out such an offence against her family, produced in her a sensation of mortification and disgust. How could she be grateful for his having thought of her under such circumstances? How could he undertake such a scheme while planning to carry Julia away from the protection of her friends? How could such duplicity be possible? She could reconcile it only by recalling how he had previously carried on a flirtation with both Maria and Julia simultaneously, and put it all down to his style of sporting with women.

Chapter 20

Sir Thomas had now been gone above a week and the Mansfield ladies had received no further news after his first letter informing them that he had arrived safely in London. He was not of a disposition to dwell on the details of so delicate a matter. His wife had every confidence in his ability to bring everything to a satisfactory resolution without needing particulars, and he knew that anything he wrote would be read by Mrs. Norris and by that means spread about the entire parish. Likewise, Edmund's letter confirming his own arrival in London had stated only that he had seen his father and that the business which had taken Sir Thomas to London was still in progress.

However, they soon had better news of Sir Thomas by his surprise entrance into the drawing room after supper one night, so late that Mrs. Norris had already gone home. Upon seeing him, Lady Bertram was suddenly overflowing with animation. He greeted each of the ladies, then sat down across from Julia and spoke very seriously to her. "You will be married in the morning." Julia seemed a little surprised in spite of her professed expectation that her father would arrange just such an outcome. Fanny too was surprised, as Sir Thomas had arrived home alone; but neither of them spoke. Julia looked at her father expectantly and he offered the following further information: "Your betrothed is at the Parsonage, where he will spend the night. You will be in church promptly at eight and depart with him afterwards. That is all." He left the room before anyone had a chance to ask him any questions and Julia retired immediately after.

It was over. Julia was to be married. How Sir Thomas had finally prevailed on Mr. Crawford would always be a mystery to Fanny, but it did not signify. The ordeal would be over in the morning and Fanny hoped tranquillity could be restored to their lives.

She was in the East room the following morning alone, unsure of whether she was expected to go to the church or not. It was too early for Lady Bertram to be in the drawing room, according to her usual habit, but Fanny felt she should check, in case she was wanted. When she arrived the room was empty. Her uncle soon appeared and said, "I do not ask you to come to the wedding, but nor will I forbid it. It is your choice."

She trembled a little, she knew not why. "Does Lady Bertram go?"

"Yes, but you need not be guided by her actions. What is your own choice?"

"I will go if I am wanted."

"I will be at hand to support Lady Bertram."

"Then," she hesitated, unaccustomed to making decisions, "I do not think Julia would wish me to be there."

"Very well," he said. "We will walk from the church after the wedding, as the carriage will be conveying the happy couple to the post, so do not expect us back quickly." She nodded and he left the room.

A few moments later Fanny watched from the drawing room window as the carriage took Sir Thomas, Lady Bertram, and Julia to the church. Julia's trunks had been placed in it and her horse tied to it as well. As she watched it travel slowly towards the church, she concluded that Mr. Crawford must have travelled back with Sir Thomas yesterday and left his own equipage in London. She watched the carriage until it was out of sight, then sat alone waiting for her aunt and uncle, but no one appeared. When she thought enough time had passed she looked out the window to see if she could perceive them walking towards the house, but there was no sign of them. She sat down again to her work, imagining perhaps that they were caught up in conversation with the Grants. Not long after, she heard the door open as Baddely showed a caller into the room. She looked up to see Mr. Crawford standing before her.

She absolutely started and for a moment was immoveable from surprise. She could not help exclaiming, "Mr. Crawford! What are you doing here?"

"Good morning, Miss Price. I have come to give you a message from Lady Bertram. She is not equal to the walk back and wished me to tell you that she and Sir Thomas will wait at the Parsonage for the carriage to return from the post."

The only explanation for his presence that Fanny could conceive was that he had stopped on his way to the post and that Julia had remained in the carriage while he delivered this message; but it seemed very odd, the house was certainly not on the way to the post from the church and surely a servant could have been employed. Yet, it was so like what she knew of him to make such a display – to call on the woman he had been professing to love immediately after marrying another. She was a little angry and replied dismissively, "Thank you. Please give my best wishes to Mrs. Crawford."

He started and looked at her in bewilderment. "I beg your pardon, there is no Mrs. Crawford."

After looking at him for a moment in confusion she exclaimed, "You did not go through with it," then quickly said, "No, then why would the carriage be in use? Pray, what is the meaning of this?"

Now he looked at her in confusion, unsure for a moment how to respond. Then, his eyes widened. "Dear God, have you been thinking that I …? All this time?" His breath quickened. He paced the floor in front of her for a moment or two then stopped to look at her. "Truly?" She only looked at him in continued bewilderment. He resumed his pacing. "Of course. Of course, you would believe this of me. It must have been the most natural thing in the world to your mind."

At last she said, "Mr. Crawford, please speak plainly!"

He stopped again abruptly and looked at her. He collected himself and said, "Yes, that seems to be what is necessary here. Let us speak plainly." He sat down beside her. "You seem to be under the misapprehension that I was to marry your cousin this morning."

She looked at him in surprise. "How could it be otherwise after you eloped with her?"

"I did not elope with Miss Bertram," he replied.

Fanny was struck by this declaration as an impossibility, and replied almost involuntarily, "No. I know you did. How can you deny it? How can you expect me to believe you?"

He regarded her for a moment, then said, "Consider: what motivation would I have to tell a falsehood that could be so easily discovered? If you do not learn the truth from me, surely you can apply to your uncle or your cousin." Fanny said nothing, but looked at him expectantly. "When Miss Bertram left Sotherton, I was in Northampton looking out a horse to buy for my sister so that Bertram's mare might be restored to you." She turned away from him, a little embarrassed to hear him openly admit what she had suspected.

He stood up again and walked to the door to make sure it was securely closed, then returned to the sofa. By the time he sat down again, Fanny had regained much of her composure. He asked her, "How is it possible that you are truly in ignorance of the particulars, having been in the midst, as you were, of all the turmoil resulting from the event?"

She could not meet his eyes. "I did not wish to know the particulars," she replied.

"And now," he asked, "what is your wish?"

"I must know the truth, Mr. Crawford."

"Very well. It is now commonly known," he began, "among those who are aware of the event, that Miss Bertram left Sotherton Court with Mr. Yates and Sir Henry."

She gasped, "What, with both of them?"

"The three of them left Sotherton together. Both gentlemen being independent and full of acting, had actually determined on joining a theatrical company that was to tour the continent. Miss Bertram saw no reason why she should not join as well and left Sotherton with them."

"But her note said she left for love. Was not it her object to marry?"

"She confessed to me that she meant her love of acting. She never mentioned marriage in the note. Everyone assumed that to be her object, which was what she intended. And I do not doubt that she had every idea of marrying one or the other of the two gentlemen."

Fanny was visibly shocked but said nothing.

"I have spoken to both of them since the event and from what I can gather they were rivals for her attentions and affections. She may have enjoyed their rivalry a little too much and not wishing to end it, would not come to the point and make a choice."

Fanny dropped her head into her hands in agitation. "Could it really be so? How abominable!" Then she looked at him and remembered a similar rivalry between Julia and Maria.

He seemed to comprehend her thoughts. "After speaking with both gentlemen, I have been given some idea of the feelings such treatment created in them. I can only imagine how much more severely the more delicate sensibilities of young ladies might be affected." She said nothing. "That is not to say the gentlemen were without fault or that her ill-treatment excused their subsequent behaviour. Even I, Miss Price, … even I can attest to its being a most shocking and abhorrent thing to have done.

"It seems, when they arrived at their destination they found nothing more than a man with a modest house who had collected around him a band of would-be actors with little talent and no means of even getting to the continent, much less of touring it. Apparently, the self-proclaimed manager of this pathetic company had been hoping to attract the interest of just some independent young gentleman, such as the two who arrived with your cousin, to fund his ambitions. In fact, when I was there, he attempted to engage my interest in this endeavour. Miss Bertram even told him I was a great actor! I quickly put an end to his entreaty.

"When I found Miss Bertram, neither of her gentleman friends was with her. Yates had been the first to leave the company after two days. He did say that he urged Miss Bertram to go with him but she refused. Sir Henry stayed only one more day, which, according to what he told me, he spent in attempting to convince her to leave as well. I know little of what passed between them, but it seems there was a quarrel, and if Sir Henry is to be believed, it ended in Miss Bertram telling him to go without her. Still, there can be no excuse for his leaving her utterly alone and unprotected in a strange house full of every kind – among such a mixture of strange persons, many low-bred, uneducated, coarse, ill-mannered – and very few of them women. I saw the conditions in which the lot of them had been living together. Thankfully, she had the good fortune to be taken under the protection of the mistress of the house and in the care of that excellent woman is where I found her."

Fanny was in utter shock. None of these particulars had been known to her. She had been too unwilling to enter into the subject for disclosure to be possible. She urged him to continue, saying, "But how did it fall upon you to find her there?"

"Bertram knew where I was lodging in Northampton. He met me there the day they had gone to Sotherton and discovered her missing, told me of the event, and enlisted my assistance. I had knowledge from something Yates had written in one of his letters of an acting company forming in a village near Northampton and I immediately suspected it as their object, but we could not be certain of it, and Bertram was very doubtful that it could be possible. He was convinced that Miss Bertram's object was marriage and made inquiries in Northampton in an attempt to confirm his suspicion that she was bound for Scotland. Thus, whilst he pursued the course he thought more likely to lead to his sister I offered to see what I could find out about my own suspicions, reasoning that even if I could only find Mr. Yates, he might have intelligence as to her whereabouts. But I did not know which village. I had to make inquiries. There were difficulties, obstacles. It was some time before my inquiries led to her."

"But Edmund said nothing of this in his letter from Northampton."

"I am not surprised. He was very distressed at the time, and the letter was undoubtedly written in haste. He did not think my supposition likely and, I am sure, would not wish to raise the family's hopes or their fears. Bertram soon found out that Sir Henry's carriage had taken a road out of Northampton and he resolved to make inquiries along that road. We later learned that upon arriving in Northampton, Sir Henry – in a moment of ill-judgement and apparently at Miss Bertram's insistence – had sent his carriage back to London to avoid being discovered; they continued to their destination in a hired carriage, and he was later forced to return to London by the same means. Bertram, with no knowledge of this subterfuge and being fairly certain of Miss Bertram having left Sotherton in Sir Henry's carriage, believed following it would lead to her discovery. Thus, while he made inquiries in an attempt to trace the carriage, I engaged in my own search, which led me to the village of ____ and to the very house.

"Once I discovered her, I found she had no desire to leave. A circumstance which gives some credibility to the accounts of the two gentlemen. She could not have been comfortable there, so I can only attribute her resolution of staying to stubbornness and perhaps fear of returning to her father; but I imagine she must have already begun contemplating some way of getting back to Sotherton, though she made no such admission to me. Since I did not know exactly where Bertram's search had led him, I judged it best to bring her directly to Mansfield. She, however, professed no intention of leaving, and as I was unwilling to leave the place without her I confess to having employed some of my … former arts to persuade her to come with me. It was the only way she would go willingly. She was very angry with me when I brought her home."

"Good God," cried Fanny, when he had done. She sat back on the sofa contemplating all she had heard. After a moment she said, "How is it possible I knew none of this? How could I have formed such wrong impressions?"

"You were here when I brought her home. Did you truly think I could return her to her family myself after running away with her?"

"I confess, I did think it very audacious."

"But not beyond what you thought me capable of?"

"No," she whispered looking down. "I thought perhaps your connection to her family had at last motivated you to return her to them."

"A reasonable supposition, perhaps, if I had merely left her at the door and driven away; but I entered the house with her, I addressed her mother and wrote to her father …"

"I know," replied Fanny, anxiously. "Perhaps your actions should have given me reason to doubt my assumptions; but there were other facts that supported them. You were in such high spirits the night before Julia ran away and so secretive as to your purpose, it all seemed to make sense after the event. And the express I received from Mrs. Rushworth the next morning promoted the idea."

"Mrs. Rushworth wrote to you? I understood no one at Mansfield knew anything of the matter until my sisters returned from Sotherton the day after."

"Oh," said Fanny. Obviously, he had not been made aware of certain details. "She did not tell me about Julia."

Now it was his turn to be astonished. "She sent you an express the morning her sister ran away but did not mention the event?"

"I am not at liberty to discuss it," was all Fanny could think to say. She felt very strongly that if Sir Thomas had not shared the note with Mr. Crawford, she certainly should not do so.

"But what she wrote supported your idea that I had eloped with Miss

Bertram."

"Mr. Crawford, please."

"Very well, I will not press you." He regarded her for a moment in silence. "I suppose then that your belief in my guilt is the reason you would not speak to me the day I brought her home?"

"Yes," she replied. "And, I take it, Sir Thomas was never looking for you?"

"No. I was not at the Parsonage when he came to speak to me. I had been very eager to return to Northampton to conclude my business and he knew enough to begin his search in London. I met him there afterwards, where I gave him all the particulars of my part in the matter and told him what I knew of the two gentlemen. Sir Thomas spoke to both of them at length and neither denied his part in the event. I always knew him to be severe, but I never imagined he could be so formidable. By the end of it Sir Thomas had his choice of the two and he demanded that Sir Henry marry her. He acquiesced and travelled to Mansfield in my charge yesterday. I was to make sure he did not run away. He was not even permitted to bring his own carriage. I think Sir Thomas was over-scrupulous on that point, but who can blame him? It was perhaps, a fitting twist of irony. In truth, Sir Henry was resigned to his fate; the marriage articles had already been signed and the license obtained. Yates, I think, was a little disappointed in spite of everything."

"And so she has married Sir Henry? And now I may call her Lady …?"

"Lady Chandler. They are gone to his house in town and I believe Mr. and Mrs. Bertram have been given leave by Sir Thomas to wait upon them. I do not despair of their being tolerably happy together. I spent some hours with him yesterday and he spoke quite fondly of her and with some regret of his ill-judged abandonment. He did acknowledge some lingering resentment towards her but he does not seem to be of a disposition to let those feelings get the better of him."

"I do hope it may be so, Mr. Crawford," replied Fanny in quiet agitation. She was restless. After a moment, she rose and walked to the window where she stood in contemplation. At length, she spoke. "But is it all true? It must be. Oh, how wrong I have been! How very wrong have been my suppositions. I am quite ashamed to think of the notions I indulged."

"You have nothing to be ashamed of, Miss Price. You had little knowledge of the facts and it is only your sense of delicacy that prevented you from seeking more."

"But my mistakes go far beyond lack of information, Mr. Crawford. I did not require facts to make suppositions of your involvement, to lay the whole of it to your charge. And you the hero in the case rather than the villain!"

He laughed at her characterization. "The hero indeed! To hear you say so makes it all quite worthwhile."

"I judged you unfairly."

"You never would have believed as you did, if I had not given you reason to suppose me capable of it. Though I hope you will believe me when I tell you that even at my worst, I would not have left any young lady alone in such a place." He paused before adding quietly, "My habits have been of a different kind." He sighed and continued, "I cannot begin to imagine what he must have been thinking. Perhaps it is owing to his having no sisters, to never having had a young lady in his protection, and he was very eager to leave the place, and very angry at her, and she adamantly refusing to go. It was an impulsive thing to do without any thought beyond the moment." He looked at Fanny again and saw her anxiety. "But, it has all turned out well."

"Because of you. Her recovery, her restoration to her family, the preservation of her reputation. It is all owing to you. And meanwhile I was believing something very different. I have been blind, wilfully blind to the truth and allowed my own bias to mislead me." She paused, then suddenly asked, "Can you forgive me?"

He laughed at this. "Me forgive you?" he exclaimed. "My dear Miss Price there can be no occasion for anything of the kind."

"You are not angry?"

"Do you imagine I could be angry with you?"

"I feel so ashamed."

Mr. Crawford shook his head. "You have no reason to feel ashamed. Sir Henry, Lady Chandler, Mr. Yates, and others perhaps, have reason to feel ashamed. But you do not."

"The more grievous mistakes of others do not excuse mine, Mr. Crawford. Even with everything I knew of both you and her – the events of last summer – I should never have allowed myself to believe what I did with so much conviction based upon so little in the way of facts."

"The events of last summer?" he asked. His having caught those words so readily heightened her embarrassment and she was unprepared to answer him. After having so severely and unfairly misjudged him, she had no wish to assail him now with accusations concerning his behaviour the previous summer. "Come," he said, upon seeing her hesitation, "we have made great inroads of truth today. Let us not stop here. Let me know your thoughts on how I conducted myself last summer."

"I was not there. I did not observe ..."

Here they were interrupted by the unceremonious entrance of Mrs. Norris already mid-sentence in explaining why she had not arrived earlier when she raised her eyes to the scene before her and stopped.

"Mr. Crawford, good morning," she began anew. Then looking at Fanny she asked, "Where is her Ladyship?"

"Lady Bertram is at the Parsonage with Sir Thomas," said Mr. Crawford.

"Sir Thomas is back from London? And at the Parsonage, at this hour? What can be the meaning of it?"

"Perhaps you have not heard. Miss Bertram was married this morning."

This was enough to require the lady to find a chair. "But how is it possible? I knew nothing whatever of the matter. Can it really be?" These were followed by further exclamations of surprise and delight and shortly thereafter a resolution of going to see Julia herself.

"But she is gone to London, ma'am. Sir Thomas' carriage has taken them to the post at ____ whence they will hire a carriage and travel to Sir Henry's house in town."

"And so I have missed her!" lamented the lady, "Deprived of even conveying my congratulations. That was most unfair. Sir Thomas might have informed me; he should have known I would wish to be there." She stopped herself and looked from Fanny to Mr. Crawford and back again. "And how came the two of you to be here?"

"Miss Price did not attend the wedding. Lady Bertram felt unequal to the walk from the Parsonage and they are awaiting the return of the carriage. As she was expecting Lady Bertram to return home directly, I walked over to give her news of the delay."

"That was very kind of you sir, I am sure." They talked on in the same style for some time, as Mrs. Norris was forced to reconcile herself to Julia being married, and to her not having witnessed it. Meanwhile, Fanny sat in silence attending to her work and contemplating all she had learned. Mr. Crawford only left them after Sir Thomas and Lady Bertram returned.

Chapter 21

Now Fanny's head was truly full of surprise and confusion. Everything she had been supposing since Julia's return home, nay since her disappearance, was overthrown. It now occurred to her that it was possible for one's sense of delicacy and propriety to be too great. Hers had prevented her from learning the truth. A truth that had not been concealed from her in the least, but rather had only been unknown to her because of her own avoidance of the subject. For the first time since she had known him, Fanny now longed to see Mr. Crawford, she was anxious to continue their conversation and to have the opportunity of discussing the matter with a clearer head – unclouded by the shock and bewilderment brought about by her own false assumptions.

The next day brought little serenity to her mind. She was restless and distracted and could not settle to any occupation during her morning solitude before breakfast. She felt absolutely ashamed of herself for her assumptions pertaining to Julia's elopement and wondered what else she might have been wrong about.

How many times had she found herself alone with Mr. Crawford when she had nothing to say to him? And now that she longed to speak with him, there could be no hope of their meeting with any privacy. Even if he would call in the course of the day, which she considered entirely possible, her aunts would be present and she had little hope that some pretence sufficient for a private conversation of any length could be contrived.

As she walked down to breakfast, she resolved to get the matter out of her head. She told herself that she had already received the most important intelligence he had to communicate. And when she thought about it further, she realized there really was nothing more to be said between them. In fact, the interruption of their *tête-à-tête* had probably saved her from further embarrassment.

Having settled this point within herself, she felt prepared upon entering the breakfast room, to be as attentive to her aunt as she had ever been. Therein, however, she found Mr. Crawford, quite alone – a plate with the remnants of breakfast in front of him and the newspaper spread before him. He looked up, and upon perceiving her, smiled, put down his paper, and said, "Good morning Miss Price."

Fanny felt the colour rise to her cheeks. She could attribute it only to the embarrassment of her shameful assumptions. "Good morning," she replied, moving to the sideboard.

"I am here on an errand for Mrs. Grant; I have brought a note from her to Lady Bertram. Sir Thomas only left the room a moment ago on some business with his steward."

"I see," said Fanny.

He said nothing further until she was seated at the table. Then he asked, "Are you well?"

"Yes, I am quite well. Thank you."

"I do hope that our conversation yesterday has not been too distressing for you."

"No," was all she could say.

"Then, I hope we will have an opportunity to continue it very soon. I have not forgotten."

Glancing at the servant, Fanny replied in a low voice, "As grateful as I am to have learned the truth of recent events, I believe the less said about them the better."

"Perhaps that is true, but I hope you will consider that it was an unwillingness to speak of them that led to your misunderstanding."

She looked at him. "I do not know what else there is to be said now."

He leaned towards her and whispered, "I believe you were on the verge of telling me how I behaved last summer."

"I could not tell you anything of the kind as I have no knowledge of it. All of my information has been from a source that has proven to be unreliable."

"If you have nothing to say, then I hope you will do me the honour of listening to my version of the tale. Then at least you will have it from both sides."

"I suppose I owe you that much after misjudging you so abominably."

"You owe me nothing, Miss Price. If you are inclined to give me a hearing, I hope it will not be out of a feeling of obligation."

Soon after this exchange, Sir Thomas walked back into the room. Upon seeing his niece, he said, "Lady Bertram is unwell and will not be coming down today."

Fanny immediately rose from her seat, "Shall I go to her?"

He motioned for her to sit back down saying, "Mrs. Norris is with her already. She is simply fatigued from the events of yesterday and indeed the past weeks. I trust she will feel better tomorrow." Then looking to Mr. Crawford, he added, "She has Mrs. Grant's note and is writing a reply. Mrs. Norris will be down with it shortly, if you would be so good as to wait." Mr. Crawford had not the least objection to waiting and Sir Thomas left them to return to his steward.

When he had quitted the room, Mr. Crawford explained to Fanny, "The

Grants are contemplating a short visit to the Bertrams in London. Mrs. Grant and her Ladyship were talking of it yesterday. I believe Mrs. Grant has offered to convey anything Lady Bertram might wish to send to the Bertrams or to bring anything she might desire from London."

The first question that occurred to Fanny was whether he was to go with them but she dared not ask it. They sat in silence waiting for Mrs. Norris, neither wishing to begin talking again only to be interrupted as they had been yesterday and both keenly aware of the presence of the servant. When Fanny was finished eating, she did not know whether to sit in the drawing room by herself or go to the East room. Supposing that she might be wanted during the course of the day, she decided to sit in the drawing room. She excused herself and left the breakfast room before Mrs. Norris appeared.

She half expected that when her aunt came down to deliver the note she would seek her out in the drawing room to give her an errand, or several errands. But after sitting alone for a quarter hour she wondered that her aunts could still be writing their note. She stood at the window to see if she could perceive Mr. Crawford walking or riding away, but to no avail. When someone finally entered the room, it was that very gentleman.

She turned from the window, with the cold morning sunlight glowing behind her; and his state of mind on seeing her, with his feelings all anticipation of the promise of a full morning's private discourse, was such as to make him believe that she looked as angelic as he had ever thought her to be, but he knew better than to say so.

"I have received Lady Bertram's note and will be off to deliver it unless it would not be too much of an imposition for me to sit with you a little while."

"I promised to give you a hearing, Mr. Crawford," she replied taking a seat, "and now seems to be an opportune moment."

He sat down opposite her. She took up her work. He began directly. "I do not know what you have been told about last summer, though I have a suspicion as to the opinions you have formed, so I will tell you what happened as well as I can." She nodded her assent. "You may imagine my surprise when I discovered that Miss Bertram was staying within two miles of Everingham in the family of my newest neighbour, Mr. Dixon. He told me himself, though not realizing at the time he was disclosing anything untoward, that the idea of coming into Norfolk had been hers. When he had first resolved on taking a house in the country for the summer, Miss Bertram wrote to Miss Dixon suggesting it. When he told me this, I began to suspect her design. I believe he eventually did as well.

144

"We saw each other several times. She seemed intent on making sure all my neighbours knew of our prior connection. She was very different when not with her sister, much more forward. She claimed such an intimacy with me. I did not know how to act, which was rather a new sensation for me. I did not know how to show indifference towards her without giving offence. Eventually, others of my acquaintance began to say things which seemed to indicate that there was more between us than really was, or that there would be.

"I will not deny that I had been in similar situations before, and I confess I was not always blameless in bringing them about – as you yourself have observed; but I had always escaped, often to Everingham. Now, I found myself in need of escaping my own home – my usual refuge. When I received word from your brother that he was to be at Yarmouth, I thought to visit him there, but such a scheme would not serve as his being her cousin might provide her with an excuse to somehow involve herself in the visit. Then I received the letter of invitation from my friend Blake to a shooting party at his estate. Nothing could have been more perfect. And the dates coincided with Mr. Price's expected arrival, so I secured him an invitation. Thither I went, as soon as I could get away. When I returned to Everingham Miss Bertram and the Dixons had gone."

He looked at her expectantly. "I thank you for the account," she said without looking up. "But this explains very little. If your neighbours had an idea that … if they had expectations pertaining to your treatment of Miss Bertram, then something must have given rise to them."

"I do not believe I did anything to single her out. I danced with her once or twice, but I never paid her any particular attention. I knew or suspected enough to be guarded in my behaviour towards her. And whenever she spoke of our prior acquaintance, I always made a point of naming the other members of the family with whom I had also been connected. Though, there was one thing more I could have done …"

Fanny looked up.

"While I was in London last year – I am sure you know from my sister's letters and indeed from what you observed during your visit there – I told everyone of my situation, … of my feelings, in short, of all that had passed between us. When I returned to Everingham, I was in very high spirits. I felt very good about my prospects. I was prepared to do the same with my acquaintance in Norfolk as I had done in London. I had no secrets to keep. I was happy and I wanted everyone to know why. The first people I happened to tell were Mr. and Mrs. Morgan, my neighbours at Everingham Parsonage. It was Mr. Morgan who convinced me not to speak publicly of it by the simple expedient of asking a question I had not yet bothered to ask myself: whether the object of my affections would wish me to speak of them so openly. The answer to this question I could readily supply and I resolved to be happy in silence.

"And so my general acquaintance remained ignorant of my true feelings and were therefore at liberty to attribute any feelings they wished to me. In truth, my situation in being young, unmarried and independent, together with my cheerfulness on coming back into the neighbourhood, her arrival a few months thereafter, and the knowledge of our prior acquaintance may have been enough for many to form an idea of a match. Such ideas have been formed with far less provocation, I dare say. And I do not know what she might have said in confidence to the young ladies thereabouts to add to the impression. I can say, however, that I did not show her any sign of particularity. My suspicion of her design gave me reason to take great care not to single her out. And – I am sure you will believe – I know how to pay particular attention to a woman when I wish to. I have my faults Miss Price, you are well acquainted with them, and perhaps I did deserve to be made a little uncomfortable in that way, but I did not mislead Miss Bertram last summer."

They were silent for a long moment. At length, Fanny said, "I confess I do not know what to believe. I have seen such contrariety in your character. You have shown extraordinary kindness of late, yet you have no scruple in laying the whole of the blame for the expectations of your neighbours on Lady Chandler."

"I speak only the truth. I know you have no reason to believe it, but if there was an expectation, it was wholly her doing, her machinations."

"I do have reason to believe it," said Fanny quietly, recalling all Julia had confided in her about her intentions and what Edmund had told her of Mr. Dixon's disclosures.

"But you cannot wholly acquit me?"

"As I said, I do not know. But it is of no consequence what transpired between you last summer. She is married to Sir Henry now and you have performed a great service to this family."

"It is of consequence to me if you think I have acted wrongly."

"But you have admitted to acting wrongly."

"In the past yes, but not since … I hope, not since our meeting at Portsmouth. Have not you seen the difference? Have not you seen the effect of your influence at Portsmouth?"

She shook her head in confusion; then after a long silence, she paused in her work and looked up at him. "Last spring," she began, "*after* we met

146

at Portsmouth," she added, looking pointedly at him, "you brought your sister to Mansfield and then you quit the country rather suddenly."

He looked genuinely puzzled, stood and walked to the window then, looking out of it, said, "I must confess to some confusion, Miss Price. I had thought I was doing right in that circumstance."

"You were," she said quickly, "you did. But *why* were you obliged to go away so suddenly?"

"Because Mrs. Rushworth and Miss Bertram set out to meet me on purpose and afterwards, that night …"

"Do not say it, Mr. Crawford, I do not wish to know."

"Then why did you ask me?"

"The particulars do not signify. All that matters is that something happened … between you and Mrs. Rushworth."

"No, Miss Price. You are quite mistaken. Nothing happened between us." He sat down again across from her. "I was on the verge of explaining it to you the day I left when I saw you outside the Parsonage, but I did not think you wanted to hear it." He paused, then in a calmer voice said, "During the night I received a note from Mrs. Rushworth." Fanny's eyes grew wide. "She sent it to me by a servant. In the middle of the night. In it she expressed a desire of arranging another meeting. A clandestine meeting – without her sister. That is the truth. I can produce the note."

"You kept it?"

"I was about to burn it when my sister convinced me I might want it someday as proof of what had passed."

"I see," she said thoughtfully. She had to admit to herself that his explanation was perfectly consistent with her recollection of the conversation between his sisters on the day of the event. "But I do recall accidentally hearing you say that Mr. Rushworth would be justified in calling you out. If you were blameless, why would you say such a thing?"

"I was referring to my earlier behaviour while she was engaged, which I have since learned to regret, and which was the foundation of the event to which you alluded. My actions precipitated hers. She was motivated by feelings I created; feelings which had not by then been sufficiently overcome." He sighed. "I knew I should not have returned to Mansfield in May."

She looked at him and said, "Then you must have felt yourself in some danger of …" She stopped herself abruptly, looked determinedly down at her work, and said nothing more.

He studied her for a moment in silence, then said, "This will not do; you shall have the whole history." He paused, but she made no objection;

thus, he began, "You were a witness to all that happened before Mrs. Rushworth was married. After her marriage, I did not see her again until Mrs. Fraser's party in London. I had hoped to meet her as a friend. She, however, was very cold towards me. Her manner made it evident that she was wounded ... deeply wounded." At this Fanny ventured to look up at him. "Her resentment, it was clear, was stronger than I had supposed. I readily concluded that I should not have stayed for the party and resolved immediately to go to Everingham; I regretted not having gone there directly upon returning from Portsmouth. After seeing her, I knew we had better not meet again until time had worked its effect on her feelings."

Fanny said nothing.

"That resolution even prevented me from going to Richmond at Easter, as I do every year. My sister wrote to me that Mrs. Rushworth had secured an invitation to be there at that very time and was staying in the home of a family of my acquaintance with whom she had just grown intimate. I wrote my apologies to my uncle the same day, almost in the same moment that I received Mary's letter. He was very displeased. A few weeks later, Mary wrote to ask me to bring her to Mansfield. I knew of Tom's death. I knew the whole family would be here. I resisted her at first, but in relenting, I reasoned that every other consideration would surely give way to the family's great loss. Whether I gave too much credit to Mrs. Rushworth's feelings as a sister or too little to the strength of her resentments, I cannot say. I can assure you, however, that the only danger I sought to avoid was on *her* side." He leaned forward a little before continuing, "Given my former behaviour towards her, I perhaps should be ashamed to confess that I never felt anything like what you have evidently been supposing."

"But you are *not* ashamed," she said, without looking up from her work.

"Of never having felt anything for your cousin, no, I am not; but of behaving towards her as if I did, I am."

A long silence followed this extraordinary declaration. At last Fanny broke it saying, "Then, if what you say is true, you were blameless in the event of last May."

"No, Miss Price. As much as I would wish to agree with you – especially when you are inclined to acquit me of wrongdoing – we both know that neither of the events we have been talking about would have occurred if not for my previous actions; but I have acknowledged this to you before now."

"That is true; but surely both ladies must bear some responsibility for

148

their own subsequent behaviour."

"I am not so much reformed, Miss Price, as to venture to disagree with you there."

"So I have been wrong again. I have misjudged you again."

"For the last time, I hope. Pray, is there anything else? Any other act of wrongdoing you believe I have committed since our meeting at Portsmouth?"

"Do not tease me, I beg you."

"Miss Price, I do not tease you. I ask in sincerity. If there is anything else let it be in the open."

"There is nothing else," she replied, almost in a whisper.

He leaned forward in his chair and caught her eye. "I am very glad to know it."

She made no reply. They sat in silence for a long while. Fanny was lost in her reverie, thinking over all that had been said by her companion who sat watching her work. At last, she broke the silence when she thought to ask, "When do the Grants go to London?"

"On Monday next and they will return on Saturday. I will be going with them. I have no wish to leave but it would be odd for me to stay behind alone in their home, and it will be pleasant to see Mr. and Mrs. Bertram again. Besides, I am expected at Twickhenham for Easter."

They continued speaking on various subjects. It was a long while before Fanny began to wonder at the length of time they had been left alone, uninterrupted. She had been enjoying the latter part of the conversation but she felt she had been forgotten by her uncle and aunts. Upon checking the clock, she resolved to inquire after Lady Bertram. Mr. Crawford took the hint and observed that the Grants must be wondering where he was as well.

Chapter 22

When her companion left the room, Fanny went up to Lady Bertram's chamber to look in on her aunt. She found her asleep with Mrs. Chapman nearby. Mrs. Norris was nowhere to be seen. She went to her uncle's room but the door was closed and, hearing muffled voices within, she did not wish to disturb him. Although it was not yet time to dress for dinner, she went to the East room to reflect on all she had heard. It was not long before Sir Thomas found her there.

"Fanny, I wish to speak to you for a moment."

"Yes sir," she said, sitting down.

"I have not mentioned the unfortunate business with Mr. Crawford since your return from Portsmouth, except for one brief conversation, and I do not wish to force your confidence – I mention it now only as a means to judge whether I can forego the real subject I want to discuss with you."

Fanny felt her colour rise. "Has he said anything to you?"

"No. Not at all. But he has done a great service to our family and I am disposed to extend him every courtesy, though not at the expense of your feelings. I know that after breakfast he visited you for some time in the drawing room. I thought it might be a conversation of some import, and therefore I made sure you were not disturbed." She looked surprised. "I trust I did not judge wrongly?"

"No sir. We were conversing. There were things he wished to tell me."

"I see. And there is nothing else?"

"No sir."

"Very well then. I have been in conference with Mrs. Norris today, to talk to her about your situation."

Fanny was alarmed. What could he mean? Was it possible he was renewing the plan to have her live with Mrs. Norris? Surely, that could not be; she was so necessary to Lady Bertram.

"When bringing you here as a child, I took it upon myself to raise you and educate you, with the intent of providing you the means to obtain a good establishment. However, there is one essential part in gaining that objective that I cannot do myself. You must be introduced to the world. You must mix in society."

Fanny felt mortified and could not stop the tears that had begun to flow.

"Do not misunderstand me, child. We do not wish to be rid of you. You know Lady Bertram would be very sorry to see you go. But I do not feel I would be doing my duty by you if we did not at least provide you the opportunity to try for an establishment of your own. It would be very wrong, after taking you away from your home and family, not to introduce you properly into the world. I have always been prepared to make provision for your future as necessary, but it would be most unfair to deprive you of any chance for independence.

"Lady Bertram is not of a disposition to exert herself in that way and I know that Mrs. Norris took Maria and Julia out while I was in Antigua. I spoke to her, therefore, in hopes of her doing the same for you; but after my conference with her, I am of a different opinion. I do not think such an arrangement would benefit either of you." He sighed. "The conclusion of my conversation with her, therefore, has led me to consider alternatives. It troubles me greatly that I cannot trust either of my daughters with such a charge; and when considering whether Mrs. Bertram would be suitable," Fanny started at this, "I remembered whose sister she is and began to think her interest might be against you."

He paused long enough for Fanny to interject. "I am obliged to you for thinking of me, sir, for exerting yourself on my behalf, but truly, I see no reason for you to distress yourself further on the matter. I am perfectly content with things as they are. And Lady Bertram, I think, would be made very unhappy if I were to marry."

"Fanny, I am pleased that you have your aunt's happiness in view; but you are young; you cannot spend your life sitting next to her day after day, year after year. All of the other young people have gone and Lady Bertram does not visit anyone. I know it frightens you but you must exert yourself to meet new people or, I fear, you will be very unhappy in the years to come, and by then it will be too late."

Fanny did not know what to say. "Truly, sir, I beg you to reconsider."

"You must be introduced into society. On this point, there can be no argument. I have not yet determined how it is to be accomplished but some means must be settled upon. Nothing can be done until after Michaelmas, but at that time, something must and will be done."

Fanny was resigned. She made no reply. Her uncle left her full of a new source of agitation. She reflected to herself that she should be pleased to finally have the opportunity to engage in those amusements which had been so long withheld from her. But she scarcely knew anyone in the neighbourhood. She had heard some of the families talked of by her cousins, but she had not grown up visiting with them, and had only met a few of the principal families once at the Mansfield Ball. It was not as if she were merely new to the neighbourhood; she had been fixed at Mansfield for ten years, and everyone knew it. Yet, she knew almost no one outside of Mansfield Village; and now as a woman she was to go out among them for the first time, with such inadequate foundation of acquaintance and with the obvious design of seeking a husband. This is what repulsed her: the appearance of a mercenary intent. She was not a Miss Bertram, who could go into society with all the confidence which beauty, rank, and fortune could bestow. Everyone knew her situation, that she was a poor relation of Sir Thomas; and everyone would now know that it was his design to marry her off. And how was she to get partners at a dance with no acquaintance? The Mansfield Ball, she now understood, had been a sort of coming out for her; there had been a general sense of obligation to dance with her. But now it would be all contrivance, interference, and embarrassment. And who was to be the chaperone charged with the execution of such stratagems? All of this was the source of her anxiety.

This conversation with her uncle at the very least provided Fanny with a distraction from constantly dwelling on her grievous misjudgement of Mr. Crawford and all that he had disclosed to her. Her meditations were divided wholly between these two subjects.

The family's intimacy with the Parsonage during this period was as strong as ever, Fanny saw Mr. Crawford a few times before his departure for London. They did not speak further on the subjects of their last two conversations, but the tone of those conversations had re-established the sort of intimacy that had begun to form between them before Julia's elopement. Now they spoke of more pleasant subjects such as Portsmouth and Everingham. These conversations served as a distraction from her uncle's plans for her, but she nevertheless worked herself into a severe state of anxiety over the matter.

On the Sunday before they were to depart for London, the Grants and Mr. Crawford dined at the Park. After dinner, while the others talked of the impending journey, Mr. Crawford sat next to Fanny and briefly alluded to their previous conversations, saying quietly, "I am sorry to be going tomorrow, but I cannot tell you how pleased I am that we have cleared the air between us."

She wanted to ask him whether he intended on returning with the Grants at the end of the week, but she dared not. She had not even noticed that she had, of late, grown fond of his company. Nevertheless, she made no reply to him other than a nod of acknowledgement. She had been meditating on her conversation with Sir Thomas and whether there might be any way to change his mind.

"Yet, you are still distressed by something," he observed. "Is there anything I can do?"

"No," she replied hastily. "It is … it has nothing to do with you."

"I am pleased that I am not the cause of your vexation, for once, Miss Price; but still, you are vexed and I do not like to see it."

She remained silent.

"I understand you do not wish to confide in me, and I will not press you to do so except to say that it may help to talk about it."

"It is only that … my uncle insists on having me introduced into society."

"I see," he replied, comprehending the full meaning of Sir Thomas' design. "And you do not wish for such a distinction?"

"I do not think it is necessary."

"It is not necessary."

It took a moment for her to fully comprehend his meaning, but when she did, her colour rose and she could scarcely utter the, "Mr. Crawford, you mustn't … I did not mean …" that finally emerged.

He smiled a little. "Forgive me. I know that is not what you meant." After another pause, he continued, "Most young ladies would be quite thrilled with the prospect of balls and parties."

"I am not most young ladies," she replied, thinking of her situation.

"Of that, I am well aware," he said meaningfully.

She said nothing.

"Perhaps it will not be as unpleasant as you fear. You enjoyed the Mansfield Ball did not you?"

"I did, but …"

"But Mr. Price was there."

"Yes."

Soon after this exchange, Mr. Crawford's attention was called away by the others. Fanny was once again left to her own thoughts and went to bed before the company departed for the evening.

The next day her first thought when she awoke was that Mr. Crawford was going away that day – had probably already gone. She did not know when or if he would be back. Of all the times he had come and gone from Mansfield, this was the first time she did not rejoice in his departure. She would miss him. It was a startling realization.

After breakfast, she spent the day in the drawing room with her aunts. She could think of nothing but her uncle's scheme. She felt helpless. She wished there was a way to persuade him to give it up. But she knew nothing could be done. She believed he would never give up what he considered to be a duty unless she were actually married. But she supposed that nothing worse could happen than that she would be forced to go out a few times, nothing would come of it, and Sir Thomas would eventually give up the idea and let her live out her days as she was now.

These vexations continued to plague her mind throughout the day and she resolved to retire to dress for dinner a little early, to have some time for solitude. When she entered the East room, she immediately noticed a letter sitting on the table with her name written across the front. Her heart began beating rapidly. She knew who must have left it. He must have come in while she was at breakfast. She eagerly opened the letter and read the following:

> Miss Price,
>
> Please forgive me for taking the liberty of writing to you and of leaving this letter for you in your room, as I intend to do before departing for London in the morning. I leave Mansfield with a heavy heart and I do not know when I shall return. I write because there has been enough misunderstanding between us. While I rejoice in the progress we've made in overcoming it, I wish to dispel whatever confusion may remain. You once expressed curiosity about the change you have observed in me and I told you I longed to explain it fully. I seek your indulgence to do so now.
>
> You are already aware that when I left Mansfield last year to take my sister to London, I happily told anyone who would listen of my feelings and my situation; and that the parson at Everingham, Mr. Morgan, stopped me from doing the same in Norfolk. But this was by no means the end of the subject between us. We spoke again when I returned to Everingham after visiting you at Portsmouth.
>
> Since Mr. Morgan was the only person to whom I could speak about my feelings – and I was eager to be talking about them to someone – I told him of having seen you in Portsmouth and of the hope I had derived from the visit. I expected him to honour my perseverance, to encourage my suit, and to give me his assurance of my eventual success. Instead, he looked grave and asked with great solemnity whether I truly wished to hear his opinion and whether I would attend to it. I assented.
>
> He then spoke to me very seriously. He wondered that I

should persist in a suit that must be unwelcome, and expressed doubt as to my avowed feelings. This I could not abide; but I was feeling cheerful, and I laughed off his doubts and reminded him of all the hints he had given me about matrimony. He then asked me questions about all that had passed between us and having established the facts – at least according to my representation – he proceeded to set forth a very different view of their meaning than I had been indulging. I naturally insisted that I must know my own heart; but his argument was rational, and nothing I said in my own defence would satisfy him.

We spoke again and again, and it took some time before I allowed the justice of any of his doubts. My zeal to prove I was right kept me engaged in the conversation and his sincere, gentle, affectionate manner prevented my becoming really angry. Our conversations went on for many days before I gave due consideration to anything he said. But when I did, when I was willing to seriously examine my own conduct, I made a sobering discovery. Till that moment, I never knew myself. I then saw with striking clarity that I had continued to importune you with my attentions against your express wishes, that my actions had brought you discomfort and misery. When I made my addresses to you, I had no doubt of your acceptance; your refusal only added to my fervour; and the challenge of overcoming it was to give even greater proof to my abilities. Mr. Morgan's doubts revealed to me that my own behaviour was not consistent with the feelings I professed to have and was instead calculated to please myself, rather than the object of my affections. These meditations naturally led to others.

At first my reflections were only of you, of my treatment of you, until it occurred to me to wonder why you had refused me to begin with. The answer, of course, was that your disapprobation of me, was not founded upon my treatment of *you*, but on how I had treated others. This led to even more mortifying self-discovery, for there was no redeeming motivation when it came to the others. It was all selfish, cold-hearted, vanity. And I then began to understand that once one begins with the object of satisfying one's own vanity, there is never an end of it; nothing is ever enough; there is never satisfaction. I used to make women in love with me because it gave me pleasure, not pleasure in their company or in their tender feelings; it was the power to make them love me that I was addicted to, with little thought to the pain I inflicted. This was the pleasure I sought, and a dark revelation about myself.

I have been a selfish being all my life, and left to my own devices for much of it. In truth, I had no good example of matrimony in my youth, no good example of compassion or of sympathy. And I was never handsome; of this, I have always been aware. All the beauty my parents had to impart went to my sister's share. Though, what was withheld from me by nature in looks, was given back to me in the form of other abilities; and these I learned to use with great efficacy. I gloried in making women, who at first would not give me a second look, unable to stop thinking of me; but I never cared for any of them. To own the truth, my success in changing their feelings lowered them in my esteem.

And so it was with your cousins. It was never my intent to injure them. What I told you before was true. I did not believe I *could* injure the eldest. Nor was it my intent to induce a rivalry between them. I enjoyed the attention, and as I have confessed previously, I closed my eyes to the damage that must so naturally result. But eventually, only after realizing the shameful truth about what I had been doing, I learned to think of it, to comprehend the pain caused by my actions. This was made possible by my own feelings – a better understanding of myself and of you led to a better understanding of the meaning of your rejection. Where, previously, I had every confidence of eventually winning you, I now despaired of ever being capable of even improving your opinion of me. Pain and helplessness followed, and it was these feelings – my own genuine suffering – which enabled me, at last, to see the pain I had caused others.

There were moments while I was alone at Everingham, when I thought I might tear my own heart out. Such was my torment. And a helpless torment it was; made all the worse by the knowledge not only that I had brought it upon myself, but that I had inflicted the same torment upon others. I worked on them with charm and gallantry until they longed for my attentions, until they expected more, expected everything, and then I fled. I see myself now as you have seen me: selfish, thoughtless, vain. Everything that is the reverse of the feelings I so boldly claimed.

The sensations I found myself subject to as a result of my designs on you were entirely new to me. Pretence, disguise, affectation – these I knew only too well; but of genuine affection I knew very little. And with no example to teach me how to act, I could not at first distinguish it from what had previously bounded my experience. I had not learned the profound satisfaction of real, selfless, attachment.

What I have written here may seem inconsistent with what you know of me, but it has been the result of many months' reflection. I hope you can believe that the change you have observed in me is very real; that once I saw my past behaviour for what it was, I was repulsed by it. There is no going back to it. There is not even the temptation.

You once admonished me for not knowing myself, and I confess, at that time, I did not. I hope you can see that I now do. I have at last begun to acquire the most valuable knowledge we could any of us hope to acquire – the knowledge of self. And it is all owing to you; for this I will always be grateful. I am the same man with the same temperament and the same heart. Only now I know I am unworthy of you.

I have given some thought to our conversation this evening and I hope you will reconcile yourself to your uncle's wishes. You are aware of my general opinion of your situation. But in this case, I believe Sir Thomas may be right. I believe you know that nothing would make me happier than to end your current distress by doing away with the reason he believes you must be introduced into society. But I know your feelings. Since you cannot be happy with me, I hope with all my heart that you may find happiness elsewhere; or that you will at least give yourself the chance to do so. I will only add, God bless you.

I remain, yours, always, Henry Crawford.

Chapter 23

The effect of this letter on a heart such as Fanny's can be well imagined. Her hands trembled upon opening it, the tears started before she had finished the first paragraph. She read through it once so quickly that she could barely comprehend one sentence before starting the next. She read through it again, with more patience and more composure, and was even more astonished by its contents. She could never have imagined that such a man could know himself so well, or could provide such an extraordinary and frank account of the faults of his own character.

He had chosen his moment well. Less than two weeks had passed since their conversation which had given her to understand how grievously she had misjudged him; and he, whether wittingly or not, had availed himself of the goodwill she must feel towards him in consequence of such a gross injustice.

He loved her. She could no longer admit a doubt of it. He had shown it all along, but she had been wilfully blind to it. The difference since Portsmouth was that he had shown his feelings only to her and no longer displayed them before others; this, together with his more subdued, gentler manner towards her had been such a marked change from his previous behaviour that she had been able to convince herself he no longer loved her. Yet, in his letter, he spoke of his love for her as a simple fact, without ever making a declaration. Indeed, as she thought back to their conversations, he had alluded to his feelings more than once – even last night, yet she had chosen not to consider the meaning of such allusions or to take them seriously. She now faced the undeniable truth that Henry Crawford loved her, had loved her for well over a year, and loved her still.

She thought of her own feelings for Edmund and how much she had feared their revelation in contrast to how readily Mr. Crawford openly acknowledged his feelings to her in spite of knowing she did not return them. Truly, she could not say what she felt. She no longer loved Edmund. That much was quite clear. Her feelings for Mr. Crawford were in such a state of confusion. How could she define them? She felt gratitude towards him for all he had done for her and those connected to her. As far as she knew, he had kept her heart's secret; and last night she had confided in him willingly. She had begun to enjoy his company. She missed him.

She knew not what to think of the change he had undergone; yet, she could not bring herself to doubt the sincerity of his disclosures. He had acknowledged his former habits and disavowed them in the strongest terms. And it seemed more than an empty assertion, he acknowledged that he was repulsed by them, that there was not even a temptation to return to them. His repentance seemed genuine.

This one fault – his inclination to sport with the feelings of women – had been the root of all her disapprobation of him. She could think of nothing else to his discredit; as a brother, as a friend, he had always been praised and loved. He had a generous heart and a cheerful disposition. And now he had learned the value of serious reflection.

At first she thought it regrettable that he had required a push from Mr. Morgan to examine his own behaviour, but then she considered how rare it is for anyone to undertake such a thorough examination of self, even with hints from those around them. The more she thought about it, the more remarkable it seemed.

A glance at the clock brought her back to the present and she quickly dressed for dinner and went down to the dining room, but she could scarcely think of anything but her letter for the entire evening and indeed the ensuing days.

The week passed quietly and Fanny found that she looked forward to the Grants' return from London. They arrived on Saturday but she did not see them until church on Sunday. Mr. Crawford did not return with them. Fanny had not expected him, and was therefore a little surprised by her own feeling of disappointment. They brought her a letter from Mrs. Bertram, who wrote as follows:

My Dear Fanny, How happy we have been to have the Grants in London and how sad we are to see them go tomorrow. We have had a week of such gaiety. We have been to the theatre and to a private ball. Though my brother has been out of spirits, which I can only attribute to his having left you at Mansfield. I must resort to conjecture because he will not talk to me about it. He no longer confides in me. I am quite out of humour with him. He will not stay beyond Saturday. He shall join the Admiral at Twickenham and return to Everingham after Easter. And there he shall remain, I suppose, through the summer. Edmund and I will visit him, I dare say. It has been an age since I have been to Everingham. I will prevail upon you yet to come with us. Mrs. Rushworth and Lady Chandler were both at the ball we attended, and Mrs. R invited our whole party to dine. Henry would not go. He claimed to have a prior engagement, but I suspect there was none.

When I suggested it was on your account he would not confirm it or speak to me at all on the subject. It is very vexing to me as we have always been in one another's confidence. I think, perhaps, between Everingham and Mansfield, he has been spending too much time in the country. He needs a diversion, something to restore him to good cheer, and I do believe this dinner party would have been just the thing. Mrs. Rushworth returned to all her glory in Wimpole Street. Happily, Lady Chandler's elopement seems to have been wholly forgotten by everyone and both she and her husband appear to be quite satisfied with the marriage state. I imagine she will have a brood of ten or twelve children before her sister has one. Of course, the lot of them spoke of nothing but the Sotherton Theatricals all evening. They are determined to resume the activity upon returning to the country, but I fear they may have lost one of their best players in Mr. Yates. We are all invited to Sotherton Court for a performance of whatever play they fix upon next. Perhaps they will arrange the performance to coincide with Sir Thomas' visit. I have discovered that the Grants had a secondary motive for coming to London. Dr. Grant has been, for some time, hoping to ascend to a stall at Westminster and it appears that his hopes may soon be answered. I will certainly miss my sister, but it would mean that Edmund and I could go to Mansfield Parsonage. He and Dr. Grant were shut up for some time yesterday working out all the particulars of the arrangement. Only think how close we shall be; and with Mrs. Grant settled in London, frequent visits to town would be made easy. How well it shall all be arranged. How comfortable we shall be at Mansfield. But I must help my sister with preparations for her journey tomorrow. Give my love to Sir Thomas and Lady Bertram. Yours, etc., Mary Bertram

Fanny found the news that the Bertrams might be moving to Mansfield Parsonage very unwelcome. Having them at Thornton Lacey had been sufficiently close for Fanny to witness quite enough of their conjugal felicity. She knew it would not bother her so much now, but she could not immediately reconcile herself to the change. She could not imagine the

160

quarrels between them would cease simply by moving from one parsonage house to another, and she had no more desire to be a witness to their marital discord than to their marital joys.

The Grants being home added some animation to Mansfield. The two families continued to see one another frequently; and soon they were all settled into a regular course. Fanny was able to ride more often as the weather grew warmer. Whenever she did, however, she could not help but think of Mr. Crawford and his extraordinary kindness that had restored Edmund's mare to her use. Further reflection since his having left Mansfield had allowed her to fully comprehend the meaning of his admission of what his mysterious errand in Northampton had been. She remembered the evening before his departure perfectly. He had been delighted in the prospect of his business – and his business had been to make sure she had a horse to ride.

His letter, she was by now in a fair way of knowing by heart. She studied every sentence: and her feelings towards its writer were at times widely different. When she remembered his former behaviour she still felt indignation; but when she considered how unjustly she had condemned him, her anger was turned against herself, and his feelings became the object of compassion. His attachment and his constancy (the very word she once thought so unsuited to him) excited gratitude, the acknowledgement of his faults and the changes he had undergone excited respect, and perhaps even a degree of admiration; but, though she could not for a moment repent her refusal, she discovered, to her own mortification, that she would not object to seeing him again. This was followed by a succession of equally mortifying discoveries: she found that she missed their quiet intimate conversations, and even his attentions and solicitude.

He was in her thoughts far more than she liked. Yet, what was there to divert her? She spent all her time at home with her aunts and occasionally seeing Mrs. Grant until she and her husband left for Bath and Fanny's circle became even more contracted. There was nothing new upon which to fix her mind until the Bertrams returned from London. At her first opportunity, Fanny spoke to Edmund about her uncle's plans for her. She knew Sir Thomas listened to his son, and she reasoned that if anyone could change his mind, it would be Edmund. She spoke of her anxiety at the prospect of going out into society and her distaste of doing so with the design of finding a husband; she spoke of her contentment in her situation and assured him of her certainty that she would never regret not marrying. But Edmund could not be persuaded to intervene on her behalf. He agreed with his father.

No sooner had the Bertrams returned from London than they began to look towards Everingham; for, as summer approached, the lady's condition now made it desirable to travel sooner rather than later, as she expected to be confined in October. Edmund retained the curate who had been doing the duties of the parish at Thornton Lacey while the Bertrams had been in London in the expectation of being away several weeks in the summer, but was carrying out his duties himself while at home. Fanny was surprised he was willing to be away from the parish so much. He reasoned, however, that there would be less opportunity to travel after the arrival of the child and, if they should have occasion to move to Mansfield Parsonage, it was best to leave Thornton Lacey in the hands of the curate already established there. For her part, Fanny could not regret the distance between Mansfield and Thornton Lacey that prevented daily intercourse.

Nevertheless, whenever they did see her, Edmund and Mary both had begun an almost constant attack upon Fanny to persuade her to join them in going to Everingham, and had gone so far as to convince Lady Bertram of its being a good idea. Sir Thomas did not require convincing. Everingham, of course, was no longer an object of repulsion to Fanny and she could not but admit, to herself at least, a curiosity to see it. But she could not justify running the risk of giving its owner the wrong impression by making such a visit. Moreover, she had no wish to travel with Mr. and Mrs. Bertram, though her discomfort no longer arose from tender feelings towards Edmund.

During this period, however, Fanny received a letter from William that gave her a very different notion on the prospect of accepting the invitation. After giving her his usual account of his doings, he added the following before closing his letter:

I am once again to be given a week's leave at Yarmouth in June. It is, of course, not enough to make the journey to Northampton but Mr. Crawford has invited me to Everingham. He says that he expects Mr. and Mrs. Bertram to be in residence while I am there. If you can contrive to go with them, it would be the most perfect scheme. I cannot imagine that they should not invite you. I hope I am not asking too much of you in urging you to go to Everingham. I know your history with its owner must make you uncomfortable with the idea of staying in his home. But it has been so long since we were together and I would rejoice in seeing you above any other pleasure.

This changed everything for Fanny. Edmund and Mary, of course intended to remain at Everingham longer than a week but the prospect of being with William again made almost anything worthwhile. In the end, there was nothing to consider. She would go.

Chapter 24

Edmund and Mary were overjoyed when Fanny gave them the news that she would accompany them to Everingham, but Mary would tease her relentlessly for only agreeing to accept the invitation after learning William would be there. Fanny could not help but reflect that as an added benefit of going away, she would not be required to accompany her uncle and aunt on their visit to Sotherton Court which was now being arranged.

Fanny was as eager as always to view any new country and as soon as she was beyond the familiar, she was awake to every difference in the countryside that could be observed. The journey was two days and, unfortunately for Fanny, the company with whom she travelled made it seem longer rather than shorter. Mrs. Bertram, who had traversed this country many times, had less interest in looking about and more interest in sleeping, owing to her delicate state; but Edmund made an effort to converse with Fanny about any object of interest that caught the eye of either. As they began to approach the environs of Everingham, however, Mrs. Bertram became much more animated and began pointing out familiar sights and places to her companions. For her part, Fanny grew apprehensive as they approached Everingham. Now, as they passed through the country she had been most eager to see, she found she scarcely took notice of anything. She could not readily identify the sensation. It was, perhaps, a mixture of eagerness and dread.

She had long admitted to herself that her feelings towards Mr. Crawford had changed. She had even been able to acknowledge that she had missed him. They had shared moments of openness, even intimacy that mortified her a little now, looking back on them; yet at the same time she had grown comfortable speaking with him. But now, as she approached his home, the home that might have been hers, there was no sensation of comfort. Instead, she experienced a contrariety of anxieties wavering between fear that her coming might give him false hope and concern that he would be offended by her having really only come to see William.

She tried to attend to Mrs. Bertram's conversation as they passed through the village and shortly thereafter began the approach to the house. At last they arrived. Mrs. Bertram exited the carriage first, Fanny heard Mr. Crawford's voice as he greeted his sister. Edmund motioned her to step out next. When she did, Mr. Crawford was not ready to hand her out. He was still looking at his sister and as he turned back towards the carriage his expression changed to one of utter shock. He paused for the briefest moment staring at Fanny as she stood ready to alight from the carriage, then quickly offering his hand, said, "Miss Price!" as his expression changed again from surprise to delight.

"Mr. Crawford," she said, taking his hand and stepping down.

He seemed unable to speak for a moment, but then recollecting himself said, "Forgive me, I understood that you had declined the invitation; I had no idea you would be one of the party but I am very pleased to see that you accepted after all."

Fanny now was mortified. She looked to Mrs. Bertram, but she only laughed and said to her brother, "Did not I tell you that Miss Price changed her mind about coming when she learned Mr. Price would be visiting Everingham?"

"No," said Mr. Crawford, "you neglected to include that piece of news in your letters; but I am very pleased to be the means of bringing Mr. and Miss Price together."

Edmund heard only the last as he exited the carriage and upon being fully informed began to scold his wife, while Mr. Crawford led them all into the house. When they reached the drawing room, Mr. Crawford first asked about their journey and after some little conversation went to speak to his housekeeper about the addition of a guest. The others took the opportunity to refresh themselves, and afterwards Mr. Crawford and Mrs. Bertram showed Fanny and Edmund much of the house. As they looked out of one of the windows in the upper gallery which gave a favourable prospect of the grounds, including the new young trees below, Mrs. Bertram whispered to Fanny with a smile, "Of all this you might have been mistress." Fanny looked back at her but said nothing. By the time they had seen the principal public rooms, it was time to dress for dinner.

They soon sat down to a family dinner during which Fanny was content to be a quiet observer. The others talked animatedly among themselves. All three had much to say. Mr. and Mrs. Bertram attempted to draw Fanny into the conversation once or twice but did not press her. At length after the exhaustion of many other topics, Mrs. Bertram mentioned her wish to walk to Everingham Parsonage the following morning and call upon Mrs. Morgan. The mere mention of the name brought the blush to Fanny's cheeks and she dared not raise her eyes to Mr. Crawford, but she thought she could hear a smile in his voice as he assured his sister that he would be delighted to walk to the Parsonage in the morning.

Fanny had to admit a great curiosity to meet the Morgans but she found that she also felt a great deal of anxiety the next morning as they walked towards the Parsonage. They were shown into a spacious drawing room, where they found Mrs. Morgan and several children of varying ages. The lady looked a little surprised when Fanny was introduced to her but greeted her with a warm expression that carried a hint of familiarity. They were joined within moments by Mr. Morgan and their eldest son, a young man about three or four and twenty. Upon meeting Fanny, Mr. Morgan had the same expression of surprise and familiarity as his wife and even ventured to smile and cast a knowing glance to Mr. Crawford that Fanny hoped none of the others noticed. For a man who had recommended more circumspection in his friend, he seemed to give little thought to reserve himself.

As they settled into conversation, Mr. Crawford and Mr. Morgan began talking of estate business with Mr. Bertram, while Mrs. Morgan and Mrs. Bertram talked of their common acquaintance, with the former relating all the local news to the latter. In the meantime, Fanny began a conversation with Mr. James Morgan, who she found to be a pragmatic, plain spoken young man who was to be ordained at Christmas and would take over another, smaller living currently held by his father on a neighbouring estate. Thankfully, he betrayed no hint of any knowledge of what had been passing between his father and Mr. Crawford the previous year. Fanny would have been content to continue the conversation but she soon discovered that the ladies were talking of walking into Everingham Village to visit one of the shops Mrs. Bertram remembered from her childhood, as the gentlemen intended to ride over to survey one of the tenant farms they had been discussing.

On the way to the village, Mrs. Morgan expressed her approbation of the errand which the gentlemen had undertaken. She was telling Mrs. Bertram how pleased she was that Mr. Crawford had come into his own as landlord and master of Everingham. "When he came of age, we were delighted with his enthusiasm for Everingham. He began improvements shortly after taking up residence, which seemed to foretell a commitment to improving the lives of those who are dependent on the estate as well. But once the improvements to the house and grounds were completed, he was absent so much that, to own the truth, we began to fear he had no intention of being actively involved in the management of his property. But in the past year or so he has spent a great deal more time at home, not only making additional improvements, but taking an interest in his tenants and neighbours and, I dare say, keeping the mischief of Mr. Maddison, in check."

Mrs. Bertram expressed her pleasure at Mrs. Morgan's approbation of her brother's recent attentions to his property, but added, "I am sure you were happy to have him at Everingham all of last summer."

"We were surprised, as he had spent almost the entirety of the previous summer away, but very pleased."

"My husband's sister, Miss Julia Bertram was staying nearby with some cousins. I trust you had occasion to make her acquaintance?"

"Oh yes, she was a lovely and elegant young lady. I did not have much opportunity to speak to her but I saw her several times. I hope she is well."

"Quite well, her recent marriage has elevated her to the name of Lady Chandler."

"I am always happy to hear of any worthy young lady being well settled."

"My dear Mrs. Morgan, you must forgive me for taking the liberty of speaking openly of a delicate matter, but we are old friends and I must be satisfied on one point. I wonder whether you ever noticed any attachment between Miss Bertram and Mr. Crawford?"

Mrs. Morgan was thoughtful for a moment then answered, "For my part, I did not. Not on his side. But I wonder what could have engaged your curiosity on such a point."

"I confess I had reason to suspect Miss Bertram of having designs on my brother and his letters from the time seemed to bear out my suspicions. You said you did not observe an attachment on his side, but what of the young lady?"

"I cannot say what her intentions may have been. I do recollect that Mrs. Webb, whose eldest daughter was on intimate terms with Miss Bertram and Miss Dixon, once mentioned the possibility of a match between them and my own surprise upon hearing her say so, for I did not see it." Upon hearing this, Fanny could not help but apprehend that it supported Mr. Crawford's statements about his treatment of Julia last summer. Mrs. Morgan added, "But, I may have had the benefit of intelligence unknown to her."

"Pray, what intelligence do you speak of?" asked Mrs. Bertram eagerly. Fanny now had a brief moment of dread.

"Knowledge of Mr. Crawford," replied Mrs. Morgan, after a quick glance at Fanny, "a better understanding of his character from his growing intimacy with our family, especially with Mr. Morgan. They have become such friends. The two have been often closed up together deep in conversation. I believe it has done both of them a great deal of good."

"Well then," said Mrs. Bertram, "I can only conclude that my supposition must have been entirely correct, and congratulate myself on the occasion."

Though the conversation had produced information that must be of some interest to Fanny, she could not regret the change of subject that followed.

Chapter 25

During the next few days, Fanny frequently found herself in company with the Morgans; the two families met almost daily either at one or the other of their houses or to explore the grounds of Everingham together. On these occasions, Fanny most often settled into conversation with Mr. James Morgan, perhaps because none of the others gave him much notice – a situation she knew something about. The two would sit or walk on their own and converse quietly while the others talked amongst themselves. Fanny found his forthright manner refreshing and there was no discomfort or anxiety, no awkward or confusing feelings, only pleasant, interesting, light conversation. He spoke with respect for his chosen profession, but could not conceal the pragmatism of his own views. He would be ordained because his father had the means of giving him a parish, but he also spoke of the importance of forming a strong connection with the neighbouring landowner in the hope of retaining the living beyond the death of his father.

Fanny and Mr. James Morgan found no shortage of subjects on which to converse. He was a willing and attentive listener whether she was rhapsodising about the natural beauty of the landscape or discussing her favourite literary works. In her private thoughts, Fanny reflected on the amount of time she had been allowed to converse with him alone. She did not wonder about Edmund or Mary, but it had been Mr. Crawford's habit at Mansfield to contrive to speak quietly to her when they were in company together. She discovered that she missed his attentions and his cheerful manner; but she was no longer surprised by such mortifying discoveries when it came to her feelings for Mr. Crawford, she was rather becoming accustomed to them. Sitting and talking with Mr. James Morgan was a pleasant diversion from thinking too much about what such feelings might portend.

One evening when the two families were sitting together after supper, Fanny, looking out the window, observed the clearness of the night sky, and wondered whether it would be favourable for stargazing. When Mr. James Morgan confessed he had never looked up either day or night except to determine whether he should carry an umbrella, she expressed her surprise and doubt. Nevertheless, he agreed to accompany her outdoors – in view of the house – to see if she could spot any of the constellations that were familiar to her.

Meanwhile, inside the house, when Mr. Crawford was able to get Mr. Bertram's attention, he motioned for him to look out the window. "What do you think of that?" he asked quietly.

"I think they are becoming fast friends. I am happy she has found someone with whom she can easily converse, but I fear he stands little chance once William arrives."

Mr. Crawford replied contemplatively, "True. That will be the test."

"What are you suspecting? They have only just met."

"Certainly it is too soon for them to have formed an attachment, but perhaps with time ..."

"You sound as if you are hoping for it. I would have thought you would be against anything of the kind."

"I have resigned myself to her feelings towards me, but I would wish her to find happiness, if possible."

"What is his fortune?"

"He has none of his own but will take over a secondary living of his father's when he is ordained. The income is certainly not enough to marry upon, and the Morgans have many other children to provide for."

"I do not know what my father intends to do for her upon her marriage, but I imagine he would be open to doing something. Are you certain he has no prior attachment?"

"None that I am aware of."

Fanny, of course, knew nothing of this exchange. But the next morning, Edmund invited her to walk with him in the garden with the intent of discovering more about her feelings for the young Mr. Morgan.

He began by asking her generally how she was enjoying her stay. She acknowledged that her time at Everingham had been agreeable but she had not yet seen William. "I am sure it will be a delightful week, but it hardly seems enough time. It will be over too soon, and then we shall return to Mansfield."

"You sound as if you are not looking forward to returning."

"I will be happy to be at home again and to see my aunt and uncle. But I am dreading some of what the autumn will bring. You will be welcoming a child, and I will rejoice with you, but I do not yet know what lies in store for *me*."

"You speak of my father's intent to have you introduced into society."

"I have no wish for it; nor can I be certain of the manner in which he plans to carry out his design. But it does not signify. There is nothing I can do to dissuade him."

"There is one thing ..." She looked at him in confusion. "If you were to form an attachment before the autumn, then there would be no reason for Sir Thomas to proceed with his plan."

She was a little affronted by his hint and as her colour rose, she said, "Surely you cannot still be thinking of Mr. Crawford."

"No, but it seems he is still thinking of you." Fanny was beyond surprised that Mr. Crawford had spoken of his feelings to Edmund after saying nothing to anyone about them for so long. But her reflections changed drastically when Edmund immediately continued, "He wondered whether you might be forming an attachment with Mr. James Morgan." Fanny's eyes widened but she could not find words to respond before Edmund continued. "His observation was not made in the spirit of resentment. He sincerely hopes you can find happiness. I know you have only just met Mr. Morgan, but if there is any chance that it could lead to an attachment, I am sure my father can be persuaded to delay or cancel altogether whatever plans he has formed, as the situation warrants."

"I am gratified by the interest both you and Mr. Crawford have shown in my romantic prospects," replied Fanny, "but I dare to hope I can be allowed to form a friendship without being suspected of any other ambition."

She soon ended the walk and with it the conversation, then fled to her room for quiet reflection. She was angry. But why? What had Edmund said that was offensive? And surely Mr. Crawford's motives were to be commended, given what she knew of *his* feelings. It was the fact that they had discussed it between them that offended her. And now, she was sure she would be too self-conscious to continue her intimacy with Mr. James Morgan. She would constantly be wondering whether either of the other two gentlemen took notice of the time she spent talking with him. There could be no more comfort, no more ease in their conversations. She sighed to herself. Indeed, she would have to avoid him now, just to dispel any notion of their forming an attachment.

Immediately upon resolving that she could not allow Mr. Crawford to persist in the suspicion that she was attached to Mr. James Morgan she searched within herself for the source of those feelings. Why did it signify whether he thought they were attached or not? This led to the most mortifying discovery she had experienced yet. Could it be possible she wanted him to be assured she remained unattached? Could it be possible she hoped he would renew his addresses? This was a new matter entirely upon which to reflect. She did not expect that it would be difficult for her to bring on a renewal of his proposal, should she wish to – as he had openly admitted his feelings to her on more than one occasion and had stopped just short of making a second offer to her in his letter. The more important question, the decisive question, was whether she would accept him. This she could not readily answer, which in itself constituted a substantial change in her feelings – they were no longer an unequivocal negative, and that was all she could say for sure at present.

Chapter 26

Despite all her preoccupation, Fanny had little opportunity to put into practice the resolution she made regarding Mr. James Morgan, as her brother soon arrived at Everingham and consumed all her attention.

Fanny had not seen William since he had sailed from Portsmouth while she was there visiting her family a year and a half ago. She awaited his arrival with eager anticipation, pacing before the drawing room windows that overlooked the front sweep, listening for the sound of a carriage. When she at last perceived his approach, she ran and met him at the door. The others remained in the drawing room to allow her to have William's full attention for the first few moments of their reunion. They returned to the drawing room together.

The remaining part of the day was spent quietly at home. First, Fanny had to thank her brother again and again for sending her the writing set. Then, William related the tale of the capture of the French merchant ship which had supplied it and spoke of his other recent adventures. Fanny could have listened to him forever. She then told William of having met John in London and Mr. Crawford spoke of his quest in finding him. And William and Mr. Crawford shared memories of their time at Hollingsworth together. After dinner, Mrs. Bertram played the harp and William listened with pleasure. Fanny scarcely left his side throughout the evening.

The following morning, Fanny and William walked out alone together. There seemed to be no end of things to talk about. At length, he observed to her, "Mr. and Mrs. Bertram appear to be tolerably happy together. I hope I may conclude your fears to have been unfounded."

"I can hardly say," replied Fanny. "They do seem happy; but there have been quarrels between them. I know this because Edmund has spoken to me about them."

"But do you really think her intentions mercenary?"

"I believe she loves him. She loved him since before Tom's illness. But I am not certain she was prepared to accept him until he became the heir to Mansfield Park. It was the way she spoke of Tom's possible death that was so disheartening, particularly after the unhappy event."

"It was rather indelicate of her to say those things; but if they love one another, as you seem to believe they do, then they may be expected to work out their differences in time."

"They are undoubtedly in love," replied Fanny, "but I have never thought them suited. I suppose, however, it is none of my concern."

"You are allowed an opinion on the subject."

"My opinion is of no consequence. I believe you were correct in your advice, it was not my place to interfere. At the time I wrote to you, I was in the unenviable position of having been made the confidante of both, which I believe was the chief source of my distress."

"That was very unfair to you, but it seems to have all turned out well."

The following day, Mr. Crawford had planned a large dinner party with the hope of raising enough couples for a little ball after dinner. Fanny was a little apprehensive about the evening. She knew the Morgans and had met the Webb ladies once, briefly, the previous week, but there would be some guests with whom she was wholly unacquainted. However, when Mr. James Morgan chose a seat next to her at dinner she was relieved to be able to sit next to someone with whom she was acquainted and with William on her other side she could not have been more satisfied.

In the drawing room, after dinner, Miss Webb immediately sat next to Fanny and began talking to her. "My dear Miss Price," she said, "I have been longing to talk to you again since our meeting last week. I hope your visit has been a pleasant one so far."

"It has indeed been very pleasant. I can scarcely believe that it is half over already."

"You must be delighted to have your brother here! I declare he is rather dashing, and from what I hear quite the adventurer. How you must worry for his safety."

"Oh yes," replied Fanny, "he has been to many places, near and far; and I do worry a great deal, particularly when I have not had a letter from him for a long time."

"Does he enjoy dancing? I think we shall have a dance this evening."

"Yes, he enjoys it very much and rarely gets the opportunity."

"I am happy to hear it. I dare say he will soon have the pleasure. And pray, how is your cousin Miss Bertram? I hope she is well."

"She was married in the spring," replied Fanny, "to Sir Henry Chandler, and has been residing in London."

"Indeed? That is a bit of news! I am very happy for her. She seemed quite eager to get married when I knew her. In truth, we thought she might make a match last year, but it all came to nothing." Fanny could not help feeling some curiosity to hear Miss Webb's account of the events of last summer, but she dared not encourage her to say more. "And now she is married and titled! I am sure she is pleased with her situation; and Miss Dixon must be happy to have her in London. I have been pressing my father to go to London, but he refuses. I should very much like to see it. I imagine you have been there many times."

"No indeed, I have only been to London once, and only for a few days last December."

"You have been more fortunate than me."

"I prefer the fresh air and natural beauty of the country," replied Fanny.

"But there is no one to talk to in the country, or at least in this country. Perhaps in Northamptonshire you have a more varied society, but here there is scarcely anyone worth talking to. One sees the same people so often and none of them has anything new to say or any alteration in person or situation." Then she looked around the room and said, "You may choose any lady in this room, save your own cousin's wife, and I could tell you what she would say if you were to approach her for conversation. You may put me to the test if you wish. It was a game I played once with Miss Bertram and Miss Dixon, though the gentlemen were in the room at the time as well, which made for a far more interesting experiment. Of course, I was right each time! How we laughed; indeed, what a delightful time we all had together last summer."

"I am quite content to take you at your word on the matter, Miss Webb," said Fanny.

"No no, we shall have none of that," laughed Miss Webb. "You shall call me Charlotte."

The gentlemen soon joined them, the dancing began soon after, and Miss Webb did indeed dance with Mr. Price. Fanny was a little apprehensive about the ball. She did not know whether Mr. Crawford meant to dance with her or how she would feel if he did. She danced first with Edmund and then with Mr. James Morgan. Afterwards, Mr. Crawford approached her and asked for the next. She accepted, and as she lined up with him she noticed William looking at her with concern. She managed a smile and received one in return. She and her partner spoke but little, and Fanny had mixed feelings when the dances were over. On the one hand, she was glad to be free of the anxiety created by his proximity, but on the other she had to admit to herself that dancing with him had not been wholly unpleasant.

When tea was served she had a chance to talk to William. "You seem to be enjoying the dancing," she observed to him.

"Yes," he replied. "And you as well." Then in a quieter tone, he added, "I have not mentioned Mr. Crawford to you for fear of distressing you; but after seeing the two of you dancing together just now without, I thought, the appearance of any awkwardness, I hope you do not mind my saying that, from all I have observed since arriving, my anxiety in pressing you to come to Everingham appears to have been unwarranted."

175

"We have been much in company together since Edmund's wedding. And it has been many months since he has ceased the behaviour which distressed me in the past."

"I am very glad to hear it. I would not like anyone causing you distress, but from someone I consider a friend, it would be especially painful."

"You may be easy on my account. I am indebted to him for bringing your gift to me and for his discovery of John in London, and I can never forget what he did to secure your promotion."

"I will allow you to be grateful for the first two, but I am well aware that you suffered for my promotion. He did not do it for me."

"I do not regret it; and any suffering I endured was worthwhile, I assure you. All of that is over now, but you continue to advance."

"My dear Fanny, you are too good; and I cannot express how happy I am to see the two of you on friendly terms. I shall say no more about it."

"Then tell me, how did you like your partners this evening?"

"I liked them all very well," he replied. "Miss Webb seems to be a very lively sort of girl."

"And quite pretty," said Fanny.

He smiled. "Indeed."

The conversation broke up as the tea things were taken away. Miss Webb approached them and claimed Fanny's arm. "Mr. Price," she said playfully, "I insist you stop corrupting your sister with this manly talk. She must have the company of other women. Come Fanny." With that, she led Fanny away, laughing.

"Now," said Miss Webb to Fanny, "are you engaged for the next? Who would you have ask you? I dare say there are so few gentlemen dancing we shall none of us get away without dancing again with the same partner. I do not believe there could be anything untoward in such a small party if Mr. Price were to ask me again." She looked around the room for that gentleman, but observed another. "Mr. Crawford is looking over here. I hope *he* is not thinking of asking me again."

Fanny was not certain of her companion's sincerity but taking her at her word said, "Was he not an agreeable partner?"

"Oh, I did not mean anything like that. But he is always about and I have danced with him many times. He is very polite, but how can anyone think him handsome? If a gentleman is obliged to be plain he ought at least to make up for it with a little gallantry."

Fanny could not help being a little amused at the comment, in spite of herself, and replied only, "Surely he has not always been so reserved?"

"I would not say he is reserved. He has always been lively enough.

Though, I could never understand why Miss Bertram was so wild for him, but it appears from what you told me that she has done better for herself."

"I have not met Sir Henry myself but Mr. and Mrs. Bertram were pleased with him when they made his acquaintance in London, I believe."

The musicians were now taking their places, and the conversation was broken up by both ladies being approached for dancing.

The next few days with William were delightful to Fanny. They dined at the Webbs' – where Miss Webb and Mr. Price continued to become better acquainted – and at the Morgans'. The week was not long enough. In spite of taking long walks together every morning, and spending the whole of each day and evening together in a variety of pursuits, Fanny felt she could never get enough time with her brother. At last, the week was over and on the last night of his visit the Everingham party remained at home, sat down to a family dinner, and spent a quiet evening of music and conversation.

Chapter 27

William departed early. Fanny had awoken to breakfast with him, and she was delighted to have him to herself during those final moments. After he was gone she went into the garden alone, where Mr. Crawford soon joined her. They had not spoken in privacy since her arrival at Everingham, which felt strange after the frequent intimacy of their conversations at Mansfield. Yet, it felt so natural for him to seek her out now in her moment of melancholy following her brother's departure.

He said nothing at first, and only sat down next to her. At length however, he spoke, "I would ask whether you enjoyed your visit with Mr. Price, but I know that you did. I could see how happy you both were while he was here."

She smiled and replied, "Thank you for inviting him here, and for inviting me."

Now he smiled and said, "It was my pleasure. I know you do not get to see him often."

"I suppose I should rejoice in the time we had together rather than lamenting his absence."

"He has only just left us. I think you are entitled to a little sadness over losing his company. I am sure when the sensation passes, you will be supported by all the fond memories of your time together. And you may look forward to your next meeting."

"Who knows when that will be," she replied.

After another few moments of silence, he stood and offering her his hand said, "Will you walk with me?"

She acquiesced and they made their way to the start of the avenue and traversed its length. At first they spoke only of William's visit, recalling the events of the past week. And on expressing his expectation that she would continue to enjoy her remaining time at Everingham, despite William's absence, he observed that she had made some friends since entering the neighbourhood. She wondered whether this was a hint regarding Mr. James Morgan, and in order to avert any suspicion there, she mentioned that she had been getting to know Miss Webb.

"I did notice the two of you talking together the evening they dined with us. Did you find her an agreeable companion?"

"I did not find her disagreeable," said Fanny, "but I confess I was surprised by the intimate way she spoke to me after so short an acquaintance."

"I hope you were not made uncomfortable."

"No, not at all. We spoke of my cousin Lady Chandler. Miss Webb mentioned their friendship last summer."

"I do recall that they were frequently in close confederation together, but that is often the way with young ladies, I believe."

"I do not know," said Fanny. "But I will tell you that what she said to me of my cousin's visit last summer was in accord with some of what you had previously told me."

"I am glad of any circumstance that raises my credibility in your view," he replied.

They walked on quietly until they reached the end of the avenue, and then turned to face the house. "It is lovely," said Fanny.

"The trees are coming along," he replied. "I dare say in another twenty or thirty years, they will begin to look as they should." Then he smiled and added, "Just in time, I suppose, for the younger Master Bertram to cut them down."

Fanny started at the idea of the trees being cut down so soon. Then she was about to protest that he would leave the estate to a son of his own, but thought better of it. Instead, she simply said, "I am sure you will instill an appreciation for these trees in whoever inherits Everingham."

"I will do my best."

She stood in silence enjoying the view. She felt a sense of serenity standing with him amongst the trees, the gentle breeze caressing her form. It had been some time since they had shared this sort of intimate conversation. She thought of the last time they had spoken quietly together. It had been before he left Mansfield Park. And the following day she had found his letter. He must have been wondering whether she had read it and what its effect had been.

At length he spoke. "Shall we return to the house?"

They began walking again and after a few moments, Fanny gathered her courage enough to say, very awkwardly, "I want you to know, I read your letter."

"I am glad you did. I hope you were not angry with me for leaving it."

"No."

"And did it soften your doubts about me?"

"Yes," she replied. She said nothing further but stopped walking and looked at him.

After a moment of silent expectation he said, "Is there anything else, Miss Price? You look as if you wish to say something more."

She made no reply and looked away from him.

"I hope that after all the frank conversations we have shared, you would feel no need for reserve."

She ventured a glance at his face. "It is not a matter of that." Then looking down again, she added, "I ... I do not know what to say."

"Rather, there is something you wish to say but you are uncertain whether you should say it?"

She continued to look downward and still would not speak.

"If you do not wish to speak, I will not press you; but if there is something you want to say, I hope you will say it."

"How can you hope I will say something when you do not know what it is? Perhaps it will turn out to be something you do not like."

"If you are inclined to speak, I would rather hear it than not, whatever it may be. I listen at my own peril."

"It is only that I ... I find myself ... confused."

"Confused?"

She would say nothing further.

"I wonder what you find confusing. I have made no secret of my feelings – from you at least."

She shook her head. "I am not confused about *your* feelings," she said quickly, as she felt the warmth of a blush on her face.

He looked puzzled for a moment. "Are you confused about yours?" he asked cautiously. She made no response. He inhaled sharply before whispering, "Have your feelings changed?"

After a long pause, she sighed and said quietly, "Have they changed? Yes. I mean ... I have learned to think better of you." She would not allow herself to say more. He might choose to be open about his feelings, but she could not meet his frankness. It would be wrong to give him false hope. She had already said, or intimated, too much.

He was quiet for a moment, then said earnestly, "I thank you for telling me this," but pressed her no further.

They walked silently into the house; and after this conversation the gentleman, for his part, gave no further thought to the possibility of her finding happiness with Mr. James Morgan.

The last week at Everingham was spent much in the same manner as the first. There were no more private conversations between Fanny and Mr. Crawford, save one very brief moment immediately before her departure.

"I will be at Mansfield in November, for the christening," he said to her with a glance towards his sister, as they stood outside the carriage.

"Will not you go to Thornton Lacey?"

"I suspect the Bertrams will no longer be at Thornton Lacey by that time, but either way, I intend to impose myself on whichever sister is at Mansfield Parsonage. Until then, I hope you remain well."

"Thank you."

They all said their final goodbyes and within moments the travellers were in the carriage and on their way. Fanny watched through the carriage window as Mr. Crawford walked slowly back into the house.

Chapter 28

The matter of Westminster was settled favourably for Dr. Grant before the summer's end and the Bertrams were moved into Mansfield Parsonage well in advance of Mrs. Bertram's lying in. Of course, this meant that Fanny was now constantly in company with Mr. and Mrs. Bertram. She was asked to the Parsonage almost daily and ever more frequently as Mrs. Bertram progressed closer to her confinement. Mrs. Bertram no longer spoke of her brother to Fanny as a lover, but nevertheless mentioned him very often. Fanny had become accustomed to hearing him spoken of and therefore, could not quite explain the little flutter in her breast at the thought of his return, whenever Mrs. Bertram spoke of his expected visit.

At Michaelmas, there was an addition to the household, in the form of Mrs. Taylor, a lady Sir Thomas had engaged as a companion for Fanny, who now was obliged to partake of the gaieties she had long dreaded. Lady Bertram could not be displeased to have an addition to the assemblage of ladies in her drawing room by day, but she soon learned to feel Fanny's absence in the evenings. Mrs. Norris viewed the matter differently than her sister. She was nigh apoplectic when she learned that Sir Thomas had undertaken such an expense for Fanny's sake (and, in all honesty, almost resented that she had been asked to take on the duties herself without compensation).

Mrs. Taylor proved to be a pleasant companion, and thankfully was more subtle than Fanny had feared in pursuing the true objective of their outings. Fanny obediently went where she was told to go and was at last able to enjoy the delights of society. She began to make new acquaintances and saw again some of the young people who had attended the Mansfield Ball almost two years ago. What she hadn't anticipated when dreading the prospect of husband-hunting was that she might find some friends along the way. Among these was the youngest Miss Maddox, who was in her first season out. After conversing together at the first assembly they attended, they began to look for one another at subsequent balls.

And so Fanny learned to dread her outings with Mrs. Taylor less as the weeks went on. She made friendships at public assemblies which led to invitations to dinners and private balls, or to spend a day at the home of one of her new friends; and she danced with many gentlemen, with less contrivance and intervention by Mrs. Taylor than she had feared would be required. But she had not encountered any gentleman who she had thought of – or who she could suppose had thought of her – after their dances had ended.

In late October, Mrs. Bertram was safely delivered of a healthy boy. It was the wish of Sir Thomas and Lady Bertram to have their daughters at the christening. Likewise, Mrs. Bertram invited both her sister and brother. And so it was, that a large family party was again assembled at Mansfield in November.

Mr. and Mrs. Rushworth arrived on the same day as Sir Henry and Lady Chandler. Mrs. Bertram expected her own sister and brother the following day. As Dr. Grant could not leave his duties, Mr. Crawford was to bring Mrs. Grant from London. And, as young Master Thomas was making his debut at Mansfield Park that evening, the Bertrams had left word at the Parsonage for them to join the party there upon their arrival.

After dinner, the drawing room at Mansfield Park was as animated as it had ever been, as everyone talked of all that had happened since they had last seen one another. Julia, being most recently married, spoke at length of her domestic concerns and announced her own expectation of adding to their number within a few months. Fanny was pleased to see that she and her husband appeared to be happy.

It was into this scene of lively cheerfulness that Mr. Crawford made his return to Mansfield society. The room suddenly became quiet when he and Mrs. Grant entered it, but the newcomers were welcomed cordially and greeted by everyone in turn. Mr. Crawford made his bow to Fanny in form but barely spoke a word to her. For her part, she was happy to see him and was learning to no longer be surprised by such sensations. But it was strange being in this room with him and not speaking with him. So many times when they had been in company together, he would engage her in quiet conversation. In contrast to those intimate moments, there now seemed such a chasm between them. To her feelings, it was just as well. She would not have him seek her out for private discourse in such a setting. With the presence of the former Miss Bertrams, Fanny faded into the background, where she had spent so many years in former times; but she did not regret the change. She sat quietly by, enjoyed the music when it was played, and retired early without, she thought, anyone noticing.

But Sir Thomas had noticed. He had been noticing a great deal of late. He had noticed Fanny's and Mr. Crawford's growing intimacy during the weeks following Edmund's wedding and had allowed whatever existed between them to take its course as his past intervention had, he now thought, been misplaced. The disclosures contained in Fanny's letters had given him a fair idea of what had been carrying on at Mansfield during his time in Antigua, and he was awake to how his daughters behaved in Mr. Crawford's presence now. There was something, some discomfort that perhaps was only perceptible to someone looking for it, in both his daughters, but perhaps a little more in Mrs. Rushworth than Lady Chandler – which was contrary to his expectation. Mr. Rushworth, for his part, did not appear happy with the addition of Mr. Crawford. Sir Henry, however, was very content to converse with him at length. And, while Sir Thomas had not yet wavered in his conviction of Mr. Crawford's being very much in love with Fanny, he wondered that he had hardly even looked at her this evening, which was quite a difference from the quiet conversations he had become accustomed to seeing them share. Mr. Crawford was far more withdrawn than Sir Thomas had before seen him and scarcely spoke to anyone all evening. All in all, however, he had no cause to reproach any of the young people, and all comported themselves as they ought.

During the course of the evening, Mrs. Taylor, who had quickly learned that Lady Bertram tolerated Fanny's absence better when she had several days' notice of it, was telling her about the assembly they would attend later in the week. Some of the young people heard part of the conversation and took up the idea of all of them going. This development increased Fanny's anxiety pertaining to the assembly. She already felt embarrassed about going out in search of a husband and the idea of her relations bearing witness to it made her uncomfortable; but, she reflected that in all probability they would scarcely notice her. She could not help but wonder whether Mr. Crawford would go as well, and if so, whether he would ask her to dance.

In the end, the Rushworths, the Chandlers, and both Edmund and Mr. Crawford all attended the assembly. Mrs. Bertram regretted not being able to attend but it was still too soon after her confinement for dancing. They were obliged to travel in two carriages, the Chandlers and the Rushworths together and Edmund and Mr. Crawford with Mrs. Taylor and Fanny.

Soon after her arrival, Fanny was relieved to be asked for the first dances by Mr. Stone, a gentleman with whom she had danced previously. Once that was settled, she found her way to Miss Maddox, and introduced her to her friends. When the dancing commenced, as she took her place, she saw that Mr. Crawford was standing up with Miss Maddox and smiled her approval.

Afterwards she had such a succession of partners that she was quite fatigued by the time tea was served. And after tea, she was very surprised to be asked to dance a second time by Mr. Stone and began to wonder whether perhaps Mr. Crawford meant not to dance with her at all. She saw him look at her, and she saw Mrs. Rushworth say something to him, but they were too far away for Fanny to hear.

Upon seeing Fanny stand up with Mr. Stone again and seeing Mr. Crawford take notice of it as well, Mrs. Rushworth had not been able to help herself from observing to him, "Fanny looks very pleased to have been asked to dance a second time by that gentleman. It is a sign of particularity, I believe. Perhaps Mrs. Taylor will prove to be worth the expense after all. I hope you shall not be terribly devastated by the event."

"On the contrary, I would be very happy for her."

She laughed. "Have you not yet begun to tire of playing the part of the hero?"

"You are mistaken, Mrs. Rushworth, it is not now, but when you knew me before that I was playing a part." He hesitated a moment here, but considering he might never have a fairer opportunity to put the past to rest, he continued. "I have long since regretted my own folly during that time, and it is my fervent and sincere hope that no real damage resulted from it."

She looked at him in surprise, but his words perhaps had a different effect than what he had expected. Rather than being comforted by his apology, she was affronted by his apparent dismissal as folly of what had previously passed between them. She only smiled as she glanced at the dancers, then seeing Fanny look their way she observed, "Ah, Fanny has seen us talking together. She does not look pleased. Perhaps it is jealousy."

"I am sure it is not."

"Are you so certain of her feelings?"

"Not at all; but she, I believe, is certain of mine."

"Oh yes, everyone knows your feelings. You have made no secret of them."

"It was, perhaps, ill-judged to express them so publicly."

"Indeed, and unfortunate for you, for when the world knows your heart, it likewise knows when your heart is broken."

"Perhaps the world would rejoice. I am sure there are some who would see it as no more than I deserve."

"Perhaps," she agreed, "or, perhaps a worse fate awaits you, perhaps she will marry you after all, and make you miserable for the rest of your life."

"That is not possible," he said simply, then bowed and walked away.

After their dance, Mr. Stone lingered with Fanny a little before returning to his own party. Fanny was rather relieved to have no partner for the next pair of dances as it gave her the opportunity of resting a little. As the dances concluded, Mr. Crawford at last approached her, saying, "Miss Price, if you are not too fatigued, I hope you will dance the next two with me." She smiled and assented.

"You seem to have enjoyed your evening," he observed when they stood up together. She acknowledged it to be so. "Then, being obliged to go out has not been as bad as you feared?"

"No, it has not been entirely unpleasant and, indeed, the experience has been quite different from the expectations I had formed."

"That is the case with most things, I believe."

"Perhaps. I suppose it is possible that I allowed myself to get carried away by my anxieties."

"And some good has come of it; you have made some new friends."

"I have. I see Miss Maddox quite often, I hope you enjoyed your dances with her."

"She is a very pleasant, amiable young lady, who values your friendship greatly."

"You spoke to her of me?"

"She spoke to me of you, yes, in the highest terms. And I am pleased you have made so favourable a connection."

"I have been little accustomed to that sort of companionship, but I have been happy to have someone to talk to at these events; indeed, her entire family has been very kind to me."

"Then I am disposed to approve of them all."

She smiled, but said nothing. Here was the Henry Crawford who had lately been absent from the Mansfield drawing room. Here was the cheerful sweetness she had come to expect from him. As she acknowledged this to herself, she suddenly realized she had grown used to not only his gentle amiability but also to his candid yet subtle reminders of his own feelings. She censured herself for having fallen under the spell of such flattery and was silent for the remainder of the dances.

After these dances Fanny was ready to go home and as neither of the gentlemen who had come with her had the least objection to doing so, she asked Mrs. Taylor to order her carriage directly. On the way home, Mrs. Taylor spoke of nothing but Mr. Stone and his having asked Fanny to dance a second time. She had suspected that he admired Fanny when they had danced together at the previous ball and now she viewed his dancing with her twice as proof of her suspicion.

This was in keeping with Mrs. Taylor's usual style of talk on the way home from a ball, but she and Fanny had always been alone. Fanny did not like having the evening's events canvassed openly before the two gentlemen. She could not help stealing a glance at Mr. Crawford while the topic was under discussion between Mrs. Taylor and Mr. Bertram, but he appeared entirely unaffected by it.

Chapter 29

The ensuing days brought all the family together almost constantly. Fanny had been spending a great deal of time at the Parsonage since Mrs. Bertram's lying in, but now that Mrs. Grant was there she could see no occasion for continuing the habit. Nevertheless, the men of both houses went shooting by day, the women met nearly as often, and the families dined together each evening. Despite this close intimacy, Fanny scarcely spoke to Mr. Crawford again until the christening, and even then, he spoke to her little more than civility required.

The morning after the christening was fair and Fanny took the opportunity to go riding. After being out a little while, however, she noticed another rider approaching and soon recognized him as Mr. Crawford. "Miss Price," he said, when he was close enough for her to hear, "I am very pleased to see you out in the fair weather." He brought his horse alongside hers and they rode on together with the coachman behind.

"It is a pleasant day," she replied quietly.

"I hope you do not mind if I join you for a while."

"Not at all, but you do not wish to be with the other gentlemen?"

"I have had enough of shooting for the present. We have been such a large party for so many days in succession that I wonder your uncle has any birds left on his property. I had some business in the village this morning and felt like going for a ride afterwards. I needed some solitude, perhaps."

She was tempted to observe that riding with her was not solitude, but she thought better of it. They rode on slowly, speaking quietly of the christening, the assembly, and other events of the past week. He spoke more to her now than he had in the whole of the time since his return to the country, and Fanny found both her companion and the conversation to be pleasant. At length, however, he wondered whether she was getting the exercise she needed walking at such a slow pace, and they urged their horses to a trot the rest of the way to Mansfield. Upon arriving they left their horses at the stable and he walked with her back towards the house.

As they came around the corner of the stable, however, they could perceive Mrs. Rushworth and Lady Chandler walking towards the house as well, returning from a call at the Parsonage. "Perhaps I should return to the Parsonage directly," he said suddenly.

"If you wish," she said.

"What I wish is to know what you would have me do. But I know better than to ask. You once told me that I must judge for myself, but I have greater trust in your judgement than in my own."

"I cannot say what you should do, Mr. Crawford. Only you can decide whether it is prudent for you to avoid my cousins; whether you fear any danger from their company."

"The only danger I fear, Miss Price, is causing more pain than I already have."

"You believe that is still possible?"

"I am not certain. What is your opinion?"

"I believe so much time has passed and their situations have undergone such a complete change that neither of them should still be indulging the resentments of the past."

"I do not disagree with you and I would wish to credit them both with having forgotten any past grievances, but Mrs. Rushworth said something to me at the ball when Mr. Stone asked you to dance a second time that made me think some resentment may yet linger."

"Then you have greater knowledge on which to draw than I do, which is why you must judge for yourself."

He looked down and appeared hesitant to speak, but after a moment said, "When she spoke to me in that way, I tried to apologize to her for the past."

"Did you?" asked Fanny in surprise.

"To no avail. The damage, it seems, cannot be undone." He glanced towards the ladies who were walking ever closer. "I will go, but I would wish you to know my motivation. If I consider only my own feelings I would not have their presence influence my conduct."

"Then this is why you have been so quiet lately?"

"Yes, not only for their sake, but for yours as well. I feared that seeing the two of us in conversation together could stir old resentments for which you might be unjustly mistreated. But I am very glad to have met with you today." With that he bowed and returned to the stable to get his horse.

Fanny went inside and her cousins appeared in the drawing room shortly after. Unfortunately, Mrs. Taylor had been talking to Lady Bertram and Mrs. Norris about her hopes for Mr. Stone, yet again. Mrs. Norris wanted to know his income, to determine perhaps whether his attentions to Fanny warranted indignation; but Lady Bertram wanted only to know how close to Mansfield he lived. Mrs. Taylor's answers to each were satisfactory: he was an attorney who lived in the nearby market town. When the former Miss Bertrams arrived, they were called upon to give their impressions of Mr. Stone. They readily complied but seemed little inclined to pursue the topic, though Mrs. Rushworth did hint that she had little hope for the gentleman, observing that she had seen Fanny being at least as receptive to the attentions of other men.

Fanny could scarcely believe Maria would make such a declaration and could see that Mr. Crawford may have been correct about her lingering resentments. Yet, she wondered that her cousin could feel such ill will towards herself; she certainly had done nothing to deserve it. Nevertheless, she listened in silence, determined not to make matters worse by being affronted. As she took up her work, she suddenly had an idea for a new project and, cutting out a fresh square of linen, began to embroider upon it.

Later, when the other ladies retired to dress for dinner, Fanny remained in the drawing room to finish a little more work on her new project. A few minutes after the other ladies had gone, Mrs. Rushworth returned to the room to retrieve her copy of *La Belle Assemblee* which she had left behind.

"Are you still working?" she asked upon seeing Fanny.

"I am just finishing up a few stitches," replied Fanny, a little surprised that Mrs. Rushworth had addressed her.

"You must give yourself time enough to dress so that you might look your best for our neighbours at the Parsonage."

Fanny looked at her curiously. "It does not much signify how I look," she replied putting down her work, "I am scarcely ever noticed by anyone."

"There is one amongst the Parsonage party who looks at you quite often," replied Mrs. Rushworth. "I would warn you about him, but it is not necessary as he has already made you an offer, so his attentions to *you* must be sincere."

Fanny stood as she replied quietly, "I never sought his attentions."

"No, and you proved it quite thoroughly by rejecting him. I do not know which is more curious, that you refused him or that you continue to admit his attentions after having done so."

Fanny approached Mrs. Rushworth and reached out her hand. The lady reciprocated, almost instinctively. "My dear cousin," said Fanny, "do you truly not know? I refused him because of what he did to you … and to Julia." With that, she released her cousin's hand and fled the room.

The rest of the evening was unremarkable. The moment between Fanny and Mrs. Rushworth in the drawing room did not instantly heal all resentments or make the ladies best of friends, but it perhaps gave them each something to think about.

Fanny's cousins left Mansfield a few days later and she could not regret it. Mr. Crawford and Mrs. Grant remained at the Parsonage, however, and Fanny saw them often. Mr. Crawford's manners became more animated. He spoke more to Fanny whenever the families met and she found the change pleasing; she welcomed the return of their former intimacy. To her, everything seemed more comfortable now and she found herself reflecting on how very sad it was that there could be such awkwardness and discomfort among women brought up together in the same house. Her cousins had never been friendly towards her, but it seemed that the influence of Mr. Crawford on all of them would have a lasting effect. She found herself wondering whether time could do away with such resentments, and in the process she discovered that when she thought about her future, Mr. Crawford was in it, and when she thought of whether her cousins' resentments could be overcome, she wondered whether they could ever be reconciled to her as Mr. Crawford's wife.

Once the Rushworths and the Chandlers had gone away, Mrs. Grant soon began to talk of returning to London herself. Fanny knew Mr. Crawford must go with her, but could not help wondering whether he would return to Mansfield or go to Everingham.

The week following the departure of her cousins brought a new source of joy to Fanny. Invitations were received at both Mansfield Park and the Parsonage to a ball to be given for Miss Maddox. Fanny had known that Mr. Maddox had been contemplating giving a ball for his daughter, and was very pleased to receive the invitation. The Parsonage party called on the ladies of the Park to share in all the felicity the expectation of a private ball generally gives. And when Mr. Crawford had a moment to speak with Fanny in relative privacy he took the opportunity to secure her for the first two dances. She was happy to know he would remain in the country at least until the ball.

Fanny was gratified to be engaged for the first dances and was further gratified the next day to receive a note from Miss Maddox inviting her to spend the morning with her the day of the ball. She readily accepted and on the appointed day, she and Mrs. Taylor set off for the Maddox home after breakfast.

Fanny and Miss Maddox spent a long but pleasant morning. The house was alive with preparations for the ball and the young ladies were anxious with anticipation. They went to Miss Maddox's room to look at each other's gowns and so that Fanny could help her friend decide on which gloves, slippers and jewellery to wear. Once they were alone, Miss Maddox almost immediately began hinting at an attachment between Fanny and Mr. Stone.

"He is great friends with my brother Charles, you know," said Miss

Maddox, "and he had dinner here last week and asked me a thousand questions about you." Fanny was a little surprised. She had not thought Mrs. Taylor's expectations with regard to Mr. Stone to be well founded. Miss Maddox smiled. "He wanted to know your fortune, of course, but none of us could answer."

"But I have no fortune."

"Everyone knows your situation, of course; and we all agreed that surely your uncle must intend to do something for you. Otherwise, why would he undertake the expense of Mrs. Taylor?"

"I have no such expectation," replied Fanny, feeling very uncomfortable about being the subject of such a conversation.

"Nevertheless, I would not be surprised if he should ask you for the first two dances."

"But I am already engaged for the first two to Mr. Crawford," Fanny replied with heightened colour.

"Poor Mr. Stone," cried Miss Maddox with a smile. "I am sure he expected the privilege of opening the ball with you, but it might do him a little good to have to wait for the second pair of dances. And, I do believe, if he asks you to dance a second time again tonight as he did at the last ball, we shall know his intentions."

Fanny smiled back, but hoped to avoid any further conversation on the subject of Mr. Stone. Mrs. Taylor had also expected Fanny to open the ball with Mr. Stone. She looked upon them happily when he made the application almost immediately after his arrival, and was rather surprised to hear Fanny decline due to a prior engagement. It was, however, but a temporary disappointment and the gentleman was assured of Fanny's hand for the second pair of dances. He then left her to seek out another partner for the first.

At last, the ball began. Fanny's feelings were much more comfortable than they had been at the previous assembly, when she had been anxious about whether Mr. Crawford would dance with her. Now they danced together with unalloyed pleasure. And afterwards, Fanny had a partner for almost every dance until supper, when Mr. Stone approached her again; and she was a little mortified by his continued attentions. He was not an unpleasant partner, but Fanny had no wish to encourage speculation about his intentions. When she glanced at Mrs. Taylor however, she saw her talking animatedly to Mrs. Maddox while looking towards Fanny with an approving smile.

The dancing resumed after supper and Fanny became quite fatigued as the ball carried on late into the night. She was almost as happy for the respite from dancing when she did not have a partner as she was to be asked to dance. Once again, Mr. Crawford applied to her after she had been sitting out a pair of dances. She was a little surprised at her own pleasure and by the return of her energy as they lined up for the dance.

"You seem to have enjoyed your evening," he observed.

"I have. And have you enjoyed yours?"

"Very much," he replied. "You look well, less fatigued than at the last assembly."

"I do feel more energetic this evening."

"And how was your morning with Miss Maddox?"

"Very pleasant. I enjoy her company."

"She appears quite satisfied with how the evening is turning out."

"I believe she is."

"And Mrs. Taylor also appears very satisfied. I do not think I have ever seen her so animated."

"She presumes too much, I think."

"I suppose then, that I too have given her something to think about by dancing with you a second time."

"I do not think she sees *your* dancing with me a second time in the same way."

He smiled but only replied, "You shall soon discover her thoughts, I believe."

"At least I shall be alone with her on the drive home this time."

"I know you did not like the conversation last time. I did not like it either."

Fanny could not help but smile softly but made no reply.

After these dances were ended, Fanny requested her carriage and sought out Miss Maddox to take leave. The latter immediately began to express her raptures on behalf of her friend over the events of the evening. Undoubtedly, she believed Fanny to be receiving her hints and encouragement with joy; and she squeezed her hand as she whispered, "I would not be surprised if he calls on you very soon to make his declarations. You must write to me once it is all settled."

Fanny only smiled and was very relieved when her carriage was announced. Mrs. Taylor talked of nothing but Mr. Stone for the entirety of the drive home. She was quite satisfied with the conquest of the gentleman and perfectly ready to give herself credit for the match. The only alloy to her triumph was in Fanny's lack of enthusiasm. She could elicit nothing in Mr. Stone's favour from her young charge. Fanny was as ready as any girl her age to talk over the fashions and the music and the supper; but of all

192

the innumerable young ladies Mrs. Taylor had known, she had never met one who so little liked to talk of her dance partners or speculate as to her future prospects. This, Fanny had no inclination for, and she said very little in response to Mrs. Taylor's hints. But the lady's joy was unabated. The thought had not entered into her head that Fanny might not accept the first offer of marriage made to her.

For her part, however, Fanny was soon tolerably reconciled to her own feelings. The contrast of what she felt in response to Mr. Stone's obvious attentions gave her clarity with regard to her feelings towards his rival. She had been considering her own feelings with great solemnity of late, and questioning all her previous assumptions. Aside from her objections to Mr. Crawford's former behaviour, she had been convinced of their being incompatible by dissimilarity of inclination, habits and taste; yet, she had since learned through her conversations with him and witnessing his lifestyle at Everingham, that they had more in common than she had previously thought, and the differences could be turned to the advantage of each by expanding the minds of both. As for their tempers, she had to acknowledge that on this point, Edmund had been correct – though she imagined he had been thinking more of his own situation when he had given his opinion that two people with dissimilar tempers could nevertheless be suitable companions. And while Edmund's marriage itself did not absolutely prove his theory, Fanny nevertheless grew more open to the possibility of its being correct in her own case. She now believed Mr. Crawford's constant cheerfulness could serve to support her own spirits; and her more serious, quiet manner might bring the calm and serenity he sometimes lacked. The liveliness of Mr. Crawford's spirits no longer oppressed her, ever since he had taken a gentler approach in addressing her. She acknowledged to herself that she had found many of her conversations with him pleasing, and had grown comfortable in his company. Indeed, she now believed her former views as to their compatibility may have been influenced by her ill opinion of his character; and as her opinion of his character had improved, so did her views of their compatibility. In short, she no longer thought him unsuited to herself.

She knew what she had to do, the question was how to do it. Notwithstanding all the very open conversations she had shared with him she could never be so bold as to openly invite him to propose again, however assured of his wish to do so she might be. He had learned his lesson after his last proposal perhaps too thoroughly, and seemed determined not to impose upon her again in that way. Yet, he had remarked more than once on his wish to speak more plainly but for her disinclination to hear his declarations. Thus, the invitation must be made, but it must be subtle, it must allow for the possibility, however small, that he might choose not to renew his addresses; she could not place him in a position that denied him the power of choice, however openly he had hinted about his own feelings.

On his and Mrs. Grant's last evening before returning to London, the Parsonage party was engaged to dine at the Park. In the East room after dressing for dinner, Fanny opened one of her boxes. It contained a necklace, nestled atop a folded handkerchief, the one Mr. Crawford had handed her the day of Edmund's wedding; she had cast it aside and forgotten about it until finding it in a corner some days later. But the necklace was her object. She had never worn it since the Mansfield Ball two years ago. She withdrew it from the box, recalling how Miss Crawford had given it to her, had acknowledged it to have been a gift to her from her brother, and had later admitted that the idea of giving it to Fanny had been entirely his. She put it on, then, looking at herself in the glass, she could not help but smile. She was certain Mr. Crawford would notice it, but she felt secure that he could choose to ignore the hint, if he was so inclined – and tomorrow he would be gone, with no embarrassing display on either side. It was about as subtle an invitation as she could contrive. Her mind made up, she went down to dinner.

The necklace served its purpose as well as Fanny could have hoped. She perceived that Mr. Crawford noticed it instantly. He caught her eye, but said nothing. He was uncharacteristically silent the whole evening and looked grave and contemplative. She wondered whether he might be considering his options. It would be very wrong of him after so many hints to refuse to follow through on them when given the opportunity. And yet, she could scarcely doubt him after all his attentions and solicitude towards her, and his sometimes less than subtle expressions of his own feelings. It occurred to her now that he had at last convinced her of his sincerity. If that had indeed been his only object, then one more wrongful act to his credit would signify very little and no one else need know; her former doubts would be vindicated and she would never regret him.

When deciding to wear the necklace she had only sought a fair opportunity for Mr. Crawford to notice it, she had not considered whether he would have time to act on the hint before his departure for London in the morning and now she doubted there would be any such opportunity. But perhaps it was for the best; the time spent away would allow him to carefully consider whether he indeed wished to renew his proposals. And if he should not return, she would know his decision. But as she reflected on the latter possibility, she could not convince herself that this would be the outcome of all that had been passing between them over the past two years. Indeed, if she had been able to believe such an outcome was possible, she would not have worn the necklace.

Mrs. Bertram also noticed Fanny's necklace and, upon seeing it, spoke fondly of her own memories of the Mansfield Ball. Fanny feared Mrs. Bertram might guess her purpose in wearing it and she did look from Fanny to her brother once or twice when talking of it, but if she wondered why Fanny suddenly chose to wear the necklace again on this particular evening, she said nothing of it.

Chapter 30

Mr. Crawford departed for London the following morning. He had not stated the exact date of his intended return to Mansfield, but he had said he would be back very soon. Fanny expected him to be gone a few days, or a week at the most. She imagined he might be deliberating on whether to propose to her again. On the fourth day of his being gone, however, Mrs. Bertram began to wonder at his not yet having returned. And, after a week, Fanny began to wonder if he had decided against her.

She dared not ask Mrs. Bertram if he had written, and after the first week had passed, Mrs. Bertram finally mentioned that she had received a letter from him, but it contained no news other than that he had been detained in London. Fanny wondered what could have detained him and her imagination began to get away from her. For the second week of his absence, she was perfectly willing to give him the benefit of the doubt. But as she entered the third week, she began to take seriously the possibility that he meant not to return at all.

She took out the letter he had written to her and read it again in an effort to suppress her doubts. How could anyone write such a letter without sincerity? She reflected on all the things he had said to her, all the hints of his feelings, all the acts of kindness, all the smiles, and these reflections served to renew her confidence in his intentions. Yet she could not reconcile them with his continued absence. He had complete freedom to go wherever he wished and had certainly exercised it liberally ever since she had known him. Even Mrs. Bertram said she could not imagine what could be keeping him in London. If it was a matter pertaining to Everingham then he would have gone to Everingham. Likewise, if his uncle had convinced him to stay longer, he would undoubtedly mention that to his sister; and he had defied the Admiral in the past. Fanny could think of no reason that would compel him to stay in London against his will and so concluded that it must be his wish to remain there.

To add to the mystery, Mrs. Grant had written that Mr. Crawford was no longer staying in her home. Upon receiving this letter Mrs. Bertram felt certain her brother must have gone to stay with their uncle. This was not an encouraging supposition. Fanny knew the admiral to be against marriage and to have engaged in conduct that could only set an unfavourable example to a young mind that might be conflicted. She knew Mr. Crawford loved and admired his uncle, and that if he should speak to the admiral on the question of matrimony, the latter would most assuredly try to talk him out of it. If he had been wavering before as to what he should do, the advice and entreaty of so near a relation might settle every doubt. In that case he would return no more.

Indeed, upon learning that Mr. Crawford was no longer in his sister's house, Fanny could not help but wonder whether he had fallen into his old habits in London. Surely, he would have been in company with old friends and acquaintances, and women with whom he had perhaps carried on flirtations in previous times. She read his letter again. How could he go back to such habits after having acknowledged them to be wrong, after expressing such regret and disavowing even any temptation? Yet, he had not been spending much time in London; it would be much easier, she supposed, for him to disavow temptation when it was not immediately before him; but could he be steadfast in his resistance when surrounded by his old acquaintance? Then she grew ashamed of herself for these reflections. After two years of constancy, how could she doubt him after only three weeks of absence?

By the fourth week, however, Fanny had resigned herself to the probability that Mr. Crawford would not return to Mansfield and would not renew his addresses to her. Mrs. Bertram had received another letter from him confirming his residence at his uncle's house, but he gave no further information to explain his continued absence than what he had previously written. And surely, it would be within his power to send some hint to Fanny through his sister, if he wished to. Every attempt Fanny made to give him the benefit of the doubt resulted in the same conclusion: there was no rational way to reconcile his continued absence with any intent to act on her invitation. Fanny could not help but think of Maria two years before, when she had hoped Mr. Crawford would declare himself, but instead he had fled, or of Julia's disappointment the previous summer. She began to wonder how she could have allowed him to take her in at last when she had the benefit of knowing of his previous behaviour. She was determined now to put the whole matter out of her mind. She had already recovered once from disappointed love and was sure she could do so again.

These reflections were a heavy burden on her mind, but she was not left without other sources of agitation. The month following Mr. Crawford's departure from Mansfield had by no means been uneventful. After dancing with her at yet another ball, Mr. Stone had ridden to Mansfield, with all the gallantry of a lover, to call on Fanny and to meet her family. For her part, she made every effort to discourage him, but Mrs. Taylor's behaviour towards him sent such a contrary message and Fanny's own demeanour was so gentle and serene that the gentleman could not have known how little welcome his attentions were to their object.

On the second such visit, Mrs. Taylor suggested that Fanny show Mr. Stone some of the grounds. Thus, they walked alone together in the shrubbery, but upon their return Mrs. Taylor's hopes in the outcome of the meeting were disappointed. Nonetheless, a positive engagement was made for him to return for dinner in a few days' time and enough hints passed between the gentleman and Mrs. Taylor to make his intentions clear.

Mrs. Taylor was so certain that he meant to offer for Fanny on this meeting that she told Sir Thomas to expect the application. She recounted the conversation to Fanny, "Sir Thomas was very pleased to hear of our progress with Mr. Stone. I am sure he feared we might end the season without a proposal and that we would have to try again next year. It shall not be one of the great conquests of all time, to be sure, but a very respectable one for you, my dear, and one which your uncle approves. It will all be settled on his next visit. By this time next week, you will be an engaged woman."

This kind of talk of Sir Thomas' approval provided Fanny with new sources of anxiety and reflection. What did she owe her uncle? Was she being selfish in not even considering Mr. Stone's addresses? He was a good man and a respectable one. There was nothing objectionable in his character to give her the same grounds for refusal she had stood upon the last time she received a proposal. What excuse could she give Sir Thomas? Could she justify continuing to be a burden upon him when she could have an establishment of her own? Her uncle had gone to the trouble and expense of bringing Mrs. Taylor to Mansfield for the sole purpose of getting Fanny married. She could not help but feel it would be ungrateful indeed to refuse a respectable offer with no good reason.

She again felt helpless – and again reflected that she had been placed in this position through no action or choice of her own. Indeed, her situation of dependence, she felt, deprived her of the luxury of choice. And, she had no one with whom to discuss her feelings and her doubts. Edmund would only encourage and expect her to accept Mr. Stone. And the thought of her cousin brought on the most mortifying prospect yet: it was upon Edmund and his wife whom she would eventually become dependent should she refuse Mr. Stone. Almost anything seemed preferable to that.

The idea of marrying without love had always been repugnant to her. But these reflections on her duty to her uncle together with Mr. Crawford's continued absence began to open her mind to different ideas. After two unsuccessful trials of being in love, the possibility that perhaps liking and respecting someone was enough seemed tolerable. After all, Edmund had married for love and nevertheless suffered discord in his marriage. The opportunity to fix her fate once and for all which lay before her held some appeal; yet to rush into an engagement so soon after her disappointment seemed ill-advised. She had not ceased to think of Mr. Crawford, or to expect him to appear at any moment; though her rational self had accepted that he would not return.

Fanny was still in this state of indecision and uncertainty on the morning appointed for Mr. Stone's visit. She awoke to the thought that the day had come which would decide her fate. Later, as she was alone in the East room before breakfast writing her letters and trying not to dwell on the choice the day was likely to bring, she heard a knock at the door. It was such a rare occurrence that it made her start. She invited whoever had knocked to enter, and when the door opened, she saw Mr. Crawford standing before her alone.

Her heart quickened and she arose in agitation as she said, "Mr. Crawford!"

"Good morning, Miss Price. Are you so surprised to see me?" he asked, closing the door behind him.

She could not answer him for a moment, then noticing his attire she exclaimed, "What has happened?"

"My uncle," he replied. "My uncle has died."

"Oh," she said, now understanding this must have been the reason for his long absence, but why had he said nothing to his sister? "I am sorry, so sorry to hear it."

"Thank you. He was very ill when I called on him upon arriving in London. Indeed, I meant to stay only one night in town but when I went to his house that first evening after dinner, I found him gravely ill."

She looked at him expectantly, but instead of speaking further about his uncle, he said, "I shall tell you everything about it, but first I must speak to you on another matter. I will delay my purpose no longer."

Fanny's heart began to flutter. She could guess at his purpose. And without further preamble he took a step towards her saying, "Miss Price, you know my feelings … you know that I love you. I came here to ask you now what I should have asked you before I left for London: whether you would do me the very great honour of accepting my hand."

Fanny was now under such a tumult of emotion, from the feelings of despair over the past few weeks, the confusion created by Mr. Stone's attentions, the news of the death of the admiral, and now yet another reversal of her beliefs regarding the gentleman who stood before her, that she could not immediately respond to his proposal and instead began pacing the room in agitation.

"You have been away for so long," she said at last. "I had no news of you. I thought …"

He looked at her for a moment but she would not finish the sentence. "You thought I meant not to return?"

She shook her head. "I do not know. I cannot say. So much has happened. And, Mr. Stone …"

At this he started, "You have not engaged yourself to him?" he asked quickly.

"No … no, I have not, but he … he has called on me a few times and … he is engaged to dine with us today."

"I know. My sister mentioned his visits in her last letter." He paused a moment then added, "I regret that I had to leave you to wonder at my intentions. Though I do wish you could have had greater faith in me."

"You have been gone above a month, without any explanation."

"I know very well how long it has been," he replied with feeling, "and what you must have thought of me." She made no reply. He continued, "When I saw my uncle, he begged me to promise him that I would not tell my sister of his condition and I could not help but acquiesce to this final wish, though I knew it would cut off my only means of getting news to you of my reason for not immediately returning to Mansfield." He paused but she still said nothing. "When I first saw him, he was confined to his bed, yet he would admit no one, not even the physician. He was quite alone and at first unwilling to see me, though he did not have the power to prevent me from entering his room. Nevertheless, he would not speak to me calmly or admit the physician until I made him the promise he demanded, which I did, partially out of fear that his agitation over the matter would only serve to worsen his condition."

"But how is it that you were not sooner made aware of Admiral Crawford's illness? He, perhaps, did not want to tell you, but I had been led to believe he did not live alone."

Mr. Crawford sighed heavily. "He never bestowed the privileges of a wife on that lady, and so it would be unfair to expect her to undertake the responsibilities of one. It would have been very good of her to write to me with news of his illness, but in the end I cannot blame her for not doing so. He was, in fact, quite alone when I found him. She had left him before my arrival, and the servants had been ordered to turn away all his friends, and to reveal his condition to no one.

"According to my uncle, they quarrelled. When she saw that he was gravely ill, she inquired as to whether he intended to make any provision for her future maintenance. When he refused to summon his lawyer, she packed her belongings and left the house. This may have contributed to his reasons for eliciting my promise. I think he imagined Mary calling on him in his final days with the expectation of receiving something on his death. But he was very ill and feverish and not thinking rationally. After my arrival, of course, I brought in the physician, but it was too late. He lingered only these few weeks before his death, and he spent them almost entirely in restless, fevered agitation. The funeral was yesterday, I arrived at the Parsonage very late last night."

"I am so sorry," repeated Fanny.

"I have to go back to London. The admiral left all his affairs in disorder. There are many matters I need to attend to on his behalf. I came here only to speak to you and it is my intent to depart again tomorrow. If you need time to consider my proposal, then you shall have it – as much as you require." She looked away from him, shaking her head.

"What is it?" he asked gently.

"I have been doubting your constancy because you were gone a month, yet you have been so patient for so long, and now still, after everything, you continue to be patient with me."

He smiled. "I believe you are worth the wait, Miss Price."

She returned his smile and then in a sudden flash of remembrance, she said, "I made you a gift."

"Have you?" he asked with obvious surprise as she crossed the room to retrieve it.

"Yes," she replied, pulling a handkerchief from one of her boxes and handing it to him. She had embroidered his initials in one corner, entwined with a vine of leaves. "A new handkerchief to make up for the one you gave me."

He was speechless for a long moment upon receiving it; then, looking at her, he said, "Is this …" but his voice caught and after a moment's pause he started again, "You mean to accept me, then?"

"Yes," she replied quietly.

Now he breathed in deeply and whispered, "Truly?"

"Yes."

After another pause he asked again, "Are you quite certain?"

"Are you hoping I will change my mind?"

"No," he said quickly, closing the distance between them, "of course not."

He took her hand and kissed it gently. Neither said anything for a long moment.

At length, the gentleman looked at the handkerchief again. "Surely you have not been working on this while doubting that I would return."

"No, I finished it before you left for London."

He looked a little surprised. "This is not the work of a moment. How long have you been decided?"

She was a little embarrassed and only replied, "In truth, I started it before I was decided, or at least before I knew I was."

He looked at his gift again and putting it in his pocket, asked "You wore the necklace on purpose then?"

"You know very well that I did."

"I have long known that you disapproved of my having convinced my sister to give it to you, and perhaps it was wrong of me; but ever since our last meeting I have been unable to regret it." He raised his hand to caress her cheek and whispered, "You know not how the image of you wearing that necklace has sustained me this past month."

"Your uncle's illness must have been a difficult time for you."

"I spent many long nights in the sick room hoping that whatever feelings motivated you to make such a gesture could withstand my continued absence – and the attentions of another."

"I confess, I had begun to believe you would not return."

"I wanted nothing more than to return to you. You had given me hope, more than hope. The necklace was a very clever device."

"Yet you believed I could make such an invitation without being certain of my own response."

"I confess I was much more sanguine that evening than I was this morning. But you must forgive me for doubting that you could accept me after I spent so much time certain that you never would." After another brief silence, he continued, "I should have spoken before I left for London, but I did not want to rush such a conversation and I intended to return directly."

"I thought you wanted time to consider whether to act on my invitation."

"Did you?"

"You were so grave and quiet that evening."

"I was astonished and overwhelmed. But I never for a moment wavered in either my feelings or my wishes." Then smiling he added, "I believe I resolved to renew my proposal within perhaps half a minute of seeing you that evening."

She only smiled in response. Another long silence ensued between

202

them, which was at length broken by Fanny, "If I do not go down to breakfast soon, Mrs. Taylor will send someone to check on me."

"Very well," he said with a sigh. "I will call on you and the other ladies in the course of the morning and tomorrow I return to London." She nodded her understanding. Then he said, "I will be back."

"I know you will," she replied meaningfully.

Then, after a lingering look, he walked to the door. But when he reached it, he turned around, moved swiftly back to where she stood and swept her into his arms. He held her thus for a moment and whispered, "Thank you."

When he released her, she only smiled. He returned her smile and left the room. Then, she moved to the window to watch him walk towards the Parsonage. She thought she could see him take the handkerchief out of his pocket and look at it again as he was walking.

Chapter 31

Upon Fanny's entry into the breakfast room, Mrs. Taylor exclaimed, "There you are. I was about to send for you. It would not do to have you indisposed today."

"I am well," replied Fanny.

"Indeed, you look very well. Your colour and bloom appear better than I have seen in many weeks," and looking at Lady Bertram she added, "I can guess why."

"It is all being done very properly," said Lady Bertram. "I only hope Mr. Stone will not take you too far away, Fanny."

Fanny's heart sank at this comment. But even as she reflected on the great distance between Mansfield and Everingham, Mrs. Taylor was reassuring Lady Bertram that she would be settled nearby.

Now Fanny felt compelled to speak up, to attempt to curb the expectations of the ladies. "My dear aunt, we must not speculate as to Mr. Stone's intentions."

"Speculate?" cried Mrs. Taylor, "He has made his intentions quite clear. He would be using you – and indeed all of us – very ill if he has been coming here without meaning anything by it."

"Indeed, he would," affirmed Lady Bertram. "And Sir Thomas expects him to offer for you."

"Has he spoken to my uncle?" asked Fanny with alarm.

"Not yet, I think. Sir Thomas did not say so."

Fanny could say nothing further. She knew she would never convince her aunt of anything contrary to Sir Thomas' expectations. She was relieved Mr. Stone had not spoken to Sir Thomas; and she only hoped he would have the good sense to speak to herself first, before applying to her uncle.

The ladies were joined in the drawing room by Mrs. Norris and spent the morning in their usual employments. But Fanny could not settle her mind. She was happy but nervous and confused as well, waiting expectantly for Mr. Crawford's promised visit but not looking forward to Mr. Stone's, and dreading the possibility of their calling at the same time. It was well past luncheon when Mr. Crawford finally arrived with his sister and young Master Thomas. Once they were all seated, Fanny worked diligently, scarcely raising her eyes, lest her embarrassment should betray her. But the other ladies were distracted first upon finding out that Mr. Crawford was among them once again and then upon noticing his attire, of which they, of course, required a full explanation. He answered all their questions and, along with his sister, accepted their condolences graciously.

After the subject was exhausted, it occurred to Lady Bertram to include him in the invitation to dinner which had already been extended to Mr. and Mrs. Bertram. This gave Mrs. Taylor an opening to remind Mrs. Bertram, with a glance towards Fanny, that Mr. Stone was expected for dinner as well. She had, in fact, already begun looking at the clock in anticipation of his arrival in time to settle everything with Fanny before dinner. Fanny felt all the awkwardness of being the subject of such a pointed reference even more acutely due to the presence of Mr. Crawford in the room. After many more minutes of agitation and checking of the clock on the part of Mrs. Taylor, Mr. Stone at last arrived. He was welcomed with enthusiasm by all except the unacknowledged lovers. For her part, Fanny only tried to maintain her composure while Mr. Crawford, though not enthusiastic, was perfectly civil.

Mr. Stone chose the seat closest to Fanny and the other ladies conversed amongst themselves with the obvious intent of allowing them some privacy. Mr. Crawford said nothing at first. Fanny did not dare raise her eyes from her work as Mr. Stone spoke quietly to her of some improvements he was contemplating to his own humble abode. She did not dare to venture a glance at Mr. Crawford, and therefore had no idea whether he was looking at her, but she felt his presence keenly. She now understood why he had chosen to call so late in the day, he had wanted to be there during Mr. Stone's visit. And his presence along with his sister's made it impossible for Mr. Stone to contrive a moment alone with Fanny – much to Mrs. Taylor's vexation.

Fanny felt her colour rise, and she could perceive that Mr. Stone noticed it and smiled, probably under a misapprehension as to its meaning. Then at last she heard Mr. Crawford speak. He entered into the conversation of the other ladies with his usual cheerfulness. He sounded as if he had not a care in the world and Fanny wondered at his abilities; how different he was now from their conversation in the East room earlier. Yet, his light-hearted manner of speaking now helped curb her own awkward feelings so that she could at least converse civilly with Mr. Stone.

To Fanny, the afternoon seemed interminable, but at last Lady Bertram rose to dress for dinner. Mr. Stone announced his intent of walking into the village to pass the time until the dinner hour. Mr. Crawford offered himself as a companion, as he had no need to alter his own apparel. Fanny was a little surprised and wondered at Mr. Crawford's motivation. For his part, however, Mr. Crawford had no intention of speaking to Mr. Stone at all about the obvious reason for his presence at Mansfield, but it was Mr.

Stone who brought up the subject.

They had been talking of Sir Thomas and of the former Miss Bertrams as they walked along, when Mr. Stone asked, "Do you know what his intentions are for his niece? I cannot find out what her fortune is."

"I do not believe she has any fortune," replied Mr. Crawford.

"A man in my position cannot afford to aim very high," said Mr. Stone with a sigh. "But a girl in Miss Price's situation, who comes from a respectable family, with an affluent patron, would suit perfectly – if only her uncle would give her something. She is pretty enough, I dare say, well mannered, quiet, obedient, all excellent qualities in a wife. But you have been acquainted with the family for some time, I believe, what is your opinion? Will her uncle give her anything?"

"My opinion, Mr. Stone, is that you aim higher than you imagine."

"Then you do think Sir Thomas will provide for her," Mr. Stone responded hopefully.

"You misunderstand me. I have no idea what Sir Thomas intends."

"I do not know what to do. Should I speak to the uncle first or the niece. What would you do in my situation?"

Mr. Crawford could not help but laugh a little at the irony of the question. But, perceiving that it might be in his power to save Fanny some measure of distress, he responded earnestly, "I would, under no circumstances, speak to Sir Thomas without having first secured the hand of the lady." He left unsaid that he had tried that stratagem himself in the past without success.

"Then you think I should propose to her?"

"I did not say that."

"You think I should not?"

"I lay it down as a general rule, Mr. Stone, that if a man doubts as to whether he should propose to a woman or not, he certainly ought not to do so."

Mr. Stone only laughed off this piece of sagacity. "That is why you are still single, I suppose."

"I only mean that marriage is not a state to be safely entered into with doubtful feelings."

"But what is to become of us men if we are to marry only when we never have any doubts? Nay, we would all be single forever under such a rule! Besides, I am not in doubt as to my wish to marry; it is only the lady, and more specifically her fortune, of which I am in doubt."

"Perhaps the decision to marry should be deferred until after one has met the right lady rather than the reverse."

"How romantic you are! I cannot afford to be so. Many ladies can be *the right lady* once a man has grown tired of living alone. You can have no trouble, I am sure, in procuring whatever company you like at any time you wish; but a man such as myself – making his own way amongst the gossips of the country – must have a wife to secure any convenience of that kind." Mr. Crawford, for all his worldliness, was a little shocked by the frankness of this rather pointed reflection and made no reply. After a few minutes of silence, his companion continued, "I will not be able to do it today, unless I can contrive a meeting with her before dinner."

"Are you assured of a favourable reply?" asked Mr. Crawford. Here Mr. Stone looked at his companion with great wonder, as if just discovering a new idea. It had not, in fact, occurred to him that she might refuse him. Mr. Crawford laughed again and said, "It is conceivable for a woman to turn down an offer of marriage."

"I know it is, of course. A woman of fortune, perhaps might. But not such a one as Miss Price; in her situation, I think she must take what she can get."

"And are you assured of her having no prior attachment?"

"I was given every assurance of it by Miss Maddox. They are such intimate friends and, you know, young ladies always tell one another those things. "

"Has Miss Price given you any encouragement?"

"As much as her quiet manner will allow; she blushed when I spoke to her today. And Mrs. Taylor has been very encouraging."

"Then perhaps you should propose to Mrs. Taylor."

Mr. Stone was affronted. "Perhaps I should have kept my own counsel. An independent man of fortune such as yourself cannot comprehend the difficulties facing those of us who have not the same good luck."

"I cannot enter into your reasoning, but I will not dispute your conclusion: I am, perhaps, not the best person from whom to seek guidance in this matter."

"I tried talking to Mr. Bertram the last time I was at Mansfield, but he offered me very little advice. And now you have added to rather than lessened my anxieties by introducing the possibility that Miss Price might refuse me. I cannot suppose she would, but it would not hurt to have a better understanding of her feelings before I declare myself."

"I could not agree more. "

"Then you will help me?"

"In what way could I possibly be of help to you?"

"You must observe her carefully this evening, to discover her sentiments towards me, and then tell me whether you think my attentions to be in vain."

"I do not know if you would like to hear my opinion."

The gentlemen talked of other things on their way back to the Parsonage and went in the carriage with the Bertrams to dinner.

Fanny was sitting alone in the drawing room when they all entered. It was an uncomfortable reunion but only for a brief time, as they were soon joined by her uncle and then the other ladies. At dinner, Mr. Stone, of course, chose a seat next to Fanny, much to her dismay and Mrs. Taylor's delight. The evening, however, was not as difficult as Fanny had feared. It was uncomfortable, but she was able to maintain her composure. And Mr. Crawford, exhibiting his usual cheerful manner, appeared so at ease, so comfortable, and spoke to everyone with such self-possession, that no one could suspect him of anything but indifference towards Fanny or Mr. Stone's attentions to her, and her own anxiety was lessened. If his behaviour had rather been marked by jealousy or resentment, it would have increased the severity of her distress.

In the drawing room after dinner, Mr. Stone was as properly attentive to Fanny as anyone could have expected him to be. Her betrothed left her to her fate, choosing instead to address himself entirely to Mr. Bertram with an air so unperturbed it might have unsettled any lady capable of vanity, but to Fanny it was her only source of comfort. She found more complete relief when Mrs. Bertram, in consequence of Sir Thomas and Lady Bertram sitting down to cards with Mrs. Taylor and Mrs. Norris, moved to a seat near Fanny and began talking to her quietly. After a few minutes, Mr. Stone left her to join the other two gentlemen. This happier arrangement prevailed until, after a while, Mrs. Bertram was called away by Lady Bertram to answer some questions pertaining to young Master Thomas. Mr. Crawford, shortly thereafter, allowed Mr. Stone's attention to become wholly engaged in discourse with Mr. Bertram, and availed himself of the opportunity to cautiously approach Fanny.

She had taken up her needle work and dared not look up on his approach. "I hope this evening has not been too trying for you," he said quietly.

"No," she replied. "It has been a little uncomfortable, but I believe I shall survive."

"I had intended not to say anything about our situation until after my return from London. I do not think it would be fair to you to make such a disclosure and then go away again and leave you to deal with whatever consequences await us, whether good or evil. And, there is the matter of

208

your parents. I would not have such news known about the country without first having obtained their consent, and there is no time for that now."

"I am in full agreement with you."

"I am happy to know it; but this arrangement, however agreeable to the two of us, does not account for your friend, Mr. Stone."

She finally glanced up at him. "Nothing has happened and if it does, I will know how to respond."

He smiled at this. "I do not doubt that you will, being as you are somewhat practised in such matters." She ventured another look at him – serious, almost reproachful at first, but when she saw his smile, she could not help smiling back. She shook her head slightly, but made no reply. "But you should not have to face whatever ill consequences that may ensue alone." he continued, "I wish I did not have to leave you."

"Do not be uneasy on my account; you have many other things that require your attention."

"Very well. Then, I will only add that it is not a matter of *if*, Fanny, but of *when.*"

She could not help but smile and glance up at him again when he said her name. But to his disclosure she replied, "He spoke to you of his intentions?"

"He did, and of his own volition. He thinks I am talking to you now on his behalf." She seemed surprised, but only glanced at Mr. Stone and said nothing. "I urge you, as circumstances warrant, to reveal the truth rather than endure the censure of those who may be displeased by your choice."

"If it comes to that, I shall, but let us hope it will not be necessary."

She returned her attention to her work and Mr. Crawford sat with her a few minutes longer in silence before returning to the other gentlemen. They did not have another opportunity of speaking alone together before he left for London. He did, however, speak to Mr. Stone, and in response to his inquiry gave his honest opinion that he did not think Miss Price was likely to accept his proposals.

Chapter 32

Unfortunately for Mr. Stone, he did not heed Mr. Crawford's advice. Even if he had wished to, he had come too far; his honour was engaged. He returned to Mansfield the following morning and had no trouble securing a private interview with Fanny. He was surprised by her refusal and could not immediately comprehend her reasons. But she gave him to understand that she did not expect any provision from her uncle and that it would be imprudent for him to marry a girl who was penniless. He would not disagree with her on the latter point, but was unwilling at first to give up hope as to the former. He saw no reason why they should not at least find out whether Sir Thomas intended to do anything for her first. But Fanny pointed out that certainly if Sir Thomas had intended to provide her with any fortune he would have made that known to Mrs. Taylor. And, moreover, Fanny asked him how it would appear to apply to Sir Thomas on the question first and then withdraw his proposals should the answer be unfavourable. In the end, Mr. Stone left Mansfield Park with the mixed sensations of disappointment in her rejection and satisfaction in having escaped an imprudent marriage.

Fanny was relieved to have the interview over with but did not look forward to answering for her choice to Mrs. Taylor. When she returned to the drawing room, however, she found only her aunts and quickly learned that Mrs. Taylor was speaking to Sir Thomas in his room.

When Mrs. Taylor appeared in the drawing room, a few minutes later, she was in a good humour and on seeing Fanny she immediately asked, "But where is Mr. Stone? Has he gone to speak to Sir Thomas? I just came from his room and did not see anyone going that way."

"I believe he has gone away," said Fanny.

Mrs. Taylor looked at her in confusion, then exclaimed, "You have not refused him?"

At this Mrs. Norris looked up in disgust. "Can it be possible she has done it again? If she has, it would not surprise me. She is determined to remain a burden on her uncle."

"Again?" asked Mrs. Taylor.

"Did not you know that she refused a far more eligible gentleman who offered for her some two years ago? Why would she accept poor Mr. Stone after rejecting the likes of Mr. Crawford?"

"Mr. Crawford?" asked Mrs. Taylor in obvious surprise, looking at Fanny.

"I do not wish to speak of it," replied Fanny. "Please excuse me." With that she retreated to the East room.

She sat at her writing table remembering her conversation in that room after Mr. Crawford's first proposal. If her uncle sought her out now, she wondered whether she would be forced to disclose her situation and if she did, how he would respond. She felt much less prepared for a confrontation than she had imagined while discussing the possibility in the drawing room with Mr. Crawford the previous evening. How she wished now for his reassuring presence. At length, she heard a knock at the door followed immediately by Sir Thomas' entrance into the room.

He sat across from her and after a moment or two of silence he spoke. "Well, here we are again, Fanny." She looked down at her hands in her lap. "I do not understand this continued defiance from one who otherwise appears to be everything I would expect from a young lady raised in this house. I have done what I could, and it has yielded results; but I had hoped – notwithstanding your protestations when I first spoke to you of my design – that you would enter into it more willingly, that you would at least be open to the possibility of establishing yourself in a household of your own. I do not know what to make of your apparent aversion to the idea of marriage. Not many girls in your position, I imagine, would risk the odds of receiving a third offer, so I must, therefore, conclude that you simply do not wish to marry."

Although Fanny had been sitting alone in anticipation of his coming, she was ill-prepared to respond; and as she was trying to think of a reply, he forestalled her with a wave of his hand. "I will not ask you for an explanation after professing that I had learned to trust your judgement. And I will not reproach you for encouraging the young man's attentions. I suspect you had very little to do with it. It was I who engaged the services of Mrs. Taylor against your wishes and it was she, I am sure, who encouraged Mr. Stone. But, more than that, I know you too well to think you would encourage the attentions of any young man if they were unwelcome to you. And to own the truth, while I would have given my consent if you had asked for it, I never thought he was good enough for you." Fanny looked up at him in surprise. "Mrs. Taylor is not happy, but I dare say she will get over it."

When he stood to leave her, Fanny walked to him and said, "Thank you," then kissed him as tears formed in her eyes. He left the room and she remained there until dinner.

Fanny almost dreaded seeing Mrs. Taylor again but, as with most things, it did not turn out as badly as she feared. Dinner was a quiet family affair, and the drawing room afterwards was even more quiet. Fanny began to feel the serenity of her mind return. She was relieved to be free of Mr. Stone's attentions and had now only to wait for Mr. Crawford to conclude his business and return to her.

He was away a fortnight and though he had written to let his sister know when to expect him, he arrived a day early. When he entered Mansfield Parsonage close to the dinner hour, he found Fanny and Mrs. Taylor sitting with Mrs. Bertram. He smiled when he saw the former, and she coloured; but neither could speak to, nor indeed even look at the other. It was an awkward meeting, and the other two ladies were by no means unaware of it. Not long after his entrance however, Fanny suggested to Mrs. Taylor that it was time for them to be getting home. As soon as they were out of the room, Mrs. Bertram inquired of him as to the meaning behind the look of consciousness that he and Fanny had shared upon meeting, but he left her unsatisfied and hurried away to dress for dinner. She did not, however, abandon the interrogation and pressed him to no avail throughout the evening.

Mrs. Taylor's attack on Fanny during the walk home was more subtle. She now began to see things in a new light. She had previously noticed Mr. Crawford's admiration of Fanny but due to the difference in their situations had considered it unlikely that he would make her an offer. Indeed, he seemed rather to check any expression of his admiration as if not wishing to raise her expectations. Then, after recovering from her surprise at learning of Fanny's previous rejection of the gentleman, she felt certain there could be no hope of a renewal. Yet now she perceived that there was clearly more between these two than she had ever suspected, and she began to formulate a possible explanation for Fanny's refusal of Mr. Stone. She tried to find out her young charge's sentiments towards Mr. Crawford as they walked home, but with no success.

The next morning, the Mansfield ladies had been sitting in the drawing room for some time and Fanny wondered that Mr. Crawford had not yet called, for she felt sure of his doing so in the course of the morning. Mrs. Taylor had an errand in the village but Fanny managed to get out of going with her and as soon as she was gone, went instead to the rose garden, where there could be an opportunity for private conversation should Mr. Crawford have the good luck to arrive while Mrs. Taylor was away; for, ever since Mrs. Taylor's arrival at Mansfield, neither of her aunts had felt particularly obligated to take notice of her whereabouts. She had not been out of doors for long when Mr. Crawford appeared.

"Miss Price," he said, "I am glad to have found you." He sat down next to her and after a few moments of awkward silence, said, "I have been aking out and looking at the handkerchief you gave me every five minutes since I left Mansfield; and I confess, if I had not had it with me I might have been disposed to doubt my own memory of the meeting in which it was given."

"Then I am glad you had it with you," she replied, raising her eyes to him with a smile.

"So, you have not changed your mind?"

She looked back at him in surprise. "No, I have not. Have you?"

He laughed lightly. "Me? Never."

She only smiled in reply.

"Come," he said, rising from the bench, "let us walk a little." They began walking past the rose garden into the grounds beyond as he spoke, "And now, at last, I may give all the expression to my feelings that has so long been denied to me."

"I believe sir, that you have been expressing your feelings all along."

"Not as I wished to, I assure you. I have allowed myself only such little hints as would give you the barest affirmation of my constancy, and give one with your natural modesty and delicacy assurance enough to make so audacious a display as to wear a necklace."

Fanny could not reply. She was unaccustomed to this lively sort of teasing, though she had no objection to learning to put up with it in time. For now, she conceded that he must be allowed the indulgence after having been repressing his feelings for so long, and responded only with a deep blush of embarrassment at the picture he painted of her audacity. This he considered sufficient encouragement, and the avowal of all that he felt and had long felt for her immediately followed.

She had not heard him speak so directly since the dark days of his first proposal. How different was her situation now, how different her views from what they were then. His addresses now were welcome. She had learned to depend on the little hints which he found so insufficient to express his own feelings; subtlety was more suited to her quiet, nervous temper. But now to hear him declare himself so openly, so passionately, and with a sincerity that rendered beauty to his natural abilities, was gratifying to her. When he had done, she felt unequal to make any adequate reply and a long silence ensued between them.

At length however, he asked, "How soon may I speak to your uncle?"

"Whenever you wish."

"And your father? Shall I write to him or shall I go to Portsmouth?"

"I believe a letter should serve. It is fortunate that he has already made your acquaintance."

"Yet another favourable consequence of my visit to Portsmouth," he observed with a smile. "Have you spoken of this to anyone? Were you obliged to disclose it?"

"No. I have not mentioned it to anyone. And you? Have you told your sister?"

"No. I did not wish to say anything without first consulting you. Though Mary interrogated me mercilessly yesterday after our chance meeting at the Parsonage."

"I hope you were not made too uneasy by the circumstance."

"Uneasy?" he said, laughing. "I am happier than I have ever been, than I ever thought I could be, and my felicity could not be diminished merely by having to forestall the curiosity of my poor, uninformed sister." Fanny made no reply and after a pause he continued, "I will speak to your uncle and write to your father today, but we shall not make it generally known until after receiving Mr. Price's consent." Fanny agreed. "At that time, I shall speak to Bertram about setting a date unless, if you should prefer … if there is a way, perhaps, for someone else to do the honours."

"That is not necessary on my account," she replied. "I shall not be made uneasy by his performing the service, I assure you. All of that is long over."

"I knew it must be or you would not have accepted me, but I see no reason for you to endure any distress that can be avoided."

"The only distress I can foresee would be in attempting to explain the reason for such a request." He nodded his assent. "I would have you know that my feelings have undergone such a complete reversal, that I have long since ceased to think of him in that way. And I cannot tell you how very grateful I am that you have never (I presume) revealed your suspicion."

"I never have spoken of it. It was a secret I should not have known." She made no reply, and after a few moments of quiet contemplation he spoke again. "It is a fitting twist of fate, I believe, that I set out to awaken in you the first sensations of the heart, not knowing of your prior attachment and never expecting to become attached myself, but it was my own heart that was awakened. You must know that I have never had feelings of this kind before; in truth, I had often doubted that such feelings were possible. I never thought such a woman existed. I have long since comprehended the true value of your character, and after having done so, who could resist loving you?"

"One did at least," she replied, but almost wished she had not said it.

"Only because he was raised to think of you as a sister; and I am the happy beneficiary. I have long understood that the only reason I had any

214

chance at all was because of how little you have been known to the world, for I have no doubt that any man who really knew you must love you."

"You must not speak so, it is not true."

He smiled, "My dearest Fanny, I told you in my letter I had at last seen myself as you saw me; my only wish now is that you could see yourself as I see you."

She blushed again and replied quietly. "But it does not follow that every man would see me in the same way. I met many young men on my outings with Mrs. Taylor who did not think of me at all."

"Fools, all of them!" he said with a mock indignation that almost made her laugh. Then more seriously he added, "I suppose I cannot offer Mr. Stone as an example as he neither loved you nor knew you. I believe you require more than a few dances to really know someone, though it is not uncommon for matches to be formed on very little more."

"I do not see how anyone could consent to marry someone whose character was not thoroughly known to them, or without a foundation of affection and mutual understanding."

"I am very happy to know your views on the subject," he said with a smile.

It occurred to her now that she had not yet acquainted Mr. Crawford with her own feelings; she had accepted him, but she had not given him the assurance of telling him how she felt. He had been reassuring her of his feelings for so long with no requital, that she now felt the injustice of her own reserve. Thus, she added, "My feelings towards you have also changed."

"I have guessed as much," he said cheerfully. Then, not wishing to silence her he added, "But I have no objection whatsoever to you explaining the change to me in great detail."

"I shall never be so eloquent as you."

"I do not wish for eloquence."

She began very awkwardly, "I … I do love you." She heard his breath catch when she said it. But, she was at a loss in the next moment to express herself sensibly.

"You needn't say more," he said quietly, noticing her hesitation.

"But there is more to say," she replied. "I wish you to know that I admire your willingness to undertake such a reformation as you described in your letter, to have allowed yourself to not only see and acknowledge your own faults, but to correct them. It shows, I believe, extraordinary strength of character. You have proven your ability to judge rightly, you have been steadfast, and you have shown kindness and generosity."

"I thank you for speaking of me in such terms. It gratifies me exceedingly that you see me in so favourable a light, but I believe I shall never feel worthy of you."

"But you are," she said quickly. "Indeed, it might be argued that those who undertake to correct their defects, may demonstrate greater worth than those who are never put to such a test."

"But this is not the only test of character. If you are speaking of yourself, I believe you have been through many trials of a different sort."

"I was speaking generally. I would never presume to place myself among those who have no defects to correct."

"I have not seen a defect in your character."

"I hope that when you do, you will bear it with the same patience you have shown heretofore; and that, for my part, I can learn to follow your example of fortitude in pursuing a correction."

"I have no doubt you will do all that is right and good and proper should such an occasion ever arise."

"The point is, however, that you should not feel unworthy. Look at all that you have done for others – for your sister, for my cousin Julia, for William – in contrast to myself."

"You have done as much as it has ever been in your power to do, and will do more when empowered to do more. You did a great deal for your family, I believe, when you were in Portsmouth, your sister especially; and here, you are indispensable to Lady Bertram."

Fanny was affected by this observation. "Not indispensable, I think, but it will be hard for her to see me go."

"But you need not go far. We can remain in Northamptonshire. I had thought to secure a home for us in this neighbourhood, if you wish."

"But you have a home at Everingham."

"Indeed. Yet, I do not think you would like to be at such a distance from Mansfield. I would not have you give it up for my sake."

"And do you think I would have you give up Everingham for mine? No. Your home is at Everingham, and mine is with you. Besides, you would miss your little trees."

He smiled at this. "They are *your* little trees, Fanny; they always have been, as I think you well know."

"Then I must be there to make sure they are well tended."

"I cannot argue with your reasoning. Alas, I hope your poor aunt will bear it well. But, you know, I shall bring you into Northamptonshire whenever you wish." He paused for a moment of contemplation, then said, "Perhaps Everingham would feel more like your home if your sister,

Susan, came to live with us."

Fanny stopped walking and looked at him in wonderment. Tears formed in her eyes and he gently brushed them away, saying, "What is this?"

"Forgive me," she said, turning away from him. When she was able to speak she continued, "I would not have you think I am surprised by your generosity, only that you should anticipate so readily what I would wish for."

"You are not accustomed to it," he said soberly. She felt the rush of a few more tears as he said it. "That will soon change." She was too overcome with emotion to make any reply. In a lighter tone, he added, "You must remember, I have had plenty of time to think about all the ways in which I might please you." He gestured for her to resume walking, as he continued, "I amused myself with the idea even when I first knew you had such a sister, while at Portsmouth."

Fanny smiled. "I thought of it then too." He seemed surprised. "I imagined you would be willing to allow it."

"Did you? I am gratified to learn that you then entertained any thought of that kind."

"I believe that was when I first started thinking of you more favourably; but, in truth, I was very happy at that time for any reminder of Mansfield. And, I confess the only regret I had on leaving Portsmouth was the loss of Susan's companionship."

"I believe it will do you good to have her with you at Everingham; and, perhaps, the change will do her good as well."

"Then I will write to my mother as soon as you receive an answer from my father. I am sure she can have no objection."

"If that be the case, then we shall travel to Portsmouth to fetch Miss Susan in our way to Everingham."

"Thank you," she said.

They walked a little further until they reached a small copse that lay beyond the gardens where he stopped and turned to face her, saying, "Now you will see the extent of my scheming and of my nefarious intent, for I have purposely brought you to this little wilderness to be out of view of the house."

She looked at him and said, "I am not afraid of you, Mr. Crawford."

"You persist then with 'Mr. Crawford?'" he asked playfully.

"By what name would you have me address you?"

"Many possibilities come immediately to mind, but perhaps you might try 'Henry.'"

"Henry," she said a little awkwardly.

"Very well done," he replied, smiling.

"I do not know if I can get used to it."

"I believe you shall."

He removed his hat and her heart quickened with anticipation. He placed his hand on the side of her face and gently drew nearer to her till his cheek was almost touching hers. He whispered into her ear, "Fanny, 'my ever new delight.'" The words were familiar, but she was not in a state of mind at present to place them. She was trembling, but his other hand reached behind her shoulder to steady her and she felt his breath on her skin as he kissed her cheek gently, again and again.

At last, he drew back and took her hand in his. She felt flushed and breathless, but as she caught his eye, she suddenly said, "Milton."

He smiled. "Yes." After a pause he added, "I shall read the whole of it to you, if you wish."

She caught her breath without knowing why and only replied, "I would like that."

"But not until after we are married," he added, "so that we may choose the properest time, place, and manner for such study."

Fanny could make to reply. They stood thus for a moment longer, the gentleman holding her hand in his, then he sighed and drawing her arm into his again began walking back towards the house, "I have no wish to end our conference, but I am impatient to speak to your uncle, which I shall do directly."

"It is for the best, I think," she said, "Mrs. Taylor must be back by now, or will be soon, and will be wondering where I am."

"Ah, poor Mrs. Taylor," he said, "what will become of her?"

"She has been doing her best for me, I think," said Fanny. "I hope it will not be too difficult for her to find another position."

"You must forgive me for hoping she had rather been doing something a little less than her best and for thinking she looked a little too favourably upon Mr. Stone."

"What is this? Did not you counsel me to accept my uncle's design? And if I am not mistaken, I believe you were looking out for a match for me at Everingham."

He was surprised, and after a moment's thought he said, "I meant what I said on both occasions. But I thought I had been speaking to Bertram in confidence; I never imagined he would share my suspicion with you."

"I know that you meant what you said, and I felt all the kindness of the sentiment, though I did not like that you had been talking to him about

218

ne."

"I had not thought of it in that light."

"You mistake me. My discomfort had nothing to do with feelings for *im*."

He was silent for a moment then said, "I see. I had no idea, I had by *hen* resigned myself to your refusal and had nearly given up all hope."

"But you must have begun to hope again before I wore the necklace."

"It was at Everingham when you revealed to me that your feelings had *changed* – and I will not hesitate to point out that I have told you this even *hough* you have not told me when you started on your embroidery *project*."

"It was the day after the christening, but I was not yet absolutely *certain*."

"So before the Maddox Ball."

"Yes."

"I had thought, for a while at least, that you might have been receptive *if* Mr. Stone's attentions."

"Did you? I never meant to give you that impression."

He was thoughtful for a moment then replied, "The impression, I think, *arose* more from my own imagination than your behaviour. I did not *perceive* any sign of particularity on your part, but my failure to notice *your* previous attachment made me cautious; if you had feelings of that *kind* I knew you would never display them. So I allowed the possibility *hat* I simply could not perceive your pleasure in his attentions. In truth, *once* my hope had been reawakened I feared that I had been allowing *myself* to hope too much and almost constantly attempted to reason myself *against* it."

"I am sorry to have left you in a state of uncertainty for so long, but I *elt* very strongly I could not act until I was absolutely certain myself; in *ruth*, I should not have said anything to you at Everingham."

"I am very glad you did. Even if nothing had come of it, knowing your *opinion* of me had improved, hearing you say it, would have made a little *misplaced* hope worthwhile."

They walked on in near silence until arriving at the door to the house. *Before* entering, Mr. Crawford said playfully, "This is your last chance to *change* your mind before I speak to Sir Thomas."

"Oh no," she replied. "It is far too late for that after your scandalous *behaviour* in the little copse."

He was so unaccustomed to her saying anything in a teasing manner, *he* almost believed her to be sincere, and for the briefest moment was alarmed. But he saw her smile and could not help but smile himself. "Take care or you shall encourage more behaviour of that kind."

She was a little embarrassed, but when she thought of how long he had loved her with so little in the way of encouragement, she could only reply, "I look forward to it."

This simple phrase at last seemed to completely undo the gentleman – accomplished as he had long been in the art of clever repartee; and she, a novice at it, had all the satisfaction of, for once, having put *him* to the blush.

He only added, "Do not go far. I am sure Sir Thomas will wish to speak to you as soon as I tell him."

"Undoubtedly," she said. "I shall be in the drawing room." Then, touching his hand, she added, "Good luck."

"Thank you," he replied, "but I fear you shall need it more than me."

With that they entered the house and parted in the hall. He went to her uncle's room and she to the drawing room whence she expected to be summoned at any moment. Lady Bertram asked her whether Mr. Crawford had found her and she informed her aunt that he had been kind enough to accompany her on a short walk before going to see her uncle. Mrs. Taylor came in just as Fanny had finished answering the questions of her aunts and thus learned nothing of her walk with Mr. Crawford.

Fanny would have liked more time to order her thoughts in preparation for the interview with Sir Thomas, for she knew he would demand an explanation of her; but a very few minutes after Mrs. Taylor's return, Baddely entered the drawing room. Fanny was the only one not surprised by his summons.

Once she was in her uncle's room, Sir Thomas began thus, "I find myself bewildered by the news I have just received, though it does perhaps shed light on other recent events." He paused and Fanny waited in silence for him to continue. "You must know that after I read your letters and spoke to Edmund, I began to better understand the events leading up to your refusal of Mr. Crawford; and while I no longer blame you for doing so, I must confess to feeling a particular fondness towards the gentleman who single-handedly restored my daughter to me, notwithstanding his previous offences. Nevertheless, as I stand in place of your father, I must be satisfied on one point. I must have an explanation as to your change of heart. What can have happened to overcome your objections – objections that even he acknowledged were justified?"

"He has corrected the defect that formed the foundation of my previous dislike. Over the past two years he has been steadfast. And, in addition to

220

what he has done for this family, he has shown me kindness, in many ways, great and small."

"He has corrected the defect that you would not reveal to me?"

"Yes," she replied quietly.

"And how can you be certain that it has been corrected?"

"Two years of constancy has shown it; and whenever I have been in company with him since my return from Portsmouth, I have seen no evidence of it. Moreover, he explained to me of his own accord that he recognized the defect in himself and has been striving to correct it."

"That is extraordinary, indeed. But, if he corrected this defect to win you, how can you be sure it will not return once he has succeeded?"

"I do not think he was motivated by any such expectation. He explained that he corrected the defect because it was wrong, and that once he recognized it in himself he was repulsed by it; at the same time, he confessed to me that he had lost all hope of winning me and even urged me to reconcile myself to your design of introducing me into society."

"Did he? Then I wonder what could have happened to rekindle his hope."

Fanny blushed and looked down at her hands.

"Well then," her uncle continued, "he has persevered beyond all my previous hopes, for I gave up the idea long ago. Indeed, I could perceive nothing between the two of you lately to prepare me for this. But are you quite certain it is what you wish? That you will be happy? I would not like to see you regret your choice – as others have done."

"I am certain. I have had much time to think it over."

He regarded her for a moment before saying, "Very well, I will send him a note with my consent, as far as it goes. He has returned to the Parsonage to compose a letter to your father and he has requested that nothing be said to anyone until he receives a response from Portsmouth, which is all very proper – and, I will acknowledge, quite different from the way he viewed matters two years ago."

"Yes sir."

"You will be missed at Mansfield, and not only by Lady Bertram."

"Thank you," she replied. "I will miss all of you as well."

With that she was given leave to return to the drawing room.

Chapter 33

The days following these events were happy for Fanny, but there were still vexations. She waited anxiously for news from Portsmouth. She did not doubt that her father would give his consent, but she disliked the secrecy at home. Her own consciousness, together with the constant watchfulness of Mrs. Taylor made private conversation with Mr. Crawford almost impossible.

During this interval, a morning dawned that was mild for January and looked fair for riding. Fanny mentioned her intent to do so at breakfast, saying she would check with the coachman about a convenient time to set forth. Mrs. Norris observed that the coachman's rheumatism had been acting up and scolded Fanny at length for not considering the poor man's condition.

The ladies left the breakfast room shortly thereafter and upon their rising to go, Sir Thomas motioned to Fanny to stay. Once the door had closed behind them, he simply said, "There is no reason to trouble Wilcox if Mr. Crawford will attend you, Fanny."

She was a little surprised but only said, "I am sure Mr. Crawford will have no objection to riding out with me, if he is not otherwise engaged."

"I am sure he will have no objection," replied Sir Thomas, without looking up from his newspaper.

Fanny quit the breakfast room after this exchange and went to the East room to compose her first note to Mr. Crawford inquiring whether he was at liberty to attend her for her ride. On this matter, he was very obliging and arrived punctually to accompany her at the appointed time.

Rather than taking the familiar circuit Fanny had been accustomed to riding with the coachman, Mr. Crawford led her along a sunny lane he had discovered on his rides in the neighbourhood. They rode side by side at a walk so that they could converse along the way. The gentleman inquired as to the events at Mansfield while he had been in London. "I know from Mary's letters that Mr. Stone finally came to the point, against my excellent advice, but you have not spoken of it."

"I think your advice came too late. He had already gone too far in his suit to give it up without being censured by Mansfield at least, if not all the neighbourhood."

"If the neighbourhood knew enough to censure him if he did not propose, then I can imagine its response to his having been refused. But I am more concerned with how you were affected by the event."

"I had the advantage, I think, of being more prepared for his application than he was for my refusal, notwithstanding your excellent advice. I emphasized my own lack of fortune and the imprudence of the match. In the end, he seemed satisfied and we parted cordially."

"I do not suppose Mrs. Taylor took it well."

"She was indeed vexed. And when she mentioned my refusal in the presence of my aunts, Mrs. Norris gave her to know that I had already refused a more eligible offer."

"She must have been quite shocked by that bit of news. But did Sir Thomas learn of the event?"

"Mrs. Taylor told him. But thankfully he was not angry. Nor did he ask me for an explanation. I do not think he was fond of Mr. Stone."

"I always thought your uncle had excellent judgement in such matters," replied the gentleman with a smile.

"I confess I was dreading the conversation with him, but it was not as bad as … as I supposed it might be."

"You were going to say not as bad as the last time you refused a proposal."

"Only insomuch as that previous conversation formed the foundation of a fear that turned out to be unwarranted on this occasion. And in the height of that fear, I very much wished for your presence."

"Then I am very sorry I could not be here."

"When you were here, the day Mr. Stone dined with us, your manner put me greatly at ease. It was a relief to me that you could be so calm and composed, rather than being affronted by his attentions to me."

"Why should I be? No man is offended by another man's admiration of the woman he loves; it is the woman only who can make it a torment. And, you behaved in perfect accordance with our conversation earlier that day. I could see that his attentions gave you no pleasure, even if he could not – though I had the advantage of knowing your heart."

"In any case, it all turned out well," replied Fanny. She then turned the conversation, "I have answered for the events at Mansfield during your absence, but you have said nothing of your time in London. I hope you were able to resolve matters without too much difficulty."

"Like you, I had less trouble than I feared. The admiral's accounts were in disorder and he had not met with his agent in months, but I soon set things right. I was able to settle with his creditors and servants and there were a few other matters that required my attention, but thankfully it all proceeded smoothly."

"It sounds like a great deal to accomplish in a fortnight. I thought you might be away longer."

"I wanted to be done with it quickly. It was not a pleasant business. And I was very eager to return here." After a brief pause, he continued, "Fanny, Admiral Crawford made me his only heir. Other than a few small bequests of personal items to some of his friends, he left me all his fortune and property."

Fanny did not know what to say. She had no idea what the admiral's fortune had been nor what other relations he might have had. Then after a moment's thought she said, "Surely he left something to your sister as well."

"No. Nothing. It was a difficult blow. I always admired him, in spite of his faults, and I had not thought he would completely neglect her. I shall make over some share of the inheritance to her, though I do not like going against his wishes."

"I do not think you are going against his wishes by exercising the discretion to do with it as you will which he bestowed upon you in making the bequest. Indeed, he must have known you would give her something."

"I believe you are right. I have yet to decide how to divide the inheritance but I cannot do other than share it with her. And, she shall, of course, have use of the house in town and the cottage at Twickenham, whenever she wishes."

Fanny thought of poor Edmund and all the quarrels between he and his wife over whether to go to London. Having use of a house there would certainly make it difficult to keep her in the country.

He continued, "And my sister is not the only one who shall benefit. I wish to do something for your family as well."

"That is very generous of you, Mr. Crawford."

"Pardon me," he said, "who is this 'Mr. Crawford' you speak of?"

She could not help but smile. "Henry," she said. "It is very kind of you to think of my family."

He returned her smile. "That is much better," he said, "I am very happy to do what I can for those you love."

They left the lane and walked a little further along a brook that had been running beside it and now veered away from it. After a few more minutes, Mr. Crawford stopped and said, "Do you have any objection to giving the horses a rest here?"

"None whatsoever," she replied. Then smiling she added, "But Wilcox never stops to rest the horses."

"I should hope not," he replied, returning her smile.

He dismounted, then helped her down, but kept his hands on her waist even after she was on her feet.

They stood thus for a moment in silence, which was broken at last by Mr. Crawford who said only, "Fanny."

"Yes, Henry?" she asked. He made no reply. "What is it?" she said, "You are not usually the quiet one."

He only smiled and in reply, bent to kiss her. In that moment, however, her horse swatted its tail in their direction, brushing it against them. They both broke out in laughter. Mr. Crawford took Fanny's hand and, walking a few steps away from the mare, he said, "I believe that may be the first time I have heard you laugh."

"Is it really?" she asked, contemplatively.

"It is my new favourite sound," he added, turning to face her again.

She smiled and blushed a little. "I suppose I do not laugh very much."

"We shall soon remedy that," he replied. "Let me see …" he continued thoughtfully for a moment. Then he said the following:

There once was a pretty young miss
Whose lover tried for a kiss
But her horse gave a flail
With a swish of its tail
Depriving the young man of his bliss

Fanny laughed again. "Very well done," she said. "Clever man! Poetry on the spot! I thought I knew all your charms."

"No indeed," he replied, "you have not yet discovered them all." With that, he kissed her successfully.

Afterwards, she pressed her head to his shoulder and he wrapped his arms around her. They stood thus for a few moments. At length Fanny pulled back again to look at him. "I used to think you were not serious enough and you have since learned to be more serious. I believe, perhaps, I have often been too serious, but you will teach me to laugh more."

"We shall each have a beneficial influence on the other," he replied. Then, checking his watch, he asked, "How long do you usually ride for?"

"Never this long," she replied.

"Then I had better not impose further on the good will of Sir Thomas."

He helped her onto her horse and they returned home.

A day or two later, Fanny was summoned to her uncle's room not long after breakfast. When she entered, she found Mr. Crawford there alone. He smiled as he held up a letter.

"I trust my father has given his consent."

"He has indeed," replied Mr. Crawford, handing her the letter, "He wrote separately to Sir Thomas as well."

Fanny read the letter which contained not only her father's hearty approval but a note to herself from her mother as well. She had not feared they would withhold their consent, but the occasion brought relief nonetheless in allowing the disclosure of her situation to be made to the rest of the family at Mansfield.

By the time the news was given, Mrs. Taylor had seen enough to be the least surprised by it and Mrs. Norris was, perhaps, the most surprised. The former left Mansfield within a week, with a letter of recommendation, the full pay she would have had a right to expect had she actually made the match herself, and a great deal of confusion over why she had ever been engaged to come to Mansfield in the first place. As for Mrs. Norris, what can be said of her amazement that a man who had been rejected once by a young woman wholly unworthy to have ever received his addresses, should demean himself so far as to make a second application to the same woman? It was enough to shock her into silence at last; and, for once, her response was met with universal satisfaction.

Lady Bertram had more difficulty reconciling herself to the match now than she had two years before. She had learned to miss Fanny while she was away at Portsmouth; and after having been lately given every assurance that Fanny would settle nearby, it was difficult to accept the distance between Mansfield and Everingham. She would be sad to see Fanny go, but Little Thomas would soon serve as a diversion and in later months and years his almost daily presence in her drawing room animated her considerably. Sir Thomas would miss Fanny even more, perhaps, than his wife; he felt her value more in her absence than he ever had while she was living under his roof; and in all probability, he eventually learned to regard her as just what he would have wanted in a daughter.

Fanny immediately wrote to her mother who readily gave her consent for Susan's removal from Portsmouth. A letter from Susan herself was enclosed with her mother's, in which she expressed her delight and gratitude for the invitation. Fanny also wrote to her brothers William and John with the news of her engagement. Both sent her letters of congratulations. William especially expressed his great joy in the union of his beloved sister and the friend he had every reason to admire and respect. John was not the least bit surprised by the news but in his congratulatory reply kept to himself his wonderment as to what had taken so long for Mr. Crawford to come to the point.

Mr. and Mrs. Bertram were both surprised at the length of time they had been kept in the dark about the engagement. Edmund understood the motivation behind the secrecy and agreed in general with the idea of obtaining parental consent before making such matters known. He was as pleased that Fanny had finally come around to taking his advice as he was to see that they appeared genuinely happy together; and upon congratulating his brother-in-law, he observed, "I hope you know how fortunate you are." Mr. Crawford smiled as he assured Edmund of his being aware of his own good fortune.

Mary was offended by the long silence of both her brother and her friend on the matter, but the knowledge that Henry and Fanny would be with her for only a few more weeks, together with the news that she would receive a share in an inheritance she never expected, hastened her powers of forgiveness. However, she did feel obliged to have a serious talk with her brother; and on her first opportunity of being alone with him after learning of the engagement, she congratulated him on having finally succeeded with Fanny.

"I must commend your perseverance. I have never seen you give up on making any woman like you once you set your mind to it, but you never were required to work so hard or persevere so long for it. Even I did not expect you to persist for as long as you did. I hope the triumph has not come at too high a price."

"That is an interesting choice of word," he said with a smile. "And what do you imagine is to be the *price* of securing my own happiness?"

"I do not doubt your happiness now, Henry, indeed there must be great satisfaction in finally succeeding in attaining what has so long eluded you. But I confess that I fear whether such happiness can last."

"You were quite sure of my lasting happiness when I first told you of my intent to marry Fanny."

"Yes. I then thought she would suit you by being a grateful and obliging wife. But she has since proven herself to be headstrong and over-scrupulous."

"My dear Mary, how can you speak so? I know very well that you love Fanny as a sister already."

"It is true. I love her and I love you, but it does not follow that the two of you are well suited. You have an independent, lively spirit and she is so morally inflexible."

"I wonder what moral transgressions you expect me to commit that she might disapprove."

"One never knows," she replied. "What does she not disapprove? You certainly have not been living your life up to now in accordance with her fastidious views."

He then laughed lightly. "And where do you think she learned her lessons in morality? It was from your husband. The man you chose to marry virtually formed all of her opinions himself. Yet you seem to be content with your choice."

"Perhaps, but Edmund has at least proven to be more flexible in his views. Remember, they were both against the play but he changed his mind; and he did not wish to go to London last year, but I convinced him."

"If I understand you correctly, you are saying that your husband's moral rectitude is not an impediment to your happiness because you have learned to charm and finesse him into acting against his own judgment, so that you might have your way in spite of it?"

"What choice do I have, Henry? I am a woman. We cannot have our own way in everything, as men do. I am sure you shall not wish to always live in retirement at Everingham. When you wish to go to London or Bath or any other place, you are free to do so whether your wife likes it or not, and to take her with you or leave her behind, just as you please. It is not so with me."

"You paint a harsh picture of me as a husband. But if, in your view of things, I shall have everything according to my own wishes, then why are you so anxious for my happiness?"

"Is it so wrong of me to fear for the happiness of my only brother? You are happy now. But you are not thinking of the many years ahead, when the passion you feel at present will have diminished with time and familiarity. Then, what will you be left with? You have never been a man of domestic habits, always flying about the country in search of fresh company and amusements; and if there is a woman who could be content to go nowhere and see no one, it must be Fanny Price."

"Those ways are not of her choosing, they have been forced on her."

"Perhaps that is true, but she will always prefer a quiet country life; and once the novelty of marriage has worn away, once you have grown used to possessing that which you have so long desired, you will find the confined and unvarying society of Everingham very dull indeed. You will become restless. You will long for the days of your freedom and the liveliness of London drawing rooms; and Fanny will be too afraid of London society corrupting either you or her or the both of you together with all your children, to agree to set foot in town."

"Mary, I am grateful for your kind solicitude for my future happiness, but your fear is unwarranted. Do you suppose I do not know what I am doing? Why do you think I avoided marriage for this long? Perhaps it does not seem very long in measure of years, but those years have been filled with opportunity. Everyone of my acquaintance, whether in town or in the country, has tried to marry me off to some girl or other, all of them pleasant, pretty, and good-natured; everywhere I go, I am told who among them I shall marry. Yet I have resisted all these machinations because I knew only too well what is comprehended by entering into the state of matrimony and I was not willing to risk my future happiness by pledging myself forever to any of the women who were cast in my way. If you believe I have pursued Fanny only for the exultation of conquest or that I would pay for the triumph of conquering the stubbornness of one heart with a lifetime of misery, then you do not know me at all."

"I did not mean to offend you, Henry. It is only that I know what it is like to live with someone who has vastly different views than oneself."

"Your fears are misplaced, I assure you. Fanny and I understand one another. I had hoped you could be happy for us both."

"I am happy for you, and for Fanny. Truly I am. I only wanted the assurances you have now given me."

He looked doubtful.

"Perhaps I have not been able to forgive her for refusing you, and for making you wait two years before accepting you."

He took her hands and replied, "I hope you will find it in your heart to do so before we depart Mansfield. You and Fanny must remain on the best of terms for my happiness to be complete."

The effect of this conversation was less than satisfactory for both parties. The next day, Mr. Crawford visited the ladies at the Park and stayed until Lady Bertram retired to dress for dinner. Fanny rose with her aunt and when Lady Bertram left the room, the gentleman motioned to her to resume her seat saying, "Stay and sit with me for a moment," as he moved to a seat closer to her.

"Is something the matter?" she asked. "You look very grave."

"No. I do not think so. It is only something my sister said yesterday. I have been unsure whether to mention it to you."

"I hope you know you may talk to me about anything."

"I do. But I am nevertheless pleased to hear you say so. It is of great importance to me that we should be able to confide in one another."

"Then tell me what is troubling you."

"I would not say it is troubling me. I do not share in Mary's fears. But Fanny, I want you to know I do not expect you to go to London every year."

"Then you shall go without me?" she asked.

"Good God, no," he replied. Then seeing her smile, he said, "You are teasing me again."

"Forgive me," she said.

"No, I shall not forgive you for that; but remember, I did warn you of the consequences."

She only smiled again, then becoming more serious, said, "So your sister is concerned that we will quarrel about going to London?"

"Not exactly, the concerns she expressed to me were more general; but she did speak of London. Perhaps it was in her mind because it has been a point of contention in her own marriage."

"Edmund mentioned to me that they quarrelled about it."

"We shall leave them to work out their own quarrels. As for ourselves, I do not think several months or even several weeks in London would be healthy for you. And to own the truth, I have not missed London society as much as I might have expected. I have enjoyed spending more time at Everingham. But, is it your desire to always be there?"

"We cannot. You have already promised to bring me to Mansfield whenever I wish it."

"And anywhere else it pleases you to go."

"But what are your own wishes?"

"I do not deny that I would not object to sometimes mixing in a broader society than what is afforded at Everingham and I think it would be good for you as well, and for Miss Susan. I would like to take you to see a play, many plays, concerts, art exhibitions, all things you have never had an opportunity to do or see, which Mary takes for granted. I do not think a fortnight in London once in a while would be detrimental to your health; or we can go to Bath or Portsmouth. You have an active, intelligent mind and a discerning taste, and you should have the opportunity to exercise them beyond the confines of Everingham. Am I wrong in supposing you would wish to see more of what the world has to offer?"

"No, not at all. You make it all sound quite fascinating. And I know you are accustomed to moving in larger circles."

"I do enjoy good company, Fanny – which is one reason I have chosen to marry you – but do not misunderstand me, I have no objection to making our home at Everingham. Most importantly, however, I wish you to always tell me your own preferences when it comes to such matters, and indeed in all matters."

"You know that I always will. And, I believe I shall be happy to go anywhere so long as you are with me."

He could not help but smile at this. "Well then," he said, standing and taking her hands to draw her to her feet, "I was correct in what I told Mary.

we do understand one another."

"I believe we do."

"Now," he said, drawing closer to her, "what shall I do about you teasing me?"

She only smiled as he bent to kiss her.

Chapter 34

Fanny left Mansfield Park with a heavy heart; she would miss her home and her aunt Bertram especially. The Crawfords stayed a few days in Portsmouth following their marriage, then took Miss Susan Price with them to Everingham where they lived happily for some four or five years before Susan formed an attachment with Mr. James Morgan, and was settled within five miles of her sister. The living once thought of as not enough to marry upon was discovered to be quite sufficient under the clever management of Mrs. James Morgan. Nevertheless, her husband's patron presented him with a second living on the same estate, providing the additional income which became necessary as their family expanded; and upon the death of his father, many years later, Mr. James Morgan took over the living at Everingham bringing Fanny and Susan together again.

The Crawfords, in the intervening years, continued their intimate friendship with Mr. and Mrs. Morgan. The two gentlemen especially remained on the best of terms; only Mr. Crawford's wife could have a greater hold on his gratitude and esteem. Mr. Morgan's death was a difficult blow to Mr. Crawford, who took solace in being able to offer the living to his friend's son and provide his widow and other children with a house in Everingham village.

William Price continued to advance in his profession. He spent as much of his time at Everingham as he could, and in later years settled nearby. John Price also continued to advance and Fanny saw him whenever she was in London. And through his connection with Mrs. Crawford he was eventually introduced to Miss Hamilton who, while marrying to secure her own happiness rather than solely to disoblige her relations, nevertheless found her joy on the occasion undiminished by their disapprobation. Mr. Crawford offered what assistance he could to Fanny's parents, although any increase in income was unlikely to produce much improvement in their situation under the poor management and bad habits that prevailed in their household.

After her removal to Everingham, Fanny saw but little of her Mansfield cousins. Mr. and Mrs. Bertram visited Everingham almost every year and Mr. and Mrs. Crawford visited Mansfield as often. The Bertrams spent more time in London each year and by that means the subject matter of their quarrels was expanded. As more of Mrs. Bertam's London acquaintances became known to him, Edmund had the additional distress and mortification of seeing her engage in flirtations with other men. Believing it must arise only from her natural amiability and that she must be unaware of how her behaviour appeared, he made his feelings known to her; but she only laughed at him for being over-scrupulous and dismissed her own behaviour as what everyone was doing. Edmund had difficulty reconciling his wife's easy acceptance of such behaviour with its repugnance to his own feelings, which in itself may be a little surprising given how long he had been acquainted with her character. And whether, perhaps, Edmund, in later life, ever arrived at the conclusion that he had not made the wisest choice of wife, or whether he learned to view Fanny as the highest standard of what a wife should be, is not for this work to tell – let other pens dwell on guilt and misery.

Mrs. Rushworth, after several more years of marriage, at last obliged her husband with an heir; he promptly returned the favour by being seized of a heart attack which brought on his death. Had his wife known that producing an heir would have such a favourable effect, she would indeed have done it much sooner. Nevertheless, she was free to marry again before age thirty and this time, it can be hoped, would be more circumspect in her choice of husband.

Lady Chandler, not having been any more circumspect than her sister in choosing a husband, had far greater luck in not having to pay for the foolishness that precipitated her marriage by being miserable in it. She lived happily with her husband for many years and was blessed with a large enough family to perform any play which inspired her fancy; for, her failed experience with joining an acting company had by no means deterred her from the activity. And Sir Henry's guilty conscience of his ill-judged abandonment in the attempt, together with his feelings of genuine affection for her and his own enjoyment of the activity, supplied him with every motivation to indulge her in its pursuit.

Mrs. Norris continued to live at the white house in Mansfield Village for many years after the deaths of her sister and brother-in-law; and as the Lady Bertram who succeeded her sister had little use and no affection for her, she no longer enjoyed the same privilege of liberal access to Mansfield Park she had formerly, and generally saw her nephew and his wife only at church whenever they happened to be in the country. She partook of her solitary dinners at her little house, however, with great fortitude of mind and little forbearance of heart; the closed door of the spare room would be a source of pain whenever she happened to pass by it – which occurred, of necessity, several times a day – in bringing to mind the very great regret that, alas, she had no friend to stay in it.

Mr. and Mrs. Crawford lived happily at Everingham and travelled often to fashionable towns of societal animation and remote destinations of natural beauty, alike. Fanny indeed learned to love plays and other similar amusements that were at last within her reach. Her husband continued in his devotion to her throughout their lives and she became just as devoted to him. They often took walks along the avenue at Everingham together and with their children, who watched its trees grow to become a defining part of their family home and a symbol of the mutual affection of their parents.

FINIS

From *Mansfield Park*, Chapter 48:

Could he have been satisfied with the conquest of one amiable woman's affections, could he have found sufficient exultation in overcoming the reluctance, in working himself into the esteem and tenderness of Fanny Price, there would have been every probability of success and felicity for him. His affection had already done something. Her influence over him had already given him some influence over her. Would he have deserved more, there can be no doubt that more would have been obtained; especially when that marriage had taken place, which would have given him the assistance of her conscience in subduing her first inclination, and brought them very often together. Would he have persevered, and uprightly, Fanny must have been his reward—and a reward very voluntarily bestowed—within a reasonable period from Edmund's marrying Mary.

– Jane Austen

Made in the USA
Las Vegas, NV
04 January 2025

15719881R10134